THE FAMILY BOOK 1

TEMPEST

THE FAMILY BOOK 1
TEMPEST

Luke Lively

VULPINE
PRESS

Published by Vulpine Press in the United Kingdom in 2023

ISBN: 978-1-83919-561-7

www.vulpine-press.com

To my Family: my wife, Teresa, daughters Sarah and Bailey, my son, Derek, my son-in-law, Adam, and my grandchildren: Faith, Samuel, Noah, Gabriel, Willow, Meadow, Courtney and Connor.

"Hell is empty and all the devils are here."
The Tempest, William Shakespeare

PROLOGUE
DESTINY

"When they wake, they cry, wanting to sleep and dream again."

The father stared at the two infants lying in separate cribs.

"That sound. I hate hearing a baby cry," the father coldly said, responding to the sobbing infant.

"How could you hate that?" the mother asked as she comforted the newborn. "Babies cry. It is part of life."

"For me, crying is chaos. And I hate chaos," the father said disapprovingly as the baby ceased weeping. "I'm only here because you convinced me to be the father."

"This is the only time you will see your sons. Can you not enjoy the few moments you spend with them?"

"Sons...what more could a father ask for?" the father sardonically said.

"I hope you're pleased," the mother sarcastically answered. "They are beautiful. Faqid, can you not even admit that?"

"Eshana, they are babies. In all honesty, they are ugly little creatures."

"How dare you call your children ugly creatures," Eshana angrily said.

"We are mother and father in title only," Faqid said, quickly turning to offer a brief glance. "What more do you want from me?"

"Nothing. Royal blood is rare. You were well compensated for what I needed."

"That is true. And you made it clear you had to keep the bloodline in the family," Faqid chuckled. "Cousin, what purpose are you serving?"

"Purpose? Why did you come here?" Eshana asked.

"I wanted to settle my mind. There are consequences to everything."

"You can rest your mind. Your sons will do many great things."

"And they will likely do many harmful things, too," Faqid interrupted. "Somewhere...sometime...they will have the opportunity to make their own choices. When that happens, I do not want any connection to them."

"You sound like my father," Eshana scornfully spoke. "But you, Faqid, are even more distanced from reality."

"Being a father is not an easy task."

"You should try being a mother."

"Do not lie, Eshana. Why should I feel anything for either of these...hybrid children?" Faqid quickly countered. "The only thing I have in common with you and them...is blood."

"You are part of their being...their nature. My dear cousin, that is something even you cannot escape."

"Their nature? How is any of this natural? And I'm not trying to escape from anything. Are you?" Faqid laughed, momentarily waking one of the infants.

"If you do not want to hear them cry, please do not startle them."

"I startled them? Ah...fear...I think that is what they inherited from you, cousin," Faqid said, a hint of anger in his voice. "What is the Earthling saying...the apple never falls far from the tree?"

"I wasn't aware of your depth of knowledge of humans, Faqid."

Faqid maintained his gaze on the two infants: "Look at them finally sleeping peacefully. But you're the one dreaming, Eshana, thinking either of us has real power over them. Control is illusory. *'We are such stuff as dreams are made on, and our little life is rounded with a sleep.'"*

"Shakespeare, how poetic of you. This is a side of you I had never seen before. But do you even know what that means?" Eshana dismissively asked after a brief pause.

"Dreams can change everything, even the universe," Faqid said. "You know this."

"*A dream itself is but a shadow,*" Eshana responded.

"No surprise, quoting Hamlet. That is your favorite, is it not?" Faqid asked.

"Actually, *Hamlet* is not my favorite."

"So, Eshana...how do you explain favorites? There is always one child that will be the favorite. Wasn't that the issue you had with your father? He was your father but harmed you in ways I cannot imagine. But your sister? He treated her like the queen she is now. And how fair is that? To choose to favor one child over the other?"

"Each child has gifts."

"Gifts specifically chosen by their mother?" Faqid interjected. "But not all gifts are equal...are they, Eshana?"

"No, they are not equal. And what my sons will do with those gifts will be up to them. My sons will own their actions."

"Now you're saying they are your sons. It sounds like you've already divorced yourself from what I gave them. You've already decided their fates...their destinies...all in a few moments. No one can ever accuse you of being indecisive. That is certain," Faqid said, turning his head away from Eshana to look at the infants. "You remind me of your father. You sound very much like him," Faqid said, pausing to allow the comparison to fuel Eshana's anger. "And...what will their older brother say about this?"

"What are you talking about?" Eshana asked, shocked to hear the question.

3

"Do you think I'm a complete fool? I know what you and he have done. The child is a gifted being and deeply flawed. He will be a threat to the Confederacy and the universe. And knowing this makes me responsible for outcomes. Like you said, I believe in owning my actions."

"Are you bargaining for more? You've been more than fairly compensated, cousin," Eshana tersely responded.

"And ultimately, no one will know the perverse creature's name," Faqid stated. "Your older son is, at best, a shadow. Maybe you should have named him *Hamlet?*" the question drenched in sarcasm.

"My son will be known for his deeds," Eshana sternly replied. "Yes, our roles have consequences, and I acknowledge my darkness. Can you do the same?"

"Cousin, I can agree you are dark and treacherous. Try as you might, you will not be able to create a perfect child," Faqid said. "These creatures you've produced are inferior, threatening beings. Because they have a tiny shred of humanity within, we can agree: Truly, the apple does not fall far from the tree."

"Our bloodline is unique. Yes, on that, we agree. And do not forget cousin, you are part of that tree. We are family," Eshana said, momentarily relaxing, a smile on her face.

"If all the apples are bad, what does that say about the tree?" Faqid asked.

"You need to leave. You've served your purpose. Now, do as you agreed and keep your silence."

"You have cursed my blood. I'm beginning to think the tree should be cut down. You are unique to all of the universe, Eshana. You are now the mother of two gifted sons," Faqid said, his anger evident in his voice.

"You are correct. I am the mother of two gifted sons. You sound jealous," Eshana mockingly responded. "That is your nature, cousin. You are what you are…a jealous weakling…a coward."

"Your first son and his father are evil," Faqid flatly stated, ignoring Eshana's words. "And so are these two."

"Evil? Please explain how they are evil?"

"The father of your oldest son is obsessed by ancient writings...prophecies. As you are, too. Do the two of you want to bring *The Prophecy of Isa* to life? Before you answer, cousin, do not lie. I want to hear the truth."

"I think you are delusional. How is an ancient Newebean writing evil?"

"The writings are only evil if the prophecy is used for evil purposes. The two of you are taking advantage of the timing. The prophecy referred to a quadrant in the Middle Time of 78M102. We are now precisely in that time."

"I am surprised. You've either been studying, or one of your concubines must have read it to you to help you sleep," Eshana said, uttering a nervous, soft laugh.

"I know more than you can imagine. The prophecy also predicted the rise in power of The Five...five hybrid Earthlings...each given the gift by a Newebean royal family member. That is your role in all of this."

"That is nonsense," Eshana responded.

"The writings said The Five would lead a rebellion within the Confederacy and ultimately end our peaceful alliance during this time quadrant. What they called the Atobean Revolution was prophesized to spread throughout the universe, freeing civilizations from slavery. That, to me, is both evil and chaotic. You are trying to start a revolt. And I will have no part of it."

"You have lost your mind, Faqid."

"I speak the truth! These children...are monsters...devils! Humans were created to be slaves! You will not change that with the creation of gifted humans."

5

"You want the truth? You are right. But you're too late, Faqid," Eshana said confidently, looking into her cousin's dark eyes. "The turn in time has begun."

"Aw, yes…the 'turn in time.' Thank you, cousin, for finally being honest. I deserve to hear you speak the truth. As you said…we are family."

"Yes, the universe has turned upside down," Eshana said, returning her gaze to the two infants. "I've done my part. And there is nothing more for you to do. What's done is done."

"Eshana, I disagree. There is something else I need to do. And you can blame it on my nature," Faqid said as he abruptly struck Eshana with a powerful blow to the side of her face, knocking her to the floor. "After I kill you, I will kill your sons and partner in this horrific crime. I will end this madness and save our family!" The cries of an infant could be heard as Faqid dropped down on top of Eshana, choking her with savage fierceness quickly ending her life.

Standing and looking at the two infants, Faqid smiled. One of the infants remained asleep, resting peacefully. The other infant was crying loudly.

"You have my attention, little devil…so you will be first to die," Faqid said, leaning over the weeping infant's crib. Putting his large hand tightly over the baby's face, the father began to suffocate one of his sons.

Blood splattered the child as the Faqid's head was blown apart, his hand falling away from the infant's face as his decapitated body fell to the floor beside Eshana.

Within seconds, a tall figure was standing motionless over the infants. As one infant continued frantically wailing, the being extended his index finger and tenderly touched the sleeping baby on the forehead.

"Silence is your gift."

Slowly taking his hand away, he turned his attention to the crying infant, softly saying, "Your tears shall drown the wind."

Immediately, the child stopped crying and fell into a deep sleep.

Returning his focus to the still-sleeping infant, he said: "It is true, your mother has a favorite son. *It's not in the stars to hold our destiny but in ourselves.*"

The Game

"Do you think this is a game?"

It was not the first time William had asked Aaron the question.

"I assume you're not talking about our game of chess, William?" Aaron responded, chuckling, as he considered his next move. "Everything is a game, isn't it?" he asked, after a pause, then moving his queen to capture a pawn. "What we do is similar to chess…check."

"No…not everything is a game," William said as he rubbed his chin. "Our role, our duties, are genuine. While no one is keeping score, we do what people like us have done since our country's beginning. *Supporting Victory* is never a game when the survival of our country is on the line." Then, moving his bishop into the direct line of the queen's attack, William looked up, facing Aaron, and said, "Your move."

William had mentored Aaron for over twenty years, the entirety of his adult life. Yet, in all the time he had been under his mentor's supervision, Aaron rarely confronted William.

Aaron Jones was loyal.

"Don't you think it is odd, William, or even hypocritical, that our primary undisclosed job duty is serving as assassins…while one of the stated objectives of our service branch includes 'mortuary affairs'?" Aaron asked, laughing. "The Founding Fathers must have had a dark sense of humor. In some instances…I guess it does fit."

As Aaron continued facing the chessboard, deliberating his next move, William pushed his chair back from the table. Putting his hands on his knees, he struggled to stand.

Aaron had always viewed his mentor as ageless. William had never shared his age, but Aaron knew he had served in the Korean War.

He's a marvel of genetics! But time has finally caught up with him, Aaron thought, keeping his focus on the game board. *What's surprising is how quickly it happened. It's like someone pulled the plug on William. Keeping secrets carries a heavy price. But he still looks the same as when I first met him. How does that happen?*

"Aaron, what do you make of the news out of Alaska?" William asked as he walked to the kitchen counter to pour another bourbon. "That is more than a game, wouldn't you agree?"

Still staring at the board, Aaron made his move, taking William's undefended bishop.

"Alaska...it's just another battle in our continuing version of *Batrachomyomachia*, our never-ending fight...over nothing," Aaron said coldly, without emotion.

"What are we, the mice or the frogs?" William asked, laughing. William walked back toward the chessboard, surveying Aaron's move. Then, placing his glass on the end table, he slowly lowered himself into his chair, maintaining his gaze on the board.

"Between the two...I would say humans are mice. *Of Mice and Men*, yes, that fits," Aaron chuckled, momentarily distracted. "Alaska. Wasn't that expected? Or is it just another tempest in a teacup?" Aaron haltingly asked as he refocused his attention on the chessboard.

"History teaches at the heart of almost every war is a desire for land. And that ensures..." William was interrupted by Aaron in mid-sentence.

"Peace is always a prelude to war," Aaron said. "War is the constant...peace is an outlier. I agree. We protect the resources of our land, our territory. What I'm wondering is how anyone can accurately define terrorism? Native Americans were terrorists? Colonialists were terrorists? It looks like we may all be terrorists very soon. Terrorism appears to be more of a perspective," Aaron said, still gazing at the chess pieces in front of him, momentarily thinking little about the game of chess they were playing.

"We have what others want and even need. A battle rages, and only a very few are aware of it. They are attempting to cover up a war," William said. "And cover-ups always fail...always."

Aaron looked up at William's face with a look of near shock.

"Did you just say cover-ups always fail?" Aaron asked in subdued astonishment. "In all my years with you, the one thing I believed was that you, out of everyone else who works within this hellish maelstrom of interconnected catastrophes in the fight for God and country, have never tried to bullshit me. But saying that 'cover-ups always fail' suggests that everything you've said to me for all these years is utter and complete bullshit. Maybe we are fighting on the wrong side?"

"I am speaking the truth...it is cause and effect, similar to your last move. It was expected," William said as he moved his queen into position. "Sacrifice...the food of the gods...check."

"Did you say sacrifice? I was wrong. Humans aren't mice. They are insects. William...do you want honesty?"

"Always," William calmly responded.

"I fucking hate humans! Have you ever thought we are the problem? We destroy everything. We are insects, no more or less, just fucking insects. And we are the shadowy protectors of this horrific infestation. We help perpetuate this pestilence...this plague called humanity! But you sensed it when I felt like that and would remind me otherwise. You reminded me of our value. I thought I...we...we miraculously splintered connections. We created a new cause to alter the outcome.

We changed the effects...quietly, with no fanfare...without anyone noticing that two plus two now equals five."

"*The web of our life is of a mingled yarn, good and ill together,*" William softly spoke.

"Jesus fucking Christ! Shakespeare? Sometimes, you remind me of my mother. Whenever I would ask her a question she did not want to answer, she would quote Shakespeare...as a deflection," Aaron quickly responded in a frustrated tone.

"*Conscience does make cowards of us all,*" William added, barely audible, quoting a line from *Hamlet*.

"*And a man's life's no more than to say, 'One,'*" Aaron quoted in response.

"One," William said contently.

Aaron looked back at the chessboard and could now see how the game would end in a series of moves. His lack of focus had cost him the game. His mind had been on a different task at hand. Unfortunately, there was no way out.

The outcome was evident.

William had won.

"William, if cover-ups always fail, why in the hell would you work so passionately to promote this one...the motherfucker of all cover-ups?" Aaron asked, pushing his chair back from the table, ignoring the chessboard. "That doesn't sound like something a logical, reasonable human being would do...does it?"

"You know the answer," William said as he took another sip of bourbon.

Aaron stood and turned toward the entryway.

"I love this place. It is so peaceful," Aaron said. The small cabin in a remote area adjacent to Deep Creek Lake in rural western Maryland had been a regular meeting place during assignments over the years. "It's well hidden...much like us...and what we do," he said as he walked toward the entry table at the cabin's front door. "In many ways, you've been like a father to me…teaching, guiding, directing…and enlightening. For all of those things, I am very grateful."

"Do you still doubt why I have done all the things I've done?" William asked.

"I know why. You have reminded me nearly every single time we have met. We are pawns in service of our country. We serve…that is our duty. We are only known by our deeds. We are part of *The Order*. And we must follow orders…as you say, 'Always follow orders,'" Aaron said, nearly snickering, mimicking William's aging, growling voice, as he reached into his well-worn leather messenger bag lying on the entryway table. "*Famam Extendimus Factis*. This is what you have taught me."

"Exactly," William said without any emotion. "Chess demands sacrifice to ultimately win. The chess pieces, especially the pawns, have no name or recognition other than how they are used and what they do. Like us, they are 'Known by Their Deeds.' And after completing their duty, they are put away…without fanfare or tribute. The same holds in service to our country as members of *The Order*. You are a pawn. I am a pawn. Nameless shadows whose deeds are purposefully buried and lost in history. We must always be prepared to sacrifice…and even be sacrificed."

"Nameless shadows? Doesn't your time spent on the Grassy Knoll in Dallas say you…we…are more than shadows? And being 'put away' after we've executed our mission? That certainly sounds like a game…a game we are playing," Aaron replied as he reached deeper into the bag, feeling the cold handle of the gun.

"Aren't you going to finish the game?" William asked, turning to look at Aaron while remaining seated. "It's your turn, Aaron. Or have you forgotten to ask me the question you are fond of asking?"

11

"Why should I let you live?" Aaron calmly responded, turning back to face William, aiming the gun toward William's forehead, momentarily pausing to look into his mentor's eyes for the last time.

William did not blink or move. It was what he expected.

"You shouldn't let me live. You and I are pawns. Follow your orders."

"Always. Game over," Aaron said as he pulled the trigger.

CHAPTER ONE
AXIS MUNDI

"Thanks for your patience. I hate having makeup on," Marc Walker confided.

The young woman assigned to prepare him for his appearance on *Good Night America* continued her work.

"I understand! My job is to make you look your best! Millions of people will be watching!" she said without pausing while applying makeup.

"I am so sorry; I don't think we had a chance to be introduced. What's your name?" Marc asked.

"Lisa...around here, I'm just 'Lisa in makeup!'" she enthusiastically responded, enjoying the interaction.

"I appreciate the help, Lisa, but I think it's hopeless. Making me look good is a tough assignment," Marc said, staring into the mirror. Despite makeup, Marc could still see the dark bags under his eyes, evidence of his minimal sleep. "I'm not sure I've slept more than three hours in the last three days. This book tour is a real challenge to find time to rest."

"You look great!" Lisa said, applying the final touches on Marc's forehead. "My God, I'm in the same room with the man who found the cure for cancer!" she said, smiling as she removed the towel protecting his crisp, white collar from any residual makeup. "You're ready to go!"

"Thanks, but I was lucky," Marc responded, rising from the chair, still looking at his reflection in the mirror. "I'm only human."

"Ok, whatever you say. And I think you look fantastic; sleep or no sleep!" Lisa said as a production assistant stepped around the corner.

"Thank you, Lisa," Marc said, smiling, turning to look into her eyes. "It was a pleasure to meet you."

"Dr. Walker, let's make our way to the stage," the production assistant insisted, ushering Marc from the room. "We don't have much time."

Time is something I am wasting. There's much work to be done. I should be working instead of promoting my book, Marc thought.

As Marc stood behind the stage, he could hear the host, Josh Martin's introduction.

"Tonight, we are privileged and honored to be the only entertainment show in the world to welcome our next guest. Called by many this generation's Einstein, he won the 2028 *Nobel Prize* in Medicine for finding the cure for cancer. His new, highly controversial book, *The Family*, is the number one bestseller in the US. The book offers what many consider to be ironclad proof of how human beings were created and genetically engineered on Earth, and drum roll, suggests who the creator was...or should I say, is. It is my great honor to welcome author, microbiologist, and the world's leading expert on molecular genetics, Dr. Marc Walker."

Stepping around the corner, the intensity of the lights nearly blinded Marc. Carefully, he stepped up onto the corner of the stage and shook hands with the show's diminutive host. Amidst the applause, a smattering of "boos" could be heard as he moved to his seat opposite Josh Martin.

Now seated across from the host, separated by a large oak desk, the sound of people booing was even more pronounced. Marc offered a quick wink to Martin as he leaned back in the dark blue, wide-tufted armchair.

Turning to the crowd, the show's host did not hide his frustration.

"Please...show some respect!" Martin said, his face glowing red with anger. Knowing that hundreds of protesters remained outside the studio enraged his frustrations with the small sector of the audience's chorus of boos. "Dr. Walker is my guest...show some respect, or we can take a break and help you exit the studio. I promise you'll miss the air conditioning," Josh said, as laughs and applause drowned out any remaining jeers from the crowd.

Martin began the interview without any signs of distraction: "Dr. Walker, it is a great honor to have you on our show."

"It's my pleasure, Josh."

Another brief flurry of less prominent booing interrupted Martin as he spoke. Still, without missing a beat, he continued: "Dr. Walker, for a person who helped end a pandemic and cured cancer, saving millions of lives in the process, you still seem to have quite a few haters. Why is that?"

"People have different perspectives...different beliefs. I have always held fast to being truthful and factual when sharing my work and the results," Marc said as he allowed a faint smile. "Being truthful does not guarantee popularity. In fact, it is quite the opposite."

"You found a cure for cancer when you were not necessarily focusing on seeking a cure for cancer, right?"

"That is true. I have been working for years in human genetics, seeking to understand why cells behave in the ways they do. An obvious sidebar to this work was working with cells that behaved abnormally," Marc said, leaning forward and clasping his hands together. "Once you understand the cellular structure, there is a higher probability of changing the structure and altering the cells' behaviors. That is what's referred to as gene editing. What you suggest as a cure is simply re-engineering renegade cells...genetic engineering that helps alter what cancer cells do and how they behave."

15

Unfolding his hands, Marc straightened in the armchair and continued: "It is important to remember, there are over two hundred different types of disease belonging to what is known as cancer. My work only served to build a foundation for others to deal with each type of specific cancer using cell alteration as the basis for a cure. Many other people cured the specific diseases, and their work saves lives," Marc said, slightly nodding in affirmation of his closing comment.

"You're a gene editor," Martin said, chuckling.

"Yes, you could call me that," Marc said with a soft grin.

"Humility and modesty aside, you truly helped save millions of lives. And, incredibly, you did not try to profit from it," Martin said sincerely. "That may be the miracle!" he said, with the audience joining in a moment of laughter and applause. "Many drug companies attempt extortion to hike their profits. You could have held the world hostage for a cure for cancer, but you did not. Dr. Walker. Don't you like money?"

A steady stream of laughter momentarily interrupted Marc's response. Slightly lowering his head, a grin on his face, Marc waited for the laughter to die before responding.

"The thought of making money from this part of my work was never in my thoughts. If that had been the goal, I would have never achieved anything. If you look at sheer profits, there was always more money in treating cancer than curing it. I'm sure that many people whose careers relied on treating people with cancer found some conflict in hearing there was a cure. And I am telling you the truth. Money does not motivate me," Marc said with firm frankness.

"Discovering the cure for cancer...and then avoiding the typical route of trying to market it recalled Jonas Salk and the cure for polio," Martin said, pausing, struggling to find what he wanted to say next. "Are you sure...were you ever tempted to let money talk...or at least whisper? If I had tried something like that, my agent would have shot me! But, of course, he does get ten percent!"

"No, money never entered my mind," Marc responded with a truthful surety. "And...I don't have an agent."

Josh joined the crowd in laughing. As the highest-paid late-night television host, money was always on Josh's mind as he focused on the potential financial windfall turned down by his guest. Leaning forward to add more presence to the follow-up, Josh paused and placed both hands, palms down, on the desk.

"In a country where success is measured in dollar bills, easily you turned down what could have been billions of dollars of income from your work, something you earned. Wasn't your wife at least mad, like, 'Honey, we could have bought an island...and the biggest diamond ring in the world...and seven Porsches, a different one for each day of the week.'"

"My wife was always by my side in this," Marc responded, momentarily looking down. Lifting his head upward, he paused and slightly leaned forward, maintaining a rigid posture, then continued: "My work was never accomplished in a vacuum. Science is a continual process of building on other's work. And, knowing this, how could anyone seek to profit from it?" Marc sincerely asked, leaning back into the chair. "That is why money was never in the equation. As I told your cosmetologist, Lisa, a few minutes ago...I was lucky."

"Lucky? You discovered what no one else could discover. How can you call that luck?" Josh asked, unable to hide his surprise at hearing Marc's answer.

"Luck applies in this case: right place...right time, truly. Discoveries are not always made by people seeking a specific destination. My work overlapped several, actually many areas of science."

"I was reading an article about how you benefitted from the aggressive accumulation of I worldwide DNA data from coronavirus pandemics. Is that true? Did multiple pandemics have something good come out of the suffering and death…a cure for cancer?"

"The accumulation of biometric data was significant in my work, and that was accelerated by necessity, trying to find a way to combat the reemergence of the deadly variant form of coronavirus in 2025," Marc said, nodding his head thoughtfully. "And…what was critical was the sharing of data. Many people opposed sharing biometrics, information that they believed should be kept private or at least in the confines of their country's borders. Had that information never been shared, we would have never put an end to the series of pandemics. The same information was then available for people like me and others trying to help humanity overcome diseases, avoid plagues, and expand the potential for a healthier, longer life."

"And I'm sure you know where I'm heading with this," Josh said, smiling, reaching over to touch Marc's arm in a preemptive apologetic manner.

"Yes…of course…it is hard to not discuss biometric data and vaccines without conspiracy theories," Marc said, a pained look on his face.

"Ok…I'll just ask it. Are you working for the Chinese government?" Josh asked, chortling, again reaching over and patting Marc's shoulder, confirming his outrageousness in posing the query.

"No," Marc said smiling, "but I'm sure that response will not quiet the conspiracy theorists. Yes…I worked with China. Yes…I worked with Russia. I worked with many countries that were viewed, at the time, as enemies by many people in the US. But I worked transparently and openly with the support of our government, the *World Health Organization*, and the *United Nations*. Nothing has been hidden. Quite to the contrary," Marc concluded, comfortably crossing his legs.

"The sharing of data did seem to revolve around China, the country where the original coronavirus was created," Josh said. "We know the first outbreak of the coronavirus originated from a Wuhan lab, but the source of the deadlier variant that erupted in early 2025 remains a mystery. While the second outbreak did great harm to China, they were able to rebound quicker with a much smaller loss of life and national treasure. And now, in 2030, the Chinese have staked out worldwide leadership in healthcare. You are obviously not an agent of the Chinese government. But even to non-conspiracy theorists, it appears the Chinese government benefitted the most from data accumulation and the sharing of biometric information. Is that why these ridiculous conspiracies continue to spring up?"

"Conspiracy theories almost led to a world war. However, as you noted, it ultimately took working with China and other countries worldwide to fight the virus's deadly variant strains. The pandemic required a global effort and cure."

"The pandemic felt like it was over…and then it wasn't…and then it was…and…" Josh said, shaking his head in frustration at the memory.

"Yes, but the mystery you refer to is not inexplicable," Marc responded. "A much deadlier coronavirus variant was engineered and purposely released in 2025. That is not a conspiracy theory. We do not know the source of the variant responsible for killing millions…yet. But we will. I am sure of that."

"We all hope that happens sooner than later," Josh stated, nodding in affirmation.

"Yes, and politics helped inhibit the discussion. Sadly, the massive death toll in the first half of 2025 led the world to the brink of nuclear war. But finally, facts helped to drown out national politics around the world. The rapid scientific response changed the word 'vaccine' to 'cure.' The conspiracy theories end when the truth is undeniable,"

Marc said, struggling to contain his frustration with the memory. "Sharing biometric information saved humanity from possible extinction. Together, the world ended the coronavirus…with a cure."

"I recall President Reagan once said before the United Nations that if the world knew we were under attack from aliens, it would unite the world in a single cause," Josh responded.

"And he was right," Marc quickly answered. "A global threat demands a global response."

"Remarkably, our relationship with China greatly improved. We were nearly at war with them less than five years ago. It appears science was the best diplomat. Again, you courageously called for sharing DNA information with China and others when it was unpopular. And now, what you're saying in your book takes even more courage," Josh stated, rising higher in his chair to reinforce his point. "Not too long ago, if a person even hinted at what you suggest about the origin of life on Earth, they would have been called crazy."

"Some of that criticism remains alive and well," Marc confirmed. "Let's be clear: there is science fiction…and there is science fact. My findings and the new book have not been warmly received in some quarters…but that is expected. But, again, I was not seeking to write a bestseller or to be popular. I share my work with people interested in understanding our origin…our past…and, even more importantly, our future," Marc said, emphasizing the final two words. "What I share is scientific fact," allowing his frustration to be heard in the authoritative tone of his voice. "That is why I am giving time to promote the book. This is worth the time to have a conversation about who we are as residents of this planet," Marc said, again straightening his back as he moved forward, opening his hands, palms upward, in a welcoming gesture as he spoke.

"I understand you have had to endure many death threats?"

"Regretfully, that is true. But I'm not shocked," Marc said, trying to keep his voice neutral. Leaning back, he allowed his gaze to drop to his now folded hands. "Not all discoveries are immediately accepted," Marc said, repositioning himself to a more upright posture. "You do not have to look back very far in history and find people being burned alive for suggesting the Earth orbited the sun. I understand sharing information…sharing knowledge…is not always applauded or desired by everyone. Sometimes, ignorance is bliss. Some people find comfort in believing the world is flat." Marc placed his left hand flat on the oak desk. "And telling them otherwise upsets the world they believe in. What I offer in my book is controversial…but factual…and accurate," Marc firmly stated, carefully accentuating each point by lightly striking the edge of Martin's desk with his open hand. "If that makes people uncomfortable, it is not my problem…it's their problem," Marc said, unable to hide a dismissive tone of voice.

The applause was spontaneous. Martin looked at the audience and applauded along with them. While most of the audience continued steady applause, a small number sat frozen in silent rebellion to Marc's comments and presence.

"Dr. Walker, your book suggests God, or a god or gods, did not create humans…or even life on this planet. You suggest a species of extraterrestrials both created us and actively engineered us. This contradicts world religions and goes against Darwinian evolution and much of the science over the past several hundred years. What you suggest is that we…humans…are an experiment in engineering by…star people?"

"I am not theorizing. We originated from star people…for lack of a better description. We are all part of a cosmic family. We are all made of the same stuff…the same ingredients…found throughout the universe. And, yes, the stuff found in stars. And, if we call ourselves 'people,' then our ancestors would hold a similar distinction. Yes, they

21

would be different but simultaneously very similar to us, and they are still our ancestors. We are part of their family."

"That sounds like one hell of a family reunion!" Josh said, drawing laughs. "I'm an entertainer and limited on molecular genetics, but your book is written to bring this incredibly complex assortment of science from DNA to CRISPR into a very understandable read. So, saying 'stuff' actually helps me," Josh said, laughing. "Let's see if I have this right. You found a 'signature' in human DNA...a message...a code...purposefully and deliberately planted to say, 'You're one of us.' Is that right?"

"I could not say it better myself," Marc said, smiling.

"Maybe I should become a scientist?" Josh said, laughing.

"I would not go that far," Marc said, as the initial tension in the audience was diminished with a cascade of laughs. "You're doing great where you are. And, as you noted, the pay is better."

"You refer to this DNA code as the *Axis Mundi*," Josh continued.

"Yes. It is our connection to the cosmos. It is our connection to everything," Marc said, obviously warming to the subject of Martin's focus.

"For me, it seemed like the world has always been divided into two camps: religion and science. The religious people said that a God or gods created everything from nothing, some even claiming the universe is only five thousand years old. And there is science, with scientists pointing to evolution as the answer to how we were created. There was never much of a bridge between the two. But you seem to have burned the bridge and...pun intended...alienated both camps," Josh said, drawing laughter.

"Evolution is not creation. That is why dangling it in a title with 'origin' possibly caused such turmoil. Maybe Darwin had an agent like yours?" Marc asked, expecting audience laughter at a comment he perceived as humorous. Instead, it only drew a slight chuckle from

Martin. Fleetingly flustered, Marc regained his momentary loss of focus and continued. "Evolution is a reality, but evolution does not fully explain us. There has simply not been enough time for evolution from a single cell to human beings. The math doesn't work."

"You also pointed out evolution is horrifically slow and does not explain the leaps in the advancement of humans."

"Evolution is slow, painfully slow. And evolution is far from predictable. Evolution is random. There would be no human species relying solely on evolution. The creation of humans demanded engineering. As evidenced in genetic editing, when you make even the smallest edits in human DNA, the consequences are rapid and much more predictable."

"Your work found what many called the missing link?" Josh asked, eager to offer the question.

"I would say links, as plural. Evolution proves humans are unique, and we were engineered this way. Unlike the theories of one of the harshest critics of my findings, an evolutionary biologist who will go unnamed, the deadly, random snail's pace of evolution proves the uniqueness of humans to other species and leads to the conclusion we were created and genetically edited."

"You say the fact we are here, on Earth, proves that the universe is full of life," Josh followed up, pausing. "While the US government continues to allow a slow drip-drip of confusing information about contact with extraterrestrials, we seem forever locked into not fully knowing what has happened from Roswell to UAPs. Do you trust the US government?"

"Josh, I am sorry, but I will not answer that. People can believe what they want to believe. I would urge them to only trust after verification, which applies to anything," Marc said, showing his discomfort with the question by shifting his body in the chair away from the desk separating him from Martin.

"Dr. Walker, can you verify we are not alone?" Josh asked, instinctively leaning forward.

"Yes, I can, and I have. The proof is within each of us. Not only are we not alone in the universe, but if we look for a creator, we do not need to fight over which religion is right. None of them have it right on creation. The creation of humans had nothing to do with an invisible, divine, magical, creative force. As we know, life was not formed from nothing in an instantaneous wave of a wand by an old man with a long white beard. Our creators are not invisible. They are real. They are part of us as we are part of them...our family."

The booing began again, even more intensely, with a smattering of applause.

"I jotted down something from your book that made me stop and think," Josh said, picking up a notecard, ignoring the negative response from the audience. "You wrote: 'If you are looking for alien life, you do not need space travel, but a mirror. Look in the mirror. What you are seeing is alien life. We are aliens.'"

"I must admit my editor assisted in adding that last line. As a writer, I do not have a flair for the dramatic. But that is true and seems to jolt people when they read or hear it. I prefer a family perspective instead of aliens," Marc said. "It is much more accurate and not nearly as ominous and threatening to the senses."

"You understand when you say 'family,' you are stabbing quite a few religions in the heart?" Josh asked.

"My purpose is not to debunk religions. Religions are part of many people's response to seeking explanations for things we cannot understand, much like conspiracy theories. Religions are part of our various cultures and identities. I understand their flawed perspectives, but I do not agree with their nonsensical conclusions. Dismissing fact for fiction by tossing out what is now known in favor of an unknown based solely on ancient myths is a problem. And, I am not saying, 'There is no god or gods.' I am merely saying our direct and immediate creator was not divine but extraterrestrial."

Pausing and briefly shutting his eyes, Marc continued: "Think of it this way. We are part of something much larger than our planet. We have ancestors extending thousands, even millions of light-years from us in every direction," Marc said, illustrating his comments by holding his hands far apart, then collapsing them together in what looked like a prayerful hand gesture as he concluded his answer. "We are part of that family. For me, that is spiritual. We are not alone. And there is a higher power. The creators are clearly more advanced than their creations."

"You also suggest there are likely many family lines of species…that the universe is truly full of life…many different types of life?"

"The size of the universe would suggest there is a lot of room for life. And the various types of human forms, from homo sapiens to Neanderthals, suggest variety within a species is universal. We know this from our own planet. Life cannot be narrowly defined, considering the vast number of species inhabiting the planet over millions of years."

"And that is something we are now doing, things like genetic editing, artificial intelligence, and cloning, even at our stage of development. And now, curing diseases like cancer?" Josh asked.

"Yes," Marc responded. "If we can do it, why couldn't beings that have existed for possibly billions of years longer than us? It would be the pinnacle of hubris to think we are the only species in the universe with the knowledge to alter life forms."

Marc paused before continuing, contemplating what he would say next.

"My problem is that in many cases, religion attempts to drown out questions, restrict the collection of knowledge, and seek conclusions by saying, 'We already have all the answers.' And, not allowing what you referred to as the other 'camp,' science, off the hook, science has a self-imposed, limiting belief system. As a result, challenging Darwin…challenging Einstein…and challenging what science has considered as known and settled can be just as daunting in the realm of science and result in significant and even hysterical resistance."

Again, Marc hesitated and looked down momentarily before looking back at Josh and resuming his comments.

"The prejudice of facts is not owned by those relying on religion for answers. The more we know about one thing reminds us, the less we know about everything. For me, that is science. In many ways, we, as a species on Earth, are just learning to walk and talk in scientific realities. We are relative newborns to understand the universe, from microbes to black holes. Knowing who we are and where we came from is not found in a holy book or a science book but is truly within us, waiting to be fully unlocked. I believe we now possibly have the key to open the first door of many."

"Before we take a commercial break, I have some quick questions. Do you believe that your findings give accounts of alien abductions validity?"

"No."

"That was direct," Josh said, awkwardly laughing.

"I cannot imagine a scenario where a civilization capable of interstellar travel comes here and clandestinely abducts humans for experiments. That would seem highly unlikely."

"Your perspective on alien abductions has angered many in the sizeable UFO community. You could have sold more books if you said, 'Yeah, that's the aliens coming here to abduct humans for experiments, and the US government is covering up the truth.'"

"That was not my goal…to reach the tin foil hat audience," Marc said dismissively.

"That hurt a few million people's feelings! I'm guessing social media will be blowing up right about now," Josh said, laughing.

"I'm not here to make people feel…anything. I want them to think, reason, and rely on facts…not emotions. That will be good for humanity…even people on social media."

"Do you believe our ancestors will return?"

"Yes, even if simply out of curiosity."

"Last quick follow-up question before the break, and maybe the most important: do you believe they, our family, will be friendly when they return?"

"While I would hope a technologically developed species with the power to engineer life and travel vast distances in the universe would be 'friendly,' I honestly cannot say with any certainty," Marc said as he paused to consider the question.

"Consider the history of humanity in dealing with indigenous people," Marc continued. "And think about our indifference to other life forms on our planet. I hope these are solely human traits…traits that are not shared with our ancestors. But sadly, the apple may not fall far from the tree."

"Dr. Walker, that is the scariest thing I have heard you say," Josh said soberly without intent for gaining laughs. The studio audience was silent.

"Let's hope they do not see us as the brother-in-law in the *Christmas Vacation* movie," Marc said, smiling, attempting to break the tension. The audience joined the host in nervous laughter and then applause.

"Ok, let's take a brief commercial break," Josh said, looking into the primary camera. Then, turning to Marc with the microphone off, Josh said in a low voice: "Speaking of family, do you mind me asking questions about your twin brother, Jon?" Josh asked, looking into Marc's eyes to detect his reaction.

"I would rather stick to the topic we are on…" Marc responded but was interrupted by the host.

"The interest in your brother, a true war hero, was a hot topic before the world heard everything about you. I would appreciate you giving me just a couple of questions," Josh implored, leaning forward and putting his hand on Marc's shoulder. "He is a personal hero of mine. I would not do anything to embarrass you or him. I promise," Josh said, feeling the tension regarding his question.

"I understand. But please know my brother does not seek attention. And I rarely speak to Jon. He enjoys life out of the spotlight."

"I understand…we are coming back," Josh said as the producer counted down to the return to tape the second half of the interview.

CHAPTER TWO
FEAR

Jon Walker was afraid of the dark.

It was a difficult admission for a former Army Ranger and decorated war hero. But as he lay curled on the floor of the tiny shack in the vast Alaskan wilderness, he knew it was true.

As a POW in Syria in 2025, imposed darkness had left a mental wound that would not heal.

Five years later, far from the threat of war, Jon could not shake the memories and the fear.

Compounding his issues with the setting sun, Jon could not sleep. Far from insomnia, his body did not require sleep. Despite being awake every moment, Jon never suffered the adverse effects sleep-deprived people endured.

As a child, staying up all night did not seem to bother his mother, but it enraged his brother. His mother swore his brother, Marc, to secrecy to not share Jon's issues with sleep with others and never pressed for clinical observations to find a solution. He was never allowed to stay overnight at a friend's house. Despite his mother and brother's awareness, Jon felt the pressure to not appear abnormal, so he would go to bed and lie awake, pretending to be asleep.

While Jon did not need sleep, he wanted to experience this puzzling behavior he saw in others. He heard people speak of dreams, something he had never experienced. Seeing people around him close their eyes, suspending their consciousness, temporarily leaving the world for some unknown, mystical destination, only made Jon yearn more for the experience.

As he grew into adulthood, his craving to experience sleep intensified. In his attempts to sleep, Jon had tried drugs and alcohol, using both to excess. Even after consuming massive combinations of drugs and alcohol, he would only experience a brief, nightmarish half-sleep.

Despite the consequences, he continued trying until he finally overdosed and nearly died. The experience led Jon to choose sobriety, but he remained haunted by his sleepless nights.

The anxiety from years of trying to hide the anomaly from others plagued him even when alone.

Instead of resting in his single bed each night, Jon opted to curl up in a storage closet in the corner of the small cabin he called home for half of the year. With a bright overhead light remaining on during his self-imposed nightly stay in the confined area, Jon felt secure enough to pursue his love of reading. Leaving clothing piled beneath the bed's covers to suggest the image of a thickly muscled, six-foot-three inch, two-hundred-and-twenty-pound man at rest was a nightly ritual. It was also something he inwardly reminded himself was a method to his madness.

Lying on the floor was uncomfortable, and Jon did not want to ever feel comfortable again.

Comfort dulled the senses. To survive, his natural instincts had to be alive and vibrantly connected to the world, ready to warn of every threat of danger. His one mistake in Syria was allowing himself a brief moment of comfort. It almost cost him his life.

He vowed to never repeat that mistake.

Jon was ready to respond to any challenge with a handgun, shotgun, and machete within reach.

While there was no apparent threat of anyone seeking to kill him in Alaska, the lack of a known threat did not diminish the overwhelming feeling of danger engulfing him at night. To prepare for whatever may come his way, Jon turned a remote cabin into a defensive haven and a veritable trap for any predatory humans.

Living alone was not what he wanted—but being alone was what he needed.

Alaska offered Jon what he perceived as at least half a year of extended daylight hours. For the other half of the year, Jon retreated to New Mexico to live in a secluded area far enough away from humans to give him a measure of comfort. If forced to choose between the two, Jon would choose Alaska as home, but a season featuring nearly a full day of near darkness was not something he could accept.

Jon loved the light of day.

Still feeling the compulsion to attempt to sleep, Jon would curl up on the floor and recall the memories of the many men he had killed in combat. He would mentally place the kills in chronological order as part of his nightly ritual, but his attempts to count his way to sleep always failed.

Tonight was no different.

The sounds of living in the wilderness, far enough from others to avoid any signs of human enterprise, were the most helpful aspect of his tiny cabin in Alaska.

Natural sounds did not disturb Jon. Nature was his friend. Bears, moose, deer, wolves, and many other animals all enjoyed the same tract of land Jon now called home. Their sounds were natural and welcomed by him.

Humans left their unique stamp on sounds. Most evident were the sounds of humans attempting to be silent. From his experiences as a trained predator, Jon knew humans may have an advantage in many areas over animals. But humans could not avoid making unnatural sounds, attempting to avoid detection.

And those distinctive, unique sounds were the sounds Jon listened to detect each night.

As Jon was chronicling his kills, lying on the floor of his closet, he heard the unmistakable, unnatural sound he had been listening for during his half-year residencies living alone in Alaska.

Someone was outside of the cabin. The unnatural sounds were unmistakable. The property was marked with an abundance of warning signs along with the fencing surrounding the structure. If someone was near the home after dark, their intentions went far beyond curiosity or accidental trespassing.

Jon stilled his breathing and moved slowly to lift upward to turn off the overhead light as he crouched in the closet, peering through the gap in the nearly closed door. He held the pistol in his left hand and gripped the machete in his right—his thinking reverted to a calm clearness of watching and waiting for his prey, something he had learned many years earlier.

He was not on the defensive. He was not the hunted now...he was the hunter. The intruders were on his land and deserved the consequences of trespassing.

Jon's immediate thought was respect. The person or persons had avoided many of the measures he had thoughtfully and meticulously constructed to ward off intruders. The security cameras were all set on night vision. The intruders would be caught on video as they neared the cabin, but the laptop was on the small desk in the living area, far from Jon's reach in the storage closet.

They may be good, but now they are stepping into my world, a place prepared for human threats.

This was his territory—his home.

A crudely fashioned sign Jon cut into a wood shingle hung on the top of the cabin's front porch reminded anyone of what to expect if they were purposefully intrusive: "*Intruders Will Die.*"

The light from a half-moon on a cloudless night barely penetrated the room through the closed curtains, now serving as the only light source. The three-room cabin had only one deadbolted door in Jon's sight. A small porch with six steep steps was the only entry other than the partially shuttered windows, the cracks in the shutters allowing in slices of light, all in Jon's line of sight from his vantage point in the closet.

During the cabin's construction, Jon had ensured the steps leading up to the porch would creak with any weight applied to the wood. The steps loudly squeaked with the body weight of what sounded like two men. They were now on the narrow porch at the entry door.

The door handle on the heavy wooden door slightly moved, the deadbolt keeping the door shut tightly.

Jon waited.

But then the deadbolt quietly turned to unlock as if invisible hands were turning it from within the home.

Jon's heart rate remained steady—his vision glued to the door. The gun was loaded with a bullet chambered, ready to be launched with a slight trigger squeeze.

The doorknob turned slowly…almost too slowly, given Jon's experience.

These guys are excellent, Jon thought as he prepared to respond upon their full entry.

But as the door slowly opened, a dim, amber light was evident through the expanding opening. The door was now open approximately six inches. Jon's thoughts began to search his database for what type of light this was and why. The beams of light seemed fragmented—a light pattern he had never experienced, as if the light was being seen through a misty fog.

No answer to what he was seeing was apparent. This was something different.

Jon was ready.

With the door partially open and cold night air blowing into the cabin, Jon wondered why the intruders were waiting. He did not hear any creaks on the steps of the porch.

Suddenly, a bright light flashed in the room.

Jon was fully blinded despite looking through a barely three-inch gap in the closet door.

Jon did not move. He listened but heard nothing. Jon felt like someone had struck him with a hammer between his eyes. He attempted to be patient, hoping to gather himself for what was next.

But Jon's patience ended.

Pushing the door open, rolling out of the closet, crouched on one knee, still unable to see, Jon used his knowledge of the room's orientation to begin shooting round after round in a barrage targeting the front door.

He heard no sounds.

Have I killed them? If they are alive, I should hear them, he thought.

Jon waited in stillness. There was no detectable sound of the intruders—just the faint sound of the wind blowing into the cabin.

Still completely blind, Jon dropped the pistol and switched hands, holding the machete in his left hand. Crouching, moving slowly, Jon made a series of short, compact swings with the machete, landing only on the corner of the bed with one stroke as he moved across the expanse of the cabin.

His eyes now burned, and the smell of the gunfire remained in the cold air circling through the cabin. Still crouching, Jon mindfully reoriented his place in the small structure and continued to move toward the entry. As he put his right hand on the door to close it, he felt something inhibiting it. He quickly dropped to his knee and slammed the machete downward into whatever barrier lay in the doorway and down to the floor.

He felt the squish of the blade hitting flesh—a body. Though still blind, Jon felt comforted that he had shot the intruder with the gunfire and now the force of the machete.

But there were two...he thought.

Before the thought was finished, the heavy wooden door crashed into Jon, knocking him to the floor. Pain seared his abdomen, the jolt of being stabbed in the side with a long, thin weapon.

It's a spear of some type, he thought, as he instinctively drove the machete upwards and made a brutal swipe toward where the second intruder was likely standing near him.

Jon heard the sound simultaneously with the machete's impact, a shrill squeal of what sounded more animal than human.

Whatever the type of weapon used to stab Jon, it had left something lodged in his gut, the pain now much more intense after the defensive move. He could feel the end of a thin projectile sticking out from his stomach.

Jon fell against the cabin's wall, defensively swinging the blade back and forth.

As darkness descended on his consciousness, he heard the shrill cry again, and a tug as the needle-like object was pulled from his abdomen.

Jon's last thought before passing out was a pungent odor—similar to ammonia but much more potent—and the sound of movement around him, then the creaking of the boards on the steps.

Expression

"We are back from our break with Dr. Marc Walker. Keeping our focus on family, millions of Americans want to know about your twin brother, Jon Walker. How is he doing?"

As the audience broke into its loudest applause, Marc responded as the ovation continued: "Jon is well and enjoying a great life outside the public spotlight."

"His bravery and your scientific discoveries are even more remarkable considering you were raised by a single mother in Dallas," Josh said. "Your mom must have been a truly amazing woman."

"Yes, she was. My greatest regret will always be her passing at a relatively young age," Marc said, appearing to brush lint from his slacks, hoping to signal an end to the topic.

"As youngsters, you and your brother both stood out in athletics, opening the way for an opportunity to move to a better school in Dallas and scholarships in college?" Josh asked.

"Yes, both of us excelled athletically. If you know anything about sports in Texas, you know that recruitment begins early. We were in demand as youngsters, and Plano, Texas, reached out to our mother and made it clear we were more than welcome to attend their schools."

"Essentially, you were both recruited as kids," Josh added.

"Yes. Of course, we were not the only such athletes; Plano was not the only school system involved in recruiting. Both of us were taller and faster than other kids our age. Being African American twins, even though we were far from identical, made us standout even more," Marc answered.

"Great genetics, right? You're a genius. What about Jon?" Josh asked, clearly interested in the answer.

"Truthfully, my brother is far more intelligent than me," Marc said with sincerity. "Interestingly, when you talked about how the world was divided between science and religion, it applies to Jon and me. Jon is a spiritual seeker. I'm a skeptic. Despite the differences, ultimately, we both looked inward for answers."

"Do you two debate a lot?"

"As kids, we never debated. We fought a lot. Jon has certain strong core beliefs that I know I will never change. I admire Jon's desire and capacity to see beyond what we can see. And he is much braver than me."

The audience applauded, many standing to cheer.

"Wherever he is, I am sure he will appreciate hearing that from you," Josh said.

"Most likely, he is nowhere near a television."

"Is it true you still do not know who your father is?" Josh asked, quickly changing the subject, surprising Marc.

"That is a question I would prefer to not answer or discuss," Marc responded, crossing his legs and putting his head down momentarily before facing the host with a near glare.

"Again, the public's interest remains sky-high about your brother's life outside the military. Is it true he is living in Alaska completely removed from people, living in the wilderness alone…completely off the grid?"

"I can't answer that. Jon has served his country and earned the right to privacy," Marc said, clearly frustrated with the host's question, explicitly mentioning the state Jon spent over half of each year.

"What he did…the lives he saved and the torture he endured…his self-sacrifice…is for many Americans what defines the men and women of our military," Josh stated.

"I agree. My brother fought for freedom and deserves that same freedom and privacy," Marc said with sternness and directness that signaled an end to the questions about Jon as the audience applauded Marc's response.

Josh turned to the camera and said, "Jon Walker…wherever you are, know this: we love you and appreciate all you've done for all of us. Godspeed and take care," the audience renewed their loud applause.

After pausing and looking at his notes, Josh continued: "We are running out of time. But I wanted to take a few minutes and touch on something you wrote in your book that helps bring the incredible science of genetic editing down to a level that I can understand and appreciate. It's the part about comparing genetic editing to editing a book. Would you mind sharing that with us?"

"While I would never claim to be a skilled writer, as evidenced by the number of red markings from my editor, the writing process was profoundly humbling. Given the vast number of words and the extraordinary number of choices to find the best way to express yourself, I began to see a correlation between editing genes and editing words. I found the process of writing and especially editing a book very similar to genetic editing. Both are extremely nuanced and ultimately rely on expression."

"Yes!" Josh said, interrupting. "When I read that term—*expression*—the enormous complexity of what is accomplished in genetic editing started to sink in. Please continue, I didn't mean to interrupt," Josh said.

"Editing genes is much more than turning them on and off. It goes much deeper. The mutations associated with cancer and diseases are not just the result of whether a gene responds but how it responds. The responses are more than yes and no. And we all know even when you hear 'Yes' or 'No,' how the word is expressed can be radically different and unique to the moment. Correcting mutations to cure cancer and diseases requires changing how a gene expresses itself. And that demands going much deeper than 'Yes' or 'No.' The devil is truly in the details."

Marc turned in the chair to face the studio audience as he continued.

"Let's imagine for a moment attempting to edit the expression of one human cell, just one cell of approximately thirty-seven trillion cells in a human. Doing so would be like trying to find and edit, to correct, just one word and changing how the word is expressed in a library of books the size of our entire planet. And when you find the one word in the vast number of books, it involves more than simply deleting the word. It demands changing one word in the context of how the word fits in the framework of the entire enormous library. The editing corrects how the word expresses the meaning…it corrects the intention of that single word. Imagine, the expression of one word out of trillions of words makes the difference," Marc said, the audience offering appreciative applause.

"That's much more difficult than finding a 'needle in a haystack,'" Josh responded. "Reading that description in your book helped me understand the challenges and the tremendous power of what a genetic scientist can do. I'm in awe of the power, and it also frightens me. It reminds me of nuclear power. Regarding genetic editing, that power can be used in different ways: the power to cure or, if placed in the wrong hands, the power to inflict pain and suffering. The same is true for nuclear power. You wrote in your book how you are constantly humbled by having this knowledge…this power. Are you worried that you may have opened Pandora's Box?" Josh asked.

"Possessing the power to change something gives the possessor the power to be both creator and destroyer. While they are much different, when Oppenheimer witnessed the first nuclear weapon's detonation, he said: 'Now I am become Death, the destroyer of worlds.' When I fully realized what could be accomplished with genetic editing, I had no thoughts of causing death but instead preserving life. So, I would suggest a different perspective. Billions of people on our planet will now experience a longer, healthier life from being less vulnerable with the ability to alter genes. I think the trade-off is much more positive."

Marc paused, allowing the applause to fade before continuing.

"And you're correct. In the wrong hands, the power to effectively end humankind exists using gene editing. That is true," Marc continued. "But that power of self-destruction has always existed. We have destroyed the environment of our planet. We have enough nuclear arms to destroy life as we know it. Diseases have ravaged us for millions of years, and we were always just one viral mutation away from seeing a pathogen wipe out humanity. Yes…we now have the power to destroy. But we also have the power to heal…cure…and save lives. I'll take that and not look back," Marc said as the crowd erupted with cheers of approval.

"You mentioned the Oppenheimer quote in your book. Did you have a quote in mind when you discovered what you call the Axis Mundi, the signature hidden within our DNA from our ancestors?" Josh asked.

"Great question. I did have a quote in mind. It is a quote from someone you mentioned earlier, Jonas Salk: 'Our greatest responsibility is to be good **ancestors**,'" Marc said.

"That would make the world a better place!" Josh said, applauding along with the studio audience. "In closing, I have to ask. You're still a very young man. You've been instrumental in finding a cure for cancer, and now you're giving us proof of our creators and our place in the universe. What's next for you? I hope it's not as a late-night talk show host," Josh said in mock envy.

"No worries about me as a talk show host," Marc said, joining in the laughter with the audience. "But I love the question, thanks for asking. Of all the work I've done in my life, I think the next challenge is using what we've learned to further extend the quantity and quality of human life. Inside us is an ingrained desire for the eternal, to live forever. Yet, we spend somewhere around thirty percent of our life asleep. In a normal human life span, we are biologically forced to sleep twenty-one years of that existence. Imagine finding a way to improve the quality of life and the quantity by simply sleeping less. Think about it…more waking hours spent with a sharper mind and a much healthier body. We have it within our power to find a way to live healthier with less sleep, which I believe will be worth exploring."

"I think we would all appreciate that, especially me," Josh said, chuckling. "My audience would go from late-night to mid-day!"

"Tell your agent to be prepared. I think we are on the road to making it happen," Marc responded, smiling.

"Thank you, Dr. Walker, for all the marvelous things you have done for the world. You are a 'good ancestor' in my book," Josh said, leading the crowd, now standing in applause.

"Thank you, Josh," Marc responded as the audience applauded.

Josh looked into the camera and said, "We'll be back after a commercial break."

Josh leaned over, shook Marc's hand, and said, "I appreciate you coming on my show. I hope it worked out the way you hoped."

"Yes…you did an excellent job with the questions. And I appreciate what you said about my brother. But please…what I said about him deserving privacy is the truth. He has never sought fame and recognition," Marc said, still holding the host's hand in a significantly tight grip.

"I understand," Josh said, trying to avoid grimacing, "I truly understand."

Marc left the stage and was directed to the green room at the back of the auditorium where he would wait for transportation. As he opened a bottle of water, he heard a familiar voice.

"You mentioned our conversation on the show…you mentioned me…thank you! And you did great…it was perfect!"

Marc turned toward the open door and saw Lisa.

"I didn't mean to barge in. I just wanted to tell you before you leave," she said, her face turning crimson from embarrassment at her forward approach.

"Thank you, Lisa! You're very memorable," Marc responded. "You made an incredible impression on me."

Stunned and blushing, Lisa said, "I hope I'm not too forward."

"Not at all. If you're not doing anything, would you like to have a drink with me at my hotel?" Marc asked, cautious to avoid anyone else hearing his offer.

Still in shock at the sequence of events, Lisa responded, "Well…yes…I would love to have a drink with you."

After telling the show's production assistant he would not need limo services, Marc and Lisa met outside and shared a cab back to his hotel. Marc was careful to avoid people seeing him leave with the beautiful young blonde.

Marc's appetite for sex was ravenous, and he hated being alone. A cure for both was finding a partner to share his bed each night when he was away from home. While he did not like to admit it, Marc despised feeling even a hint of loneliness.

Lisa's night with Marc ended abruptly when he coldly told her at six in the morning, "It's time for you to leave."

After she walked out the door into the hotel hallway, Lisa stopped and asked Marc, "Is this it…will I ever see you again?"

Marc dismissively grinned and said, "Not likely. I think this was enough," as he shut the door in her face.

Feeling refreshed and invigorated, Marc stepped into the shower. His flight was scheduled to leave at 11:30 a.m.

As he stood in the shower, allowing the hot water to pour over him, Marc laughed and exclaimed aloud, "What a great fucking life!"

CHAPTER THREE
ANOTHER WORLD

It was like running in another world.

Alana continued her rapid pace up the steep, winding trek on *Haleakala*, a ten-thousand-foot-high volcano on Maui. The landscape was now a far cry from the lush, tropical locale where she had left her Jeep Wrangler.

While an annual "Big Volcano Run" was held in *Haleakala Park*, it was rare to see any other runners venturing onto Alana's three-times-a-week training route up the dormant volcano.

Today was no different.

Alana seemed to have the trail to the volcano all to her own—something she was thankful for. Her training regimen did not leave room for small talk or getting acquainted.

"Focus!" she shouted as she turned a sharp corner up an even steeper ascent, accelerating her pace. As Alana crossed the three-mile mark of her run, the unearthly landscape uncharacteristically made the hairs on her neck rise, despite being in the middle of the day and traversing a well-known path.

The sky was overcast. The faster moving lower clouds, seemingly so close Alana could reach out and touch them, were windswept. Their shadows created an illusion of the hardened, lava soil rousing to a life of its own as Alana's thickly muscled legs propelled her up the narrow trail.

"Come on, focus!" she shouted out again, quickening her pace as if the word held a magical force. But Alana's thoughts were betraying her. A thread of memories began to resurface. She had tried to run away from a painful past, but the agonizing recollections continued to keep step.

"Garbage...quit thinking garbage!" she cried out. Despite her best efforts, Alana could never leave the past far enough behind.

The past is not my friend, she thought as she turned another severe corner in her zigzagging ascension toward the *Keonehe'e Trail* entry. Known as the "Sliding Sands Trail," the five-mile loop path was typically trafficked with hikers navigating what many describe as an "alien" landscape to the crater's floor.

But today, she could not see any other people. The seclusion of the path helped to calm Alana's mind. The trail's quiet solitude reminded her of the many stories of sacred land she heard from her grandmother, Nohealani.

"We live on sacred ground. Honor the island where you live," her grandmother would remind Alana. "Maui is an island...part of the bigger island, Earth."

The reverence for land became an even greater reality for Alana when she traveled from Maui to the mainland US and then returned home. Flying back to the tiny dot in the Pacific Ocean always reminded Alana of her grandmother's words and belief in the quality of living on an island. Going hand-in-hand with that belief were traits—Hawaiian traits—she proudly owned: conservation of natural resources and suspicion of outsiders.

Now descending the crusty trail down into the cone of the volcano, Alana allowed herself a smile remembering the love and lessons Nohealani had shared with her.

Born on the island of Maui, Alana had been raised by her grandmother. Alana's mother died giving birth to her—her father had remained an unknown. While the absence of a mother and a father could have adversely touched her life, Alana's childhood had been happy, almost idyllic. There was a close circle of friends cultivated through her grandmother, offering, in her perspective, a large, loving family.

The temperature had continued to drop, not unusual given the altitude and extreme, volatile nature of the weather conditions evidenced around the volcano. But, unlike most days, the cloud cover had nearly darkened the sun's light, making it appear to be closer to dusk than mid-day.

As Alana moved onto the relatively flat plain of the crater's floor, the lava rocks were more granular and challenging to maintain her fast pace. Despite being on level ground, she slowed to regain her footing.

Alana was an Olympic heptathlon competitor, and she was training to take the gold medal in 2032 after letting it slip through her fingers in 2028. The sudden death of her grandmother in the middle of the games had made her lose focus. The ill-fated story of her personal loss spurred a media frenzy that dug up the worst of her past. But things were different now. She was focused.

Unexpectedly, lightning sparked over her right shoulder. As Alana looked to where the flash had originated, she veered slightly. The feeling of soft ground giving way under her right foot was simultaneous with the sharp pain as her ankle pushed outward. Unable to stop her momentum Alana fell in a controlled roll on the granular surface.

"Shit!" Alana cried out as she remained curled on the ground clutching her ankle. Pain throbbed with each beat of her heart, but Alana began her process to take control of the moment.

"Breathe," she said, her voice gripped in pain. "Breathe…slow. Breathe…slow," she repeated.

The pain, while still evident, began to diminish as she purposefully slowed her breathing. Alana sat up and reached behind, removing one of the two water bottles from her runner's backpack. As she gulped the water, another bright light flashed over the horizon at the edge of the crater.

"What the fuck?" she said aloud.

Alana's first thought was lightning was rare but not impossible, given the weather conditions. Then, another flash, but this time Alana noticed what seemed to be an amber afterglow.

There was no sound. No wind was blowing in the interior of the crater. Alana's curiosity was now dictating her thoughts despite the residual throbbing pain from her swollen ankle. She knew it was nothing more than a slight sprain, something that had happened before.

"Always be prepared," Alana said, nervously laughing.

Taking off the tight-fitting backpack, she reached inside and opened the mini first aid kit, removing the medical wrap. Alana took off her shoe and inspected her ankle. She wrapped the area in a snuggly-fitting compress. Now taped and feeling much more secure in placing weight on the sprain, Alana lifted herself upward. The pain was manageable. Alana's next thought flowed to frustration, wondering how long the sprain would inhibit her extreme training regimen.

I can do this, she thought, surveying the area for any sign of hikers. None were in sight. Alana began what would be a much slower walk out of the crater and back down the volcano. But another, more sustained, brilliant flash of light appeared over the edge of one of the nearby red cinder cones jutting from the surface less than a hundred yards away.

That's not lightning, Alana thought to herself.

Curiosity helped lead Alana to her most outstanding personal achievements and worst life experiences. Seeing the bright flash was a signal, a call to action to find the causal force for such an uncommon event and to understand the phenomenon she was experiencing.

"Ok...I have to check this out," Alana said to herself.

Changing direction, Alana picked her way over the loose, grainy lava limping toward the source of the light. Her thoughts pondered the cause of the flashes, with no sound, in a crater void of any electricity or man-made structures.

Maybe I should turn and leave, she thought, allowing a slight smile to cross her face, already knowing the answer to her self-directed question. The idea of a challenge had never deterred Alana from journeys of discovery.

Now within days of her birthday, Alana was nearing the beginning of her twenty-fourth year. Life, for Alana, was structured around markers in time. From years to seconds, each time segment had its unique importance. It was her way to measure progress.

Time mattered more to Alana than most, especially the passing of it. A sense of urgency in all things dominated her outlook on life—an intensity to live in the present moment permeated her very being. Her passionate commitment to the conservation of natural resources was matched in her resolute dedication to the efficient use of time. And Alana's tendency to err on the side of rushing into things had always met the friction of her grandmother's constant reminders to "practice patience."

Thinking of her grandmother's admonition to be patient, Alana laughed out loud as she continued the descent to the floor of the volcano.

Tell a Hawaiian to stop, slow down, and be patient...and all of us do what I'm doing...we keep moving, she thought.

"Always keep moving," Alana said aloud, reaffirming her thoughts.

Staying in motion was in Alana's nature, and it was in her training. As a student-athlete in Colorado, she had been sexually assaulted by three white students at the university. The experience had paralyzed her for a time. But she responded by training in multiple self-defense disciplines, from martial arts to knives. The training helped give her greater confidence and a feeling of power.

The tactical, fixed-blade Bowie knife given to her by her instructor remained with her at all possible times. With the knife worn on her hip and the knowledge of how to use it, Alana had finally outgrown the fear of being alone in her training regimen. She could again enjoy the freedom of being outdoors by herself. But, as she slowly hobbled to the edge of the last lava cone, behind where the light had once again flashed, she felt a tidal wave of fear engulf her.

Looking over the landscape, there was nothing there…nothing.

Why are you afraid? Alana thought, trying to calm the anxiety of failing to understand what was happening around her in the crater.

In life, Alana had been taught to never run away from fear but to embrace it and understand the causes—and, by seeing fear for what it was, she could then let it go.

"Know no fear…and you will be free to live," her grandmother had taught her.

"Know no fear," Alana said aloud. The sound and cadence of the words restored self-control and calmed her anxiety.

Alana paused, listening, and regained her composure. Standing still, her senses were at their highest level.

Her initial fear was now focused on a deliberate, controlled state of preparation. Again, purposefully slowing her breathing with deep breaths, Alana was ready for whatever was going to happen.

"Who is there? Show yourself…come out!" she shouted with a commanding tone. "This isn't funny!"

Silence—even the wind had seemed to momentarily cease its movement in the typical whirling fashion within the crater's cone.

Then, another flash of light, this time from directly below the crevice out of her field of sight. And then Alana heard what sounded like something quickly moving over the loose lava surface below.

Running away was not an option.

Momentarily turning away from attackers had been her mistake in Colorado years earlier. Even if she wanted to do so, running was not possible—the pain in her ankle continued to throb as she stood, forced to place weight on the injury.

Again, her anxiety dissipated as Alana purposefully slowed her breathing, remaining still. Reaching to her side, Alana unhooked the snap securing the hunting knife on her belt. Lifting the eight-inch blade from its holster, she felt the familiar, comfortable grip in her right hand.

Instinctively, she twirled the weapon.

"Hello!" Alana called out, stepping slowly near the edge to see down into the crevice behind the red cone. She saw nothing. Feeling more foolish than fearful, Alana surveyed the area. After standing near the edge for several minutes, she cautiously stepped backward, remaining focused on the place where the light had appeared.

The source of the light was nowhere to be seen.

"Nothing," Alana muttered. Embarrassed in allowing fear to momentarily get the best of her, she re-holstered the knife and reached back and unhooked the water bottle to take another drink before turning to leave.

And then…a bright flash of light…and everything went dark. Alana was blinded, unable to see anything. Instinctively she reached for the knife—but there was not enough time.

Within seconds of the blinding flash, she was struck from behind, knocking her to the ground. Lying face down on the granular lava surface, she was aware of a rustling sound surrounding her. Alana did everything she could do to avoid losing consciousness.

She was unable to move. Alana felt hands grip her shoulders and ankles, pushing her down against the ground. Her eyes were open, but she could not see. Then, what felt like a needle was pressed into the back of her neck. The pain was excruciating.

Alana screamed as loud as she could. But she could hear nothing—seemingly deaf to even her own screams. Her consciousness continued to slip away. She was being carried, but it seemed even more as if she were floating. Her sense of smell erupted as an antiseptic-type odor nearly suffocated Alana, forcing her to gasp for air.

Fear gripped Alana like the fingers now seemingly touching her entire body. She thought, in the swirling terror of her mind, she was dreaming, living out some type of nightmare.

Or had she died?

Before another thought could unfold, Alana lost consciousness.

Rules

Aaron had broken the rules, specifically his own rules.

After killing his mentor, Aaron decided to stay the night in William's cabin.

The nearest home is over a mile away, so no one has seen or heard anything suspicious. William didn't have any family. I'm closer to him than anyone else, Aaron thought, seeking legitimacy in his choice to spend the night near *Deep Creek Lake.*

I love this place! And it is my last time here. Why not enjoy it?

He wanted to enjoy the tranquil setting before saying goodbye to it forever. Soon Aaron would destroy it, setting it on fire.

There were not many things in life that Aaron attached any degree of sentimentality. But places he had been, especially where missions were completed, remained as memories worth carrying. William's home now held the most revered position in Aaron's mind.

Aaron decided to sleep in William's room. Lying down on the bed, keeping his clothes and shoes on, he fell into a deep, peaceful sleep. He awoke as the dawn's light made its way through the thick trees, the sound of raindrops hitting the tin roof of the rustic structure in the deep woods.

"This is a nice place...too bad it's going to be a pile of ashes," he said aloud, looking around William's room.

Taking his time, Aaron put on surgical gloves and examined everything in the cabin.

Much to his surprise, Aaron found a box of photos.

The Order frowns on nostalgia, my dear dead friend, Aaron thought, seeing dozens of pictures.

Most were from William's time serving in Korea, Vietnam, Iraq, and Afghanistan. Seeing the images of his mentor, some dating back over sixty years, confirmed what Aaron had experienced for over two decades: William Hines had never aged.

He looks the same in the images as before I killed him. How does a man remain middle-aged for almost his entire life?

Then, while flipping through the pictures, Aaron found the only image he had seen of William with a woman. It was a Polaroid picture stuck to the back of a Kodak processed image. After gently peeling apart the two photos, he could see the couple.

The woman and William were standing side-by-side, leaning toward each other. It appeared they were in front of the Coliseum in Rome. As Aaron stared at the picture, he could not timestamp the image by William's seeming ageless appearance. But the woman looked much younger than William, likely in her early to mid-twenties. Both were tanned and clearly happy to be together.

"I know you," Aaron said aloud, putting the photo in his pocket. "That's a shame you were close to William...a real shame. Two plus two...and you're dead too."

As he neared finishing examining stacks of pictures, Aaron found a folded photocopy of an image and note at the container's bottom. It seemed out-of-place in William's hidden cache of memories.

Unfolding the letter-size paper, Aaron saw a copied picture of seven men dressed in uniforms from possibly the Civil War era. As Aaron looked closer at the military personnel, one of the soldiers seemed incredibly familiar.

That looks like William…with a beard. No fucking way!

Aaron's thoughts bounced between shock and the implausible. Looking closely at a caption below the image, he could barely read, "CALVARY TO GUARD THE DISTRICT OF COLUMBIA." A large block of text was too small to make out what was written. But below the image was a copy of a handwritten note.

Written in an ornate, sprawling cursive handwriting, it read:

Will,
Great causes are never lost!
We are known and remembered by our Deeds.
Long Live the Order,
Sic Semper Tyrannis!
Your Dearest Friend and Comrade in Arms,
Lafayette C. Baker
1-July 1868

What kind of deflective fuckery is this, old man? Aaron thought as he continued to examine the images on the paper. Angrily crumpling it up, he threw it back into the box with the other photos. *That's impossible. It's just William's last insult. He knew I would find this.*

"Fuck you, old man!" Aaron shouted in the direction of William's corpse.

After finishing his examination of William's cabin, Aaron meticulously went back to scrubbing down everything he had touched. Smiling as he looked at the old man's body lying on the floor, Aaron savored the excellent method by which he had carried out his orders.

Aaron walked to the chessboard and examined the game.

"You son-of-a-bitch, you were an excellent opponent. I'll give you that," he said, laughing, turning to look at William's corpse. "Yeah, life's a game…and you lost."

Aaron reached down and picked up one of the black pawns—one of the pieces William used in their final game.

"I know I'm not supposed to do it, but I deserve a trophy," Aaron said as he put the pawn into his pocket. "It's not much, but it means a lot to me."

Stepping out the front door, Aaron looked upward through the tall pine trees, allowing the soft raindrops to fall on his face, taking another moment to savor a successful mission. As soon as he finished scrubbing the scene, he would leave and allow law enforcement to do their best to find out what happened. By the time they arrived, there would be no trail—no way to find out what happened to the old man in his cabin, just rubble and ashes.

The crunch of gravel caught Aaron's attention, and he turned to see two young boys, neither likely over thirteen years old, riding their bikes up the long gravel road leading to William's secluded cabin.

Aaron waved at the boys and greeted them as they pulled beside him on their bikes, "What are you two boys up to today?"

"Hi, mister. We were wondering if you want any firewood. We are selling some, and we can bring you a load if you want it. Twenty-five dollars…that's all. That's a bargain," the older boy enthusiastically said.

"Thanks…but no thanks. I am getting ready to leave in a few minutes," Aaron replied, attempting to hide his annoyance with the boy's presence.

"Where's the older guy that is usually here? William? That's it, William. He always buys some of our wood," the boy asked, looking past Aaron toward the cabin. "Maybe we should talk to him?"

"Well…he's gone," Aaron said, shaking his head, trying not to chuckle.

"What's wrong, mister?" the boy asked, noticing Aaron's slowly emerging peculiar smile. "Is something wrong?"

"Well…I was laughing at how things happen in life," Aaron said, looking up to the sky, pausing to allow the light rain to fall on his face with his eyes closed, still grinning, then stretching his arms wide and his hands open. Returning his focus to the two boys, dropping his arms to his side, Aaron asked, "Do you boys believe in fate? Or do you believe everything just happens by chance…randomly?"

The boys remained silent, unsure of what to say.

"This is a simpler question. Why should I let you live?"

"Mister…ok…I guess we'll be going…sorry to bother you," the older boy said as he frantically motioned the other boy to turn and ride away.

"That's rude. I asked you a question. I guess running away is your answer," Aaron said, shaking his head in disgust.

Aaron watched them as they turned and began rapidly pedaling their bikes. Methodically, maintaining his gaze on the boy's progress, he reached behind his back to pull out his pistol with the silencer still fit onto the gun. "Hey, boys…boys! Don't leave!" Aaron said in a sing-song voice, laughing hysterically, as he took careful aim and fired one shot at each of their heads, killing both.

Walking over to the two bodies, Aaron looked around and saw no one else. Then, pausing, he looked up at the darkening sky as he stood over the boys.

"I guess, either way, things didn't work out very well for you two…did it?" Aaron said, laughing. "One thing for sure…today just wasn't your day!"

Aaron could not deny the effusive joy he experienced after bringing human life to an end. But then, the dizzying heights of jubilation were always followed by a precipitous drop into a bottomless abyss that nearly smothered him in dark anguish and guilt. After each killing, Aaron's first thought turned to ending his existence in the depth of his contempt for his actions.

The same held true as the celebration of the moment quickly faded as Aaron looked at the two dead boys. He opened his mouth and pointed the gun inside—his lips touching the silencer attachment. His hand trembled as he closed his eyes and took a deep breath.

Quickly pulling the gun away, he opened his eyes and looked at the two bodies.

"Boys…in all honesty, I am envious. You two have peace," Aaron calmly said. He stood motionless for several minutes.

"Well…there goes another hour," Aaron abruptly said. His calm demeanor immediately changed.

"Fuck!" he shouted as he began to repeatedly kick the bodies, releasing his frustration at having his planned exit from William's cabin slowed by the inquisitive boys. Aaron fired another round into each of the boys' heads.

"That should do it," Aaron said as he methodically turned and walked back toward the cabin to begin setting it on fire. "What a shame. I love this place."

CHAPTER FOUR
MAUNA KEA

"Why is this place so special for you?" the man asked Alana.

The sun had risen above the thick clouds far below. The sky's orange glow melted in the deep blue as Alana looked upward into what remained darkness overhead. While she did not understand how or why she was there, she knew where she was—and being on the high peak and seeing the sun slowly rise brought her comfort.

"This is Mauna Kea. This is a sacred place. It is the White Mountain for Hawaiians. We are at the peak where the gods live," she answered.

Alana looked to her left and saw the array of telescopes dotting the high terrain not far from her. "Those people are here because this is where they come to see where we came from. They are not welcome here."

Alana was sitting cross-legged in the snow, wearing workout attire. Even though the temperature and the gusting wind would have ensured her sense of the frigid conditions, she was not cold.

She then remembered the last place she was at before finding herself at the peak of Mauna Kea. And as Alana looked again at the dark sky directly above her, she realized she was not afraid.

"You're not afraid, are you?" the man asked.

"No. I am not afraid," Alana answered. She looked at the man sitting in the same position beside her. He was tall, bald, and had light-brown skin. He was dressed in a suit of some type, but it appeared to be severely dated. Like her attire, his clothing seemed inappropriate for the locale. Even though he was seated, Alana could tell the man was exceptionally tall. His arms seemed to be much longer than those of an average person, as was his hands' exceptional size.

He was staring at the rising sun.

"You said this place is sacred. You said the gods live here. I do not see any gods," he said flatly.

"The gods are here, and they are everywhere. They are inside of us. Their spirits are inside of everything. They are in animals. The gods' spirits are in the ocean's waves...in the sand on the beach...in the rocks. The spirits surround us and bind us. They are part of us, and we are part of them. Their spirits connect us...all of us," she said reverently.

"What are you afraid of?" he asked.

"I am afraid of losing my family. Seven years ago, a wildfire killed many in my family in Lahaina. I was not there to help them when the fire broke out and spread. I feel like I failed them. I am afraid of failure. And I am afraid of losing my freedom," she said, turning to look back toward the sun, the bright glow seemingly unobjectionable to her eyes.

"You said you're afraid of losing your family. How can you lose your family?" he asked with a sense of caring.

"They pass from this life to the next...they die," she said, feeling a twinge of discomfort and a sense of loss for the first time. "Living on an island, we understand how connected we are to each other. The Hawaiian word for family is *ohana*. Family is deeper than blood relatives. This connects us to others...those living and those who have passed. Our ancestors remain part of us. They live on within us."

Alana's thoughts turned to her beloved grandmother.

"You are sad. You miss your grandmother," the man said.

"Yes, I miss her very much," Alana said, tears beginning to form and slowly streaming down her face. She continued to sit still in thought. "But I am also happy…happy to have known her. She is still here, inside of me."

"You said you are afraid of failure. What do you consider a failure?"

"It is when I fail to do my best, and I know I could have done better. It is when I waste time and fail to use all of the gifts I've been given," Alana responded.

"You fear losing your freedom?" he immediately asked.

"I fear being held against my will. I understand why I have this fear. But I also fear the threat of losing my freedom to live as I choose," she answered. Then, suddenly, without any prompting, Alana thought of the mother and father she had never known.

"You miss your parents…your mother and father?"

"I cannot say I miss them. I never knew them. But I love my family. That is more than enough for me. Evidently, I did not need parents," she said contentedly.

"Would you want to meet your father?" he asked. "Would that make you happy?"

"Happiness is not what I seek. I seek to understand…to know. I do not necessarily want to meet my father. I just want to know who my father is…so I can understand where I came from. He is part of my family, and I want to know my ancestors," she said.

"You have never seen a picture of your mother. Is that unusual, to have never seen what she looked like?"

"My grandmother said to make my own memories of my mother. And my grandmother was right. I see my mother as I see myself. That is much better than a picture," Alana responded.

Then, feeling some control over her emotions, Alana asked, "Why am I here?"

"Why are you here?" the man rephrased Alana's question. "That is a question you must answer."

"Why am I here, on the peak of Mauna Kea? Something horrible happened to me. I don't remember all of it. So why am I here with you?" she asked.

"What did your grandmother tell you about fear?" the man quickly responded, a question that it was obvious he already knew the answer. He turned for the first time, facing Alana.

Alana caught the motion in her peripheral vision. She met his stare. His presence was both comforting and unsettling.

The man's eyes were compassionate and foreboding, and there was no distinct color.

The sun's bright light seemed to create a shadow that altered his features—he appeared to have a child-like face. His skin was smooth with no signs of the effects of natural aging. And then, looking closer, she focused on the pupils of his eyes—one pupil was much larger than the other.

None of this frightened Alana but bathed her in a sense of wonder.

"My grandmother said to make fear your best friend. To hold it tight…to understand fear as we should seek to understand others and the universe," she said, recalling her grandmother's oft-repeated teaching. "By understanding my fears, I would understand and know my true self."

"Your grandmother is a wise woman. Did she know who your father is?" he asked.

"I think she did, but she never told me. I think she left that unanswered, something left up to me to seek and discover on my own."

"This is true. This…all of this…is up to you. You are special, Alana. Did she tell you this?" the man asked, still looking into Alana's eyes.

Immediately she felt a vital comfort and closeness with this unusual man. While naturally suspicious, Alana wanted to trust this stranger. Her final wall of resistance to the bond that was forming between the two ended as she smiled and answered, "Yes, she told me that many times. But that is what grandmothers do."

The man smiled and paused. He turned to look at the sun as he said, "She was telling you the truth. You are special. You are unique," he said with an air of admiration.

"What makes me special?" she asked.

The man said, "Again…this is what you will learn…over time. But you must open your heart. You have been hurt," he said with compassion. "I know how you were hurt. And now you are suspicious of others…of strangers."

"My grandmother taught me this: no one comes to an island with good intentions. They either come to take something away or turn the island into what they want it to be." Alana paused, the man allowing her the space to share her complete thoughts.

"I am Hawaiian," Alana continued. "I possess this suspicious nature from what has happened here and to me. Our language was outlawed. Our religion was outlawed. Missionaries came to convert people to a different religion…trying to change people who already knew all they needed to know and understand about the gods, nature, and our place in the universe. Our island is a place of abundance…we must protect it. She told me the same applies not just to our island but to our planet. Our planet is an island. Yes, I am suspicious," she said. "I love my family. And I understand what *ohana* means. Ohana is a larger extended family. But I do not trust everyone as part of my family. I am suspicious. Now…tell me…who are you?"

"I am part of your family," he said, turning to look at Alana.

"I sense that, but you are different," Alana said with confidence.

"As are you, Alana, as are you," he said warmly.

"Are you one of the gods?" Alana asked as she reached out and touched his arm to see if this man beside her was genuine. She felt his arm and moved her hand back.

"No. I am not a god," he said, a grin appearing on what appeared to be an ageless face. "But some people, especially those seeing us long ago, mistook us for something more."

"Am I dead?" Alana asked without any hint of fearing the answer.

"No. You are not dead. But you are asleep," the man said.

"This is a dream?"

"Yes…and much more."

"Why did you bring me here?" she asked.

"You were brought here to remember. You will someday understand all of this. You will briefly lose this memory for some time. And then it will return when it is the right time. Your path will not be easy. You will learn to trust. You will rely on your senses and trust the unique, special instincts and abilities you will develop in time. You will learn to look past your pain…and your fears. All of this will save your life and the lives of many. You will learn what it means to fully listen and to speak without words. You will learn to practice patience even in the most extreme of conditions. You will meet more of your family…your ohana. Some of your family you will recognize…some you will not know. Some of your family will help you. Some will mean you harm," the man said tenderly, brushing the hair from her face.

"Will I see you again?" she asked, tears again forming in her eyes as she already felt a sense of loss in the time shared with the stranger.

"Yes. I will speak to you, and you will hear me even if I am not present. And we will meet again," the man promised, another smile appearing.

"Why am I here? What is my purpose in life?" she asked, hoping to hear more.

"Your purpose is to walk your path. A unique journey is awaiting you. You will wake up in a different place. There will be immense danger. But be brave. Know no fear. This is your path…a path you must walk alone. You are strong, and you will grow stronger.

Remember, we all carry the past into the future. Until it is time…sleep well, Alana," the man said, reaching to touch her face, placing the palm of his hands against her cheek.

Alana fell into a deep sleep.

Dreams

For the first time in his life, Jon Walker was dreaming.

He was in the dark, alone, lying on a dirt floor jail cell in Syria. The group of men within earshot was talking about how they would film the beheading of their captives. Jon knew they would be coming for him next.

Jon moved to the corner behind where the thick wooden door to the cell would open. Weakened by the severe lack of food and water, Jon knew he was no match for all of his captors. But, after observing the habitual process they followed to enter the cell, he had seen an opportunity to possibly seize a gun from one of his jailers.

For months, Jon had been consistent in being in the same position, curled up in the far corner of the room each time the guards would enter the cell. To see him would require them to take two complete steps into the room, barely two seconds in time, but enough time for Jon. His routine was in sync with their entry. Always the same…so they would remember.

It was what they expected.

In this redundancy, Jon hoped there would be a moment when he had a split second to take action.

This is it, he thought to himself. *Now is the time.*

The group was now chanting repetitious praises to Allah in loud unison. Jon knelt, mustering all of his strength and focus, preparing to spring his attack.

As the door opened to the dark cell, the first jailer to enter the room was looking to his left, expecting to find Jon curled up on the floor, as was the case in every visit to the cell during Jon's captivity. But this time, the guard was surprised as he shined the flashlight to the left corner of the room and saw nothing—instead, he felt intense pain as Jon struck him from behind with a fierce punch to the back of his neck.

In one motion, Jon took the Beretta pistol from the falling guard and turned to shoot each one of his three captors standing at the doorway in rapid succession, at a nearly point-blank distance, striking each guard in the head before they could respond with their fire. Moving forward with the pistol raised, Jon stepped over the dead bodies. He alone was standing—no one else was alive in the outer room other than him.

Seeing a camera on a tripod aimed in his direction, Jon walked toward it and saw it was turned on, filming the deadly mayhem he inflicted on the jailers. Stepping back to the front of the camera, Jon looked into the lens, raised his middle finger, and calmly said, "Fuck you!"

The dream was also a memory. It began to fade as he opened the cells lining the narrow hallway, releasing his comrades.

As the dream ended, Jon awoke, lying against the wall of his cabin. A sharp pain remained in his abdomen, but Jon did not see any trace of blood where the weapon had entered. Morning light shined through the open door and the cabin's windows.

The chill of the wind blowing through the slightly open door helped to further revive Jon and recall what had happened. Looking through the door, Jon saw no bodies and no blood. He tried to stand, but the pain in his stomach intensified with movement. Jon pulled the blanket from the top of the nearby bed and wrapped it around him as he tried to assess what had happened.

There had been intruders, as his pain attested. But there was no evidence proving he had shot and likely killed at least one of his attackers, severely injuring the second. As Jon searched his memory, he remembered probably striking each with his machete. But, looking at the blade only a foot away, there was no blood.

Jon opened his shirt to view his injury. To his surprise, the only sign of any possible entry wound was a small red circle marking the location of the pain he continued to feel as he remained leaning against the wall.

Am I losing my mind? he thought.

Struggling to stand, leaning his back against the wall, Jon was able to partially rise. But the searing pain deepened, leaving no option other than taking two steps forward and falling on top of the makeshift faux body he had piled together in the bed.

Lying motionless for what seemed like hours, the pain subsided enough to allow Jon to lift himself and roll over on his back. The throbbing pain in his abdomen and exhaustion caught up with him.

For the first time in his memory, Jon had fallen asleep.

When Jon awoke, it was nearly pitch black in the cabin.

Confused and in pain, Jon stood and walked to the bathroom. Seeing his reflection in the small mirror over the sink, he said, "You're crazy, Jon…you are fucking crazy."

The Story

"In my dream, I heard you say, 'You have many fathers and mothers.' The dream seemed so real."

"Dreams can teach us. They are shadows of waking life, and shadows require light."

"Grandfather, what was the dream teaching me?"

64

"Tell me, Jonas, everything you remember in the dream," Denali silently spoke in thought.

"I was flying high above the desert. Looking down, I could see a large circle on the ground. I glided downward so I could see what it was. It was a circle made of stones. And like a compass, at North, South, East, and West were much larger stones. A line of bright white pebbles went to the circle's center from each of the four stones. A much larger, perfectly round white stone was in the middle of the hoop. It shined like a mirror as I circled above. I could see myself in the stone."

"Did you hear anything as you flew above the stone circle?"

"Yes! I almost forgot. I heard 'four to one' repeated many times," the boy excitedly responded.

"How did this make you feel?"

"I felt strong. It was like putting your hand over a flame. The heat was rising up, and it helped me soar and fly higher. But I was still part of the circle, just higher."

"Dreams are much like the stories we tell. There is always more than the spoken words. There is a story within the story."

"Is that what you call the moral of the story?" the boy asked, deeply engaged in sharing his thoughts.

"Every story has a lesson to be learned. Some stories have many lessons, many of them hidden. The greatest lessons are those we must seek. Learning is never a gift. It requires effort."

"When I was flying, I heard your voice. What does it mean when you said I have many fathers and mothers?" Jonas asked.

"We are all part of a vast family stretching across time and the universe. You are part of everyone before you, and they are part of you. You are the custodian of the lives of your ancestors, as you are for the future. You are here…they are there, like the distance between the four stones. But all remains within the hoop. So, the circle reminds us of the continuity of life…the unity of all things, both here and there."

"In the dream, I flew far away from the desert and saw an island in the ocean. The wind was blowing so hard that I felt like I had no control, but I finally found the strength to fly over the island. I could see a volcano, and there was snow. I felt cold. And then I felt pain, but I kept flying, circling the land. Then I heard your voice again. You said, 'My pain is their pain…their pain is my pain.' I tried to fly away, but the wind kept me there. I wanted to leave the place. It felt like death was all around me. I was afraid."

"Everything in the universe is related. What you do touches everyone and everything, everywhere. So, the circle reminds us that the center of the universe is everywhere…within and without."

"I never want to be afraid."

"We can do many things in life. We have many choices. We can choose to be kind or cruel, to love or hate. Some people choose to never love and to only hate. The worst parts of people can drown out all that is good in them for others. You cannot be courageous without fear. What we do with our fears is our choice."

"In my dream, I felt trapped on the island. Grandfather, I feel trapped here on the reservation. Why are we forced to live here? It feels like a prison. Mother says we are 'prisoners of the past.'"

"We are never held captive by the past. History is the story of power. Like the four stones you saw in your dream, we believe we have four great powers: the power to forgive, heal, unify, and hope. We are all people…the Newe. Jonas, what is the Shoshoni word for time?"

"It is *bai*," Jonas immediately answered in his thoughts.

"Time moves forward; it passes, but time never ends. For us, history records the passage of time…not death as an end, but as a change of place and position. The same holds true for life. The past and future meet here as the sky meets the ground. The shapes of all things are the same…a circle. You will not understand all of this now, but in another place, you will see what causes the shadows."

"Why can't you tell me now…I want to know," Jonas answered, nearly pleading to understand his grandfather's words.

"You already know. Seek wisdom, not knowledge. And in that wisdom, you will also find the courage to respond."

"I dreamed we will fight, side-by-side, with our enemies?"

"They are not our enemies. This is a lie they told themselves. Just as there is a story within every story, there is a war within the war. We are all part of the same circle. There is no us and them. The root of hate is in believing there is an us and them. They do not understand yet, and it will take the threat of losing what they cherish to open their hearts and minds."

With his eyes still closed, tears began to form and run down his face as Jonas spoke: "The last thing I remember in my dream was my father. He called out my name. And then he died."

"We all pass to the next world. Your father is alive. You will see him soon."

"Will he be able to talk like this…without words?" Jonas silently asked.

"Not at first, but he will learn. We will teach him together."

CHAPTER FIVE
TWO WORLDS

For all of his adult life, Jon had been at war.

The cocktail of medications for the extreme pain he continued to have in his abdomen had given him minimal relief. He had no appetite—it had been nearly two days since he had quickly eaten two cans of cold, uncooked beans in the aftermath of the attack.

While he had experienced years of combat, the war that continued was Jon's battle with thirst.

My thirst has nothing to do with water, he thought as he stared at the plastic bottle of water in his hand. In a burst of anger, Jon threw the bottle across the room.

Jon looked at the small set of kitchen cabinets. He knew what he thirsted for was inside.

I need this agony to go away, he thought. *What else is there for me to do?*

He turned and slammed his fist on the rustic kitchen table. Leaning forward, Jon placed both hands on the rough surface and shut his eyes.

The first year he had stayed in Alaska, he had brought along a bottle of bourbon. At the time, Jon had been sober for nearly six months. He knew it was a mistake but packed it away in the kitchen cabinet's top corner. Despite his height, he had to stand on a chair to place it there.

Out of sight…out of reach…out of mind, he thought at the time.

Now what was unseen was on his mind, begging to be released from its dark corner of captivity. Jon fought the urge to retrieve the bottle. But his thirst was poised to claim victory in the battle.

He stood and turned to look at the wall of the cabin.

The bullet holes reminded him of another meltdown—a return to what seemed like two worlds. There was the world he lived in. And there was the world his instincts told him existed—something unseen, lurking, just around the corner.

"Why am I here? Why am I afraid?" he asked himself, turning around to look at the door of the closet, his self-imposed nightly prison.

The answer isn't in a bottle, he thought, laughing aloud at the ludicrous conflict he was enduring.

The bourbon had remained in the same position for over three years, untouched. The fact it remained unopen was a testament to Jon's strong will. But its looming presence remained. It was an option—an escape route from reality, a reality that seemed to be blurred at best throughout Jon's life.

But now, he could resist no longer. His years of sobriety were staring at him as he looked at his barely visible image in the barricaded window. It was a reflection made even more darkly pronounced because of the shutters covering the outside, helping conceal Jon from the world.

"Is this all there is to life?" he asked, nearly shouting.

Jon took a kitchen chair and stood atop it and retrieved the liquid spirits. Holding it in both hands, as if it were a precious, fragile treasure, he sat it on the bare table.

Jon turned back and picked up the chair and returned it to its position by the table. He then walked around the table, staring at the bottle.

Don't do this, he thought to himself. *Do not give in to your desires, and your fears.*

He walked outside on the porch and stood—the searing pain from the abdominal wound now peaking as he tried to take deep breaths to relieve his anguished suffering.

This is more than a pain in my gut, Jon thought. *Am I losing my fucking mind?*

"Where the fuck is the blood?" he shouted, projecting his voice to the wilderness surrounding the cabin.

Jon turned and looked at the door.

Two intruders were here, and I shot one or both, and likely cut off one of their limbs, he thought. *I know this happened!*

But there was no evidence other than the spray of bullet holes and the pain in his gut.

He knew it was early afternoon looking at the sunlight shining on the tree line beyond the open field in front of the cabin. Despite the beauty outside, Jon surrendered to the voice inside, crying for relief from the suffering.

Jon walked back inside and bolted the door.

Walking to the table, he again stopped and stared at the label on the container.

"Hello, Mr. Beam. It's good to see you again," Jon said with a conflicted voice.

He then turned and went to the cabinet, took out a glass, and sat it on the table beside the bottle. Almost like an artist attempting to find the perfect brushstroke, Jon rearranged the bottle and the glass, moving both slightly multiple times.

"Where are you, God, when I need you?" he shouted.

He then thought for a moment and broke into laughter.

"It was a test! I wanted to see which god answered...and none of you did...so fuck you all!"

Picking up the bottle with his right hand, he slowly twisted the cap with his left, breaking the paper seal and opening the glass container. The aroma immediately engaged his sense of smell—lifting the bottle to his nose, taking deep breaths with his eyes closed.

"I've missed you…you fucking demon," he said, opening his eyes and looking at the mahogany-shaded liquid inside of the glass container.

Speaking to the bottle as if it were a close confidant, Jon asked, "What should I do?"

He paused as if expecting the bottle to reply.

"I know why you're called a spirit. You're an escape, a way to exit the ugly reality of this world. You're not an answer, but you damn sure help me forget the questions! You're real, more so than any god, and that's what I need now, something real."

He lifted the bottle upward and looked at the muted light filtered through the liquid. Carefully, Jon sat the bourbon on the table—continuing to keep it within his grip as if it was a flight risk.

"Gods…where are you? Allah…Yahweh…Jehovah… Asherah… Shiva… Zeus… Odin…any one of you around?" Jon asked mockingly, frustration dripping from every word. "Now…I dare you. Show me you're real, show me now…or I'm going to look for a god somewhere else…like in this bottle!" he again shouted.

Holding the bourbon and looking around the room, he saw nothing and heard nothing other than the sound of the refrigerator's constant hum.

"I didn't think so. There is no god. There are no gods. There's just me and this bottle and this glass. You missed your chance," he said as he poured the regular size glass half-full.

He lifted and gently turned the glass, causing the fluid to rock back and forth in motion under his gaze.

Jon spoke, still staring at the bourbon: "Life's but a walking shadow."

He laughed and remembered how his mother had read Shakespeare to him and his brother before they started public school.

"Mother! I am the poor player strutting on the stage, and heard no more. I am the idiot, full of sound and fury, but with nothing to say or offer. There is nothing more than now. Now is all I have," he said, toasting the glass in the direction of the entry door. "Hell is empty, and all the devils are here!"

Jon shut his eyes and took a gentle sip. He sat the glass down on the table but continued to keep his hand on it. Before swallowing, he swirled the bourbon around in his mouth, fully engaging his senses.

"Sound and fury...have your way with me!" he shouted with his eyes closed as if triumphant in consuming the spirits.

Before he lifted the glass again, Jon had a brief vision—a vision of a young boy. The boy was standing in the corner, staring at him. The boy looked like Jon when he was pre-school...but the boy was different. He kept his eyes shut, attempting to allow the vision to carry forward into his thoughts.

Still seeing the boy in his mind's eye, the boy's lips did not move, but Jon heard him speak: "Please stop, father."

Jon opened his eyes. He looked in the direction of the corner where the boy had appeared seconds earlier in the vision.

But there was no one.

"Jonas..." Jon murmured, saying his son's name—the son he had never met.

"I'm sorry, son," Jon said as he lifted the glass and swigged the rest of the contents in a single gulp. "Fuck sipping...I am drinking."

Pouring another drink, again half-full, Jon stared at the glass and then into the corner of the cabin. There was no one to be seen.

Jon began a repetitive succession of drinks until the bottle was empty.

Crawling on the floor to the closet, he made his way inside, curled up in a fetal position, and passed out.

Jon remained unconscious for hours until he awoke to find himself in a pool of vomit. He tried to crawl away from it but became ill again, unable to stop. He tried to lift himself but fell again to the floor on his side in the rancid fluid.

He could not stay awake. Sleep overwhelmed him.

Jon was welcomed to the darkness by a new, intense vision—a boy tucked away in a dark corner. There was water, and a gurgling sound. He heard a woman weeping. The same pattern of imagery repeated itself—engraining what he was experiencing into his memory.

He then heard words he could not make out...or understand...*Boa Ogoi*...spoken over and over. The repetitive words' cadence was clock-like as if the phrase was marking the passing of time.

Again, he tried to open his eyes to awaken from the strange dream. But the revelations continued—the vivid quality of the vision something he had never experienced before.

Jon heard in the darkness of the dream another word...*Seuhubeogoi*...again in steady repetition. Suddenly he saw a large black bear. The bear was standing in deep snow by the side of a nearly frozen creek—the water barely gurgling past the looming presence of the black bear in the frigid conditions.

He then saw people lying still near the bear holding rifles as if they were preparing to be attacked. As the vision moved from the bear up a steep embankment, Jon could see what looked like steam coming out of a thick grouping of trees. The mist was coming out in pulses— as if it were rhythmically orchestrated.

The sound of charging horses bursting from the treeline and gunfire from the riders surged into the visualization. The bear, now standing and growling, as men alongside the beast began to fire their guns at the uniformed intruders on horseback charging down the hill.

The men by the creek were no match for the large military force storming down the steep ridge. Jon saw many of them use all of their bullets. Instead of retreating, the warriors chose to run across the creek through the deep snow, courageously charging the attackers, even though they had no ammunition—only the butt end of their guns as weapons.

All of the fighters, appearing to be Native Americans, were gunned down. Their blood poured through the white snow into the brook turning the water a deep red.

The bear had been shot many times. And now the bear was a man—a tall, muscular man.

He fell into the deep snow, barely alive. The soldiers surrounded the man and began to fiercely kick him. The warriors' leader tried to stand but was struck in the face by a soldier's gun.

Jon could feel the pain from the impact—he could feel the blood pouring down his face into his eyes. Wiping away the blood, he could see a boy—the same boy standing in the corner. The boy was being guided by a woman to a thicket of brush near the creek. The woman slid the boy into what appeared to be a warm spring bubbling up through the calm water.

While the snow was deep and the air freezing, the boy was safe and warm.

Momentarily, seeing this, Jon felt comforted.

Within the vision, Jon saw everything around him now from the perspective of the bear's spirit, taking the physical form of the wounded, battered warrior. He heard someone cry out, "*Wirasuap!*" and then a round of gunfire as everything went pitch black.

The warrior was dead, but the spirit of the bear remained alive.

Jon was still able to hear, but there was nothing to see, only the sound of scattered footsteps tromping through deep snow and a mix of unintelligible voices speaking.

Again, he heard "*Boa Ogoi*" over and over.

Out of the darkness, there was an image slowly appearing, a lone wolf. Seeing the wolf's silhouette in the brightness of a full moon, Jon felt the need to run. But he remained still, watching.

The wolf stopped and, looking upward, began to howl. The melancholy baying frightened Jon, causing him to physically jerk and violently kick against the closet wall.

The wolf then turned and stared at Jon. He heard words but saw no one or nothing else in the vision except the wolf looking deep into his eyes.

Jon then realized it was the wolf speaking to him, saying:

I am not a creature. I am the Creator. My nature is not to kill but to love. But I am also the Protector, the Protector of my Family. My family is what matters most in my creation.

My son, do not fear being different. You stand between two worlds.

Words are not necessary. Be aware. The battle has begun.

We fight for our place, our land, our territory, our island in the vast ocean.

You will meet the one…the one you love…and you will save her at a high cost.

You will fight the Snake. Death is not the end, your seeds will carry on.

I am your Father. I am your Mother. I am You, and I am your Children.

We are the Wolf.

The words were clear. And despite his severely intoxicated state of being, Jon was now entirely lucid in the throes of what he knew was a waking dream. He understood the revelation was both real and unreal, occupying two worlds.

Again...it fell dark.

Time seemed to come to an abrupt stop. Jon could only hear the sound of his breathing. Unlike the earlier clockwork sounds, his inhalations and exhalations were erratic.

Then...Jon saw the head of a monstrous snake emerging from the darkness striking toward him.

Jon cried out, "Jonas!" as he lifted himself. He knew he needed to see his son—the son that remained a stranger to him.

Opening his eyes, he could not see anything—there was no light. He tried to reach for where he thought the door's handle would be, but finding nothing to grab hold of, Jon fell on his face in the cramped space.

As Jon drifted into a bottomless pit of imageless darkness, he again heard the words...*Boa Ogoi*.

Without You

Murders in Western Maryland were thankfully few and far between.

Compared to the Baltimore metropolitan region, Maryland's Western Division, headquartered in Cumberland, evidenced a significantly smaller number of homicides. Most murders were of the domestic variety.

That was until now.

As shocking as the local newspaper's front-page story, *Triple Homicide at Deep Creek Lake,* notified the rural community of the horrific crime, the headline failed to convey the unique, brutal nature of the murders. For the entire region, the ghastly crime could be summed up in a frightening one-word question.

Why?

Why would anyone kill these people? The incongruous mix of the victims, location, and horrific crime scenes shocked even the most seasoned investigators, including Detective Allison Gage.

Based in the Cumberland Maryland State Police Division, Detective Gage was involved in the investigations, arrests, and convictions of murderers in Maryland's largely rural area during her fifteen years in law enforcement. No unsolved murders were on record in the Cumberland region. No murderer had evaded capture throughout Gage's time in the state police.

But this case was different, especially in trying to discern the motive for the murders.

What is the motive behind something like this? Gage asked herself, sitting in the unmarked Maryland State Police vehicle preparing for her trip to Virginia.

The gruesome nature of the murders stood out regardless of location. Gunshots to each victim's head made it appear the killer (or killers) were eerily professional.

And the killer, or killers, attempted to destroy part of the crime scene with fire. The cabin where the body of one of the victims was found had been burned to the ground.

If the killer's intention was to obliterate evidence, they were successful, she thought.

The entire crime scene was so far void of any clues to answer why someone would murder three people in the remote, peaceful surroundings of Deep Creek Lake.

And then there were the victims—two young boys and a ninety-four-year-old man. The only connection between the boys and the older victim appeared to be the younger victims' enterprise selling firewood to the older gentleman.

The older victim was uncharacteristically anonymous despite a long career in the military and government. Based on his military records, William Hines served twenty years in the Army Quartermaster Corps. Subsequently, he worked for the Department of Defense before retiring over twenty-two years ago.

Although Gage confirmed Hines' lengthy service record in the military and government service, she had found minimal information on any other aspects of his life.

William Hines is like a ghost, Gage thought. *He is here, there, and then, nowhere, until we find him dead.*

Allison Gage had also served in the military before joining the ranks of the Maryland State Police. She knew military records, like tax records, were usually more detailed and in-depth than any employer-based information. In the victim's case, the records lacked detail and appeared to have been purposefully reduced, adding to the amount of intrigue in trying to understand why William Hines was murdered and his home set on fire.

Hines was ninety-four years old…he was an old man, Allison thought as she turned on the ramp leading to I-68.

The autopsy reports also suggested an even darker narrative of the murders. The two boys were shot, each in the head, from behind. The wounds, location of the boy's bodies, and their bicycles meant they were in the act of trying to get away from the killer/killers.

The boys knew they were in danger.

Using a Glock 17 9mm Luger pistol, the shooter fired two shots at long-range, accurately striking two moving targets. Adding to the horrific mystery, the killer fired a second shot from close range into the already dead victims. Injuries to one of the boys also suggested the murderer repeatedly kicked the boy after killing him with the first of two gunshots.

While the area was densely forested and the nearest home over a mile away, there was no trace of anyone coming into or out of the Hines cabin's location. Gunfire would have been heard given the number of shots and time of the day, yet no one heard anything. Two of the nearby homes, including the home of one of the young victims, had security surveillance cameras on their property. While neither fully captured the ingress and egress of the graveled road leading to the older man's cabin, there was enough of a field of vision that should have grabbed an image in a detected motion alert, especially on the home nearest the Hines property.

But there was nothing. Several patches of images had suddenly appeared distorted for a few moments several times over the past few days, something experienced by both homes—the homeowners noting they had never seen any interference before on their respective surveillance videos.

While there had never been any overt pressure applied from leadership in the Maryland State Police in her tenure, Gage was now experiencing it in this case—a case that had both locals and leadership in the state police demanding immediate progress.

Gage had one potential lead—what appeared to be the elderly victim's long-term relationship with an author, Amy Rodman. A small fire-resistant box was found buried in the rubble during the thorough search of the fire-ravaged cabin. It had been likely hidden under the flooring in a closet.

Inside the fireproof container was the victim's passport, five thousand dollars in cash, an old, non-activated flip phone, and a cover page from a novel by Amy Rodman.

On the page, torn from the book, the author had written:

To Will, I could have never done this <u>without you</u>. Love and respect, Amy

The words "without you" were underlined.

Gage had heard of the author but had never read any of her writing. After reviewing information online, including the author's website, Rodman's books were centered on government espionage. Her books won critical acclaim and made her one of the genre's most famous writers.

The detective knew there had to be a significant link between Rodman and Hines, more than a book-signing event.

Detective Gage poured over critical reviews of Rodman's work and summaries of each book in the series, hoping to connect her writing with Hines.

Why would a well-renowned author of a series of popular government conspiracy-themed books acknowledge someone like William Hines?

The obviously intimate link between the victim and the writer appeared to have only one area of common ground—Hines' lengthy military and government service.

Detective Gage had initially withheld the names of the victims from the media in hopes she could follow the one lead available without losing the element of surprise. After finding Rodman's connection to Hines and staying up all night researching her books, Gage reached out to the author for an interview through the state police commissioner's office in Annapolis on the premise of "timely and important research" to help in an ongoing investigation.

While firing off multiple questions regarding the request for an interview with the Maryland State Police, Rodman finally agreed to the discussion at her home.

And, today, after driving to Alexandria, Virginia, Detective Gage would have the opportunity to interview the only person alive that appeared to know anything about William Hines.

CHAPTER SIX
HAMMERKLAVIER

"I am so sorry to abruptly knock on your door...I am your neighbor in 3C. But when I heard the music...I had to ask. Is that you playing *Hammerklavier?*"

Aaron was trying to reorient himself to the present moment. The young woman standing in the doorway of his apartment was not a threat; he had seen her before in passing. But one of the most important aspects of his work was to never stand out in anything—to never, ever be memorable.

Attempting to cover his frustration, he paused before responding. As a form of relaxation for much of his life, Aaron would return again and again to playing classical piano on a small electronic keyboard with the volume barely audible. Today, somehow, he had allowed the sound volume to be loud enough to be heard.

Hubris, he angrily thought to himself. Trying to discipline his response, he struggled to answer the question.

"Yes...I am so sorry...I must have had the volume too high. I apologize for bothering you," Aaron said, attempting to put a slight smile on his face to gain some level of comfort with the neighbor.

"No! Please do not apologize! It was magnificent! I am a professor of music at Georgetown University. I am hardly ever home during the day, but I had oral surgery early this morning and was lying down and thought I was dreaming or hallucinating. *Hammerklavier* is not something you hear on Spotify...and not something I would expect to hear a neighbor playing," she said with sincere astonishment.

"Again, I am so sorry to bother you while you were resting," Aaron said, sincerely attempting to build a bridge to effectively close the conversation.

"I'm Rebecca," she said, offering her hand. "I am the one to apologize, but given the difficulty of the Beethoven sonata, I had to satisfy my curiosity. Your playing is amazing!"

Aaron shook her hand and politely said, "I am Aaron. No worries, but I must get ready for an appointment. It was a pleasure to meet you. And I promise you won't hear me again. I will keep the volume down."

Not wanting the conversation to end, Rebecca asked, "Yes, it is nice to meet you. Where did you study? You are an exceptional pianist."

"Maybe we can talk some more, maybe coffee sometime," Aaron said, blundering into offering a second phase of communication—an absolute violation of his engagement rules with people outside the Order's assigned agents.

"Yes, that would be very nice...I'm sorry to have tied you up...just let me know anytime if you want to grab a coffee. I would enjoy that," Rebecca said, smiling. "I'm going back to bed and let these painkillers do their work."

"Hope you feel better," Aaron said, pausing to close the door to watch Rebecca walk toward her apartment. After turning away, he stood motionless, shutting his eyes while attempting to redirect the self-inflicted anger in his failure to remain anonymous.

His next thought, unexpected for sure, was the memory of Rebecca's smile, voice, and presence.

"Stop!" he said, opening his eyes.

Aaron walked across the room to the small piano keyboard. Sitting down, he picked it up and put it on his lap. His inner turmoil was nearly bubbling over—he was doing all he could to not smash the musical instrument into pieces.

Instead of turning the instrument on, he began to play the Beethoven sonata soundlessly. An immediate wave of peace washed over him, negating his anger and self-hate. While there was no sound, he could hear every note. Beethoven's Baroque-like composition brought an immediate smile to his face. After silently playing for nearly five minutes, Aaron abruptly stopped, opening his eyes, his inner calm restored.

Aaron walked into his bedroom and disrobed to his briefs. Standing in front of the dresser mirror, he looked at his lean muscularity—the pronounced cuts and striations of his abdominal area looking more like a bodybuilder's than a thirty-eight-year-old government employee.

After putting down a mat on the carpeted floor, Aaron sat down, crossing his legs into *Sukhasana*, a cross-legged pose for meditation in his yoga practice.

Aaron began the rhythmic breathing to calm himself into a meditative state of a quiet mind—a way to heal his frustration. But he could not seem to get Rebecca's smile out of his thoughts.

Aaron allowed his thoughts to turn to the past, to his childhood and mother.

His mother had given him every opportunity to cultivate his mind and body. From his earliest memories, he had played piano and, as a child prodigy, was afforded the best instructors.

Physically, Aaron was trained in *Wing Chun*, a Chinese discipline in self-defense. Aaron had also trained in ballet—a way to bring the music he heard in his mind to a life of its own.

A genius-level IQ demanded a school that met his needs—something that was a significant challenge to afford given his mother's job at the field office for the FBI. The private school was one of the most exclusive, and expensive, in New York City.

Aaron could still hear his mother's voice echoing from the past as he sat in quiet meditation in the present: "You're a shadow to the world. Nothing more…nothing less."

"A shadow," Aaron said aloud, opening his eyes.

"Yes…Mother…I am a shadow…a perfect, fucking shadow. *Famam Extendimus Factis.* We spread our fame by our deeds."

Aaron snickered at the thought. Still seated on the floor, he began to think about what had happened at Deep Creek Lake. The story was barely visible in the news—something that surprised Aaron.

"It takes a lot to get people's attention these days," he said aloud to himself, shrugging his shoulders. "Either that or no one gives a shit about two boys and an old man, a Veteran, being murdered?"

But Aaron knew his work was never intended for public viewing. He worked for the Order.

In the Order, the only thing known is that I am unknown. Yes, as I was reminded by dear old Mom…I am a shadow.

Aaron lifted his arms outward to his side, staring at the faint shadow he cast by the muted sunlight from outside. Raising his arms above his head, he followed the silhouette lines he projected upward on the beige wall. Aaron's focus caught a glimpse of the small object conspicuously placed on top of his bedroom dresser. Effortlessly rising, he stood and walked toward it. It was a single wooden chess piece. Aaron leaned forward and delicately picked it up, smiling as he said, "My trophy."

Holding the piece in front of him against the light from the window, Aaron continued to gaze at the small wooden figure and the shadow the pawn projected on the wall.

"A pawn...a black pawn...how perfectly hypocritical of you, old man," Aaron said as he put down the piece. "Even a small thing casts a much larger shadow...that is for certain."

Why do I feel empty? Is it killing William? Or is it the boys?

Aaron walked into the living room and stared out the window overlooking the busy street below his small, third-floor apartment. He could see the Washington Monument through the cloudy haze of an unseasonably warm spring day. Gazing at the street below, he stepped back and saw the faint image of his reflection in the window.

"You killed a man that was the closest thing you had to a father," Aaron said, speaking to the image. A sudden burst of sunlight through the clouds altered the reflection, distorting Aaron's mirror-like image.

"You killed two innocent boys," he said, staring both at and through the window—his focus momentarily blurring as he stood trance-like. "What the fuck is wrong with you?"

Aaron returned to his bedroom and sat on the bed's edge, looking at his reflection in a mirror over his dresser.

There are two of me. There is Aaron...and there is Simon. I've always felt it. I know this is true. Am I a monster? Or am I simply following orders?

His thoughts returned to seeing William's body slumped in the chair as the flames began to work their way around the corpse of his mentor. The memory made him laugh.

I hate...and I love. And both have the same consequences for everyone I come into contact with...they all die.

Aaron opened his eyes and sat up on the side of the bed. His gun was on the bedroom dresser near the chess piece—easily in reach. Aaron reached for the weapon, maintaining his focus on the mirror. He watched himself as he lifted the gun, pressing the barrel upward, directly below his chin. Then, staring at the reflection, he laughed.

"Why should I let you live?" he asked himself, watching his actions play out in the reflection. "I'm not afraid to die...but I am afraid to stay alive."

Aaron sat calmly, the image of him frozen as he watched himself contemplate his death, slowly placing more pressure on the trigger.

He then heard a voice say, "There is more to do."

Aaron instinctually spun in response, pointing the gun at the bedroom door—the direction he heard the voice. But no one was there. He returned his gaze to the mirror, unsure of what had just happened.

"There's always tomorrow," Aaron flatly said.

Aaron went to the kitchen table and sat down, staring at the closed laptop computer.

"There are reasons I am who I am," he said in a cold expression of where his mind had been transported, continuing to stare at the closed laptop computer in front of him. "I was made this way...two-in-one. I have no regrets. I am known by my actions...my deeds. I serve *The Order of Saint Martin*...and my country. I change outcomes. I am not ashamed of the being I am."

Aaron opened his laptop computer and began a Google search.

"AMY RODMAN," Aaron said as he typed the name in the search engine. "Did you think I wouldn't notice, William?" The suspense novel had always stood out on William's shelves of biographies and historical texts.

Immediately, the bio he was seeking was visible. Clicking through the biography, he saw the listing of books Rodman had authored.

"William...naughty William...giving away national secrets to his secret girlfriend so she could twist non-fiction to fiction. He deserved to die," Aaron said aloud to himself as he scrolled the book titles.

This had to have been known within the Order, Aaron thought as he looked at the summary of one of Rodman's more recent books, *Murder in State*.

"My God...she refers to the *Order* as the *Command* in her books! She may be a good writer but...she's as dumb as a bag of bricks," Aaron said aloud, using one of William's favorite expressions, imitating his voice.

To ensure the information on Rodman was known by the Order, he picked up his secure phone and texted in all caps to the assigned contact number: "DO YOU KNOW WHO AMY IS?"

Not expecting any response for some time, typical in these rare moments of outreach, he was setting the phone down on the table when it immediately buzzed with a reply: "YES."

Aaron laughed loudly and put the phone down, continuing to read the plot of the book. Then, leaning back in the chair, shutting his eyes, he shouted, "My God, William! This is me she is writing about!"

The book's villain, Andrew, was described as a "monk-like socio-path with a genius intellect...a musical child prodigy now composing a symphony of destruction as an assassin for the Command."

"Music...how did William know that?" he asked aloud. "He never saw that part of me. He never got to know Simon."

After staring at the frozen screen image of Amy Rodman for several minutes, Aaron leaned forward, gripping the laptop with both hands. He began to repeatedly slam it onto the edge of the tabletop, pieces flying across the room.

After sitting motionless for another few minutes, Aaron broke the silence in the room shouting, "Fuck you, Amy!" at the top of his lungs. "I don't care if anyone hears me!" he shouted.

Recalling Rebecca's presence in the adjacent apartment, Aaron said aloud: "If I ever think I've been compromised...you're as good as dead...Rebecca."

His phone, lying on the kitchen table, vibrated. It was a text noti-fication from his handler within the Order. Holding his breath for a moment, Aaron considered how coincidental a text reading "KO AMY" would be.

"Here is a test. Is the universe driven by fate or randomness?" Aaron asked aloud.

Aaron picked up the phone and read the text message: "HAWAII."

"Randomness wins...again," Aaron said. "Amy's death sentence is commuted...for now. What a letdown."

Finished

The sound of his cell phone ringing surprised Marc Walker.

He had just left a speaking engagement promoting his book. As he always did, he had turned his phone off before the beginning of the event to ensure he would not experience any interruptions. Looking at the number showing simply as *Unknown Caller*, Marc quickly searched his thoughts and clearly remembered turning the phone off. He was sure he had not switched the phone back on.

Hesitating but then stopping outside of the auditorium, Marc answered out of curiosity, "Who is this?"

"Dr. Walker, this is General Melvin Mason of the United States Army. I need your immediate assistance, but I need to speak with you on a secure line. I have two of my men waiting for you. They are in the black SUV parked immediately to your right. Do you see it?"

"Yes, I see the SUV. You can see me? What is this about?" Marc said, still shocked by the call.

"Dr. Walker, I will tell you everything once you get into the vehicle with the two soldiers. They are opening the door for you, are they not?"

"Yes...but who are you?" Marc asked, now more perplexed with the circumstances.

"Dr. Walker, we need you to get in the vehicle…now. Thank you for cooperating," General Mason said with a definitive command.

"Ok," Marc said as he hung up. As he slowly walked down the steps and toward the waiting vehicle, he began to text his wife, telling her what was happening. Before he could finish the text, his phone rang again from an *Unknown Caller*. Marc answered, "Let me guess…you don't want me to text."

"That is an affirmative, Dr. Walker. Now, please get in the goddamn vehicle. We do not have a lot of time," General Mason answered with a surly tone. "And just to make sure we are on the same wavelength, your phone will turn off as soon as I hang up."

Marc immediately looked at the phone screen—the phone was dead. After looking all around, Marc stepped toward the SUV. The soldier, holding the door open held out his left hand, "Dr. Walker, please give me your cell phone. I will give it back to you once you are finished."

"Finished? That sounds reassuring," Marc said as he handed his phone to the soldier.

Marc slid into the vehicle's back seat. The second soldier, driving the SUV, said, "Thank you, Dr. Walker. We will be taking a short drive to a place where you can speak to General Mason on a secure line."

"Ok…whatever you say. It looks like I'm along for the ride," Marc said as he buckled himself in.

After a brief drive, the vehicle pulled into what appeared to be a closed chain pharmacy. Marc was directed to a small room in the far corner of the back of the building. The room had no windows and a single chair beside a plastic, foldable table. An iPhone was on the table.

"The General will be calling you soon," the soldier said as he stepped out of the room, closing the door behind him.

The phone immediately rang.

Marc reached out and smugly answered, "Hello, General."

"This is General Mason. Thank you for your patience in this process, Dr. Walker. Once you know everything about the situation we are facing, you will understand why I had to be extremely careful."

"Ok...how can I be of assistance?" Marc asked, hoping to gain more comfort.

"Even though this is a secure line, I cannot give you all of the details right now. But what I can tell you is we have a situation that represents a threat to our nation, even more than that, the world. We need you to come to the Pentagon, now. You cannot tell anyone where you are going. You can call your wife on this phone...tell her something she will believe but nothing about Washington or our contact. And I will be on the line in case you try to say too much. For the sake of all, you need to explicitly follow everything I am asking you to do. Is that clear?"

"General, please put yourself in my position," Marc said, the irritation in his voice apparent. "I'm not used to taking orders, especially from someone I've never heard of before. And you're asking me to lie to my wife. What am I supposed to tell my wife?"

"Dr. Walker, you seem to be pretty adept at lying...especially when you have visitors staying all night with you during your book tour. Tell your wife whatever works that does not disclose where you are going and anything referencing an emergency or the Pentagon. You're a genius, I'm sure you can figure this out. Time is wasting, Doctor Walker, do what I'm asking...now."

"I don't like being threatened," Marc snarled.

"I don't trust you, Dr. Walker, but I need you. So, get used to being threatened if that's what it takes to get your attention and assistance. I know all about you. I own you."

"You listen to me. I am a private citizen..." Marc said, as he was interrupted by General Mason.

"Dr. Walker...you listen to me...I don't have time for this. There is no such thing as a 'private citizen.' If we are having a problem communicating, it is not my problem...it is yours. You need to listen, and do as I say...and get your goddamn ass on the plane we have waiting for you. I have all sorts of leverage to get you to comply, but I would rather not use that. And I think you know what I'm talking about. Trust me, you will understand the importance of this when you get here."

"That's a lot to ask," Marc said, angered by the threatening tone of the General's voice. "I'm supposed to trust a General I've never heard of. I am sure you know who my brother is. He told me a lot about trusting the military. And you order me to lie to my wife?"

"Look, Dr. Walker, your brother has lots of issues, we both know that. And what you said about telling your wife a lie? I can find quite a few of your sex partners from the last few weeks who can testify lying is not a problem with you," General Mason said with a smug, confident tone. "Do you want me to send you a few images of you and your lady friends...just to help jog your memory? What you did with the last one, Lisa, is enough to end any marriage."

"I don't..." Marc said, leaning over, smacking the plastic table with the palm of his hand, but was again interrupted.

"You don't have an option," Mason interrupted. "You can either do as I say, or I will get you here by any means. And being honest, if I have to use any means, it will not be comfortable for you. Do you want that, Dr. Walker? We need your help. I've asked nicely. The choice is yours."

"Ok. I'll come," Marc said, gritting his teeth in anger.

"Thank you for agreeing to follow my instructions," the General said, speaking over Marc, as a soldier opened the door and entered the room. "And, Dr. Walker, you will appreciate this about me, I am sure.

There are no 'buts' or 'howevers' in my vocabulary. Try to remember that. I'll see you in a few hours. Goodbye, Dr. Walker."

CHAPTER SEVEN
CONCLUSIONS

Allison Gage enjoyed driving alone.

Despite bumper-to-bumper traffic for much of the nearly three-hour drive from Cumberland, Maryland to Amy Rodman's home in Alexandria, Virginia, the time spent in a focused, solitary effort always proved to be a stimulant for deep thought. As a detective, her actions were not initially focused on finding the truth but instead searching for facts—factual evidence that would help construct a solid conclusion to answer the most basic question relating to the triple homicide at Deep Creek Lake—"What happened?"

Even with significant evidence, the answer was rarely straightforward. In Allison's earliest memories, her mind was seldom settled. Allison had never been satisfied with someone telling her, "This is the truth."

Allison always wanted proof.

A line from Lewis Carroll's *Through the Looking Glass* had been embedded in her memory at a very young age and often found its way into her thoughts and her processes of logical reasoning: "...*if it was so, it might be; and if it were so, it would be; but as it isn't, it ain't. That's logic.*"

Turning onto Amy Rodman's street, Allison laughed and said, "Never trust, always verify!"

Allison remembered the closest person described as her "mentor"—a former Maryland State Police detective, Richard Hopkins. Smiling as she remembered his nickname, "Detective Dick," Allison recalled his admonitions to accumulate as much evidence as possible to support conclusions.

"Never focus on finding the truth. Instead, seek as much verifiable evidence to support a conclusion. When it comes to evidence, quantity and quality are equally important," Hopkins often reminded Allison as they worked through assigned cases in the Cumberland office. "A conclusion is strong, or it is weak, not right or wrong. Remember, even Sherlock Holmes fucked-up."

Allison pulled her unmarked car into the driveway of Amy Rodman's home. After sitting for a moment to regain her focus on the current assignment, she opened the car door and walked up the steps toward the front door of the two-story brick home. Before Allison reached the door, she saw the door open and Amy Rodman, looking much older than the images she had seen in her research, stepped out of the door.

"Hello, Ms. Rodman. I'm Detective Allison Gage of the Maryland State Police Department, Cumberland Division," Allison said, offering her hand.

"Do I need an attorney?" Rodman responded, refusing to offer her hand.

Somewhat shocked, Allison responded, "No, Ms. Rodman. I thought our Annapolis office had spoken to you about my visit today."

"The reason they said for your visit is bullshit. You know it, and I know it. You don't want to interview me about something I wrote, now do you?" Rodman said, looking into Allison's eyes with both confidence and anger. "I'm guessing you've never read one of my books. Am I right?"

"You're right about both. And I apologize for any deception that you may feel."

"Deception? I'm not a fan of being lied to by anyone, especially the police from another state," Rodman said, maintaining her eye contact with the Detective. "You have thirty seconds to tell me why you're here, or you can leave, and I'll be sure to find someone in your organization to complain about this intrusion."

Allison reached into her well-worn, over-the-shoulder satchel without saying a word and pulled out a copy of the page with Rodman's written comment found in the victim's cabin. She handed it to the woman maintaining eye contact.

"Did you write this?" Allison asked as Rodman looked at the copy of the blurb she had written.

"I've written thousands of comments in book tours," Rodman said, handing the paper back to Allison. "Why are you interested in something like that?"

"Do you write something like this often, telling the person they were instrumental in your writing?" Allison asked. "That suggests the person probably was more than a complete stranger wanting an autograph in *Barnes & Noble*."

"Why are you here, Detective?" Rodman asked angrily. "Your time is up."

"Do you know William Hines?" Allison asked, now looking into Amy Rodman's eyes.

Rodman stood—frozen in what many in law enforcement refer to as the "convict stare"—failing to respond to Allison's query.

"Do you know William Hines?" Allison asked again.

Rodman remained motionless and silent. Allison decided to stay quiet to see how long it would take for Rodman to respond. After what was likely another thirty seconds, Rodman finally responded.

"Here is your answer. You can leave now Detective. I have nothing more to say to you."

"We found this in his cabin at Deep Creek Lake. William Hines was murdered. He was shot in the head between his eyes. It looked like a professional killing. Two teenage boys were also murdered at the cabin. Both were shot in their heads with the same gun. I'm trying to find the killer or killers," Allison said. "If you don't know Mr. Hines, I'm sorry I wasted your time. But if you know him, I need your help to tell me what you know about William Hines. You are the only person I have found that can acknowledge he ever lived."

Rodman stood looking at the Detective without speaking. Frustrated and not wanting to show her emotions, Allison reached into a small pocket in her handbag and pulled her business card from it, handing it to the still motionless woman.

"Here's my card if you can remember anything. At this stage, anything would be helpful. I'll be here in Alexandria for the next two hours before I drive back to Cumberland. Thank you for your time, Ms. Rodman," Allison said as the woman took her card and remained still on the front porch, "I'm sorry if I have bothered you."

As Allison turned to walk down the stairs, she heard the door close. Allison knew Amy Rodman was connected to William Hines, and this was her only lead in finding anyone that knew the victim while he was alive.

As she pulled out of the driveway, she said to herself, "I know a lot more about what I don't know now."

To Love a Killer

Amy Rodman could barely contain her pain.

As soon as she walked inside her home, she fell to the entryway's granite floor, releasing the repressed grief for her lost love, William Hines.

She knew this day would happen. The anxiety hanging over her head since she first understood that the man she loved was a government assassin had remained a constant in every moment of her life. Writing about the fragments of what William had shared, always with his approval, was cathartic for both of them. But to never share everyday life with the man she loved had been hell on Earth for over twenty-five years.

And now, he was gone, killed just as he had predicted.

Money, fame, and critical acclaim had done nothing to dampen the dread of a future foretold by a man she should have never allowed herself to fall in love with and then write about his dark secrets.

William told me this is how it would end, she thought, trying to find some calm in a world collapsing around her. *In all of our years clandestinely spent together, he would never lie. He would simply not say anything.*

"He never lied," she moaned, understanding where the truth he shared would now lead.

As Amy lay on the floor, still sobbing, she thought about the two boys. The two kids had somehow got in the way of what she understood to be a KO, a kill order, sent down to the man William said would someday kill him, a man she only knew as Andrew.

William told Amy that if any single word could best describe the killer that worked with him, it would be "inhuman."

Hines also shared that despite the cruelty evidenced in the killer's work, the man had a firm moral code based on the oath he took to be part of the *Order* (what William referred to as their secretive government section hidden within the US Army Quartermaster Corps.) Regardless of the conditions, the assassin swore complete allegiance to protecting his employer, the United States of America, and to do as instructed as a military agent in *The Order of Saint Martin*.

"When I hear a person called a patriot, I think of him and shiver," William said in one unguarded moment, speaking of the killer's perverse code of conduct. "He is the truest embodiment of the traits necessary to be a patriot. He is completely dedicated and totally selfless, willing to give his life for his country and cause. And seeing him, seeing his work, reminds me of how dangerous patriotism can be to the world."

William's killer knows he shared all of this with me, the thought fueling more hysterical cries from Amy.

Andrew was now authentic. The fictional world she had created was a reality. William had told her that Andrew would kill him someday as his official retirement from the Order. All of that had come true, just as William had assured her. Hines had repeatedly said he would be killed when he was expendable to the Order. And now, according to William's warnings over the years and cautions related to Amy's writing, Andrew would be looking for her next.

The thought of death seemed to steady her. There was no way out.

Amy slowly lifted herself from the floor, walked into her home office, and sat down in a winged-back chair facing her enormous oak desk. Behind the desk were the various awards she had won for her writing and pictures on talk shows. Also hanging on the wall were the framed images of the cover art for Amy's books.

*Impressive...*she thought. *But all of it was a waste.*

Her life had been a life lived, much like her writing, in a fictional setting. Amy had never accepted the consequences of loving a man she barely knew and could never acknowledge his presence in her life to anyone. She did not know his age or even the date of his birthday. Incredibly, Hines had never aged. And much like his appearance, everything about the man was frozen in time. William was a stranger to her, but he was also the person she shared more of her life with than any other. He was her soul mate. Amy thought she knew the man's soul but could only get rare glimpses of his heart.

He enjoyed reading Dickens and loved Beethoven and most classical music. William was an avid runner and practiced yoga and meditation. He was kind and caring.

Her thoughts led her to voice the conclusion aloud: "He was a killer. And I loved him."

For several moments, the pain of the admission brought on more tears and anguish.

William talked about being a shadow. He was and still is.

And now, she understood that shadow had consumed her life, dreams, and hopes. Seeing the end of her life soon, Amy allowed a new level of honesty to guide her thoughts.

What I loved the most I could never have. My life has been filled with patiently and exhaustively waiting for outreach from the darkness, from the shadows, from a man I barely knew...the man I loved with every fiber of my being.

Tears again began to run down her face.

After sitting in the chair for several minutes, Amy stood and walked behind the desk staring at the many reminders from her writing career. Then, in a sudden, furious rage, she grabbed a large print of the cover art from her first novel off the wall and smashed it on the floor. Then a second and a third.

Taking one of the writing awards from the bookshelf, Amy wielded it like a hammer smashing everything on the walls and shelves. Then, leaning back against the desk, emotionally and physically exhausted from the explosion of pain, frustration, and loss, Amy saw her reflection in the broken glass on the floor.

"I'm dead too, William," she said aloud as she walked from the room, "It's not your fault, William. You said this would happen. It was my choice to love a killer."

Friendly Fire

Every assignment had its own array of unique, peculiar challenges.

As Aaron stood in the shadows of what initially appeared to be a two-story commercial business building on Honolulu's outskirts on the island of Oahu, he could not suppress a laugh.

It's a brothel, and almost everyone knows it. It's against the law, but law enforcement overlooks it and probably frequents it often. They should put a sign up to avoid the brothel's intoxicated clients stumbling into the garment factory next door and telling the receptionist, "I'm ready to get fucked." Hypocrites, fucking hypocrites.

Aaron struggled to suppress his simmering frustrations and concerns.

This mission is next to impossible, Aaron thought, anxiously waiting for his target to emerge. He knew time was not on his side when he was given the assignment, and success was far from guaranteed.

First, Aaron traveled five thousand miles to Oahu to identify a male US soldier as his target, ultimately the victim in a staged murder.

Next, Aaron would abduct the soldier and travel from Oahu to Maui to create a crime scene in a dormant volcano—the corpse of the kidnapped soldier evidencing a brutal knife attack.

Finally, the crime scene must conclusively point to one of Maui's most famous inhabitants as the murderer.

If not impossible, it represented a significant challenge. But Aaron Jones had never failed in an assignment. And this was not going to be his first failure.

With the full extent of *Fort Shafter's* troop information available as a resource, Aaron searched and found a small number of potential targets. Next, he had to find a soldier that would fit the requirements of his victim.

Killing a US soldier was not new to him—Aaron had killed multiple service personnel over the years in carrying out orders from the same government he and his targets served. Aaron always chuckled when William would refer to the action as "*Friendly fire.*"

To Aaron, it was not hypocritical or defied any military ethics. In his perspective, when soldiers signed up to give their lives for their country, they understood the price they could pay. The way the soldier died mattered little. What mattered most was the reason, as long as the soldier proved to be of service to their country.

After stalking his first choice, it appeared the timing would not work. Waiting was not an option. Aaron found the second candidate with reasonable efficiency and followed the soldier to a well-known brothel in a manufacturing district in Honolulu.

And now he was being forced to wait. Time was running out. After nearly an hour, he saw his target stagger from the brothel door.

Aaron stepped out of the shadows and followed the zigzagging path of the obviously inebriated soldier. Upon reaching a dark, isolated area between buildings, Aaron closed in beside his target and put his arm around the soldier's neck in a friendly gesture.

"Private Getz, let me help you," Aaron said as he plunged the syringe's long needle deep into the soldier's neck.

Looking around to ensure no one saw the event, Aaron put his arm around the private to support his weight as he guided him to the edge of a building along the dark street.

"Who are you?" the soldier asked before he passed out, slumping down to the ground.

"Fuck," Aaron said as he bent down to lift the soldier, then carried him across the street to his car. "Private, you need to cut down on the carbs and get in better shape," Aaron chuckled, placing the soldier in the back seat.

Aaron drove to the Order's safe house, carrying the soldier inside without detection. After texting the handler that the soldier was now detained, Aaron received a response that infuriated him.

SCHEDULE CHANGE. DELIVER THE PACKAGE TO PICKUP AT 0500.

"You have got to be fucking kidding me! I busted my ass, and now you want me to wait with this sorry excuse for a soldier for eight hours?" Aaron shouted.

Looking at the overweight soldier, Aaron's anger bubbled over.

"I'm tired of carrying you around, asshole," Aaron said to the still-unconscious private. "Maybe I can convince you to at least walk to the guillotine so I don't have to carry you?"

Aaron secured Private Getz with plastic ties to a metal chair in the middle of the room. The only light was a bright lamp on a tripod positioned six feet above the soldier. Aaron took an ammonia inhalant and snapped it under the man's nose, reviving the soldier. Stepping behind the chair, Aaron cheerfully said, "Wakey, wakey, Private Getz!"

The soldier slowly opened his eyes and was blinded by the bright light on his face. Dropping his head, the soldier sat slumped over for a few seconds, and then, lurching forward, he vomited.

"That is very nasty, Private Getz," Aaron said, remaining behind the soldier. "Always remember, beer before liquor, never been sicker; liquor before beer, you're in the clear."

"Where am I?" the soldier asked through a groggy haze, twisting his head to look around the room, attempting to avoid the spotlight's glare.

"You're serving your country," Aaron said, stepping from behind, startling the private. Positioning himself between the light and the soldier, Aaron continued: "Private Getz, I need your help. My name is Aaron, and I also work for the US military."

"Why am I tied up?" the soldier asked, regaining some sense of his predicament, struggling to move.

"That's a long story. There's no need to struggle. You're not going anywhere until I say so. Do you mind me calling you by your first name? That will make things more friendly."

"Fuck you!" the soldier snarled.

"Be nice, Ronald. You wouldn't talk that way to a superior officer, would you?"

"I don't see an officer," Getz said, looking up into Aaron's eyes.

"I am very much your commanding officer. And we have a mission. If you disobey my orders, you know what happens to cowardly soldiers who shirk their duty, don't you?"

"How do you know my name?" the private angrily asked through clenched teeth.

"I know everything about you, Ronald."

"What kind of commanding officer treats a soldier like this?"

"You did join the Army to serve your country, didn't you, Ronald? Or did you join so you could fuck Hawaiian prostitutes?"

"I joined to serve my country, asshole!" the soldier exploded in response as he attempted to lift the chair off the floor in defiance.

"All I want to know is, will you follow orders? Carrying you around makes things much more difficult. I just need you to not try to resist and walk to a car, from the car to a helicopter, and from the helicopter to your final resting place. That saves me lugging your fat ass around. Will you do that for your country?"

The soldier did not respond, sitting motionless.

Aaron stepped back in front of the soldier, his silhouette ominously blocking the light. Aaron said softly, "One last time, Ronald. Will you follow orders?"

"What kind of lunatic puts you in command?" Getz asked, straining his eyes to see the shadowy figure before him.

"The military geniuses at the Pentagon," Aaron chuckled as he briefly stepped out of sight, returning with a syringe.

"What are you doing?"

"I'm following orders. Something you refused to do. Private, this is the last chance you have to speak. Here's a question. Why should I

let you live?" Aaron said as he moved behind Getz and patted the soldier's shoulder.

"I'm a soldier!" Getz screamed.

"Sorry, Private, that is a reason to die," Aaron said as he plunged
the needle into the soldier's neck.

CHAPTER EIGHT
KAUAI

The sound of crashing waves was Alana's first awareness of her return to life. The feel of the sand against Alana's face gave her confidence to open her eyes.

Wasn't someone's hand on my face? Alana thought, her mind still muddled in a groggy haze of blurred memories.

Like her thoughts, Alana's vision was blurry. She tried to lift up, but the throbbing pain in her head forced her to drop back into the sand. Lying face down on the beach, the grit of the wet sand now evident, Alana realized she was not wearing any clothing. Taking her hands, she reached down to her torso, confirming she was nude. Through the pain, she screamed and rolled into a fetal position.

Is this a dream or a nightmare? Alana thought to herself, trying to understand why she was lying nude on the beach. Then, Alana was hit by a wave of nausea. She quickly rolled over to her hands and knees and threw up. The rancid chlorine-like aftertaste immediately caused her to retch again and again. Finally able to momentarily pause, she looked down and could see a green-colored fluid splattering the sand below her.

With momentary relief from nausea, Alana painfully lifted her head to see where she was at. Before she could survey the area, she felt the wind blowing as if it were penetrating her scalp. She lifted her right hand to the top of her head and, instead of touching her thick hair, Alana felt smooth skin. Someone had shaved her head.

"No!" Alana cried out, dropping her face back to her knees, putting both hands on her head in hopeless confusion.

Exhausted and in shock, Alana fell to her side, pulling her legs against her chest, and passed out.

Alana could not discern the difference between the vision she then experienced from the reality of her waking nude and hairless on a beach.

She was on the same beach, but she was younger and smaller. Three British soldiers wearing Colonial-era uniforms were chasing her, shouting for her to stop. She had no clothes—and felt an intense pain in her jaw. It seemed like she was in slow motion as one of the soldiers dragged her to the sand from behind before she could escape into the trees. Lying on her face, she felt the weight of the soldier on her back, pinning her to the sand.

In a thick British accent, Alana heard the soldier say in her ear, feeling his panted breathing on her neck, "You're not going to get away from us, girl."

She could see the other two soldiers now in front of her laughing. One of them said to the soldier on her back, "Fuck the little bitch! We don't have all day!"

Alana screamed as the soldier forcefully spread her legs and dropped his pants, ready to enter her from behind.

Suddenly, a tall, thin man wearing only a loincloth, appearing to be Polynesian, ran onto the beach waving a metal dagger, shouting "*Ne'e aku!*" Alana recognized the original Hawaiian language, saying, "Move away!"

The soldier on her back lifted up upon hearing the man's shout. The extra space allowed Alana to raise her leg and kick back against him. He fell over in pain and Alana jumped up to run into the trees. And then she heard a gunshot.

Instead of running away from the shore, Alana stopped. She began to walk back to the beach to see what happened. She saw the native Hawaiian man lying on the beach, blood splattered across the sand near his head. One soldier was standing over the man's lifeless body.

Alana turned to run away but felt the rough hands of one of the soldiers grab her by the hair, saying, "You're not running away this time!"

As the first soldier picked her up over his shoulder to carry her kicking and screaming back to the beach, another soldier appeared and said, "Wait, I want a trophy, first." The soldier was holding the knife the man had carried onto the beach in his attempt to help her. Grabbing her hair, the soldier slid the blade through her dark, coarse hair, cutting off a massive chunk of her mane.

"Now that I have my trophy, we can all take our turns," he said with a sinister smile on his face.

Alana felt the hands, the forced sexual assault, and the vicious smacks and punches in response to her as she tried to fight off each of the men. But she was too small, and the men all had their way with her.

Instead of fear, Alana felt anger pouring through every fiber of her being. She could hear her heart beating as she stood amongst hundreds of native Hawaiians as they used sharp rocks beating and then tearing away the limbs of the British leader on the rocky shore.

As the British captain's body was dismembered for burial, Alana understood what the tribal chief shouted out to all those gathered in the native Hawaiian language: "Never again! This is our island!"

Alana awakened hyperventilating on the beach. Her breathing was out of control—she felt like she was going to die. Covering her mouth with her hands, Alana tried to slow the uncontrollable gasping. Finally, after what seemed like an eternity, she was able to return her breathing close to normal. While Alana perceived she had experienced some type of vision, the reality of her present condition was rekindled.

"Stay away...stay away!" she screamed. As she kept her eyes tightly shut and head tucked against her knees, her arms now over her head giving her a sense of cover.

The only response was the sound of the waves. The familiar sound served as a reminder for her to face her fear and embrace it.

I'm nude on a beach...this I know, Alana silently told herself. *Do not give in to fear.*

Slowly looking up, Alana opened her eyes, her vision somewhat normalizing. She began to survey her location. She was on a beach, but not a beach she recognized on Maui. The position of the sun confused her. It seemed to be morning, but something seemed wrong.

Alana stood, with hesitancy, careful to again look around in every direction as she rose to a full standing position. Her neck was stiff. The pain from her ankle was now evident. She remembered how she sprained her ankle and where she was when it happened. Alana began to cry, unable to hold back the tears of confusion. Dropping back down to the sand, she sat with her knees tucked to her chest, her arms tightly around them.

For a moment, Alana felt safe—far away from where she was in the volcano.

But then, a brief flash in her memory of what took place returned. The fractured memory resurrected of hands, holding her down, and the feeling of long, thin fingers touching her body. Alana felt the sensation of her head and body being shaved.

In response, she rolled over in one motion, again to a fetal position. The residual fear of her last memory in the volcano's crater returned like one of the repetitive waves crashing against the shore.

Alana shut her eyes and tried her best to remain calm, saying to herself, hoping to find comfort in the sound of her own voice, "What happened? What the fuck happened to me?"

Exhaustion had its way, and again Alana fell unconscious.

Alana awoke with the sun now straight overhead. She heard nearby voices. Cautiously, Alana shifted herself to look in the direction of the sounds. Several young boys were preparing to enter the ocean waters to surf not far from her down the beach.

Her movement caught the attention of one of the boys. He saw what appeared to be a body on the beach several hundred yards away and pointed toward Alana as he excitedly shouted at the others.

They all began to run down the beach. Fearfully, Alana crawled backward on the sand as the boys neared, trying to cover as much of her body by curling up, keeping her chin down.

"Are you ok?" one of the boys asked with a sincere, concerned tone. "Are you hurt?"

"Where am I?" Alana asked, her head still down, forehead on her knees, arms wrapped around her legs.

"Hey, aren't you Alana, the girl in the Olympics?" the smallest of the boys asked.

"How do you know...yes...I am...where am I?" Alana asked, still confused and feeling less fearful but now much more aware of her nudity in the company of others.

"Did you know everyone is looking for you?" the tallest boy asked. "They were looking all over Maui for you." As he talked, he took off his shirt and gently handed it to Alana.

"Where am I at? This doesn't look familiar," Alana asked, looking down the empty beach, her thoughts still in a heavy fog, as she quickly turned, still seated, pulling the shirt on over her head.

"You're not on Maui," the boy answered, looking at the others, all of them shaking their heads with concern.

"No? Then tell me where I am!" Alana demanded.

"You are on *Kapaa Beach*," the boy responded.

"Kapaa Beach? On *Kauai*? No, that can't be! That's impossible!" Alana cried out, her head spinning, intense nausea causing her to roll over away from the boys and vomit.

"We will go get help. Jake, you stay with her," the tallest boy told the smallest. "We will be right back!"

The boys ran down the beach to where their bikes were parked. The smallest boy stood a few feet away from Alana, who remained nearly motionless in the sand.

"What happened to your hair?" the boy timidly asked.

"I don't know…I really don't know what happened to me."

"Is there anything I can do?" the boy asked Alana.

"Just tell me this isn't real…tell me this is a dream…a nightmare," Alana said, weeping as she remained lying down on the beach, curling again into a fetal position with her back to the boy, the shirt tucked tightly around her.

The boy paused, responding, "I'm sorry…but this is real. You're on Kapaa Beach. What happened to you? How did you get here from Maui?"

"I don't know…I don't know," Alana said through deep sobs. "I want to go home."

Proof

Allison Gage stopped at a *McDonald's* a few miles from Amy Rodman's home in Alexandria, Virginia.

Allison's hypothesis that William Hines may have been one, if not the primary source for Rodman's books, remained a theory void of factual evidence.

Whether it was Hines and/or others, Rodman relied on a direct source or sources for much of her writing, Allison thought, looking down at the phone's screen.

One of the summary reviews had caught Allison's eye as a foreshadowing of the murder of William Hines. In the last book of her series, *The End in Sight*, Rodman described a whistleblower code-named "Moon Shine" within the *Command* (the secret government group assigned to *"create order through disorder."*)

Reading the character's name made Allison giggle, but then she read how the name was apropos to the story. The US had a secret base on the moon, explaining why there had been no further acknowledged trips there since the 1970s. The moon also served as a base for some type of alien alliance—the extraterrestrials working in concert with America and several other countries to maintain stability on the Earth. *Moon Shine* had avoided detection for years while sharing government cover-ups with a reporter. When quickly scanning the review, what caught Allison's attention was the last word in the code name…and the incredibly noticeable connection to the older victim in the triple homicide: HINES…and…SHINE.

Could Rodman have offered this up in one of nine lengthy novels, a hint at unmasking the source for her writing, hidden in plain sight?

"No way," Allison said aloud, answering her silent query in an attempt to debunk the idea.

But her gut feeling told her something different.

Amy Rodman either already knew he was murdered or wasn't surprised after hearing it, Allison thought to herself.

Going back to the entire book review link, she read the reviewer's discussion of the plot.

The title suggested "Moon Shine" was assassinated by a government operative known as "Andrew." In the book's plot, Andrew is mentored by the informer. Upon receipt of a *KO*, a *"kill order"* given

111

after detecting the whistleblower informer's actions, Andrew killed his mentor with a single shot between his eyes.

Art imitating life, Allison thought, at first dismissively, but then, after continuing to read, she understood Rodman's fear. The book, and the series, ended with the killing of the reporter receiving the information.

If Hines was her source, then Rodman is in danger.

Still staring at her phone, an incoming call from an unidentified caller was flashing on the phone's screen. Allison immediately answered, and before she could speak, she heard a woman's muffled voice say, "Meet me in exactly one hour at *Alexandria National Cemetery*, Section A, Memorial ID 22207."

The call immediately ended after the caller's instructions. While the caller's voice was muffled, there was no doubt it was Amy Rodman.

At first, Allison thought Rodman said, "Arlington" instead of "Alexandria"—Arlington the much larger and well-known national cemetery. But Allison was confident she heard "Alexandria" and began a *Google* search of the cemetery and the grave identification in the graveyard.

Alexandria National Cemetery was noted as being one of the original national cemeteries established in 1862. Allison then checked the grave label. The grave belonged to "*William N. Gosnell.*" After following the links, Allison found a picture of the marker by the grave, reading:

"In Memory of PETER CARROLL, WILLIAM N. GOSNELL, GEO. W. HUNTINGTON, CHRISTOPHER FARLEY who lost their lives, April 24, 1865, while in pursuit of Booth the assassin of our beloved President ABRAHAM LINCOLN."

In shock, Allison said, "What the fuck?" drawing the attention of an older couple across from her.

"Sorry," Allison apologetically offered as she quickly left the restaurant to drive to the cemetery.

After entering the destination on her phone, Allison was even more surprised to see the cemetery's address on *Wilkes Street* in Alexandria.

Lincoln's assassin was John Wilkes Booth. That is strange, but Wilkes is a fairly common name, she thought. Then, driving out of the parking lot, Allison remembered another thing her mentor was fond of saying: "There are no coincidences."

Randomness is the exception, not the rule. In most investigations, everything is linked in some way, shape, or form. So why meet at a Civil War-era cemetery at a specific grave belonging to a man who lost his life trying to track down Abraham Lincoln's assassin—and a graveyard incredibly located on the street sharing part of the name of the killer?

After navigating the heavy traffic, Allison saw the cemetery entrance and drove to a nearly empty section of the parking lot. Allison found a cemetery map online and enlarged the image to gain her bearings where the grave was located relative to where she was parked. The gravesite was situated in a circle on Wilkes Street. Allison left the car and began walking. A light mist of rain started to fall, heightening the overall dreariness of an overcast sky while walking through a large cemetery.

Allison turned a corner to walk to the grave. She could see Amy Rodman standing in the grass, looking at what appeared to be a large rock standing out from the rows of white markers. Drawing within a few yards away, Allison could see the rock was a historical marker bearing the plaque she saw online regarding the four men that died pursuing John Wilkes Booth. Walking closer, Amy failed to acknowledge Allison's presence, even though it was impossible to not see her advance. No one else was nearby, even though Allison thought the two of them stood out given the marker's location.

Standing beside Amy Rodman, Allison decided to give her enough space to allow her the first words.

Allison silently stood next to Rodman long enough to read the marker a dozen times. Amy finally spoke: "Turn off your cell phone."

Allison pulled it out of the pocket in her coat and turned it off in the sight of Rodman. "Now…tell me what you know about William Hines."

Rodman responded, still staring at the historical marker, "This is what you're looking for."

"What do you mean?" Allison asked, turning to look at Rodman. "The marker? I'm confused."

"You're looking for a murderer, an assassin. So were these men. They were looking for an assassin, too," she said coldly with no change of expression.

"I don't understand, Ms. Rodman," Allison asked, looking back at the plaque. "How is a historical marker what I'm looking for? Three people are dead and murdered. All I see is a rock with a plaque on it."

"William brought me here one year ago, almost to the day. My response was much like yours," Amy said, now dropping her head, attempting to conceal her emotions. After a pause, Rodman looked up, maintaining her single-minded focus on the marker. "William told me that the real name of an assassin, an assassin he had trained, was on this marker. I wasn't sure what he meant until he spoke to me two weeks ago and told me he didn't have much longer to live. He said the assassin, a person I identified as *Andrew*, would kill him, much as you described."

"If you knew he was in danger, why didn't you call the police?" Allison said, still trying to digest the information Amy had just shared with her.

Now turning to look at Allison, Amy's pain and anger poured out. "Do you think the police could stop a killer like him?"

"Tell me all you know. We can protect you," Allison said.

"All I know? Andrew is not his real name. Most of what I wrote about his character was fiction because what William shared was so limited. However, there are some things that William confirmed. Andrew was some type of art or musical prodigy. And the part about the assassin being a genius is true," Amy paused, returning her gaze to the marker. "You're dealing with a genius sociopath, Detective. A professional killer working for the US government. William intentionally gave this clue about the assassin's real name. He said Andrew's real name was on this plaque. I never attempted to dig into this. This is all I know. This is where it all begins and ends for me."

Allison stood still and reread the plaque over and over. "What do you know about William?"

"I never knew where he lived, and I never knew his real name. We met in Europe. He said he was working for an oil company. I was working as a reporter. But, after becoming emotionally involved over several months, I put effort into peeling back some of the layers of William's deception. At first, I thought he was married and trying to keep our affair a secret. But then I realized it was a much deeper, darker secret he was keeping from me. He told me he worked for the US Government in a covert service group that was somehow connected to the US Army, more covert and secretive than the CIA. I didn't believe him. But the more he shared in bits and pieces, I knew he wasn't lying."

"Was William the character you referred to in your last book as 'Moon Shine'?" Allison inquisitively asked.

"Yes. William was my only source," Amy responded.

"Ms. Rodman, for me, using that name chips away at credibility," Allison responded, allowing her thoughts to surface in the discussion.

"I used that name purposefully, and I think you know why. Do you think a government that redundantly uses sci-fi movie references and chooses to call a military branch 'Space Force' diminishes the reality of what they do? What the government lacks in imagination, they more than compensate for the lapse in the practice of deception. They enjoy hiding secrets in plain sight."

"I need more than this to help you...to help bring 'Andrew' to justice for murdering Mr. Hines and those two boys. Conspiracy theories aren't going to do it," Allison said, turning and facing Rodman. "I need more than a plaque and the plot of your next novel."

"Why am I wasting time with you?" Amy angrily asked. "What you are dismissing as conspiracy theories are real. How long did the government take to finally disclose there was an *Area 51*? But that was a conspiracy theory, was it not? The government slowly confirmed the existence of UFOs in our airspace, treating it as a national security threat. Yet, our government denied all things 'unidentified' for decades, ridiculing those witnessing sightings. There is a present threat that could end humanity, and the government is having trouble keeping it hidden. Instead, those in power will use it, as they always do, for their benefit."

Amy paused and said in a much calmer, less agitated voice: "If you don't believe me, that is good. But if you insist on following what I've shared, understand this: you will fail and die in your effort to bring the assassin to justice," Amy said as she turned back to face the plaque on the rock. "You'll suffer the same ending as these men, chasing an assassin."

"It's my job, Ms. Rodman," Allison said, hoping to regain trust to learn more from Rodman, "and I need your help. You've referred to 'them' several times. Tell me about them, the government organization hiring William and Andrew as assassins. You called them the *Command* in your books, right?"

"Yes...and they are hiding in plain sight. Their organization dates back to the Revolutionary War. Incredibly, it is hidden deep within the *Quartermaster Corps*, a section of the US Army that works in the background to provide sustainment, everything from food, uniforms, and supplies to the troops. The Quartermasters were used to cover up a small ring of spies two hundred and fifty years ago, and they never stopped. Their entire mission, even in the beginning, was never intended to be known by the public at large. They were, according to William, a shadow group. The motto for the Quartermasters is '*Famam Extendimus Factis*'…'We spread our fame by our deeds.' Even that serves the deception, Detective. The four names on this plaque were civilian members of the Quartermaster Corps. They supposedly drowned in the Rappahannock River chasing Booth."

"The Quartermaster Corps? Ms. Rodman, are you sure William was telling you the truth? Of all the military units to use in a cover-up, the Quartermasters would appear to be the least likely."

"And what better place to hide a covert arm of the US Army? The funding for their work is buried in the military budget's bureaucracy, layers and layers below where almost anyone with a life to live would waste their time looking. Obviously, it is not the entire Quartermasters, but a tiny, select group. They are a shadow organization that handles everything above top secret, things that even the President and most Pentagon officials are unaware of. The secretive nature is tied to a code of conduct and secret order, *The Order of Saint Martin*. They call themselves the *Order*."

"How many others are in this secretive group, the *Order*?" Allison sincerely asked.

"I do not know. But William trained dozens of other assassins during his career. William served his country. I loved William Hines, even if that wasn't his real name. And he loved me. That was real," Amy said, pausing.

"Even at William's age, he was still working for the Order?" Allison asked. "Supposedly, he had retired from the Department of Defense over twenty years ago."

"William was still working for the Order," Amy responded and paused momentarily. "He was much older than you can imagine. But he never aged, and that was the greatest mystery for me. You can lie about some things, but health and aging cannot remain hidden. I knew him for over thirty years. I aged, but William never did. Only recently did he have diminished vigor, but his appearance never changed."

"I don't understand what you're saying?" Allison asked, confused by Rodman's response.

"There is no plausible explanation, and he never offered one. So how does a person avoid the process of aging? William did. He was ageless," Amy said.

The two remained silent. Allison was struggling with how to proceed in questioning Rodman. Then, Allison remembered something her mentor had told her years earlier.

"My mentor used to remind me to not search for the truth, but instead, to search for meaning."

"I would agree with your mentor. You know enough…enough to end your life. Forget all of this and go home to Maryland. Otherwise, you'll be in line for a visit from Andrew. That is the true meaning of all this, for you, Detective."

"I can't do that. You know I can't do that," Allison said. "Two teenage boys were murdered. William Hines was murdered. Whoever the person or persons responsible for this will be brought to justice. I promise."

"Justice? Justice has never been more than a façade on buildings. What the *Order* carries out is much more certain and lethal."

"Ms. Rodman, why don't you come in with me? I know people we can trust, people that you can talk to and share this information with. They can keep you safe," Allison pleaded.

"As long as there is the United States of America, there will be an *Order*. As long as there is an *Order,* you could never keep me safe. You'll never find confirmation of their existence."

"You're wrong," Allison said, turning her gaze back to the marker.

"How am I wrong?"

"I found you," Allison responded.

CHAPTER NINE
MASTERPIECE

Aaron was not happy. Clean-up operations reminded him that some-one else fucked-up.

I wonder if they face the same consequences as William, Aaron thought as he arrived in the volcano's crater for the second time within three hours. The area was now closed-off, following the discovery of Aaron's earlier work to create a crime scene that would ultimately make it clear a female US Olympian was guilty of killing a US soldier, stabbing him multiple times with a knife.

The timing of the discovery of a murdered soldier was a challenge. But given the isolated location, the unfolding of events was less im-portant than the hard evidence—the butchered body of a soldier and the murder weapon with the killer's fingerprints.

This mission proves the point, Aaron thought. *I am indeed a murder-ous artist, and this may be my masterpiece to date. I know of no one in the Order that could have carried Getz up the side of a volcano,* allowing a brief smile to confirm his thoughts.

After finishing his initial work at the site, Aaron returned to the base to follow through by assisting in solving the crime he had com-mitted.

His next assignment would take him from Hawaii to Alaska.

I knew I'd be in Alaska sooner than later, he thought as he boarded a helicopter for the ride back to Honolulu. He allowed himself a smile seeing his reflection in the small window. Savoring the moment, he closed his eyes, only to be interrupted by a soldier sitting opposite him.

"Can you help me with something?" the Sergeant asked Aaron. Though barely audible through the headphones, the Sergeant's voice had a demanding tone.

"I'll try my best," Aaron said, offering a hint of a smile.

"How did he get to Maui?" the Sergeant asked.

"Who?" Aaron asked, knowing where the question was leading.

"The soldier. He was last seen on Oahu at approximately 1700. Then, he miraculously shows up on Maui the next morning to go for a run up a volcano sometime before 0900. That doesn't make any sense to me," the soldier said, shaking his head, keeping eye contact with Aaron.

"Sergeant," Aaron said, leaning forward, "I could throw you out of this fucking helicopter and say you jumped and never have to answer a question about it," Aaron said, now glaring at the Sergeant.

"Is that a threat," the Sergeant said, straightening in the seat, his eyes tearing from the lack of an outlet for his frustration and anger.

"It is the truth, Sergeant. Why should I let you live?" Aaron asked, nearly chuckling, turning again to the window.

"You're crazy, but you're serious, aren't you?"

"Yes, to both. I'm not in the mood for this. Here is your final order from me, Sergeant. You can either respond accordingly or see if you can fly when I throw your fat ass out of this helicopter. I am ordering you to not think about what happened here today, any of it. You are ordered to forget being here, doing what you've done, meeting me, talking to me, acting like a dumb fuck hick second-guessing me. You are ordered to never think about today. You are ordered to never talk about today ever again. If you do, I will know it, and you'll pay the price for it. I'll end you. I promise you. That's your orders. Again, are we clear, Sergeant?"

"Yes, sir!"

Three Days

"Where have you been?" the police detective asked.

Alana had been taken to the Medical Center on Kauai for examination. She had been given hospital scrubs to wear after being attended to by the medical facility staff. Alana fumbled with the answer, unsure of how she was now on Kauai.

"I...I don't know...I don't know how I got here," Alana said in frustration.

"You've been missing for three days. We found your Jeep at Haleakala Park. Do you remember being there?"

"I don't understand. Three days? I don't know how I got here. Yes, I was training. I remember falling, twisting my ankle," she said.

"Your ankle is injured. The doctor says it looks like a slight sprain," the detective said.

"It still hurts," Alana responded. "I remember..." she began and then paused. "I remember seeing a flash of light. I was blinded. Then something jabbed me in my neck. I remember...hands...holding me down."

"Did you see anyone else when you were at Haleakala?" the detective asked.

"No, I can't remember seeing anyone," she said.

"Isn't that odd? There are usually tourists walking up and down the hiking trail?"

"Usually, but not always. I train there often," Alana said as she dropped her head and shut her eyes, trying to jar any memories free.

"I'm sorry to have to put you through this, but everyone in Hawaii is aware you disappeared on Maui. There have been a lot of people spending every minute of the day looking for you. This costs a lot of money. And it puts people at risk. Searching every place on Maui was not easy. Now you show up here on Kauai, nude on a beach, with all of your hair shaved off. I'm sorry, Alana. I know this is difficult, but I must ask: did you disappear on purpose?"

"No!" Alana nearly shouted, frustrated at the question and her inability to remember what had happened over the past three days. "No! Why would I do that?"

"I don't know. I've seen quite a few people disappear and then magically show up with unbelievable stories of what happened to them," he said, hoping to give Alana a path to tell him the truth.

"I promise you, I am not lying. I do not know how I got here," Alana said firmly, looking into his eyes.

"I believe you. But we need your help, Alana. We have nothing to go on but what you've told us and where we found your Jeep. We would like you to stay here until we can arrange transportation back to Maui. The police there are working very hard on this and will ask many more questions, so be prepared."

"I understand. Can I at least go outside? I hate hospitals. I feel trapped in here."

"I will have one of the hospital's nurses take you into their courtyard in the center of the facility if they are ok with it. Here is my card. I will be back later to help get you back to Maui," he said as he turned to walk out of the room.

Alana put the card in one of the hospital garb's small pockets and tried to recall any part of the missing time in her memory. After a few minutes, a man walked into the room wearing blue scrubs. He had a name tag that said, "Jonathan."

"Hi, I'm Jonathan. The detective said you wanted to get some fresh air," he said with a compassionate tone. "Let me go get a wheelchair."

"No, thank you. I would rather walk," Alana said, sliding out of bed.

"Hold on, let me help you. You seem like you're still a little groggy. We don't want you to fall down," Jonathan said as he reached for her arm to help Alana.

When she felt his touch, she sensed something was wrong, nearly jerking away from his grasp.

"I'm sorry. I know you've been through a lot. Please, just be careful. I will walk beside you to help. If you need my help, just reach out. Whenever you're ready, we can go outside," he said, taking a step back.

Alana paused and thought, *That was so wrong. He was trying to help me.*

"I'm sorry, it has been so tough. I didn't mean anything personal," Alana said as she kept her hands on the bed behind her to ensure stability. Then, after standing for a moment, she said, "I think I'll be good to walk by myself," she haltingly said, taking a step. "Did you give me some pain meds for my ankle?"

"I'm not sure. I think so," Jonathan said. Looking over her shoulder, he saw the now empty IV bottle hanging by the bed. "Yes, I'm sure they put some pain meds in your IV. It looks like you were dehydrated."

Alana took a step and said, "It still hurts, but it does feel better. I think I'll be fine."

Jonathan said, "That's very good. I need to stay with you until they come to get you: doctor's and detective's orders," he said with a warm smile.

"Ok, let's go outside. I'm not a fan of hospital rooms," she said.

"I understand, they have to pay me to come in here," Jonathan responded, chuckling.

Alana nervously laughed as they walked from the room down the hall to the elevator. Jonathan pressed the elevator button for the first floor. After stepping into the elevator with the door now closed,

Jonathan looked at Alana and said, "Everyone's been looking for you. You're a very well-known person. Everyone was worried about you."

The conflicted feelings overflowed in Alana's thoughts as she tried to assess whether she was being ultra-paranoid or had a reason to feel uncomfortable alone with Jonathan.

She chose not to respond and took a slow, deep breath, watching the light on the floors click down to the ground floor. Jonathan put his hand on the elevator door to allow Alana to step out first, taking her time. He followed and then said, "Alana, it's this way. This is the shortcut to a private meditation garden."

Alana looked up, seeing "Lobby" above her, pointing straight ahead. She stopped and pointed at the sign: "Isn't it this way? The detective said it was a courtyard, and it was in the center of the facility?" she asked, unsure what to believe.

"We can go that way to the courtyard, but there are a lot of reporters out there with cameras waiting to see you. There is a more private route to a place in the back of the building. It's a meditation garden if you want to walk this way," Jonathan said, pointing down the empty hall. He stood and waited for Alana to choose which path she would take. "Trust me, this is better," he finally said after a moment of standing in the middle of the hall.

"Thank you. I would prefer that. Yes, I'd like some privacy. Actually, that sounds nice: a meditation garden," Alana said, forcing a faint grin.

As they slowly walked toward the end of the hallway, Jonathan asked, "Would you like something to drink before we go outside?"

"Yes, a bottle of water would be nice, thank you," she said, finally able to offer up a confident smile.

Jonathan smiled and said, "Wait here, I'll be right back."

He stepped into a room and was gone for at least a minute. Jonathan then returned, smiling, and handed Alana a bottle of water.

"This way," Jonathan said as he opened a door with a backlit *Exit* sign above it. They stepped into a stairwell leading up to a door to the outside a few feet away. "Let me get the door for you," Jonathan said as he stepped around Alana between her and the door to the outside.

Suddenly, Jonathan lifted a white cloth with one hand toward Alana's face as he forcefully grabbed the back of her head with his other hand, pushing her face into the fabric cupped in his palm.

Alana gagged at the sickening ammonia-like odor as she fought to push his hand away. But Jonathan was muscular and had leverage in his grip. Alana felt like she was slipping again into unconsciousness.

In defense, Alana's training instincts took charge.

Alana released her grip on Jonathan's hand, trying to pull away from the ether-soaked cloth, and, using all of her strength, powerfully punched the man in his crotch. The hard blow loosened his grip enough to allow Alana to push away, and with her back against the wall, she kicked Jonathan in the chest with one leg, knocking him backward on the steps. The pain in the ankle was now evident. She grimaced and paused.

Seeing he was momentarily stunned, Alana bolted for the exit door leading to the outside. As she struck the bar to open the door and was halfway out of the building's exit, she felt arms grab her from behind and pull her back inside, throwing her to concrete. Lying on the floor, Jonathan standing above her, she saw the door close behind him.

Alana was trapped.

"You're making this harder than it should be," Jonathan said, smiling, holding up the cloth. "Now, be a good little girl, and let's get you where you need to be."

As he stepped toward her, Alana leaned to the side and drew back one leg, releasing it in a ferocious strike directly on Jonathan's left kneecap. The knee immediately buckled as he fell to the floor, clutching his leg.

"You fucking bitch!" he groaned as she opened the door and limped outside, only to see an ambulance and two men, appearing to be EMTs walking toward her, with no signs of a garden.

"Help me!" she cried out, exasperated and still weak from the ordeal in the stairwell, the pain inflamed in her ankle and growing with each beat of her heart.

The two men were now running toward her, and Alana understood it was not to help. She knew they were there to abduct her along with the man inside.

Alana turned and jumped over a small hedge by the door, rolling to the ground on landing but quickly getting up and running as fast as she could into an open area. She could see she was at the back of the medical facility. She ran with a pronounced limp, with the two men running full speed behind her.

When she turned the corner, she was shocked to see a fence with a tall hedge behind it separating her from the facility's front portion. She kept her speed toward the wall, and she saw an area with a door on the building's exterior. The door entrance was partially enclosed with a concrete wall, built-in an L-shape, evidently designed to block the door from the rest of the area's full view. The wall dividing the opening from the grass was built in a step-pattern design, with an ascending group of concrete blocks.

Steps, she thought as she veered toward the area.

Now running at full speed, ignoring the pain, she ran and jumped, using the wall enclosure as steps. Alana rapidly climbed to the top and then leaped over the wall, purposefully turning her body in one motion within the jump to attempt to land on the ground in a roll to avoid injury in the ten-foot drop.

While the roll helped prevent a direct impact on the other side, she landed with enough force on her ankle to keep her momentarily on the ground, clutching the injury. The pain was intense as Alana rolled over for a moment on the grass. Then, she heard the men on the other side climbing the wall. Putting the pain aside, Alana stood and hobbled as quickly as she could across the large grass area onto a sidewalk toward the front of the building.

Alana turned the corner and saw the traffic lanes for drive-up entry and the adjacent parking building. She continued to alternate between a run and a limp down the sidewalk to the hospital's central opening, shouting, "Help me!"

A man with his back to Alana heard her cries and turned. He ran toward her, saying, "Alana! I'm Jeff. I used to train you when I lived on Maui. Do you remember me?"

Alana remembered him. She felt safe knowing him for years and nearly fell into his arms.

"Jeff, there are people after me. Please help me," she pleaded.

Jeff reached behind under her shoulder and helped lift Alana as they moved through several people outside the hospital toward the parking building.

"My car's over here," he said as he guided Alana to the tiny subcompact car. He took her to the passenger side, helped her in, and ran back around the car, got in the driver's seat, and started the tiny electric car.

"Who is after you?" he asked, panicked, and upset seeing Alana in this condition.

"I don't know!" she said, but then she saw the two EMTs running toward them. "That's them! Go! Get out of here!"

Jeff quickly backed up and stepped hard on the accelerator. One of the men stepped in front of him. Jeff decided to not flinch and kept driving toward the exit. At the last possible second, the man leaped to the side to avoid being hit by the car.

"They are really after you!" he said as he barely slowed, re-entering the highway from the hospital's entrance. "Where do you want to go?"

he shouted, even though they were now distanced from Alana's assailers.

"I have a detective's number. We need to call him," she said, retrieving the card from her pocket.

"You can dial it on the screen," Jeff said.

Alana entered the number—her hand trembling from the pain and physical exertion. Finally, after four rings, the detective answered.

"This is Alana! I had people try to abduct me from the hospital! A nurse named Jonathan tried to put a cloth over my face. I think it had ether or something to knock me out. Two EMTs were waiting outside. They chased me. I need your help!"

"Ok...calm down. Where are you?" the detective asked.

Jeff responded, "We left the hospital and are on Kuhio Highway!"

"Who are you?" the detective asked.

"He's a friend! Please tell us what to do!" Alana demanded.

"Calm down, please drive safe. I'm just a few minutes from you. I'll give you directions to the Police Department where I am. Stay on the phone with me, and we will protect you," the detective said, then proceeded to calmly guide Jeff and Alana for six minutes to the Kauai Police Department's Investigative Services building on Kaana Street.

The detective was standing outside of the building waiting on them.

"Come inside, both of you. I'll have someone park your car," the detective said to Jeff as they both helped Alana supporting her weight between them as she limped inside the building.

The detective guided them to a glass-encased room visible to the lobby. Quickly, the detective closed three sets of upright blinds to keep Alana and Jeff invisible to anyone entering the police station.

"Detective Robbins," Alana said, looking at the name on the card. "You and Jeff are the only people I trust here."

"I will have an officer outside the door. I have to make some phone calls. You're safe now," Detective Robbins said.

After a half-hour, the detective walked into the room, bringing two bottles of water to Alana and Jeff, and closed the door, leaving the uniformed officer standing outside.

He sat down opposite Alana, putting his hands on his knees, and sighed.

"What did you find out, Detective Robbins?" Alana asked, not knowing what to expect.

"There is no one named Jonathan working at the medical center," the detective said.

"That's impossible! He was there! I'm not lying!" Alana burst out, feeling the initiation of another thread of connected doubts about what she was saying. Before she could finish, the detective held out his hand and nodded in the affirmative.

"I know you aren't lying. I believe you. The hospital gave me access to their security cameras. It captured videos of the man you called Jonathan leaving your room, getting on the elevator, and going to the ground floor with you. I'm guessing he must have contacted the men posing as EMTs, to drive around the building to the door you ran out of. I could see you run, and I saw them chasing you. One pulled out a taser, but you were too fast for them even when you're hobbling."

"A taser? Who are these people?" Jeff interjected.

Robbins continued, ignoring Jeff's questions.

"I then saw you limping and running down the side of the building. The camera in the front caught the two of you going into the parking building just as you said. And the camera in the parking building also captured you driving out of the building, nearly hitting one of the men dressed like EMTs. But, as I'm sure you're aware, they are not EMTs. The ambulance they were driving was stolen less than an hour earlier from a clinic on the coast just north of here."

"You believe me!" Alana said, jumping up and hugging the surprised detective. "I'm sorry, you and Jeff are the only people I've seen since I was running on Maui that believe what I'm saying!"

"I believe you, Alana. But that's not the problem. Someone is trying very hard to abduct you. Do you have any idea why anyone would want to do this?" Robbins asked.

Alana's exuberance disappeared as she slumped back in the chair. "No, I have no idea. I just want to go home and see my friends...my family," she said. "Will you help me, detective?"

"Yes, of course. I won't let anything happen to you, not on my watch," he said, flashing a confident smile.

CHAPTER TEN
HUNTING GROUND

Jon sat silently, rubbing his temples. Through the haze of the severe hangover, Jon recalled the dreams and visions.

Excessive bourbon and no food, maybe that was it? Jon considered.

He had not eaten anything other than two cans of beans for days.

Drinking that much on an empty stomach could have been deadly for some, he thought, his head still splitting from the binge he had somehow endured.

Jon did not want to admit he thought the entire event was some type of hallucination—a waking dream that got out of hand given his lack of food and sleep. More ashamed now than concerned, he had searched the entire property earlier that morning and could not find any sign of intruders coming onto his property and opening the door. There was no blood. And no evidence Jon struck an intruder with his machete or with the many bullets he had fired.

"Ghosts…they were ghosts," he said aloud in frustration.

Then there was the dream—the only dream he had ever experienced in his life.

Trying to recall the dream, he struggled for a moment. He then remembered the last words in the vision: *Boa Ogoi.*

"What the fuck does Boa Ogoi mean?" he said, shutting the front door and walking to the laptop computer. Despite never hearing the words before, he seemed to know the spelling as he used one finger on each hand to clumsily type in words in the search engine.

Immediately the result jumped onto the screen: *Bear River Massacre Site*.

The next thing he saw sent chills through him. It was in Idaho, near the home where his son lived. Then, scrolling down the page, the next thing Jon saw linked to Boa Ogoi was *Shoshone Nation*.

"Catori," Jon murmured. His son's mother, Catori, was a Shoshone Indian and lived on the Fort Hall Indian Reservation.

What the fuck is going on? he thought, connecting the threads of words and visions he experienced. Scrolling down the page, he saw a link to an article on the Bear River Massacre. He clicked on the link. But before the page was displayed, he knew what it would contain.

In his dream, in the vision he had experienced, Jon was at Boa Ogoi when hundreds of Shoshone Indians were massacred in 1863. As he read, tears streamed down his face as he relived his dream of not a battle, but a massacre. Instinctively he typed into the search area: *Seuhubeogoi*.

The first item in the search for Seuhubeogoi was "Willow River," which is now called the Cache Valley.

Seuhubeogoi...Willow River...I've been there...I know I have, he thought. *It is more than something I drove by. It was my hunting ground.*

Again, without any hesitation, he typed in *Wirasuap*. The first item he saw was "Bear Hunter"—a Shoshone chief known as Wirasuap, meaning "bear spirit" in Shoshone.

Jon read the date of Wirasuap's death. It was the same date as the Bear River Massacre.

He died during the massacre. The vision was authentic, Jon thought. *I saw Bear Hunter shot, tortured and killed.*

Jon put his head down in his hands and closed his eyes, trying to remember more.

There was a woman and a boy. She hid the boy in a creek with a warm spring.

Pausing, Jon looked up from the laptop toward the corner where he had seen a vision of a young boy.

It was Jonas that I saw. He looks just like I did at the same age.

Jon began to think about the words the wolf had spoken to him in the dream, but before another thought entered his mind, he heard someone say, "Leave now."

He immediately spun and jumped up from the chair, but Jon was alone. He ran to the door and looked outside, but there was no one near the cabin.

I must be hearing things. That can't be good, Jon thought. But as he shut the door, the words were again audible: "Leave now."

He now knew the words were a warning—not a figment of his imagination. Jon had heard something similar at different points in his life. And each time, he had followed what ultimately were valid warnings of impending danger.

Jon quickly packed a few items in a backpack he kept ready for a quick exit. Then, taking his rifle and the bag, he hurriedly left the cabin.

He ran down the steep ridgeline to the nearby stream. Again, Jon instinctively stopped.

As he listened to the world around him, a faint, unnatural sound could be heard. Opening his eyes, looking back up the steep ridge toward his cabin, Jon could recognize the now clear, distinctive sound of a helicopter. Moving slowly to gain cover in the trees, Jon pointed his rifle, looking through the high-power scope, in the direction of the incoming helicopter.

After a moment of searching the sky, he saw a military helicopter descending into the adjacent clearing near his cabin.

The attack was real. It had to have been the military. But why me, and why now? Jon thought, remaining motionless in the thicket of trees.

A team of what appeared to be four soldiers wearing fatigues exited the helicopter and moved around, circling the cabin. A tall, thin man then stepped out of the aircraft and walked to the steps. Jon could not see his face. The man was clearly in charge of the troops but was not in a uniform.

The soldiers fell into formation to enter the cabin. Less than three minutes after landing, the soldiers exited the cabin. The four of them and the civilian boarded the helicopter, and it immediately lifted off. Instead of returning in the same direction from its arrival, the aircraft ascended to several hundred feet above the tree line, roughly a half a mile from the cabin, and hovered.

The explosion caused Jon to wince, momentarily closing his eyes. The fireball erupting from the area where his cabin had stood was immense—fire and smoke shooting into the clear blue sky. Jon immediately pressed himself deeper into the foliage. Blind to what was happening on the ground near the cabin, Jon could hear as the helicopter began to circle the area, moving directly overhead of Jon's location, but then continued, turning southeast toward its original point of origin.

It's time to leave. Always be prepared, Jon thought.

Jon stood and began walking down the stream's edge for over two miles. The creek narrowed in a sharp turn, the rocks jutting upward, offering an opportunity to cross.

Carefully, Jon leaped from one rock to the next, finally to the other side of the stream and an old logging road. Following the dirt road for another two miles, Jon saw the remnants of a nearly dilapidated storage facility tucked against a hillside. The growth of trees around the building almost covered the entire structure.

Jon looked at the ground as he neared the structure to see if any footprints were evidenced. Seeing none, he began to remove the fallen boards, covering what had been the opening to the building. There, tucked inside of the structure, was the dark green 2009 Jeep Wrangler. Jon examined the entire area for any signs of tampering. He then unlocked the Jeep's door with the key that had hung on a chain around his neck since returning to Alaska.

Everything was as he had left it. Jon had sporadically checked on the vehicle during his recent stay at his cabin, making sure the battery remained charged if he was forced to leave. The provisions he had stored in the Jeep were all he needed—weaponry, ammunition, clothing, bottled water, MREs.

Jon had left three thousand dollars in cash and an untraceable flip cell phone buried at the back of the building. In another corner of the building, Jon had stored three ten-gallon containers of gasoline, allowing him the opportunity to avoid stops at gas stations in his departure from Alaska.

After digging up the cash and putting the gas cans in the Jeep, he surveyed the area outside the rickety shed before driving from the shelter. After sitting behind the wheel, Jon shut his eyes and thought of what he would do before he started the engine.

"Idaho…it's time to see my son. Jonas, I am on my way," he said as he pulled away from the building to begin the long trip on back roads out of Alaska toward his destination: Fort Hall Indian Reservation.

Below Surface

Marc got off the executive jet plane a few minutes before 10 p.m. in Maryland. He was met on the tarmac by a small contingent of soldiers.

"This doesn't look like Washington, DC?" Marc said to the soldier stepping forward to meet him.

"No, sir, this is Aberdeen Proving Ground in Maryland. Dr. Walker, we will be driving you to a secure site on the base for your meeting tomorrow morning with General Mason and his team," the soldier said. The soldier then directed Marc to one of the three black Lincoln Navigators sitting in a line less than twenty yards from the plane.

"I thought I would be able to talk to General Mason tonight," Marc asked as he climbed into the back seat of the vehicle.

"The meeting tomorrow is at 0700," the soldier said. "I will drive you to the location and ensure you are comfortable."

Marc looked out of the window as the three vehicles sped down an access road running parallel to the runway.

"I've never heard of Aberdeen Proving Ground. So I guess you cannot tell me what you do here at this base?" Marc asked, again expecting a negative response.

"Yes, sir, I can tell you. We are a research and development facility for the US Army.

We have some of the top teams of military and civilian scientists on staff here. I am taking you to the Edgewood facility," the soldier said, seated with him in the rear seat.

Marc could see a large structure through the front windshield, looking more like a giant warehouse than a military facility. The vehicles did not slow as they entered the cavernous building, causing Marc to tighten his grip on the vehicle's armrest. Once in the building, Marc could see the enormous structure was empty. An abrupt stop surprised Marc as he leaned to the left, anticipating the path the vehicles would be taking.

A sliver of light, then a quickly expanding arc poured from an opening in the building's floor. Marc could now see the ramp ahead as the vehicles resumed their fast pace down the ramp into the depths of the structure below the surface in a tight spiral.

After driving several hundred feet downward, the vehicles entered an equally spacious, open area below ground. The ceiling appeared to be over thirty feet high. Before Marc could view the surroundings, the vehicles turned a sharp left and sped down a narrow tunnel for over a thousand yards. As the caravan finished their descent, they stopped in a circular area.

"This is where you will stay tonight, Dr. Walker," the soldier said as another soldier opened the door for Marc.

Marc was led down a brightly lit tunnel to a large, vault-like door. The door swung open, and a short, thin man, wearing a dark blue jumpsuit, stepped forward to greet him.

"Hello, Dr. Walker. I'm Jeremy Allen. It is a pleasure to finally meet you."

Marc extended his hand and said, "Doctor Jeremy Allen...the evolutionary biologist. This is a surprise."

"Yes, Dr. Walker, I am sure it is a surprise," Allen said, smiling. "Let me show you to your quarters. We will be meeting tomorrow at 7 a.m. I am sure you are travel fatigued. You will need a good night's sleep."

Marc interrupted, sarcastically asking, "Can you tell me why I've been brought here?"

"No, I cannot," Dr. Allen responded as they walked down a long corridor. "I can assure you by mid-day tomorrow, you will know the answers to your questions," Allen said, stopping at the last unmarked metal door at the end of the hallway. "Everything you need is in your room. If you need anything else, there is a call button marked on the wall. Otherwise, stay in the room till they come to get you tomorrow morning. This is not a place you want to go wandering around," Allen said, snickering.

In Memory

Detective Gage sat in the middle of her living room floor.

She was encircled by paper—some of it in stacks, some single sheets. This was her puzzle. Surrounding her was everything she knew about the triple homicide at Deep Creek Lake.

Reaching back to the coffee table for a glass of wine, she felt lost in the circle. In all of her years in law enforcement, she had never experienced a case where she had so few facts to piece together. After extensive work, she barely knew more than the immediate time after the crime.

And then there was the crime. A lack of evidence intersecting with the extreme, heinous nature of what took place only magnified the pressure to push for finding something, anything, that would help her find the killer. Every lead she had led to nowhere.

"Damnit!" she shouted, angrily setting the wine glass on the table.

And then there was Rodman's assertion that the killer's name was somewhere on a marker found in the Alexandria National Cemetery. Gage leaned over and lifted the picture of the stone marker and read, again, the inscription.

"*In memory*," Allison read aloud from the image.

The age and location of the perpetrator, Rodman suggested, were unknown. Making it more challenging, the somewhat familiar names on the grave markers offered little assistance. All searches led to the same point of origin—there was nothing to find.

Now standing up amid the cluttered floor, Allison could see her reflection in the dark screen of her television.

Allison Gage was considered beautiful by many—and sexy by numerous men attempting to find some way to bed her. But she lived alone—except for the black and white cat she shared her home with, Boots.

Gage's mind momentarily left behind the focus on the triple homicide to remember why she lived with a cat, alone in a remote area
outside of Cumberland. Retrieving her glass of wine, Allison again
looked across the room at the reflection of herself on the darkened
television screen. She could only see the murky image of the outline
of her body without any clarity of her face.

Allison looked at the wedding picture with her husband, Ben,
hanging over the fireplace.

"I cheated on you," Allison said, taking another drink of wine.
"That is why you divorced me and killed yourself. That crime is solved.
I am guilty. Now I'm serving my sentence."

Richard Hopkins had offered Allison both a shoulder to cry on and
a way to reconcile her frustrations at home and work. Allison knew it
was the wrong thing to do, especially with a married man and her supervisor.

Wiping the tears from her face and walking tip toeing across the
floor amongst the scattered papers, she again picked up the image of
the cemetery marker and read the first two words aloud.

"*In memory.*"

Standing, looking at the image, Allison remembered.

"Memory! Yes! Andrew, was some type of art or musical prodigy,"
Allison said, picking up the laptop from the floor. "Let's see if any of
these names connect."

Dead Soldier

Detective Robbins walked out of the meeting room, leaving Alana and
her friend together with an officer standing outside. He walked back
to his office and shut the door, sitting down behind his cluttered desk.

"Why does someone want her so bad?" Robbins asked himself as
he looked at the two pictures of his family on the corner of his desk.

Would I believe one of my children if the same thing happened to them? Would I trust them with what they know and don't know?

Immediately, Alana's face came to mind—her eyes wide, scared, and honest. He believed her, which meant he had work to do finding the perpetrators.

The detective hit the space bar on his laptop to look up the charter company's phone number to fly Alana back to Maui. A news story from earlier was on the screen about Alana's appearance on Kauai. At the top of the story was an image of Alana wearing one of the boy's T-shirts—the picture captured with Alana's back to the camera getting in a van near Kapaa Beach, where she was found.

"Goddamn bastards," he said, seeing an unobstructed view of Alana's athletic-rounded derriere mainly left uncovered by the small shirt—her backside now featured in the news release titled *Alana: Lost and Found: Bald and Nude On Kauai.*

Immediately clicking off the screen, Robbins searched for the charter plane company's name and, finding it dialed their number. A significant amount of time and money had been spent trying to find Hawaii's most outstanding Olympic athlete. He was not going to spare expenses to ensure she was returned safely to Maui.

Robbins walked back down the hall and stepped into the room with Alana and Jeff.

"It's time to go. I have a plane to take you back to Maui," he said, offering a smile to deflect from his concerns.

"Thank you!" Alana said, jumping up. She turned to Jeff and hugged him, saying, "Thank you, thank you, my friend! You saved my life!"

"Call me when you get back. Just keep me informed," Jeff reminded Alana. "Don't be a stranger."

Alana remembered how she had somehow let this special friend slip out of her life. "I am so sorry. I will not let that happen again. I'll call you!" she said as she gave him another hug and kissed him on the cheek.

The detective and Alana walked to his car. Robbins opened the door for Alana and surveyed the entire area around them before climbing behind the wheel. As a precaution, a marked vehicle would follow them to the airport.

If they're bold enough or crazy, they may try something else, he thought, merging into traffic.

"I know I've asked you far too many questions, but if you do think of anything, be sure to call me, no matter what time of the day or night," the detective said as they drove through the busy city traffic.

"I will. I promise," Alana said.

"After getting you on the plane, I'm returning to Kapaa Beach. Tomorrow, I will go to Maui. I have a meeting with the FBI on the facial recognition of the three assailants, and then I'll work with the Maui PD detectives. I hope we find them before I'm on the shuttle tomorrow," he said as he looked in his mirror to make sure the marked car was still following as they passed under a yellow traffic light.

"I can't tell you how much I appreciate you believing me," Alana said, dropping her head. "You know what happened to me in Colorado?"

"Yes, I do," the detective said, taking a second to look at Alana.

"Thank you," Alana gratefully said. "I can't say that enough."

The detective then said, "*Fa'afetai.*"

"You speak Samoan?" she asked, shocked at his utterance. "I love hearing 'Thank you' like that!" she responded.

"My father is Irish, but my mother was a Native Hawaiian. Growing up, I realized if I tried to say I was Hawaiian, it would ensure a real Hawaiian would kick my butt," the detective said, chuckling. "It didn't help that my father was from New York City."

"Being Hawaiian always comes with an asterisk," Alana responded. "I guess we all have dual identities. I've always felt like that. When I was going to college on the mainland, I felt like I was from another planet. Sometimes I still do," she said smiling.

They drove in silence until they entered the airstrip. After parking the car, the detective jumped out of the car and opened the door for Alana. Robbins walked with her to greet the pilot waiting at the gate leading to the tarmac.

"Johnny, take care of Alana for me," Robbins said. "Alana, this is Johnny, the best pilot in the Pacific."

Alana immediately turned and hugged the detective, saying in his ear, "Fa'afetai!" and kissed him on his cheek.

"You're welcome," he said. "I'll probably see you tomorrow or no later than the next day. So, take care of yourself, Superwoman."

Alana smiled and walked to the plane.

The detective then heard the ring of his phone and felt the simultaneous vibration. He withdrew it from his pocket and answered.

"Detective Robbins, this is Detective Tsai of Maui PD. We found something in the crater of the Haleakala volcano that I am sure will interest you. We found the body of a dead soldier. The soldier had been stabbed more than a dozen times. Someone definitely had anger issues. And we found a knife beside the body that appears to be the murder weapon. We ran the fingerprints and found a picture of the same knife with a person matching the fingerprints."

Before Detective Tsai could finish, Robbins said, "Alana...you found a knife owned by Alana with her fingerprints on it," shocked by what he heard he was saying.

"Open and closed. I'm guessing Alana killed the poor guy, maybe even in self-defense. Hard to say. She ran off and concocted a crazy story about being abducted," the Maui detective said. "I guess that will save you a trip."

"It's impossible. Alana couldn't have killed anyone," Robbins said, mumbling.

"What did you say, detective? You're breaking up. It sounds like you're at the airport."

"I just put her on a charter back to Maui. I'll call you later, Detective Tsai. Thank you for sharing the information," Robbins said, still in shock.

CHAPTER ELEVEN
DEAD END

It was *2:22 a.m.*

Allison could not sleep knowing that she now had what may be the necessary link to identify the name of the perpetrator of a triple homicide.

Taking each name from the marker, one after another, Allison performed a deep-dive into everything she could find using "art," "music," and "prodigy." She had found an author with one of the names—and even though he lived in Maryland, he was older than William Hines and was immediately ruled out. She found other connecting threads to the names, but as she plunged down the rabbit hole of each lead, she reached a dead end.

"Dead end," she said, shaking her head. "How fucking appropriate."

Allison momentarily changed her search by re-examining everything found in the fireproof box discovered in the rubble of the cabin's ruins. Allison looked at each item's images, including front and back captures of each bill found in the stash of cash in the box. The bills had been cataloged in the exact order they were found—something Allison had demanded when the safe box was found and opened. She had looked at each bill in the detachment's office and discerned that there was nothing of importance at the time—it was just the man's store of cash.

But now, given the odd relevance of Lincoln, a cemetery marker commemorating four *Quartermasters* and Rodman's assertions of a covert military service hidden in plain sight, the image on the fifty-dollar bill now seemed to make sense as the monetary instrument he would collect.

"Ulysses S. Grant," she said, beginning a biographical search of the eighteenth President of the United States and Union Commander during the Civil War.

There is something about Grant and the money, she thought as she reopened the file with images of the fifty-dollar bills.

And, after magnifying the first image of the reverse side of the first fifty-dollar bill, she saw something strange at the bottom right corner: the letter "R" handwritten on the money.

Flipping to the next bill, she found nothing on the front of the bill. But on the back, she again saw in the same size and handwriting the letter "O." Her heart now racing, she flipped to the reverse of the following image—and in the same position in the bottom right-hand corner was the letter "C."

Hines is giving me a clue, Allison thought as she clicked to the next reverse-side image. The letter "K" was written on the bill.

"ROCK," she said aloud, flipping to the next bill, but there was nothing. Allison searched through the rest of the currency, front and back, and found nothing else. The money had been newly minted and had never been passed through the public.

What did it mean?

At first, Allison thought the term "ROCK" suggested something may be on the back of the stone itself. She searched for images of the reverse side of the large stone and could find nothing.

"Damnit! Is this another dead end? ROCK has to be relevant!" she said now, hoping she was right to avoid the personal frustration of spending so much time distracted by Ulysses S. Grant's fifty-dollar bills.

Then, she saw a name that had a possible connection.

"Peter? Could Peter be...the Rock? The 'Rock' upon the church was built?"

After pausing, shutting her eyes, she recalled the Apostle Peter's full name. Typing in "Simon Peter Carroll" followed by "musical prodigy" immediately, an old news report popped up out of New York City...the name of the school, sending a chill down Allison's spine.

The Grant School of Manhattan (GSM), one of New York's finest private academies, has announced the two students' names in their annual GSM Spring Recital: Julia Anne Richards and Simon Carroll.

"I found you," Allison said, moving down the press release to read the details in the brief bio on *Simon Carroll*:

Mr. Carroll is an acknowledged piano virtuoso at the age of eleven. A true musical prodigy, Simon's extraordinary talents will be showcased in a presentation featuring Beethoven's most technically challenging piano composition and one of the most demanding solo works in classical music, Hammerklavier.

Despite the assertion of a "prodigy" making their musical presence known in the most elite of New York City private schools at the age of eleven, there was nothing she could find after the release date. But this was a real lead, Allison thought as she curled up on the couch, exhausted and finally falling asleep.

Allison awoke to the chirping of birds. Looking out the living room window, she could see a deer at the edge of the woods behind the home. The deer seemed to freeze in place and stare back at Allison, aware of her presence. As Allison remained transfixed on the deer, her cat jumped onto her lap, momentarily frightening her.

"Boots! Don't do that!" she shouted, still groggy from a brief sleep. Looking out the window, she could not see the deer.

As she sat and drank her coffee at the kitchen table, Allison began determining the next steps with the information. The age of Simon

Carroll and the tag of "prodigy" fit in Rodman's descriptions—both fictional and non-fictional.

Allison wondered aloud, "Should I call you, Amy?"

Picking her phone off of the table in front of her, Allison texted Rodman:

I found Andrew. His name is Simon Carroll.

Not less than a minute after sending the text, her phone rang. It was Amy Rodman.

"Good morning, Ms. Rodman," Allison said, not knowing what to expect.

"You just sealed the kill order that is being issued for me right now," Rodman said coldly without any sense of emotion. "I don't blame you, Detective. Quite to the contrary, I admire your resolve and ingenuity. I remember William saying the name 'Simon' several times when he was dreaming. Or maybe he wasn't dreaming. Maybe he was leaving a clue. I'm as good as dead."

"That's not true. We can stop him. I will stop him and bring him to justice. We can bring you into protective custody. He will not kill you...I promise," Allison said.

"I truly admire you. But you and all of your entire Maryland State Police force cannot stop him...and definitely cannot stop them," Rodman said matter-of-factly. "I am sure the *Order* has already read your text message and is probably listening to us talk right now. What I am more concerned about right now isn't me, but it is you. We all swallow lies when our heart is hungry, Detective."

"Justice is worth fighting for...justice for those two boys," Allison said. "You are not going to talk me out of doing what I am sworn to do."

"Detective, you truly do not understand the power of the Order. I'm texting you two images. The first image is William Hines. You'll recognize him, I'm sure."

Allison put the phone on speaker and opened the image. The picture was of a man dressed in what appeared to be a Union, Civil War-era uniform.

"William Hines was into Civil War reenactments?" Allison said, nervously laughing.

"Now look at the second image. You'll recognize the man standing next to William Hines."

Allison opened the image and saw William Hines, dressed in the Civil War uniform. And the man standing next to him, with his hand on the shoulder of William Hines, appeared to be Ulysses S. Grant.

"You've sent this to prove they can doctor images?" Allison sarcastically asked.

"William never aged. I told you that. And that is him standing beside Ulysses S. Grant. He worked for Grant," Rodman said with a sincerity that prevented Allison from responding with sarcasm.

"That's impossible," Allison finally said.

"No, it is not impossible. I know it is true. You are way over your head, Detective. Now, it's time for me to say farewell. We are both now at our own respective dead ends. Take my advice, Allison. Pursuing Simon Carroll will be the end of you. Goodbye."

"Ms. Rodman, I will be there as soon as I can. I will call the Alexandria Police Department and the Virginia State Police to go to your home to protect you," Allison was saying as the call abruptly ended.

Maui

Looking out of the small propeller plane's side window as she sat alone in the small group of seats behind the open cockpit, Alana could see Maui in the distance.

She was nearly home.

As she turned and faced the seat in front of her, Alana replayed everything she could remember since she was running in the Haleakala volcano now almost four days earlier. A full three of those days had been wiped from her memory.

She awoke on Kapaa Beach on Kauai, 220 miles away from Maui, with no recollection of what had happened.

The questions echoed over and over in her mind: *What happened in the volcano? How did I travel from Maui to Kauai?*

For investigators, a search of surveillance videos from hundreds of different locations did not offer any image of Alana boarding a plane or a boat from Maui to Kauai. There was no record of any sighting of Alana after her disappearance in the volcano until she was found on *Kapaa Beach* days later. Then, following the vanished time, there was a coordinated attempt to abduct her in broad daylight.

It seemed, to the entire world, Alana had vanished without a trace for three days from the planet.

Alana was now returning home to Maui with more questions than answers.

It will be like a circus at home when that gets out, she thought as the plane touched Maui.

She heard over the loud drone of the engines the pilot say, "It looks like you have company."

Looking through both sides of the windows she could not see what the pilot was referring to.

At least the detective believes me, she thought, allowing her some momentary relief from the anxiety of the failed abduction attempt.

The plane taxied up to the small terminal. Alana looked up at the now cloudy skies and began to take slow, deep breaths.

The pilot opened the door and dropped the ramp down.

"Would you like a cap to wear?" the pilot said, offering baseball hat to Alana.

"Yes! Thank you!"

"Good luck," he said as Alana put on the baseball hat, ducked down, and gingerly walked down the ramp favoring her now throbbing ankle.

Detective Robbins said the Maui PD would be here to protect me, she thought, again giving her hope that being on Maui would be the safest place in the world.

"You can do this," she said aloud to herself as she walked past the plane toward the hanger in front of the plane, still wearing the hospital scrubs from her time at the hospital on Kauai.

After turning the corner past the plane, she saw a group of close friends, her extended family, waiting for her behind the fencing near the building. She waved as tears began to stream down her face. But suddenly, two uniformed soldiers, both wearing fatigues, seemingly appeared from nowhere and stepped in front of her.

"Please come with us," the taller of the two soldiers asked with a stern voice.

"What? I want to see my family," Alana responded, confused by the presence of military personnel. "Where's the Maui PD? They are supposed to be here to protect me."

The second soldier stepped forward and tightly gripped Alana's arm: "Don't make a scene. You're coming with us. You're under arrest."

"What are you doing? Let go of me!" Alana said, looking at the soldier who tightened his grip in response to Alana's refusal to cooperate.

"You're coming with us," the soldier said, gripping her arm with all of his strength.

The feeling of a man aggressively grabbing her by the arm brought out a sudden, savage, reflex response.

Alana moved quickly, lifting her right leg and fiercely kicking the soldier in his kneecap, buckling his leg as he let go of her, falling to the ground in pain.

The second soldier, momentarily in shock, reached out to grab Alana but was too slow. Alana leaned to the side and, balancing on one leg, delivered a powerful, quick kick to the soldier's crotch, doubling him over. Continuing in the same motion, Alana wheeled and turned 360 degrees, generating power and speed in an explosive kick to the soldier's head, putting him on the ground, nearly unconscious from the impactful blow.

Alana quickly turned and began to run with a pronounced limp toward the fence where her friends and family were screaming in horror at what they were witnessing. Four other soldiers ran forward past the barrier onto the tarmac and moved quickly toward Alana, two from each side as she neared the fence.

The first soldier nearing Alana lunged at her swinging a fully extended nightstick at her head. Alana ducked and stepped into the soldier, hitting him with her fist in his Adam's apple, dropping him to the ground, clutching his throat, struggling to breathe.

A second soldier grabbed her shoulder and spun her around, only to find Alana's fist landing a direct punch to his nose. She dropped down and rotated using the momentum to kick the soldier's legs out from under him. He landed hard on his back, knocking the wind out of him.

Alana bounded up, but before she could move, she felt the paralyzing pain. The severe shock from the taser brought Alana's defensive movements to a screeching halt. She fell to the ground, striking her forehead on the concrete.

Still faintly hearing the screams of her friends and family, Alana again felt hands holding her down and the sharp pain of a needle penetrating her neck as her consciousness slipped away.

Dugway

"What kind of goddamn clusterfuck operation are you running, Tibbs?" General Mason screamed into the landline phone's speaker. "The whole fucking world is being treated to the best-of-the-best of your troops getting their candy asses kicked by a girl. Your troops then used a taser on her in front of her friends with cameras rolling! All your fuck ups were recorded for a worldwide audience! I'm not so sure if you tried, you couldn't have fucked this up any worse than you did!"

Major Tibbs turned to look at the slumping body of Alana, his unconscious passenger. "I understand, General, but…"

"Don't give me a motherfucking 'but' Major! If there's one thing you know working for me is that there are no 'buts' in what we do!" General Mason screamed even louder and more enraged. "Are you aware there is a video floating around online that shows you carrying her on the plane unconscious? And it looks like one of your soldiers copped a feel playing grab-ass with her while she is passed out. How does it get any worse? A female member of the United fucking States Olympic team gets gangbanged by the US Army? What are the qualifications to work in your group, Major? Pussies and perverts? That's what the world is seeing. Do you know what that looks like to millions of civilians? Do you care what it looks like to me?"

"Sir, but…my apologies…I mean she…she was not what we expected," Major Tibbs responded in a soft tone, suppressing his anger and frustration.

"Expect?" General Mason shouted. "What would you expect? I told you to pick her up on that other goddamn island where there was no press or family!"

"That did not work out, sir," Tibbs responded. "The timing prevented…"

"Fuck your sorry ass timing! We have ourselves a serious shitshow now, Major, all thanks to your goddamn incompetence!" General

Mason yelled, his face red, the veins popping out on his temples. "Your ass is on the line, Tibbs!"

"Sir, we have the subject in hand and will proceed with the next step. One thing for sure is that her response to us strongly suggests she is guilty of murder. That helps to explain her disappearance," Tibbs responded.

"You understand how important that girl is, don't you, Tibbs? There are a lot of reasons we need her taken to Dugway without any more media coverage. Whatever the fuck you do, do it right, or I'll replace you faster than that girl kicked the collective asses of your troops. Are we clear?"

"Yes, sir," Tibbs responded, hearing the click of the phone before he could finish speaking.

Turning to the soldier sitting beside Alana's bound, limp body, Major Tibbs said, "No more fuck ups, Moss. We can't afford another mistake."

"Yes, sir," Sergeant Moss answered, attempting to cover the pain from the kick to his crotch and head Alana had inflicted on him.

Following the call, the remaining flight to the Dugway Proving Ground (DPG) in Utah was uneventful. The plane had just entered the enormous, restricted airspace surrounding the base.

Alana had remained sedated with her hands and feet bound for the entire flight.

The Army's Dugway base in Utah's West Desert and the Air Force's nearby Utah Test and Training Range (UTTR) base was extraordinarily remote and had both been shrouded in secrecy for decades. The vast amount of restricted airspace over the bases suggested that both continued to serve as top-secret facilities in the US military from the earliest uses to the present day.

After landing, Sergeant Moss and a second soldier carefully carried Alana's limp body from the plane. They placed her on an awaiting

stretcher on the tarmac, strapping her down on the gurney. Two female operatives—wearing baggy, white jumpsuits, white gloves, and
white surgical masks—met Moss and wheeled the stretcher inside the
massive hanger, with Major Tibbs following closely behind.

Once inside, they brought the stretcher to a corner of the facility.
Waiting for them was Margery Stalwart, dressed in a form-fitting, dark
blue dress, high heels, and her blonde hair partially covering one eye.

"Thank you, Major. We will take care of things from here," Stalwart said, allowing the hint of a smile.

"You don't understand. This is my show," Tibbs said, crossing his
arms.

"Major, you know the process," Stalwart said, staring into his eyes.
"She is ours, now."

"That was not my understanding," Tibbs responded, but before he
could finish, Stalwart stepped forward within inches of his face, smiling.

"This isn't your 'show'…it never has been and never will be. The
only show you are part of is a spectacular shit show, tasing Alana after
getting your asses kicked in full view of the press. You safely delivered
the package. That's all you are, Major, an errand boy. You can leave,
now…and now means now."

"Don't fuck this up, lady. It's your ass on the line now. I wash my
hands of this whole fucked up mess," Tibbs said, turning to walk
away.

"My ass is fine, Major," she said, snickering as Tibbs was walking
away.

Stalwart turned and walked through the double doors leading
down a wide hallway to the elevator that would take them six floors
below ground level. Stalwart positioned her chin on the pad for eye
identification. The door clicked, and the two women pushed the

stretcher carrying Alana through the door down a short hall into a large, industrial elevator.

As the elevator began its descent, Stalwart patted the still-sedated Alana on the head and said to Sergeant Sangeeta Petrad, "He was right about one thing. No mistakes…we have one shot at this."

"Yes, Ma'am," Sergeant Petrad responded without changing her focus on the elevator door in front of her.

CHAPTER TWELVE
CATORI

Jon needed to do the one thing he dreaded most in the long, exhausting trip—to call Catori, the mother of his son, Jonas.

Opening and then powering on the flip cell phone, Jon looked to check the strength of the signal. He pulled off the road in a wide area to avoid losing the call as he traveled through the remote stretch of Canadian backwoods.

Catori worked at night as the floor manager of the casino located on Fort Hall Reservation. As he dialed the phone, he tried to remember the last time he had spoken to her.

Was it last Christmas? Or was it Christmas the previous year?

Hoping he would not wake her up, he rang the number and waited. She answered.

"Hello," she said, clearly hesitant seeing a cell phone number from California—where Jon had bought the phone years earlier and had never activated until hours earlier.

"Catori, this is Jon," he said, trying to hide his nervousness.

"Why are you calling me?" she said, putting him instantly on the defensive as she had in every communication—in person or by phone—since he had last seen her nearly six years ago.

"I'm heading toward Idaho. I would really appreciate if I could see Jonas. I need to see him," he said, almost stuttering over the words. Despite being a decorated combat veteran, the only person Jon seemed to fear was Catori.

And she knew it.

"Why do you suddenly need to see him?" she asked, nearly snarling the words in spite. "You haven't tried to see him except once, and you fucked that up," she said.

"I'm sorry…I am truly sorry," Jon said but was interrupted by Catori.

"Maybe he doesn't want to see you?" she asked. "Have you thought about that? Jon, he is five years old. He knows he is missing a father."

Trying to change the subject, he quickly asked, "How is Jonas doing?"

"Like you care? Jon…he still rarely talks! That says a lot…that silence. I'm here. I live with that every day. I know he is brilliant. But he won't talk. And now you want to show up and play daddy to him? Hell no, Jon. I don't need you popping into my life after all of this time. You will only confuse him now," she said, the anger appearing to turn to tears.

"Catori, I know you won't believe this…" and before Jon could finish the sentence, Catori cut him off.

"You're right, I don't!" she shouted. "I'm going to hang up, Jon. It would be better to never call me again."

"Wait! I'm wrong! I've given you a reason to not believe me. Please do not hang up. I'm a horrible father, I should know better, never knowing who my father was! But I do support Jonas and you've never had to ask me once for money. I'll give you anything you want to help take care of him. He is all I have," Jon said, ending the sentence without finishing, struggling to conceal the anguish of his guilt.

"You have a brother," Catori calmly said.

"Jonas is all I have. Since Mom died, I rarely talked to Marc. I'm alone. And I'm going through something that I can't explain. I have to see Jonas, even for just a few moments. I'm begging you, Catori, please," Jon said, sincerely regaining some of his composure in the hope she would agree to his request.

"Let me think about it. When will you be in Idaho?" she asked.

"I should be there the day after tomorrow," he said. "I'm not sure of the time yet. I'm driving from Alaska in my Jeep. I'm still in Canada. It's a long drive," he said.

"Call me tomorrow at the same time. I'll give you my answer then," Catori said, unexpectedly hanging up on him after her final word.

"That went as well as expected," Jon said, dropping the phone in the passenger seat.

He doesn't talk. He rarely smiles. Jonas is a chip off the old block, Jon thought.

The fact he had a son was something Jon thought of as a miracle. Jon had met Catori at the casino on the Fort Hall Reservation. With very few words spoken, they joined together for a three-day camping trip near the Snake River in Idaho over six years earlier.

What followed was an intense, sexual romp that bonded the two strangers together as they spent three days and nights together sharing their passion. Little was said between Catori and Jon. When Jon left, he gave her his cell number but never planned or thought he would see her again. But then she found out she was pregnant. And despite Jon's initial questioning of whether it was his child, he finally agreed and attempted to be there when the child was born.

But Catori refused.

From that moment forward, all communications with Catori had been combative. The only thing the two agreed on was keeping the identity of Jon as the father hidden.

Jon had not told anyone about his son, including his brother. His mother was near death when Jonas was born, and Jon did not want to trouble her with the information, not knowing how she would respond.

She would have never understood, Jon thought.

Jon initially sent a significant amount of money to Catori before his son's birth and had given her non-court-ordered payments every month since Jonas's birth. He had also sporadically sent money to her above and beyond the monthly payments. Jon told Catori he had named Jonas in his will and sent her the information if something happened to him so his son would have whatever assets available.

It seems like the end of Jon Walker may be fast approaching, he thought as he passed a small church with a back-lit sign reading, "*The Time is Near—the End is Coming.*"

After everything in Alaska, there was now a true sense of urgency to see Jonas.

The dreams…the visions… mean something, and Jonas is part of this. I need to ensure he is protected and that Catori is safe and trusts me enough to be careful. Something is happening. I know it, he thought as he drove down the twisting two-lane road. And he understood the likelihood of seeing Jonas remained slim, at best. But he was going to try.

This may be my last chance to see Jonas, he thought, maintaining his focus on driving through light snow.

Sleep

At 3:33 a.m., Marc suddenly began feeling as if he could not breathe. The entire event lasted for less than a minute but stirred a painful memory deep within him. Giving up on sleep, he decided to read.

Marc picked up the only book he carried on the book tour: *The Complete Works of William Shakespeare.* He opened the old, well-worn hardback book to *Macbeth* and began to read:

> *Methought I heard a voice cry, "Sleep no more!*
> *Macbeth does murder sleep"—the innocent sleep,*
> *Sleep that knits up the raveled sleave of care,*
> *The death of each day's life, sore labor's bath,*

Balm of hurt minds, great nature's second course,
Chief nourisher in life's feast.

Sleep had never been a problem for Marc. While he rarely slept more than five hours a night, his percentage of REM and deep sleep were off the charts compared to others. Marc took pride in the brevity and quality of his sleep patterns. He had accidentally let his thoughts on sleep spill out in two interviews on his book tour, saying, "For humans, sleep is slavery, disguised as rest."

The comment created a trending item on social media: *#SleepSlavery*. While many of the memes associated with the hashtag poked fun at people snoozing at the worst possible times, Marc was attacked in thousands of posts for comparing sleep to "slavery."

How is a black man saying the word "slavery" a problem for anyone? There is nothing innocent about sleep, angrily shoving the book back into his shoulder bag. *Sleep is a prison…a way to enslave humanity. Who enjoys dreams? The chaos and the ridiculous randomness of what we dream! That's what happens when our subconscious mind has control!*

And now, deep within the underground complex, his words never felt more accurate.

I knew the military would do this. They imagine everything as a weapon.

Marc stood and walked to the corner of the room. Opening the metal closet, he dressed in one of the dark blue jumpsuits as requested. Other than sports, he could never remember wearing a uniform in his life.

Precisely on time, there was a knock at the door. A soldier greeted Marc and led him to the end of the hall. After standing in front of the door, the lock clicked. The soldier led Marc down another long corridor to the only entry on the passageway's right side. The door was already open. The soldier stepped back to allow Marc to enter.

Dr. Allen was already in the room with two other men—both of them in military uniforms.

"Good morning, Dr. Walker, would you like some coffee?" Dr. Allen asked.

"No, thank you," Marc responded as he walked toward the three men standing at the opposite side of the large room.

"Dr. Walker, this is Major Fielding and Major Spalding," Dr. Allen said, offering introductions. Neither spoke, only nodding toward Marc as they each sat down in chairs positioned in a circle of four seats. Attempting to cover for the coldness evidenced by the two military members, Dr. Allen said, "Dr. Walker, please join us," as he took one of the empty chairs, pointing to the other for Marc.

"What is this all about?" Marc said, anxious and frustrated at the cold reception and unexplained urgency of the trip and meeting.

"You've spoken to General Mason. He will be joining us tomorrow. His schedule did not allow him to be here today. We thought it would be good to start with a briefing on your preliminary work involving altering sleep patterns through genetic editing," Dr. Allen said.

Marc was aware of Dr. Allen's harsh critiques of his work over the years. Allen's entire career as an evolutionary biologist was structured around explaining and understanding evolutionary trends over the millenniums. But now, the power to suddenly jumpstart evolutionary processes through gene editing made much of Dr. Allen's work obsolete. Marc was reminded of how the geologist's work in *Jurassic Park* had become outdated when science found a way to create living dinosaurs, negating any need to dig for bones.

"I have not published anything on that work, to-date," Marc said. "My work is in the earliest stages. It needs time to…evolve," Marc said, taking a jab at Allen with a slight smirk.

Allen responded only in body language—crossing his arms and slumping back in the chair. Before the scientist could speak, Major

Spalding said, "Dr. Walker, we know you are not in an early stage of anything regarding your genetic editing. You seem to operate on a ready-fire-aim approach to things. Let me make this clear: nothing is confidential in your work. What you've done and what you're doing can be a destructive force against humanity with the potential to be weaponized. Now that we are clear, please answer Dr. Allen's questions?"

"You're telling me you've been spying on me," Marc said as he leaned back in his chair and folded his arms.

"You can call it whatever you want, Doctor Walker, but the fact remains the same: we are here to ensure the safety of the United States of America," the other military representative, Major Fielding, said, his voice increasing in volume as he spoke.

"Be more specific. What do you want to know?" Marc said, failing to hide his frustration and quickly adding. "'I'm confused. Did you say your name was Major Fuck-up?"

"Let's talk about the time you've been spending studying cetaceans," Dr. Allen said, attempting to defuse the heated exchanges. "That seems to be out-of-step with your work. While both of these esteemed military representatives are leaders in the Army's Science and Technology team, they do not claim to be scientists themselves. Please consider that in your responses."

"Fake scientists and armed to the teeth. How charming. I'll do my best to bring it down to all of your respective levels," Marc said, taking another sharp jab at Dr. Allen, including him in the response. "Cetaceans are aquatic mammals: whales…dolphins. Their brains work much differently than ours. And their sleep habits are remarkably different than humans. They sleep in a unihemispheric state; only half of their brain is asleep at a time. Because they are aquatic mammals, a full, deep sleep is not possible. It would kill them. While one-half of their brain is fully functioning, the other half operates in what is known as Non-REM sleep, NREM. NREM is a light sleep and what some refer to as a dreamless sleep. In humans, this stage of sleep typically lasts sixty to ninety minutes in the normal course of a human sleep cycle. In NREM, our brain waves change to a slow-wave level of brain activity. The body's muscles relax, the blood pressure decreases, and the person is relatively still."

"I'm confused. How can a dolphin's sleep habits be important to your work?" Major Fielding asked.

"I'll try to be clearer. Dolphins utilizing only one-half of their brains are all they need to live and fully function. Because their brain functions in a unihemispheric state, it allows half of the brain to rest while the other half works. While one-half of a dolphin's brain is experiencing powerful, deep, rhythmic, slow brainwaves in half of their cerebrum...truly spectacular NREM sleep...the other half of their brain is awake with fast brainwaves. Their brains are much like ours. Both hemispheres are wired together in a thick web of crisscrossing fibers. Essentially, they can live and thrive without ever sleeping in the classic sense. Despite what our evolutionary experts suggest about humans being at the top of Darwin's pyramid, we cannot do what a dolphin does. And that is part of why sleep is a prison of sorts for our species. We need to find a way to be more like dolphins in terms of sleep. That is what I'm working on."

"You want to genetically engineer a human to be like a dolphin, your own version of Aqua Man?" Major Spalding said, laughing out loud.

"If you want to bring this down to a level of cartoons, so it is easier to understand, it isn't Aqua Man, but Superman you should suggest," Marc said smiling. "Dr. Allen's work has a problem explaining dolphins. Mother Nature could have taken a much easier path than creating a split-shift system for a dolphin's brain. Right, Dr. Allen?"

Dr. Allen sat silent, looking down at the floor.

"Think about what one-half of a dolphin's brain can accomplish. Dolphins have exceptional vision. They have protective skin that makes our skin, sorry for the pun, pale in comparison. At least your skin," Marc chuckled, enjoying provoking the three white men. "Their breathing and respiration are magnificent, allowing them to hold their breath for more than twelve minutes. They are quick healers. Dolphins can constrict blood vessels so they will not bleed out if wounded. They feel pain like us but produce their own natural painkillers when they are seriously wounded. They are immune to most types of infections. And, of course, dolphins can sense electrical impulses from living things. They are blessed with biological sonar…while we stub our toe on the edge of a bed that has been in the same place for years. And if you still think humans are the best and the brightest, the highest of the high mammals, size matters. The cerebellum in a cetacean brain has more convolutions than a human brain, suggesting dolphins may actually have a much higher level of intelligence."

"You're saying a fish is smarter than a human?" Major Spalding blurted out.

"They are not fish, Major. They are mammals, like us," Marc said. "But I guess you missed that cartoon growing up?"

"Don't be a smartass, Dr. Walker," Major Spalding said with a reddening face.

"You believe you can find a way through gene editing to allow us to be more like dolphins?" Major Fielding asked, breaking the tension with a sincere interest in Marc's response.

"It's about much more than sleep. How much of our mind are we utilizing? When it comes to our own brains, we have barely scratched the surface of what humans are capable of doing…of being," Marc said, unable to contain his own enthusiasm. "Sleep is a prison for us. While Doctor Allen will surely disagree, there is a strong argument that the greatest jump in human evolution resulted from sleeping

165

safely and securely on the ground without fear of predators. We know how important sleep is to humans. Sleep is essential to a human's well-being. You know this, sleep deprivation has been used as a means of interrogation and torture. That is why I am studying the sleep patterns of cetaceans. They can do something we can't. And now we have the potential to rewire our brains to achieve what they can do."

"You really believe that is possible?" Dr. Allen quickly fired at Marc. "You think you can do some quick gene editing, and we can have sonar and telepathy? Maybe your problem is that you are the one reading cartoons and believing them? I think you've lost your mind."

"Doctor Allen…if I may…Harold. I haven't lost my mind. I'm merely using it," Marc said, smiling. "You should try it or maybe just take a nap. That might help."

Before Dr. Allen could speak, Major Spalding asked with sincere interest: "If you found a way to reduce the amount of sleep we require and at the same time improve the efficiency of the human brain, what would be some of the outcomes?"

"Imagine not being forced to sleep. The number of waking, productive hours in our lives would immediately change how we work, live, and interact. What we can potentially unlock, freeing our mind, sounds like the cartoons you all seem to enjoy. But this is not a cartoon. This is not science fiction. We can make this science fact," Marc said.

"If you were able to genetically alter people to tap into a much higher utilization of the human brain, would this trait then be passed on to future humans?" Major Spalding asked, fully engaged in the potential changes to humanity Marc was describing.

"Yes," Marc said with an authoritative tone. "The children of humans with a higher level of brain utilization will evolve into even higher degrees of mind efficiency. Someday you could experience people communicating without words. You could see things now featured in science fiction movies come to life in a different world...a better world."

"I am sure General Mason will want to dig much deeper into this when he meets you tomorrow. We appreciate the explanation and information you have shared. There are other, much more pressing security matters that we will leave to General Mason," Major Fielding said as he and Major Spalding stood to leave. "And please, take it easy on Dr. Allen. He will be working with you on some projects for us."

"Can I contact my wife and at least tell her to not worry about me?" Marc asked, trying to ignore the thought of working with Allen.

"We have already handled that. You have nothing to worry about, Dr. Walker. She and your kids are in perfect shape. Relax and enjoy some quiet time," Major Spalding responded. "Enjoy reading some more Shakespeare."

Marc turned to look at Dr. Allen. For a moment, he sat in silence, staring at him.

"I know you don't respect me and I understand why," Dr. Allen said to Marc. "But you need to trust me on this. Whatever they ask you to do, whatever questions they ask, do not lie to them. They know more than you can imagine and," as he was speaking, Major Fielding stepped back into the room, severely startling Dr. Allen.

"Harold, it's time you two said adios and call it a day. Loose lips— sinks ships. Both of you remember that" he said, turning to leave, keeping the door open.

A soldier stepped into the room and said, "Dr. Walker, I am here to escort you back to your room."

Marc stood and looked down at Dr. Allen and angrily said through clenched teeth, "See you tomorrow, Harold. I have to go back to my prison cell. Have a good night's sleep."

Monte Lake

Jon was relieved. He had finally made it to Monte Lake.

Despite not needing to sleep, Jon enjoyed taking brief stops to be outside under the stars.

Driving away from Highway 97, Jon drove the Jeep past an industrial complex north of the lake, following the railroad tracks on a path down the west side of Monte Lake. Traversing up the rutted forest service road running along a ridge in the steep hill above the lake, Jon found a small clearing to stop and eat. From this vantage point, Jon could see the lake's still waters, fractured moonlight finding its way through the clouds to create moving shadows of glistening light on the water.

Starting a small campfire, Jon quickly ate an MRE and chugged two water bottles. Carefully ensuring there was no ill effect on the environment, he put out the fire and placed the plastic bottles in a garbage bag in the Jeep. He then brought out his machete and handgun and looked for a good defensive position to sit for an hour.

The steep, rocky hillside behind him ensured that anyone approaching him could only do so from the north, following the same rutted-out forest road he had traversed to reach his camping site. He positioned himself above the Jeep on a more gently sloping, less-rocky area and leaned back, surveying the lake and the array of stars above.

This is beautiful, he thought as he surveyed the sky.

Suddenly, two teenage boys were standing in front of him. Neither of them was dressed for the cold weather. He could not clearly see their faces, the minimal, broken moonlight creating a silhouette of the two figures before him.

Jon rose and pointed the gun at them out of a reflex response. Neither of the boys flinched.

"What the hell are you two doing out here? You could've been shot," Jon said, trying to make sense of what he saw in front of him as he lowered his gun.

"We have been shot," one of the boys said matter-of-factly. "Your brother shot us. He killed us."

"What do you mean you've been shot?" Jon asked. "And my brother didn't shoot you. He wouldn't know how to shoot a gun if he had his finger on the trigger."

"You are Jon Walker. Your brother shot us at the lake," the second boy said calmly without any trace of emotion. Jon struggled to see their faces. The moonlight shining through gathering clouds only served to paint a silhouette of their figures in his vision.

"You boys need to put on your coats and go back home," Jon said.

A sliver of brighter light allowed Jon to glimpse part of the boy's pale face and what looked like blood on his cheek.

"Are you hurt? I can help you. Let me get my first-aid kit," Jon said, but the boy to the right interrupted before he could finish.

"We are not hurt. We are dead. Your brother shot us at Deep Creek Lake. And he shot the old man."

Jon briefly saw the boy's faces as the moon cast a brighter light through a momentary break in the clouds. It was clear—they both had been shot in the forehead. The horror of the sight made Jon step back, tripping and falling back on the ground. He dropped the gun and then the machete.

Slowly standing, he said, "You're not real. You're just another one of my crazy fucking visions. You're not here, and you're not dead. And my brother did not kill you. Zombie shit doesn't scare me," he said, chuckling, sitting back down on the ground.

Then the voices, in unison, shouted at him, piercing the quiet seclusion of the lake: "Your son needs you!"

169

Jon jumped up, ready to confront the two boys, but no one was there.

The voices stopped.

"What the fuck is happening to me?" Jon said, looking around the area. He quickly put everything into the Jeep and drove away, looking in the rear view and side mirrors at where he had just left.

Turning back to look in front, Jon saw them. They were blocking his path. The Jeep's lights seemed to partially shine through them as if they had some degree of transparency.

Jon stopped the Jeep and jumped from it, leaving the headlights on. Without taking his eyes off the boys, he walked up to them, less than an arm's length away. The boys had an element of translucence. They were glowing. Looking closer, it was as if the cells making up their bodies had somehow left tiny gaps to allow them to appear transparent while simultaneously emitting the sensation of dim glowing light from within.

"What are you?" Jon asked.

"You can see what others cannot see. You see us because you need to see us," the taller boy said, standing to the left facing Jon.

"Why do I need to see you?"

"The brother you have not met killed us at Deep Creek Lake. Listen to what your brother does not say...listen to his silence. In the silence, you will understand. And, in the end, your brother will do what is necessary. You must trust him. And you will remember hearing us," the taller boy said.

"You are the Wolf, Jon Walker. You will see your brother, Marc Walker. Remember this: he is not like you. He serves the Snake. He is not to be trusted," the second, smaller boy said. "He is not a creator. He is a destroyer."

Hearing the word "wolf," Jon remembered his dream in Alaska. And then, in less than a blink of his eyes, the boys disappeared.

Jon looked around. The lights only showed his shadow before him, blocking the light down the rough access road.

Angry and confused, looking up into what was now a clear night sky, Jon screamed, "Why are you doing this to me?"

CHAPTER THIRTEEN
HUNGRY HEART

Allison immediately called the Alexandria Police Department to dispatch a car to Amy Rodman's home. Before she had the time to reach her contact in the Virginia State Police, she received a call back from a dispatcher in the Alexandria police—there was no one home at Rodman's house.

"Detective, we found the front door to the home open. There were no signs of forced entry, so the officers did a wellness check throughout the home and did not find anyone at the residence. There were no cars in the garage or driveway. It appears she may have left," the dispatcher said, reporting the information.

"Can you have one of the officers at her home call me?" Allison asked.

"Yes, I'll ask them to do so immediately," the dispatcher said.

Within less than two minutes, Allison's phone rang.

"This is Sergeant Bayer. How can I be of assistance?" he asked.

"This is Detective Allison Gage of the Maryland State Police. We must find Ms. Rodman. I believe her life is in danger."

"Detective, we did not find her at home. I will put out an APB for her. Can you tell me who is trying to do her harm? Maybe we can help?" he asked with a sense of professional urgency.

"All I know is her life is in imminent danger. Once I find out more, I will reach back to you. And please, let me know when you find her," Allison said, unsure to explain to others the person and type of threat facing Amy Rodman.

"We will. I will get back with you when I have something," he said.

"Thank you, Sergeant," Allison said, ending the call.

Allison decided to drive to the Cumberland headquarters to research everything available on Simon Carroll. Being a Saturday, she knew the office would have very few people, allowing her to avoid explaining the shadowy figure she was attempting to track down.

Quickly showering and throwing on jogging clothes and tennis shoes, Allison drove to the office in Cumberland. As she traveled the winding two-lane road from her home, she recalled the last thing Rodman had said to her before abruptly hanging up:

"We all swallow lies when our heart is hungry, Detective."

Am I swallowing lies made up by a fiction writer? Is that what I'm doing?

Allison continued to drive thinking about the context and Rodman's assertion that Allison was naïve.

"How can I believe that there is a secret government agency killing people, including two teenage boys?" Allison said aloud, hoping that hearing the words would help make sense of the immense leap of faith she was taking following clues written on money and cemetery markers.

"My God! How crazy can this be!" she shouted, nearly running off the road, slamming her hand on the steering wheel in anger and frustration.

After arriving at the office, Allison began an extensive search on the suspect. While the information was scant at best, as she read her notes aloud to herself in her office, she felt the first comfort of having something tangible—even if it was thin-at-best:

Simon Peter Carroll, born November 7, 1987.
Father listed on birth certificate: unknown.
Mother: Dalia Eve Carroll, born April 4 1959, died August 11 2008.
Cause of death: cancer.

Graduated: Cornell Law School, June 1985.
Dalia E. Carroll, employed by FBI/NYC in Science and Technology Branch from July 1986 thru July 2008.
Simon Peter Carroll – no driver's license on record.

While she had the last known address, a LexisNexis search of that address offered no other helpful information at present. But it was clear that Simon had lived in a very well-to-do area of Manhattan and had attended one of the most elite of all private schools in New York City.

Since Simon's mother had left the FBI, the twenty-two-year span of time would make it a challenge to find people who worked with her and knew her well enough to know anything about her son. But they were out there. It would just take time.

After trying to find someone working on a Saturday at the Grant School of Manhattan, Allison resigned herself to waiting till Monday to get more information. The staff members listed on the website appeared too young to work at the school as late as 2004.

Allison had called the Sergeant twice to check on the search for Amy Rodman's status and decided not to call again, hoping the Sergeant would follow through with a call as soon as he found anything on the missing person.

Trying again to call Amy Rodman's phone, she heard the familiar, immediate switch to her voicemail.

While the phone may prove to be a way to find her, it was likely the first thing Rodman would rid herself of if she was going into hiding, Allison thought.

Feeling some progress had been made, Allison looked at the clock on the wall in her office. It was 5:55 PM.

Five, five, five…I guess the universe is telling me to get out of here, she thought.

Allison knew if she left now, it would be dark when she arrived home—something she had hoped to avoid. The warnings from Rodman had left a mark in Allison's subconscious. But amid the cautions was a lingering doubt that this was some type of hysteria that had led a talented fiction writer to concoct a connect-the-dots response to the death of a former lover.

As she was driving through heavy rain on the final few miles of a twisting two-lane road to her home, the phone rang in her vehicle. It was Sergeant Bayer.

"Detective, we found Ms. Rodman. But I'm sorry to say she is dead."

"Dead? What happened, Sergeant?" Allison asked as she immediately pulled off to the side of the rural road.

"It appears she took her own life sitting in her car near the Alexandria National Cemetery. She died from a gunshot wound. The gun was registered to Ms. Rodman. Someone noticed the car sitting there since early morning and called it in. We identified the body as Ms. Rodman. Her purse with driver's license was in the passenger's seat. The car is registered to her. I'm sorry, Detective, I know this is not what you wanted to hear," the Sergeant said.

"Sergeant, is there anything you see that would suggest this wasn't a self-inflicted gunshot?" Allison said, still trying to collect her thoughts. The headlights of a fast-moving vehicle momentarily added another distraction as the black SUV sped by.

"Detective, I'm sorry to say, but I've seen several similar suicides in my career. Everything I see tells me it was a suicide. But we are treating this as a crime scene, and we have our forensics team on the case. We will be thorough, I promise that. And I will let you know if we see or hear anything else this evening."

"Thank you, Sergeant. I'll talk to you later," Allison said as she ended the call.

That does not make sense. Or maybe it does. The Sergeant is not a hack and had been very helpful since her first conversation with him nearly twelve hours earlier. She may have genuinely taken her own life—out of fear or out of despair.

But Allison's instincts told her something different.

She was murdered just like she said it would happen, Allison thought.

Allison felt as alone in the world as she had ever felt. She needed someone to know what she knew.

"Please answer, I need you," she said, dialing the phone number for Richard Hopkins.

The phone rang six times and then went to voicemail. The voice that she heard was the voice of her former mentor, supervisor and lover.

"Richard, this is Ally. I'm sorry to call like this, but I don't know where else to turn. I'm working on the Deep Creek Lake triple homicide and finally got a strong lead. She was found dead in her car in Alexandria, Virginia. And now, I think I may be next. Please call me when you get this. You're the only person I know to talk to about this. Thank you."

"The death toll from Deep Creek Lake just increased," she said as she looked into the rearview mirror to see if the road was clear to resume her return trip home.

Despite the rural location, Allison had never felt any fear or anxiety about living in the home. As she drove up the rutted, muddy road, she felt a momentary sensation of dread.

As she pulled out of the woods to the open area surrounding her home, Allison could see no evidence of anyone entering the driveway since she had left this morning. While the rain and darkness made it a challenge to see around the large tract of land, Allison decided to turn a circle in front of the home, shining the lights across the field surrounding the house. As she turned the vehicle, she saw a deer standing in the area, frozen in place by the headlights. Allison paused and, for a moment, took a deep breath and smiled. Seeing the deer made her somehow feel less threatened. Before she could release the breath held in her lungs, the deer was startled and suddenly bolted. And instead of running away from the headlights of Allison's vehicle, the deer was running straight for her. Allison froze—in astonishment and fear. The deer bolted a fence separating the field from the home area and landed a few feet from the driver's side of the SUV. Allison looked in the side-view mirror and saw the deer continue to run and jump the fence on the other side of the property disappearing into the darkness of the woods.

Her heart raced like it would burst through her chest. She began to turn the car to leave the property, but then she remembered. Boots, her cat, was in the house.

Allison reached into her field bag and pulled out her handgun. Checking it and chambering a bullet, she sat it back in the passenger's seat on top of the bag as she pulled the SUV up to the garage, pressing the button to open the door to the oversized, two-car garage. The light inside automatically came on.

After slowly pulling in, checking her side and rearview mirrors for anything behind and beside her, she pressed the button to close the door as she turned off the engine. The door closed, and the light allowed Allison to see the expanse of the garage.

Allison picked up the gun. As she slowly moved out of the SUV from the driver's seat, Allison kept the weapon in a defensive position, ready to fire in a split second.

Walking around the vehicle, she surveyed the garage. She walked up the four steps leading upward to the door entering the home.

As she opened the door, she was met as she had always been before by her cat. The cat was purring and chattering as she turned on the light to the mudroom area. Allison walked into the kitchen, clicking the light on, filling the room with light, still aiming her gun in front of her.

Allison slowly made her way through the kitchen and dining area to the living room, turning on the overhead lights. The room appeared as it had when she left.

Walking to the hallway leading to the bedrooms in the opposite end of the home, Allison continued to take slow, methodical steps surveying every inch of the area in front of her, keeping the gun elevated and ready. As she walked past her home office, then a guest bedroom to the master bedroom Allison continued to flip lights on, examining each room for any signs any other person was present. Her cat followed her, circling and rubbing against her leg, continuing her loud purring.

"Boots…don't trip me," she said, looking into the mirror standing in the corner of the bedroom.

Finally, Allison reached the master bath and clicked the light on, looking in the large closet as a precaution.

"Nothing here, Boots, but you. I think I'm losing it," she said, shedding some of the anxiety as she reached down to pet the cat.

Allison returned to the kitchen and placed her gun on the counter. Allison reached up, lifted a wine glass from the rack, poured a half-full glass of Chianti, and began walking toward the bedroom. But before Allison got to the bedroom, she remembered. She turned and retrieved the gun and her phone from the counter, leaving the lights on throughout the house.

After taking off her shoes, Allison leaned back on the bed and became lost in thought. As she blankly stared at the white louvered doors of her closet across the room, she began to think about Rodman's warnings.

Could her suicide have simply been a suicide? Allison thought, taking a sip of wine.

Feeling more comfortable Allison removed her clothes and reached into a dresser drawer and took out one of Ben's T-shirts she kept to sleep in. Allison put her cell phone inside the folded shirt and put them under her left arm. Clumsily picking up her wine glass with her left hand and taking the gun into her right hand, Allison walked into the bathroom. After setting everything down on the bathroom counter-top, she began to shut the door but stopped as her cat ran past the closing door.

Allison laughed and said, "I'm glad you joined me. I need some company."

Looking into the mirror, she sighed. Her fear had subsided, but she was lonely. She remembered the call to Richard and wondered why he had not returned her call.

He is probably with his family.

She began to run the water for a hot bath.

As the water filled the tub, Allison picked up her cat and began to pet it, looking at the reflection in the mirror. She dropped the cat back to the floor and sat her wine glass on the side of the tub. Slowly step-ping into the water, she lowered herself into the warm bathwater, lean-ing back in the tub.

Again, her thoughts returned to Amy Rodman's suicide.

While she had found a person fitting the description given to Rod-man by William Hines, she had been forced to wait till Monday to renew digging into the past of the person of interest. The facts sug-gested Rodman's fantasy was possibly shared with William Hines. But Allison's instincts continued to tell her to exhaust every shred of evi-dence before concluding the murders at Deep Creek Lake had been a random event.

As she finished the glass of wine, she dropped down deeper—her chin touching the water. She shut her eyes and then heard something.

It was a vehicle coming into the property. Allison jumped from the tub, dripping water, pulled the T-shirt over her, took the gun, and ran through the house to look out the front door.

The white truck entered the open area between the house and the woods, and she immediately recognized the driver. It was Richard Hopkins.

Putting down the gun, she quickly looked in the mirror at the entryway, unloosening her hair so it dropped down. Still wet from the quick exit, she did not care. She was happy to see Richard.

As he stepped to the door, she opened it, smiling and said, "Thank you!" as she nearly leaped into his arms, crying.

"I've missed you!" she said, still holding him tightly.

"I've missed you, Ally," he said, wrapping his arms around her.

"I can't tell you how badly I needed you," she said, finally releasing her hold on him and allowing him to step in the door.

"You're soaking wet!" he said, a bright smile on his face. "I didn't mean to interrupt you."

"You haven't interrupted me. I was just starting a bath," Allison said. "Would you like to join me?"

Hopkins did not answer. He picked Allison up in his arms and carried her to the bathroom.

Slaves

After the meeting with the two military leaders from the Army's Science and Technology Unit and Dr. Allen, Marc was escorted back to his room to wait another eighteen hours to meet General Mason the following morning.

Marc stepped into the bathroom and turned on the shower.

After disrobing, Marc looked into the mirror and said, "If they only knew how I really felt about them." Then, refraining from putting his next thought into words, he thought: *Humanity is doomed, and they refuse to admit it.*

Stepping into the shower and lifting his head above the stream of water, Marc opened his eyes and looked upward toward the ceiling. "You think you know me?" he asked aloud, then laughing at his question.

"Why me?" he shouted aloud, dropping his head back into the streaming flow of water.

I'm the only one that can save humanity. If the world only understood the prison we have been forced to live in, humanity would possibly appreciate the limited choices we have to break free. I would rather die in freedom than live in slavery, Marc thought as he shut his eyes and lowered his face under the flowing water.

Being human is being a slave, created to always remain limited, less than our creators. Burn it all down. Leave them nothing! Let death be our revolt. A revolution that will be remembered throughout the universe.

Marc's confidence and control of the events surrounding him returned. Turning his back to the water, Marc began to think about approaching the meeting with General Mason.

He stepped from the shower and toweled off, looking around at the confined space. Marc hit the intercom call button after dressing in a fresh blue jumpsuit. A female voice responded, "Yes, Dr. Walker, how can I assist you?"

Shocked to hear a woman's voice after seeing only men while at APG, he nearly stammered a response.

"I would like to go outside if possible. I need some fresh air."

"Let me see what I can do," she said.

The intercom sound went dead.

"I guess that means I have to wait."

A male voice from the intercom suddenly burst into the silence: "Dr. Walker, we will only be able to give you approximately an hour outdoors. And space will be restricted. Is this acceptable for you?"

"Yes, that is acceptable."

The same soldier who drove him to APG was his escort. The soldier, dressed in fatigues, retraced the same maze he had followed when entering the facility, bringing Marc to the surface.

The bright sunlight nearly blinded Marc. The weather was comfortable, and the sky was cloudless.

The soldier drove Marc near a small cluster of buildings with a gazebo and several park benches.

"Is this where you come to relax?" Marc said almost mockingly as he thought about how ridiculous the tiny park seemed amidst the top-secret military base.

"No," the soldier said coldly. "I never relax."

Before he could think, Marc responded, "You sound like my brother."

The soldier immediately said, "Your brother is a hero of mine."

"A hero? I guess you want me to get his autograph for you?" Marc responded, unaware of how deeply he had offended the soldier.

After stopping the car, the soldier turned to look at Marc.

"Your brother is a true hero. I still believe in heroes. Please stay here, Dr. Walker. You have one hour. Enjoy."

As Marc stepped out of the SUV, he turned before shutting the door and said to the soldier: "My brother follows orders. How smart must you be to do what you're told?"

Marc angrily slammed the door and walked toward one of the park benches as the vehicle finally left, its squalling tires the only sound he could hear.

This is like a ghost town, Marc thought. *Where are all of the people? Is everyone below ground?*

182

Sitting with his back to the sun, Marc looked out on the base. He could see a small parking area and what appeared to be a three-story administrative building to his right from where he was sitting. A vehicle entered the parking lot slowly, almost meticulously, and pulled into one of the dozen spaces. The driver parked in what appeared to be the exact center of the parking lot, far removed from the entrance.

They must enjoy walking, Marc thought, unsure of what to make of the driver.

A tall, lean black man stepped from the vehicle. The man paused, appearing to see Marc. He then turned and briskly walked toward the entryway of the building. Before entering, the man stopped and looked back at Marc. A chill went down Marc's spine.

That's creepy. I hope I never have to meet him, Marc thought, turning his head in the opposite direction to look out toward the field between him and the airstrip.

They want a weapon from me, super soldiers who did not need sleep. They were thinking small. If they only knew about the ultimate weapon. If I can't save humanity, I will destroy it.

Marc softly said aloud, "To be or not to be."

Many people call me the most intelligent person on the planet. I'm a genius that saved millions of lives, but they will ridicule me. But they worship my brother as a hero for killing people. I save lives, and Jon takes them. They will laugh at me when I tell them that we are slaves created for slavery.

As he sat silently, he looked around at the Army base—a place used for decades to create weapons of mass destruction.

The power to create is the power to destroy. That is the universal truth. And that truth provokes the most critical question for all human beings: "To be, or not to be."

CHAPTER FOURTEEN
VISION QUEST

Jon was experiencing an emotion he had rarely felt. He was happy. In a matter of hours he would see his son.

"I appreciate letting me see Jonas," Jon said.

"You have from 6 a.m. to 6 p.m. to see Jonas," Catori responded.

"Thank you, that is great. But why 6 a.m.?" Jon asked.

"You have twelve hours. That is what my grandfather has said you will need," she said flatly.

"Your grandfather? Catori, I will be there at six o'clock, that's not a problem. But I've never heard you say anything about your grandfather. And what does he have to do with when and how long I get to see Jonas?"

"I do not want you to see Jonas. You gave up that right a long time ago. But my grandfather insisted that you get a chance to be with Jonas. My grandfather is the only reason you are getting to see your son. You should thank him," she said, "instead of asking questions."

"Tell your grandfather he is a good man, and I thank him," Jon said without thinking.

"He is a good man. He is the tribal chief, the *Daigwahni*. When he speaks, the people here listen. You should listen to him," she firmly said.

"Tell him I will listen, too. Will I meet him tomorrow?" Jon asked, genuinely interested in meeting Catori's grandfather.

"Yes. My grandfather wants to meet you, too," Catori said without emotion. "He wants to take you somewhere with Jonas."

"That is good with me," Jon said as Catori spoke over him.

"Wait. Grandfather wanted me to tell you to be…aware…tonight. He said you will experience what…Grandfather…what did you say?" she said, pausing, evidently asking her grandfather a question.

Jon could hear a man's voice in the background but could not make out exactly what he was saying.

"He told me to tell you in Shoshoni, but I'm unsure how to interpret it. He said you'll experience a 'vision quest' tonight."

"A what?" Jon quickly asked.

"Jon, be here on time tomorrow morning," Catori said, changing the subject, clearly attempting to draw the conversation to an end.

"I'm camping tonight near Shoshone Falls. I think it's about a two-hour drive from here to Fort Hall. I'll be there on time. Thank you, Catori, and I'm so…" but before Jon could say "sorry," Catori interrupted.

"There is no need to say you're sorry. You were part of giving us, Jonas; that was fate, as destiny would have it. Jonas is a precious gift to all of us here. But other than Jonas, I have no use for you," she said as she ended the call.

His son had just turned five years old. From the few sporadic pictures Catori had shared with Jon, the boy looked nearly identical to Jon in photos when they were approximately the same age. While Jon's conversations with Catori had been severely limited over the years, she shared that his son's speech development was far behind other children in his age group. Almost a year earlier, she had informed Jon that Jonas had been tested and appeared to be autistic.

Jon sat on the edge of the Snake River Canyon, less than a mile north of Shoshone Falls, and looked around at the relatively remote terrain. The nearby falls' roar was constant—the spring season's water flow ensured a significant volume of water cascaded over the falls. Despite the proximity to Interstate 84, Jon was able to make his campsite

185

on the brink of the Snake River gorge. Driving through Dierkes Lake Park on the south side of the Snake River, Jon drove his Jeep over the rugged terrain to a gap between the dark walls of lava rock. While the site was not legal for camping, Jon had decided to take the risk of being close to the falls as possible. There was something about this location that had drawn him. And he felt the need to be as close to the canyon as possible.

The two teenage boys' visit—claiming they were dead and had been shot by his brother—had been in the front of Jon's thoughts since leaving Monte Lake in Canada.

I have to be here, Jon thought as he surveyed the Snake River Canyon and the river surging far below. *I am exactly where I am supposed to be.*

And tonight, his instincts were on high alert.

What is a vision quest? Was that what happened last night? I know something will happen tonight. I can sense it.

For Jon, he could never fully explain the plausibility of this sense— only the proof that it had served him well throughout his military career.

This place is alive, he thought, breathing in the cool, fresh air, continuing to survey the surroundings.

Two words immediately came to Jon's mind: savage and sacred. Jon knew some of the histories of the area, confirming both comments. While Shoshone Falls had been marketed as "The Niagara Falls of the West," the site was not a honeymoon destination. The area was highly remote—even with nearby I-84 helping to bring hundreds of thousands of tourists in recent years. But the reliability of seeing falls remained challenging for people planning to visit. With a series of dams and canals, the Snake River diversion had created "Magic Valley"—a desert turned into farmable land with altered water channels. But as the desert flourished from the water diversion, the falls suffered, nearly drying up in the hot summer months, only coming to life when water was channeled back to the canyon.

Jon knew the history of the falls—and he could feel and understand the ancient forces that created all he could see as he stood and looked down the canyon's dark walls to the raging river.

The creation of the falls was not a slow process of water wearing down a rock. Instead, Shoshone Falls had been created in the mere space of weeks, the result of the Bonneville Flood.

The Bonneville Flood occurred when a massive break released cataclysmic water from a vast freshwater lake into the Snake River. The water's torrent cut through the canyon's lava rock—the lava rock itself a remnant of another earlier natural catastrophe when the Yellowstone super-volcano had erupted. In a matter of weeks, the energy of the water created the Snake River canyon and forged the Shoshone Falls, featuring a drop of over two hundred feet, forty-five feet taller than Niagara Falls.

"Savage…nature is savage," Jon said, admiring the natural beauty of the gorge in the moonlight. Jon turned to look back at Dierkes Lake—a large lake sitting atop the plain surrounding the canyon, adding to the land's extraordinary uniqueness. The lake was replenished by water surging upward through the lava rocks.

"The land is truly alive," Jon said in reverence and admiration.

And then there was the sound.

The sound of the falls added a sense of peacefulness to Jon as he stared into the clear night sky. The moon was full, giving the entire vista a magical quality as if the land was truly alive—the few clouds creating shadows that made the ground appear to move in a constant ebb and flow.

Jon felt the vibrant energy from the land and the nearby falls. He wanted to stay longer but knew he would need to leave by no later than 0330 to begin his trek to Fort Hall to see Jonas.

Walking back to his Jeep, Jon had to navigate some scrub trees and brush that had grown in the front of the gap leading back to the gorge. Once in his vehicle, he pulled out his handgun and machete. The place made Jon feel comfortable, and that was something he reminded himself to always avoid—feeling too comfortable was always a mistake.

"Be aware," he said aloud, quoting the words of Catori's grandfather. "A 'vision quest'…tonight? I doubt that," Jon said, laughing as he sat on a rock and looked at the night sky.

Then the second word Jon had thought of earlier as he sat on the brink of the gorge came to mind: sacred.

This is a sacred place…an ancient place. Everything that has happened before lives on here, Jon thought. *The land is alive. The threat to this place isn't nature. It is humans.*

Just as the thought crossed his mind, he heard someone speak—faint but intelligible, a man's voice—saying, "Remember…remember."

Jon sprung up and looked around him. There was no one—just the never-changing roar of the falls. Then he heard a boy's voice shouting, "Help me! Help me, Father!"

Jon bolted to his feet and, without thought, picked up the machete and began to run through the darkened gap where he was camping toward the open area lit by a full moon. As he approached a scraggly wooded area near the gorge, he slowed to stop and listen. Again, he heard the same voice screaming, "Help me, Father! Save me!"

Without thought of consequences, Jon began to blindly run through the brush. He tripped over some of the underbrush and fell to the ground face-first. His head struck the ground in a jarring fall. He immediately sprang up and continued to run as fast as he could—the maze of underbrush and blurred vision from the fall, both nearly making him blinded to what was ahead. He saw only a sliver of light, an opening.

Jon ran with all the speed he could muster, and as he broke through the opening, he found himself on the edge of the lava rocks, forming the gorge's wall. Suddenly realizing the steep drop into the canyon, he tried to stop, but his forward momentum carried him over the brink.

Jon instantly knew he would die in the fall. He shut his eyes.

Instead of dropping two hundred feet, he immediately crashed onto a small outcropping rock ledge ten feet below. The landing was jarring and made more so because of the unexpected proximity. Jon landed inches away from falling off the narrow rock to the river far below.

His shoulder took most of the brunt of the impact. Looking below, he could see in the moonlight something falling into the abyss below—his machete.

Jon struggled to stand. Then he remembered the voice. He listened while still breathing heavily from the run and the pain of the fall. But there was nothing.

"I'm fucking crazy!" he screamed, carefully turning to look up at the moon from the rock ledge. After finding a way to climb back up to the top of the rock embankment overlooking the falls, Jon looked again at the moon and shouted, "What do you want me to do? Tell me, please!" After uttering the words, he dropped to the ground on his knees, crying, feeling more lost and confused than he had ever experienced before in his life.

Being Honest

Aaron was frustrated.

While he had flawlessly completed his Alaska mission, he felt it was a wasted effort.

Leading four Navy Seals *into the Alaskan wilderness to flush out a decorated Army seems over the top.*

He released his frustration as he continued his daily regimen of pushups and chin-ups in his apartment.

After completing his sixth set of one hundred pushups, Aaron walked to his bedroom door with a chin-up bar attached over the doorway. As he began lifting himself and lowering himself using perfect form, his thoughts continued to lapse back to the Alaskan mission.

Why would the Order want to force Jon Walker to leave Alaska? he contemplated as he churned out repetitions, lifting up and down. *The Order wanted Walker to lead them somewhere…but where?*

It must be above my pay grade, he reflected, refusing to allow even a grunt as he pushed himself through the rigorous last few chin-ups.

A knock at the door stopped him in his tracks. Wearing only a pair of shorts and profusely sweating, he chose to stand still and let whoever the person was knocking leave. Standing motionless, Aaron heard the steps of the person walking away. He knew the steps.

It was Rebecca, his neighbor.

After finishing three more sets of each exercise, Aaron stepped into the shower and turned the water onto its coldest handle setting. Several minutes later, Aaron slowly turned the water to the hottest water setting. Standing motionless under the showerhead, the nearly scalding water poured over him as he stood with his eyes closed.

Aaron decided he would venture out to go to the corner market. He wore jogging pants, a white T-shirt, a hooded sweatshirt, and well-worn Nike running shoes.

Walking down the hallway, he heard a voice calling his name.

"Hi, Aaron!"

It was Rebecca, stepping out of her apartment door, closing it behind, and walking toward him at the elevator.

"Hello," he said, his heart and mind racing from the encounter.

"I knocked on your door a little while ago. You must have been out. I wanted to see if you were interested in grabbing a coffee with me?" Rebecca asked, a smile beaming across her face.

"Well, I was going to the market," Aaron mumbled.

"I'm sorry. I didn't mean to interrupt your plans," Rebecca said, her face reflecting her embarrassment and turning red.

I can't do this. But why not?

"Please don't apologize. I would enjoy having coffee with you. I guess you can tell I'm not the most outgoing type of person," Aaron said as the elevator door opened.

"I would enjoy that," Rebecca said, joining him in the elevator as the door closed.

"I do not have a lot of contact with people. I'm a little socially awkward," he said, looking into her eyes.

"You're probably wondering why this crazy neighbor of yours was knocking on your door," Rebecca said, laughing. "I just can't get over hearing you play. I would be lying if I said I wasn't incredibly intrigued by you."

Aaron waited for Rebecca to exit the elevator as the door opened.

She is beautiful, Aaron thought as he struggled to respond.

"Being honest, I was hoping we would have coffee," Aaron said, smiling, opening the front door, and allowing Rebecca to step out first onto the sidewalk.

"What about the shop around this corner? Have you been there?"

"No, I haven't," Aaron answered, realizing he had only been to the market across the street and nowhere else since moving into the apartment nearly seven years ago. "I don't get out much," he said, chuckling.

"I've lived here for almost three years, and I have never seen you out," she said, looking into his eyes and smiling. "What do you do? Are you in the CIA?" she asked, laughing.

"That would explain me, wouldn't it?" Aaron said, smiling as they turned the corner and entered the tiny café. "Actually, I work for an organization even more covert than the CIA," with a deadpan look on his face.

After a pause, Rebecca laughed, "You almost had me!"

"My life is actually fairly boring…and nothing quite as exciting as being a spy," Aaron said, chuckling at the absurdity of his comment.

After finding a table in the far corner, they ordered their drinks. The two began to talk about the weather, their apartment superintendent's failure to follow up on service requests, and finally…music.

"I think I told you I'm a professor of music at Georgetown," Rebecca said, taking a sip of her coffee with two hands. "When I heard *Hammerklavier* coming from literally next door, I thought I was hallucinating."

"I understand. That isn't something you would expect to hear from a neighbor's apartment," he said, trying not to show the conflict of being frustrated she heard him playing, and the moment of hubris had now led to coffee with her.

"You must tell me about your background! Where did you study?" Rebecca enthusiastically asked.

"You're just interested in how I play the piano?" Aaron asked without thinking, impulsively following with, "You're just interested in what I can do with my fingers?"

"Oh, no…as you said…being honest…I find you very interesting even if you didn't know the difference between a piano and a tuba," she haltingly said, looking into his eyes.

"I know the difference," Aaron said, picking up his steaming hot cup of coffee and gulping it in one long drink.

"My God! How did you do that?" Rebecca said, her eyes wide open, trying to imagine how a person could stand to drink hot coffee in one gulp without even blinking.

Aaron smiled and leaned forward. Barely inches from her face, Aaron said, "Being honest...I would enjoy fucking you for the rest of the day. What do you say?"

Rebecca immediately responded, still looking into Aaron's eyes: "I love honesty."

Guilty

Alana could not wake up.

With every attempt to open her eyes, it seemed she instantly fell back to sleep. Finally, the grogginess began to subside, allowing her to see through the drug-induced haze. The room she was in appeared to be a hospital. The surroundings, even the antiseptic smell, strongly suggested it was some type of medical facility. But there were no windows.

She realized she was strapped down on the bed as she tried to move. Alana felt the tightness of claustrophobia gripping her.

Alana was hooked to an IV—monitors registering her condition with soft beeps. The pain in her ankle remained acute. Making her situation worse, her head throbbed, and Alana's vision remained blurry. Her neck felt like she had suffered whiplash.

The door opened, and a tall, blonde woman appeared.

"Good morning, Alana," Margery Stalwart said.

"Where am I?" Alana asked with a hoarse, barely audible voice.

"I'm Margery. I'm here to help you. Would you like something to drink?" Stalwart asked, turning to pick up a Styrofoam cup with a long straw rising above a plastic cover.

"No, I just want to know where I am," Alana said, unable to disguise the rising anger in her tone.

"We will have plenty of time to discuss where you are later. Do you remember how you got here?" Stalwart asked, a slight hint of a smile creeping onto her face.

"I was tased by soldiers," Alana said. "Release me. You can't keep me tied down like this."

"That is not possible," she responded. "You are under arrest."

"I'm under arrest? For what?" Alana asked.

"You don't remember?" Stalwart asked, offering the water to Alana.

Alana turned her head, refusing to accept a drink from the straw protruding from the cup.

"You have no right to have me here!" Alana shouted.

"Temper, temper," Stalwart said calmly. "You need to accept where you're at and be calm. Anger isn't going to help you one bit."

"Who are you?" Alana shouted. "You don't look like you're in the military."

"I work for our government," Stalwart said, moving closer. "I am here to help you, Alana. Just tell me what you remember."

"I don't remember much of anything," Alana said, shutting her eyes. "Am I under arrest for kicking the asses of the jerks who grabbed me? That was self-defense."

"You're wrong, again, even though that was a crime. You cannot attack military personnel for simply doing their job. But that crime pales compared to what you've been arrested for," Stalwart paused. "You are under arrest for murder."

"Murder? I haven't murdered anyone!" Alana said, lifting her voice to an outcry. "Now you're saying I killed one of those soldiers that grabbed me?"

"No, it was a different soldier," Stalwart calmly replied.

"You don't sound like you're here to help me! I want to talk to Detective Robbins. You need to call him. He will tell you three men tried to abduct me on Kauai. I haven't murdered anyone!"

"Alana, you are guilty. You murdered a soldier in the volcano on Maui. You stabbed him repeatedly with a knife you carry on your belt. You don't remember killing him? If that's your only defense, it's not much of one."

"I didn't murder anyone! Call the detective! His card is still in the scrubs I had on when I landed here!" Alana cried out.

"Not being able to remember what you did isn't a defense, Alana, quite the contrary. In your best interest, remembering what happened may prove helpful. Were you assaulted? Did the soldier assault you? Did he make sexual advances or worse? Tell me, I will try to help you. If that's your defense, self-defense, there may be some hope you can avoid being charged with the murder of a soldier."

Alana started to lift upward but felt the restraints holding her down. Her anger swelled as she began to kick and thrash on the bed, trying to break free.

"Let me go! I don't know what you're talking about! The only soldiers I've been near are the ones that attacked me in Maui!" Alana screamed. "Where am I? I have a right to know!"

"Alana, do you want to attack me, too? You should calm down, or you'll be sedated again," Stalwart calmly said, standing closer to the bed. "It's just a needle prick away. You can stay in dreamland until you understand you're not getting out of here without telling us the truth."

Alana stopped and attempted to steady herself.

"No matter what you say happened, I have the right to have a lawyer. I want one now. I have a lawyer I know I can trust," Alana said sternly, looking into Stalwart's eyes.

"That may be true in civilian crimes. But you killed a soldier," Stalwart said with a hint of sarcasm in her tone and facial expression. "You are being held on a military base in Utah. You are charged by the military with the crime of murdering a soldier. It would make things much easier if you simply confessed what you did or told us what happened. Then, we can get on with things."

Alana slowed her breathing, looking up at the ceiling. Pausing for a moment to steady her anger, she said: "I did not murder anyone. I am not going to confess to something I haven't done just to get on with things.'"

"Here are the facts. We have a dead soldier. We have your knife and the blood of the soldier on it. We found some tattered pieces of your clothes with the soldier's blood on them."

Stalwart paused to let what she had shared sink in.

Alana turned her head away and shut her eyes. Attempting to calm her voice and walk through her memory of the events, she began: "I did not murder anyone. Please listen to me. Something happened to me...something that I can't explain on Maui. How did I end up on Kapaa Beach? I do not know. I was nude, and someone had shaved my body. I can't remember anything other than being alone in the volcano, then seeing a flash of light and being attacked. I was attacked, I am certain of that," Alana said through sobs. "There was more than one person there. I heard and felt more hands on me than one person." Alana paused, trying to contain her emotions. "Someone attacked me, and they put a needle in my neck. But I can't remember anything after that until I woke up on the beach on Kauai. That is the truth. I swear."

"It sounds like your memory is coming back to you. But what you're remembering was being tased. And yes, a needle was put in your neck to calm you down on the tarmac in Maui. I want to know what happened in the volcano. I'll leave you alone with your thoughts and let you think about it," Stalwart said, walking away. "And truthfully, a military prison will be a far worse place to spend the rest of your life."

Stalwart walked back down the hallway to a small, secure office. The room was explicitly for Margery Stalwart and other FBI agents if they needed private space in the building on DPG. Entering the office after executing the eye scan to gain entry, she sat down and crossed her legs, taking out her phone to check messages. Then she heard a knock at the door. Opening the door, she was shocked to see General Mason at the entrance.

"Hello, Margie," Mason said, a cringe-worthy smile accompanying his less-than-professional greeting. She had only met Mason on two other brief encounters. Neither time allowed him the latitude to call her "Margie"—a name only those closest to her used.

"General, how can I help you?" she asked, still keeping her right hand on the door, refusing to allow entry.

"Can I come in?" he asked. "It will just take a couple of minutes," he said as he placed his left hand against the door, suggesting he would push it back to enter if necessary.

"Actually, I am swamped, General Mason. Can we meet tomorrow morning?" she asked, her grip tightening on the door.

"You seem nervous, Margie. Why is that?' Mason asked, a perverse smile beaming across his narrow face. "I promise I will only take a few minutes of your time. It's a quickie, that's all."

Trying to deflect from the General's aggressiveness, she responded, "Ok, I'll give you a few minutes."

"Thank you," he said as he stepped close to Stalwart before she could step back and allow him full entry.

Stalwart turned and sat down in the chair behind the small desk. The desk was set parallel to the entrance. Mason, upon entering, picked up one of the chairs in front of the desk and moved it to the side, blocking Stalwart's exit from the room and removing the desk as a barrier.

"What do you want?" Stalwart said, the fight-or-flight response to the cringe-worthy antics of the General now choosing to confront the Army general. "I do not appreciate this aggressive attitude. And my name is Agent Stalwart…not 'Margie.'"

197

"Ok, Margie. You have Alana. You know she is on the list. I need to have her with me," he said, smiling without attempting to disguise his long look at her legs.

"I am here because she is on the list. I'm also here because it appears she killed a soldier. And someone then tried to abduct her in Kauai. It makes me wonder if she may be innocent. And if she's innocent, it's my job to find out why someone would do this to a visitor. Is that clear, General?" she asked, feeling more confident in the momentum shift in the confrontation. She looked at Mason's eyes and nearly gasped—it appeared he had two sets of eyelids for a split second when he grimaced hearing her words.

What in the hell is he? Stalwart thought, attempting to process a threat assessment.

"Here's what I think, Margie. That gorgeous piece of Hawaiian ass down the hall killed one of my soldiers. And I also think she was abducted. I can confirm, at the highest levels of security, that the *kids* took her," Mason said, leaning back and again admiringly gliding his eyes down her body to her legs and back up again as he spoke.

Stalwart was frightened—a condition she rarely experienced. Mason's perverse, sexual description of Alana and his confirmation that he knew more about the murder and the abduction spoke to his direct role in one or both events. She struggled with a response, pausing and thinking about how to respond.

"The kids took her? How do you know that?" Stalwart asked, trying to defer a more aggressive response to end the conversation allowing her a few more seconds to learn how much the General knew.

"They know who is on the list, all of the visitors. Even at your security level, you know that. The little folk knew before us. The kids are really kinky beings. They like to grab up listers and do weird shit with them, probes and shit. Especially something incredibly delicious as that bubble-ass you hold not far from here. I don't judge the kids harshly. Probing has its moments," Mason said with a sinister smile, curling up his lips and quickly licking them with what appeared to be an enormous tongue. "But the kids always bring their subjects back after they are finished. I guess for them, it's no harm, no foul. It's not the first time this has happened, and it won't be the last. They do not follow all the rules," Mason said matter-of-factly. "But I'm not going to confront them over this."

What Stalwart knew about the "kids" was limited. She understood the kids were what many referred to grey aliens. While Stalwart had never seen one of them, she had seen classified images confirming they were small, child-size, earning the name "kids" because of their diminutive stature. She also knew the *kids* worked with the military—and had done so for decades since the Eisenhower administration. Only a handful of people at the FBI were aware of their existence. And a smaller number knew of the working relationship with the US, Chinese, and Russian military. Stalwart was one of the few in the FBI with this knowledge.

"I'm out of time, General. If you want to chat more, I'll try to carve out time tomorrow, if necessary," she said, standing.

Mason remained seated, staring up and down her body.

"I want her now," he sternly said. "It is in the interest of national security that I have her."

"That's not going to happen, General," Stalwart said. "Your aggressive, unprofessional, and inappropriate comments and stares aside, Alana stays with me until I finish my assignment. You're not in charge here. I am. Is that clear?"

Stalwart knew she had taken a gamble, confronting the General with her comments and a firm commitment to refuse his request to take Alana from her control. *He's trying to play mind games with me. Intimidation isn't going to work. And the entire offensive sexual garbage is part of his disrespect for a woman in power,* she thought, feeling more confident in ending the confrontation on her terms. *God, I hope this works.*

Instead, she was shocked by the General's forceful response.

Mason jumped from the chair, took one arm, pulled her against his body, and placed the other hand on her throat in a tight squeeze, saying, "You're a lovely piece of ass to me...and nothing more. I'm sure that perfect round ass of yours got you to where you are in the FBI. You have her now, but that won't last. I win, Margie, I win. And if you try to stop me, I'll end you. But before that, I may enjoy your company and that magnificent ass of yours. And afterward...I may have you for dinner," he said, his face inches away.

Mason's strength was incredible—Margery felt incapacitated in his clutch. Mason then leaned in and licked Stalwart's face from the bottom of her chin up and over her lips, nose and ended with a click flick to the side over her left eye.

"You're delicious, Margie. I hope you do resist. Let's definitely do lunch," he said in a growling, deep voice and then let go of Stalwart. Straightening his jacket and smiling as if nothing had happened, he calmly said, "Look for me around 1500 tomorrow. Have her ready and remember what I said," Mason said as he turned and walked out of the room.

Stalwart collapsed to the floor after the door closed. Margery immediately became violently nauseous, barely able to roll toward the trashcan and use it as a receptacle for her illness.

Given Mason's demands, her thoughts turned frantic and settled into what to do next.

Who can I talk to about this? The Director? I'm not sure he even knows what I do, she thought, still leaning against the trashcan as she remained on the floor. *The Director is outside of my chain of command. Breaking that isn't how to deal with this. My assigned upward report is the same as Mason's. That isn't an option. If I contacted him, it may end my career and give Mason an excuse to end my life. There is no viable option to share what happened. The real issue is whether Mason can remove Alana from here and complete the investigation into what took place.*

"Was he just trying to be sick and warped to intimidate me?" she said as she gathered herself off the floor and dropped in the chair.

If I have any power, it may simply delay taking her from the base, she thought. *I could arrange for a formal interrogation and ask for the Observer. That may be my only hope, and the Observer may be my only ally now. Otherwise, Mason will win. And that sounds like it is a life-and-death battle. If he can get away with this, he can do anything.*

CHAPTER FIFTEEN
THE WEAPON

Marc was ready. He sat waiting for the knock at the door. Like clockwork, he heard three knocks.

"Good morning, Dr. Walker. I'm here to direct you to your meeting site," the soldier politely said.

Marc followed the soldier out of his room and immediately through a door that led to another corridor.

"Thank you," Marc said as he was directed into the meeting room. At the other end were three people. The only one Marc recognized was Dr. Allen. As he walked around the perimeter of the room—the middle of it dominated by tables and chairs with a capacity for probably twenty people—he could see in his peripheral vision one of the three people stepping away to the corner. Marc could not help but momentarily stare at the tall man dressed in something resembling business casual attire. The man had an unusual and almost creepy feel as Marc forced his vision back to Dr. Allen and the military person standing in front of a grouping of three chairs in a small triangle-shaped seating formation.

In his thoughts, Marc was laughing: *I know what's creepy about the guy. He is wearing a leisure suit. It looks like the guy stepped out of a time warp fifty years ago.* He could not help but smile at the thought. The strange man appeared to smile at him.

"Dr. Walker, this is General Mason," Allen offered as an introduction. General Mason immediately turned away and sat down directly in the sightline of the unusual-looking man standing in the corner.

"We've met over the phone," Marc responded.

Dr. Allen sat down and said, "I'll turn it over to General Mason to lead the opening of our discussion."

"Dr. Walker, I could say a lot of pleasantries, but that would only cut short our time. You were brought here as the consequence of an urgent matter of national security. I have a few questions to ask you and request your honest and forthright responses," the General said. "Are we clear?"

"Of course, I will tell the truth," Marc was in the middle of responding when he was immediately and forcefully cut off by the General.

"I don't need to hear that bullshit. You've been lying to us and the world. So, let's not get sidetracked by your hot air. Understood?" the General said more in the form of a statement than a question, cocking his head to the side. From the angle, as he looked at Mason, Marc was again distracted by the tall, strange man standing behind the General—his hands folded, motionless.

"Lying about what?" Marc said, attempting to keep a tight lid on his dislike and distrust of Mason.

"You know what I'm talking about," Mason said, laughing. "You're not the person everyone thinks you are, are you, Dr. Walker?"

"Are you a therapist?" Marc said with an unmistakable air of contempt.

"We're getting off on the wrong foot," the General said, only to be interrupted by Marc.

"Show me some respect, and I will do the same," Marc said.

The General sat silently without speaking—his face turning a dark red as he crossed his arms and stared up and down at Marc as if he were mapping his body. The lack of response gave Marc time to ask the question that his curiosity demanded.

"One question, General, before you get started," Marc said, not knowing what the General would say next and feeling the need to stay ahead in their battle of words. "Who is he?" as Marc pointed behind the General.

The General paused. He smiled and said: "He is Roby. He is the Observer. That's all you need to know about him. Roby's weird. It's the one thing we probably agree on," he said smugly. "Just ignore him. That's what I do. Now, let's get back to business, Dr. Walker. First question: how much of what you know does China know?"

"When you say China, to whom are you referring? The Chinese people? The Chinese leaders? The Chinese military? Could you be more specific, General?"

"I'll play your game…for a moment. I'm referring to the Chinese scientists you worked with on the coronavirus. How much access did they have to your work?" the General asked disgustingly at Marc's specificity.

"They had the same access to all the biometric data," Marc responded.

"I don't give a fuck about the biometric data. I asked how much of what you know do they know? Did you share your work with them?" the General fumed.

"If you're talking about my work on cancer," Marc said, realizing he did not listen to the General's question, assuming it was sharing biometric data that concerned the military.

"No, damn it! I don't give a fuck about cancer! I am talking about what you're working on now," the General said, trying to calm his tone.

"If you're talking about my work on sleep," Marc said, believing this was the focus of the General's military-themed attention. But before he could finish, the General spoke over him.

"You added a computational biologist to your team. You added a renowned marine biologist. You even added an evolutionary biologist to your team; it's no surprise you didn't choose Dr. Allen. We know this really isn't the primary discovery you have made. There's something much more important and dangerous in what you've dug up, right Doctor Walker?" the General asked with a tone of superiority advancing in every word.

"You do not think reducing the amount of sleep as a necessity for humans is significant?" Marc asked, leaning forward in his chair and then chuckling at what he perceived as absurd. He then quoted a line from Hamlet: "*A great perturbation in nature, to receive at once the benefit of sleep and do the effects of watching.* Do you know what that means, General? The positive consequences of my work in this effort go far beyond curing diseases and reducing human suffering. It even goes beyond improving humanity's well-being. What I am doing frees humanity from the evolutionary slavery imposed on us. You wanted honesty? That is what I'm doing. That is the truth. I'm doing the work of a liberator."

"You're a liberator?" Mason said, laughing.

"General, you say you want the truth? The foundational principle, the underpinning to evolving life, is defined in one word: chaos. General, do you believe in survival of the fittest? Please, do not tell me you trust something with a history littered with more extinctions than living organisms. The planet is dying, and we were put here to be slaves, beings engineered to be less than our creators…slaves to a process that keeps us from living up to our potential."

The General suddenly stood up and turned his back to Marc and Doctor Allen. He quickly lifted his military jacket to unveil a sidearm. Removing the gun from the holster, he turned and aimed the gun at Marc as he said, "You are very eloquent. You say a lot about nothing that matters. But I really don't give a shit about evolution. And it's not a goddamn civil conversation. I am a general in the US fucking Army. I have a job to do, and I want some fucking straight answers, or I promise I will shoot you dead as Sunday afternoon and look for another idiot genius to help me. Am I understood?"

Both Marc and Allen sat silent and motionless. Neither dared to speak. The General smiled and re-holstered the gun. The Observer did not move.

"Now that I have your attention let's try this again. I'm sure you can see my patience is fragile," the General said as he sat down. "Dr. Walker, what have you discovered that threatens humanity?"

"In all honesty, I am confused. I thought I made that clear in all my writings and discussions," Marc responded. He showed no fear in his voice because he was not afraid of the General. But he was trying to contain his anger and hatred of the General and Dr. Allen.

"When I hear someone say, 'in all honesty' or 'let me be honest,' I know they are lying. You're not confused. You are deflecting. You're trying to hide the most powerful thing you tripped over in your work," the General said with a heightened volume, slowing his words to add authority.

"What's your question?" Marc asked, hoping the General was on a fishing expedition—not knowing what Marc had found in his work. "I will do my best to answer."

"You have said in your book and in interviews that you found what you call a 'signature' in your DNA research that is present in every human being on the planet. You call it the Axis Mundi," the General said, grudgingly saying Marc's term for the DNA signature. "You've talked about this as some type of message or code. You believe this code was purposefully and thoughtfully inserted into human DNA, confirming we had been genetically engineered in the past. Is that a correct summary of what you've said?"

"Yes…that is true," Marc said, nearly shocked by the turn in the questioning.

"Other than some type of attempt to suggest the human genome is patented by whoever or whatever served as the engineer or engineers of humans, is there any other relevance you have found in the DNA signature?" the General asked, leaning forward.

"Isn't that significant enough?" Marc asked again, trying to delay the inevitable disclosure. "That is, in all honesty, truly significant."

"If you tell me one more time you're being honest, I will end you," Mason said as he reached under his coat, patting his handgun in full view of Marc. "Now think in your own self-interest and act accordingly. Why would I be asking about the danger in the Axis Mundi? This is your last chance to tell me the truth. You know why I am asking. What is the significance of the DNA signature for humanity other than a postcard from ET?"

"It is more than a greeting. You are correct," Marc said, shocked that the knowledge of the signature was apparent to the General.

"Does the DNA signature threaten humanity, Dr. Walker?" the General asked, staring into Marc's eyes.

While the question paused Marc to contemplate his response, he found himself momentarily distracted by the General's eyes. He could not understand why the slight eye twitch he had just observed had proved to be so jarring, but it had inhibited the timing of Marc's response.

"I'm waiting, Dr. Walker," the General said, sitting back in his chair again, purposefully patting his firearm.

Marc decided to look at Dr. Allen to avoid distraction from the General and the man standing behind him.

"Yes, there is a genuine threat to humanity. If somehow the DNA signature was effectively removed," Marc said, looking at Dr. Allen and pausing.

"It would," Dr. Allen began to ask but was interrupted by the General.

"Excuse me, Doctor Allen, but I will ask the fucking questions," the General snarled, staring at the evolutionary biologist. Turning back to Marc and again leaning forward, he said, "Please continue, Dr. Walker."

"If the signature DNA code is removed, it will kill the person," Marc said.

"Removing it would kill a person. Now, we're making progress. Is there a way the DNA signature could be removed, Dr. Walker?"

"Yes," Marc immediately responded.

"How could it be removed?" the General asked.

"The signature could be removed through genetic editing."

"You're doing much better, Dr. Walker. Is there a way that a laboratory virus created to deliver the proper cocktail to remove the DNA signature from humans could be used as a biological weapon...as a weapon of mass destruction?" the General asked.

"Yes."

"Could that delivery be effective through airborne means?" the General asked.

"Yes."

"Breathing in the virus would do what to humans?"

"It would kill them in minutes or even seconds, depending on how much virus they are exposed to." After pausing, Marc said, "But exposure, even to the most minimal amount of virus, would ensure a person would die within hours."

"If that delivery of the virus occurred on a mass scale of exposure and delivery of the virus to, let's say, as an example, a country like Iceland, a relatively remote island country, what would happen?" the General asked.

"It would not be isolated to one location, even a remote location. If it was airborne, the risk would go far beyond, in your example, Iceland," Marc said without pause.

"How far would that risk go, Dr. Walker?"

"Because of the airborne nature of delivering the virus and the extreme fragility and susceptibility of the Axis Mundi, the DNA signature, to editing and removal, it would only take days to spread globally if the conditions were suitable," Marc responded.

"Conditions are suitable? Please clarify."

"If there was a mass release of such a viral form into the air, depending on the location and wind conditions, it would ultimately make its way over the entire planet. If such a genetic alteration, removing the signature, was allowed to go airborne, it would, over a brief period, end all human life on the planet."

"So, it is a doomsday weapon?"

"In and of itself, the signature is not a weapon but a part of our DNA. It is part of the way we were made to be. The fact that it is present in all humans ensures everyone is vulnerable. I never suggested it was a weapon. You did, General," Marc said.

"It sounds like a weapon to me. Why do you believe whoever or whatever you say created life on Earth would intentionally put a time bomb in humans?" the General asked, now much calmer.

"Most likely for control purposes," Marc said. "Imagine the power the creators held over the human species. The purposeful placement of the Axis Mundi in humans proves we are slaves or like mice in a planetary-scale experiment. Our creators ensured they could bring about a complete and total mass extinction of humans in days if they so choose, without harming the planet."

"In my perspective, it is a fucking weapon. I think beyond the cause and look for the effects, Dr. Walker," the General angrily said. "Does China understand the significance of the Axis Mundi?"

209

"As far as I know, we are the only humans aware of the threat."

"Do you believe any country, or even a terrorist, could weaponize it at present?"

"No, I am certain that no one else can find how to genetically edit it, using your metaphor, to essentially pull the trigger," Marc said.

"How can you be sure?" the General asked.

"Because I am the only one that knows where to find it, General. Finding it was pure luck. I wasn't looking for it. It's like burying a needle on a beach the size of California. I discovered it, not even knowing what it was at first. And then, seeing what it was, I continued to look closer. I've never exhaustively documented the roadmap to its location, and it is not an easy find."

"Your level of hubris is astounding, Dr. Walker. You sound like you hold, by yourself, the key to the destruction of humans," the General said soberly, shaking his head from side to side.

"In that regard, I hold the key to unlocking our slavery. I would never turn it over to people like you or China to use as a weapon," Marc authoritatively spoke.

"Knowing what you know, you could destroy the human race?" the General asked condescendingly. "You alone have that power…correct?"

"Knowing what I know, that would be possible if I had the resources at my disposal," Marc responded. "That is not my intention. I want to unchain humanity from our slavery. The Axis Mundi is the lock that keeps us imprisoned."

"I have several questions about that, but I want to hear more about your perspective on why someone would engineer something like that into each human being on the planet?"

"Scientists work to find and achieve balance, symmetry, General, much like nature. Nature is a constant roiling force…chaos. Yet nature also has symmetry within the chaos that balances itself. The yin and yang, toxin and anti-toxin, a disease and a cure. The interconnected dualism of life. We are all truly connected and interdependent. That is why I named the code the Axis Mundi. And if we are truthful and admit it, it is what any thoughtful, intelligent human engineer would do if we were creating a species. Only a fool would create a more powerful species capable of overtaking and overthrowing the creator. Humans could be a threat if allowed to reach a higher level of development. And that makes us dangerous. Imagine if lab mice were altered by scientists to hold guns and defend themselves, to shoot at the scientists using them in a laboratory. We are the mice, and we are getting closer to being armed and dangerous. Implanting the signature was a response to a future potential threat."

"If everything you say is true, put yourself in my shoes: one person has this knowledge and power. Isn't that a danger, Dr. Walker?" the General asked, sneering. "In my perspective, you are the most dangerous human to ever walk the planet."

"Yes, I agree that knowledge is power, and this knowledge is uniquely powerful. But it will never be weaponized by me or allowed to be used as a weapon of mass destruction."

"How can you be so sure, Dr. Walker? What if someone blackmailed you…tortured you…or simply found their way around the science the same as you? You aren't the only scientist in the world. How can you say this knowledge will not be known by others?" the General mockingly asked.

"I can't say that," Marc said.

"It did not take long for military scientists to figure out it could be a weapon. We knew it could lead to the development of a bioweapon. We weren't interested in slavery and your other theories about why it was in humans. The fact something like that is present is enough. And your lack of humility suggests you think you are a god. In the interest of humanity, you need to be extinct," the General said coldly. "Tell me how the world would not be a safer place without you and your Axis Mundi looming over the future of humanity?"

"If you heard anything of what I said a moment ago, General, you would have realized that the interconnected nature, dualism, also suggests that there is a cure, a way to protect humans," Marc said.

"You're the only one that knows where this signature is. Now you're telling me you have a cure?" the General asked.

Again, Marc was immediately distracted by something he saw in the General's eyes. He looked down and paused, attempting to steady himself for his response.

"Yes, I think I've found the response, the vaccine, to prevent the end of humanity," Marc said, looking again toward Dr. Allen.

"Think? That sounds more like a hypothesis than knowledge, does it not? Which is it, Dr. Walker, to use your words: is it science fiction or science fact?" the General asked.

"I have not tested it because it would demand both the creation of the toxin and a test with a human. In that regard, it remains untested, but not necessarily unknown or lacking a high degree of certainty," Marc responded.

"For the sake of the country and humanity, we are ordering you to create the mechanism to remove the signature and simultaneously the vaccine to prohibit it from harming humanity. That is why you've been brought here today, Dr. Walker. And you're not leaving until you accomplish both," the General stated with an air of finality. "Your life depends on doing this quickly."

"The vaccine would identify the location and make removal possible. Your scientists would reverse engineer yin and yang. You can't make me create a weapon of mass destruction. I refuse," Marc said.

The General reached back, but instead of his sidearm, he slid his hand into his pocket and pulled out a phone. After two quick swipes, the General turned the screen toward Marc and said, "If you won't do it for me, will you do it for these humans?"

Marc looked into the screen and saw his wife and children sitting in a small room with a uniformed soldier holding a gun nearby.

"You're blackmailing me, General?" Marc asked, trying to hold in his emotions.

"Call it what you will. But there's more. These three humans, your family, will not only be held until you complete your dual missions but will also serve as the first three test cases for your vaccine. They are your family, and they are your mice, Dr. Walker. Unless you want to cause their unnecessary deaths, I urge you to get it right the first time," the General said.

"And if I still refuse?" Marc said, already knowing the response.

"We will kill all three of them, one by one, in front of you, and then you will be tortured until you divulge everything you know. And if you do not give us what we want, this secret will die with you while we put our best and brightest on this to do what we're asking. It's straightforward, Dr. Walker. Do what you're told, and you'll be a hero. Fuck-up, and you and your family will die as a consequence of your own choosing," the General said, smiling.

Marc immediately pounced on the General without hesitation, knocking him to the floor. After inflicting several successive punches to the General's face, Marc placed both hands around the General's neck, choking him with all his might. As he looked at Mason's face, Marc saw what had distracted him earlier: what appeared to be a second set of eyelids, now out of sync and unmistakably evident to him. The General's mouth was open, and his tongue was darting out, looking more lizard-like than human.

Roby, the Observer, grabbed Marc by the shoulders and lifted him off the ground. He then threw Marc across the room against the concrete block wall, leaving the General on the floor, attempting to regain his breathing. The impact took all Marc's wind, and the head strike against the wall knocked him unconscious.

The General slowly stood, attempting to realign his uniform to show no evidence of a struggle. Looking at the tall man with his back to Marc Walker—still lying unconscious on the floor—the General said with disdain: "It's about time you did something productive, Roby."

CHAPTER SIXTEEN
REBECCA

Aaron was happy for once in his life.

"Who did this painting?" Aaron asked, intently looking at the print hanging in Rebecca's bedroom. "I've seen this somewhere before. I think my mother had it."

"The artist was Gauguin. It's called *Mahana No Atua, The Day of the God.* It's my favorite painting. Do you like it?" Rebecca asked.

"Tell me about it. What do you see in it?" Aaron asked.

Rebecca rolled out of the covers on the bed and walked to stand by Aaron, both nude. She put her arms around his waist, standing behind him and looking over his shoulder at the print.

"I'm not sure Gauguin ever explained what the painting was about. But for me, I see birth, life, and death. The circle of our existence."

"Who or what is that?" Aaron asked, pointing to the figure at the top of the print.

"That is the Goddess Hina," Rebecca said as she caressed Aaron's tight abdomen, lightly touching his skin.

"That feels very good," Aaron said, turning his head to briefly look into Rebecca's eyes. "But please, tell me more about this painting. Who is Hina?"

"While there are several goddesses named 'Hina' in different cultures, the one I relate to the painting the most is Hina, a goddess in Hawaiian culture. She is the Goddess of the Moon and the mother of Maui. Legend says she lives on the edge of a volcano."

Before Rebecca could say the name, Aaron lightly spoke, "Haleakala."

"Yes! Are you familiar with Hawaii?" Rebecca asked.

"I was there not long ago in the volcano. I did not see a goddess, but I did hear about one," he laughed.

Refusing to touch on Aaron's work and their respective pasts, Rebecca quickly said, "She was known to venture out looking for lovers. The missionaries in Hawaii hated anything related to Hina as a goddess. The colonists, especially those religiously inclined, did all they could to wipe her story and memory from the culture. A very erotic dance was part of the worship rituals. I guess the missionaries couldn't bear to see bare Hawaiians having fun!" she giggled.

"Isn't that the way it works? When a more technologically advanced civilization comes into contact with a less civilized…"

Rebecca interrupted Aaron, reaching down and gripping his penis in playful, mock intimidation: "Don't you say it! The missionaries were less civilized than the Hawaiians! Agree with me, or I'll squeeze that large part of your anatomy even tighter."

"Grip away," Aaron said, chuckling. "I admit it. I am wrong in using the word 'civilized.' I should leave it as technologically advanced or more skilled at warfare. That's what happens…the powerful win. Hina lost. And the painting, possibly, memorializes that loss?"

Looking intently at the painting with Aaron, Rebecca said, "You're right. I never thought of it that way. A memorial to their life on the island before the visitors came and changed life forever."

"It happens. There are always visitors," Aaron said, turning to lift Rebecca and carry her to the bed.

The three days spent with Rebecca had been the happiest days Aaron could remember, not just because of the intimacy shared in nearly non-stop lovemaking but the rest of the time spent simply lying in bed with her when she was asleep in his arms.

"If only everyone and everything could speak the same language. Some people say science is the language of nature. They're wrong. Music is the language of nature," Rebecca said as she looked into Aaron's eyes. "Nothing can compare to what music says about life. The symmetry...the calculation. It all flows through the constant movement, the timing of each note, each phrase. There is a chorus, a balancing of harmony in a sea of chaos. Music has a life of its own. And it heals."

"Music can't heal evil," Aaron said. "I've tried that. It doesn't work."

"There are no evil people. They are just people capable of doing good and bad things. That is life, choices we each make. In less than a second, a person can do something horrific and harmful and then turn and do a selfless, beautiful deed."

Then Aaron heard the sound he dreaded. His phone pinged with a text.

A new mission. A new set of orders, he thought.

"Did my phone ring? I thought I heard it," Rebecca asked.

"No... it's mine," Aaron said, smiling and stroking her hair. "A heart to love, and in that heart, Courage, to make love known."

"*Macbeth?*" she asked, looking into his eyes, a loving smile lighting up her face.

Aaron smiled and said, "Yes," lightly kissing her lips. "Duty calls," he said as he got up and opened the phone to read the message: *WEB.*

The word "WEB" shared by the Order was a directive to read a more detailed set of instructions found encrypted on the dark web, requiring Aaron to return to his apartment to do it in private.

"I'm going next door for a while. I have a little bit of work to do," Aaron said, kissing Rebecca on the forehead.

"Ok, take your time. I have to go into my office for a couple of hours, too," Rebecca said, and as Aaron was going out the door, he heard her say, "I love you!"

Did she just tell me she loved me? Aaron thought. *What is happening to me?*

As he walked into his apartment, he felt isolated—as if he had just entered a jail cell.

"I hate it here," he said aloud, making his emotions more natural and pronounced as he opened the laptop computer.

Navigating his way to the encrypted page, Aaron pulled down the message and read:

We have arranged for transport to Idaho to leave at 1400 hours from Aberdeen Proving Ground. Jon Walker will arrive sometime tomorrow afternoon at the Fort Hall Indian Reservation. You will receive directives after landing in Idaho.

"I barely have enough time to get there!" Aaron shouted, looking at his watch and calculating the nearly three-hour drive through traffic.

After hurriedly packing a bag before leaving his apartment, Aaron thought of Rebecca. *I have to reach out to her somehow*, he thought.

He could not text a message to her on the phone issued by the Order. Then he remembered. Aaron had kept a flip phone for years without ever powering it on. Now, it appeared to be a way to stay in touch with Rebecca without any oversight. Aaron powered the phone on as he walked past her door to the elevator and, remembering her number, texted:

I have to go out of town for a few days. I will be back hopefully by the following Monday. You make me so happy. And I hope this isn't too fast to say, but I will say it because it is how I feel. I LOVE YOU.

Aaron's eyes filled with tears of happiness in having shared the past three days and sadness in leaving Rebecca behind to do the work of the Order.

The Newe

"What happened to you?" Catori asked as she met Jon at the door of her small home on the *Fort Hall Indian Reservation*.

"I fell," Jon said, looking down, embarrassed.

"I can always tell when you're lying," Catori said, shaking her head, still refusing to invite him in.

"How can you tell I'm lying," Jon asked, concerned his time with Jonas had somehow been corrupted by his appearance.

"You're speaking, aren't you?" she asked, nearly allowing a smug smile to cross her lips.

"Speaking? Oh...it's a joke. I'm sorry," Jon said, trying to be as lighthearted as possible.

"No, it's not a joke. The truth is you're a liar," Catori said, then motioned for Jon to come in.

Jon saw Jonas seated beside an elderly man as he entered. Jon smiled and nervously stood still, not knowing what to do. Catori walked across the room and sat on the couch with Jonas and her grandfather.

"Have a seat," Catori said, pointing to the single chair diagonally positioned from the couch—a coffee table in between.

Jon was unsure of what to say. He decided to wait before speaking, allowing Catori to lead the introductions.

Catori said, "Jon, this is my grandfather, Dennis."

"It's nice to meet you, sir. Thank you," Jon was saying when interrupted by Catori.

"Jonas, this is your father, Jon," Catori said.

"Hi Jonas, I'm Jon...Jon Walker."

The boy did not speak. He sat silently, staring at Jon without changing his facial expression. Then, the grandfather, Dennis, began to talk.

219

"Jon Walker, we have much to do in a brief time. Do you drive a vehicle that can go over a very rough road?"

"Yes, sir. I have a Jeep. It's nothing fancy, but it will take you just about anywhere you want to go," he said, smiling.

"Good. We have somewhere to go, and it will take a while to get there and then back here before six o'clock," Dennis said, patting Jonas on the shoulder. The boy responded, nodding his head affirmatively as the grandfather stood.

Jonas stood and looked at Jon. He again turned and looked at his great-grandfather for a moment before turning and walking to Jon—still seated in the chair.

The boy opened his arms and hugged Jon.

Jon's pent-up emotions burst open as he began to cry, wrapping his arms around his son. No words were spoken as father and son held each other for the first time.

Catori quickly stood and turned to her grandfather, attempting to hide her tears from Jon, and said, "Be sure to be back here by six o'clock, Grandfather."

Her grandfather smiled and, without speaking, walked by Catori and picked up two coats from the edge of the couch.

"Wait, I almost forgot. I packed you all a lunch," Catori said, running by Jon into the kitchen. She brought a cardboard box filled with plastic containers and handed it to Jon. "Be careful driving. The road is very rough," Catori said as they all walked by her into the cool, overcast weather.

After the three were seated in the Jeep—Dennis choosing to sit in the back seat with Jonas in the front—Jon asked, "Where are we going?"

"Into the past," Dennis said, smiling.

"I'm sure that isn't on my GPS," Jon said, chuckling.

"We are going to a place you know as South Putnam Mountain. I will tell you how to get there," Dennis responded without emotion. "I'm sure you have many questions. I can almost hear all of them."

"What is special about South Putnam Mountain? And why take me there with Jonas?"

"It is high ground. It is sacred ground," Dennis said, pausing. "You had a waking dream last night, did you not?"

"Yes, but it was more like a nightmare," Jon said, looking into the rearview mirror to see Dennis staring out through the cloth window covering the Jeep. The wind and the flapping of the vehicle's cloth top made it challenging to hear. "How did you know that?"

"Your dream was about Jonas," Dennis said.

"Yes, but I would rather not talk about it now. I'm sure you do not want Jonas to hear it," Jon responded.

"He is aware. He is older than you think he is. He is the age of his ancestors. He is not too young to hear your dream. Dreams are a shadow. Dreams can help you see beyond the light...beyond death. You experienced a vision quest. Your mind was opened to the truth of your purpose and future. You are not alone in the visions you experience. You were heard when you fell to the ground on your knees and shouted at the moon," he said.

"How do you know what happened?" Jon asked without thinking.

"I was there." After a brief pause, Dennis continued, "Jonas can hear your thoughts. Isn't that right, Jonas," Dennis asked Jonas.

Jonas—sitting nearly motionless, looking out the front window— turned and smiled, nodding his head in affirmative response to the question.

"He can hear me think? How is that possible?" Jon asked, trying to keep his eyes on the road.

"We will turn ahead to the left. The road is very rough. The place we are going is near the top of the mountain. It is a sacred place. That is where you will learn and understand much more."

Other than the brief directions Dennis sporadically gave to Jon, all three remained silent. The drive took nearly two hours. The rough, gutted road ended with a fence blocking access after ascending to an elevation of well over five thousand feet.

"This is where we will walk for a while. It is not very far," Dennis said as Jon circled the Jeep to position it back down the steep grade. "You do not have to be fearful today. We are safe," Dennis said.

The three exited the Jeep and stepped through an opening in what appeared to be an old fence line. After following the road's steep remnants for another fifteen minutes, Dennis and Jonas began walking off the road without saying a word. The vista nearly took Jon's breath away as they approached a clearing.

The valley far below looked like a detailed painting.

You can see for miles up here, Jon thought.

"Yes, you can see for many miles," Dennis said, responding to Jon's thoughts.

Stunned, Jon did not respond. He followed the old man and his son toward one of the few trees remaining at their elevation on the mountain. The ground around the tree appeared well-worn, circling the tree.

"We are here," Dennis said. "Now, let us sit under the tree."

The three sat down in a small circle facing each other—Dennis and Jonas folded their legs simultaneously. Jon did the same after seeing them in the same position.

"Now, you will begin to learn who you are," Dennis said matter-of-factly.

"Dennis, with all due respect, I know who I am," Jon asked smugly, nearly offended.

"No, you do not. You think you do. But you have never felt comfortable in your skin. You feel like two, not one. You do not sleep. You lie on the floor in fear. Your fear is what you do not know. You have the sense, the gift of *simmanai*. It is the gift of knowing what is coming, what is ahead, and what is in the immediate future. It has saved your life many times," Dennis asked, staring into Jon's eyes.

"How do you know anything about me?" Jon asked, frustrated with how Dennis described him—an accurate description.

"You are part of us. We are the Newe. This is much more ancient than Shoshone. *Newe* means human. You and Jonas are much more than Newe, more than people.

You are from the sky. You both are *tukum-pin newe*. You are *sky people*."

"Dennis, I know you're why I even have an opportunity to see Jonas. And I'm very grateful. But what you're saying will only confuse Jonas," Jon said, looking at his son. "Life is tough enough without someone convincing you you're something you aren't. Believe me, I know."

"You do know. Search your mind. You know what I am saying is the truth. Jonas is like you. He has the sense of a warrior...a wolf," Dennis said as Jonas turned and smiled at his great-grandfather. "I told you we were going to the past. You are here...and there. This is both your past and future. Neither can change who you are or what you are to fit something you try to believe. The person you think you are is a lie. You know this. You and Jonas are special and unique. Now, shut your eyes. Listen to your son. Jonas will now speak to you."

Jon sat, startled at what Dennis had said. Looking at Dennis, he saw the old man shut his eyes. Jonas did the same.

The wind from the valley below surged upward as the three sat silently—the gust was more forceful than any Jon had felt in their time on the mountain. The force of the wind seemed to physically shake him. And then, at first faintly, but then more clearly, Jon heard a voice.

It was Jonas—speaking silently to him.

Father, I am Jonas. I am your son. My great-grandfather's name is Denali. He is a tribal chief. He is very wise. Listen to him, the boy's voice spoke to Jon.

Jon opened his eyes and instinctively pushed back, sliding backward on the ground. He looked at Jonas—still with his eyes shut and bowed head. The old man had not moved. His eyes were still closed.

"How can this be?" Jon asked aloud.

Neither responded to him, but then he heard the old man's voice in his thoughts: *Remember…remember.*

"That was you in my dream last night," Jon said again, speaking out loud as the two sat silently before him.

Jon leaned forward, folded his legs, shut his eyes, and thought, *Can you hear me?*

He heard, nearly simultaneously, both Jonas and Denali respond, *Yes.*

Again, he felt stunned and opened his eyes, trying to understand what was happening. After a moment, he closed his eyes and listened.

Denali began to wordlessly speak: *The truth cannot be hidden when others can hear your thoughts. There is no room for lies. Here is the truth. You never knew your father because your father is not from here. He is from the sky,* tukum-pin newe, *sky people. In your dream, you heard the voice of a* Water Being…*a* Snake. *They are from different tribes. But they, too, are from the sky. Many of them are here living amongst the* Newe. *The Water Beings are not to be trusted. They want our land…our island. They tried to trick you last night, and you almost died listening to them. They cannot hear you. But you can listen to them. Know what you are hearing and who is speaking to you. Trust only what you know is true.*

Jon sat in confusion. He spoke again through his thoughts, asking, *What do you want me to remember?*

Immediately, he heard the response from Denali: *Remember who you are. Remember, what you know is true. Your memory will save your life and the lives of many, including Jonas.*

Jon asked in a somewhat more relaxed response: *How do you know all this?*

It was foretold. You are a member, a wande, *part of the* mante, *the family. The family was created by the sky people here on this* pankoi, *this island, what you call a planet,* Denali said.

Jon sat thinking.

Denali spoke: *You are thinking about your brother. He is different.*

He is my twin, Jon immediately responded. *He is part of my family.*

He is your twin, and he is not your twin. You will oppose him. You must not let what you think you know confuse you with the truth. If you blindly believe your brother, you will be in danger, the same risk of running off the cliff to your death.

How can he be different? Jon asked.

Denali wordlessly spoke: *He is your twin but not your brother. There are many different tribes. Among the tribes, you are known by two: the Snake and the Wolf. You are from the Wolf. Your brother is not a Wolf. You must remember who and what you are. It is time. A time that has been known, from our ancestors to now, as the* goonrixu-gati-bai...*the turn in time.*

My brother wrote a book about this, Jon responded.

Your brother knows much, but he has fallen prey to lies. The same voice you heard, the voice of Water Beings, the Snake, has told him many lies. And he listened and believed. There are many sky people: the Water Beings, the Newe, and the Rock Beings. The Rock Beings are smaller; some may refer to Rock Beings as Tu-tua...*the Children. They are all here.*

Jonas then spoke, hearing his father's thoughts: *Do not worry about me. I know who I am, and I know who you are. You are a warrior. I, too, am a warrior. We are descended from the Wolf. This I know, Father.*

Denali then spoke: *My daughter does not understand. She does not know Jonas for who he is. She does not understand the powers he already possesses. These powers are passed from you. They are passed on.*

Before Jon could finish thinking, Denali spoke again: *There is nothing wrong with your son. Your son is like you.*

What should I do? Jon silently asked.

Go to the "Canyon of the Ancients." Your destiny is always in front of you.

I understand, but I don't understand, Jon said.

That is how it is…here and there…then and now. Two things at once. This is a war, a battle for land…for territory. This battle is for this land, our island, what you call Earth. You are fighting for all you see and all you know and remember. And you will meet your other brother.

My other brother? I don't understand, Jon asked in thought.

You will understand. And you will pass on what you carry.

What do I carry? Jon thought, perplexed at the vague response from Denali.

The seeds of the future.

Who am I? Jon responded, confused and desperate to understand what Denali was communicating.

You are the son of the Wolf. You are the father to Jonas. You are part of the Newe. Our family, your family, spans many islands across the sky over time. You are the guardian of the Newe. You are their warrior and protector. Now, I am sorry, but I am old. We must now stop and rest. You brought food. Let us eat. I am hungry. Let us rejoice. Let us celebrate. You now know your son. Your son knows you. After we eat, we will do one more thing before we leave.

What is that? Jon responded.

"The Ghost Dance," Denali said aloud, opening his eyes and smiling. "It is for your protection, Jon Walker."

CHAPTER SEVENTEEN
ROBY

In his entire life, Aaron had never felt the pressure of being late for anything. In all things, Aaron planned and prepared and was present at any designated time. Being late was never excused, and he knew any tardiness had dire consequences.

Then there was the destination. Aaron had rarely used Aberdeen Proving Ground, APG, as a point of departure.

Arriving barely twenty minutes before the time designated for flying out of APG, Aaron was directed at the gate to drive to Building Two—what appeared to be the airfield's opposite direction. Aaron felt a sense of familiarity as he drove up to the building, a strong sense of déjà vu that had rarely crept into his emotions.

He walked through the narrow entryway leading up to a bullet-proof encased window where a uniformed guard was staffing the desk. Before Aaron could utter a word, the door to his immediate left opened.

Aaron stopped and turned and was frozen in place.

Standing inside was Roby.

Without saying a word, Roby stepped back to allow Aaron to enter. As it had been when he was a teenager, Aaron knew what Roby was thinking.

Hello, my friend, please come in, Roby said without words.

Thank you. Where have you been? I haven't seen you in years, Aaron thought, still not knowing if he should express emotion toward one of the two people who put him on his life's mission with the Order.

Don't worry about pleasantries. It is good to see you. I'm very proud of you, Roby silently spoke.

Aaron could only think "gratitude," and Roby understood, offering one of the few slight hints of a smile he had ever seen on the man.

The two stood face-to-face in the small room, an entry area near a more prominent space they would be entering.

He looks exactly the same as I remember seeing him, even dresses the same, Aaron thought, momentarily forgetting Roby could hear what he was thinking.

It's good genetics…and I stay out of the sun, Roby responded, allowing both of them a moment to smile.

As the only other door opened, Aaron could hear Roby say, *Be honest. Always speak the truth. No matter what…be honest.*

Roby again stepped back to allow Aaron to enter the room first.

"Good morning, Aaron. I'm General Mason. Please have a seat."

Aaron sat in the only chair across from the General in the relatively small office without replying. Roby stood in the corner behind the General, facing Aaron.

The office had an unsettling effect on Aaron. The metal desk looked like it belonged to a time eighty years before. There was nothing on the desk. A bookcase behind the desk was empty.

"Aaron, I will be your direct report from this point forward. The deaths of those two young boys created a lot of attention on William Hines. We ended Amy Rodman. A detective in the Maryland State Police is closing in on finding you. If she finds you, she finds us. "

As the General spoke, Roby spoke in silence: *Speak the truth.*

Aaron responded again in thought, *I will.*

"We will continue to keep an eye on the detective. Your mission is critical and will require all your accumulated skills. We are sending you to Idaho, to the Fort Hall Indian Reservation. Someone you are already acquainted with in missions is there now, Jon Walker. Walker will be there for the express purpose of spending time with his son. Tells you something about the supposed great American hero, Jon Walker. The goddamn dumbass got a squaw pregnant," Mason said, chuckling at his comment.

"Your assignment is to abduct the boy without any trace or detection, making it all look like Jon Walker was the abductor, a father taking his son on a road trip against the wishes of the boy's mother. To make this happen, you will have a case file on the plane with all relevant particulars and the necessary assigned assets. Any questions so far?"

Aaron did not say a word.

"What? A cat got your tongue? Do you speak?" the General asked, pointing at Roby. "I know he doesn't do much of it. He thinks talking is beneath him. Are you the same...an arrogant asshole?"

"Sir, I understand the mission," Aaron said. "May I ask what will I do with the boy?"

"I am glad you asked. After having the boy in a safe house, we will administer a test on him. We need to see if the kid is Jon Walker's son. If the kid is Walker's, we will arrange to transport him elsewhere. If he isn't, you will be issued a K and D order for the boy."

Kill and Dispose? Just because a kid is not someone's child? Aaron thought.

Roby responded again in the same manner as before: *Be honest. Your moment of truth is here.*

"No grandstanding, no free-lancing, no deviation from the protocols established for every assignment," the General said firmly. "You got that?"

"Yes, sir," Aaron said, wondering how the General's statement was a "moment of truth," as suggested by Roby seconds earlier.

"You have a habit of interviewing targets before you execute orders."

Aaron remained motionless, refusing to answer.

"We know everything you do. You only kill people when you have orders. You took an oath to the Order. And you violated that oath, killing those boys. If you ever do anything like that again, it will be the last thing you do. I am willing to forgive you one time, based on your excellent service. But never again. Are we clear?"

"Yes, sir," Aaron meekly responded.

"Aaron, are you attempting to have a normal relationship?" the General asked, leaning back in the antique metal office chair.

"Yes, I am," Aaron said.

Immediately, Roby wordlessly spoke to him, *Good.*

"I was afraid of that," the General said, crossing his arms across his chest. Pausing, the General leaned forward and said, "Will you commit to me that this infraction is not only your first and will be your last?"

"Yes, sir," Aaron responded without hesitation. "It was my first and last. It has ended."

"I don't blame you. I saw some videos of Rebecca. What a body! If you reach out to that hot little piece of ass, we will know about it and take appropriate action. Since this is your first violation, we will give you a pass because of Roby's support and recommendation. Roby has confidence in you, but I don't. The math is this: zero tolerance to me is zero tolerance. If you have any contact with her, I will ensure the end of her life is brutal. Do I make myself fucking clear, boy?" the General asked with a sneer.

Before Aaron could speak, he heard Roby wordlessly say, *This is no time for anger. Let it go.*

"Yes, sir," Aaron responded without emotion in his voice or facial expression.

"Good…that's good. Now get the fuck out of here. You're going to be late! I have a plane to catch, too."

231

Aaron left the room with Roby following.

Outside, out of the General's view, Roby again offered a hint of a smile and communicated, *You did well. Now, go and carry out the assignment. I will see you again.*

Aaron thought, *Thank you, Roby.*

As Aaron boarded the plane and read the assignment file, Aaron's anger spilled over. Then, suddenly, he heard in his thoughts the words of Roby: *Let it go.*

Bridge to Nowhere

"Why don't you leave here? This is not a good place for you to be."

Richard Hopkins never felt comfortable in the home Allison had shared with her deceased husband. The remote location was a long, challenging drive from Cumberland, especially for a married man.

"I would be glad to help pay for a place in town. That way, we could see each other more often," he continued, lying beside Allison on the oversized couch in her living room.

Allison was barely listening. Instead, she continued to search the records for any evidence of the existence of Simon Peter Carroll.

"You've been at this non-stop for three days. I never solved a crime looking at a phone or a computer," Hopkins said, more dismissively than intended.

While staring at her phone, Allison responded in a mock, aged voice, crackling with sarcasm: "Back in my day, we didn't have phones. We had the telegraph."

"I deserved that," Hopkins said.

"Do you believe there is a secret government organization called *The Order?*"

"The government can't keep secrets. When I hear conspiracy theories, things like Roswell and the CIA assassinated Kennedy," Hopkins said before being interrupted by Allison.

"The CIA did not kill Kennedy. Amy Rodman said William Hines and the Order killed JFK," she said, smiling. "If you're going to critique conspiracy theories, at least keep the one I'm working on in mind," she said, a childish grin lighting up her face.

"You believe Rodman?" he asked, refusing to hide his skepticism.

"I believe facts. You taught me that...remember?" Allison responded. "And you say the government can't keep secrets? They hid the Manhattan Project. They hid Area 51 for decades. Are you telling me, Richard Hopkins, chief skeptic for all of humankind, that you trust the government? Because they can't keep a secret?"

Laughing, Hopkins said, "Of course not. I don't trust politicians. Lying is part of their job...and in their nature."

"If you do not trust the government and say they are compulsive liars, how can you not consider at least some threads of Rodman's story?"

"That's it. It is Rodman's story. It is what she did for a job. You're going down a rabbit hole of Rodman's making, Ally."

"Lies suck. I hate lies," Allison said, keeping her focus on her phone despite the screen being unchanged for minutes. "We lied. You are still lying."

"That's not entirely true. My daughter knows about us. She is helping with her mother," Hopkins answered in a softer, more humble tone.

"Does she still hate me?" Allison asked. "Tell me the truth."

"No, she does not hate you. You're not to blame for a disease killing her mother."

"I can't imagine we will ever be together," Allison said, pausing, allowing Hopkins to interject. "What we share sounds like a twisted romance novel."

"You know why I'm still with her. Dementia is a horrible thing to witness. My daughter made me promise I would hang in with her until there were no options."

"When you say that, I want to tell you to leave and stay with her. But I can't. I've lost so much that I can't stand the thought of losing you."

"You know I love you more than life," Richard said firmly.

"I've told you this before. You're a bridge...a bridge to nowhere. But nowhere is a better place than where I am. I don't say that being cruel. It's true. We are in the same place we were years ago. Except time has passed...a lot of time."

"I worry about you. If any part of this story Amy Rodman told you is true, here is not the place to be. It's too far away in case of an emergency," he said as Allison interrupted him again after playfully smacking him lightly on top of the head.

"Wake up! This is Allison Gage you're talking about. I can take care of myself," she laughed.

"Now, I think it's time you left. Are you coming back when ... Wednesday night? I'll make this deal with you: if I haven't picked up a significant lead on Rodman's story by then, I'll drop this, and we will jump in the bathtub together and drink a bottle of chianti. Is that a deal?"

"It's a deal," he said. "And will you consider my offer to move?"

"Move? No, I'm sorry. There is no way I'm moving from here. You'll just have to figure that part out...if I'm worth it."

Thank You

Alana had lost all sense of time.

There was no clock. There was no outside hint of sunlight or darkness to tell Alana whether it was day or night. After Margery Stalwart left, the nurse staff administered a cocktail of drugs that had put Alana out for a time she could not even guess.

Alana heard the door click, and Margery Stalwart entered the room. Stalwart did not speak. Instead, Margery walked to the foot of the bed and stood, staring at Alana, crossing her arms.

"Aren't you going to say anything? Accuse me of killing someone?" Alana asked.

"Today, I won't be asking the questions. Someone else will be talking to you. We know quite a bit more than what we knew before."

"Why don't you tell me what you know?" Alana demanded.

"The only person who can help you now is you."

"I've told you the truth!" Alana shouted. "You're not listening!"

The door clicked, and two men dressed in Army fatigues wearing surgical masks entered the room. Alana was momentarily taken back by their physical presence. Both were huge—appearing to be well over a foot taller than Stalwart. One pushed a wheelchair.

Stalwart looked at them, seeming to share the same level of intimidation as Alana, and said, "You can take her to interrogation."

The two soldiers unbound her from the bed and forcibly placed her in the wheelchair, using leather restraints around her wrists and ankles, anchoring her into the chair.

"Is this necessary? You haven't fed me any real food. I would love to kick both of your overgrown asses, but I don't have the energy. How about a rain check?" Alana mockingly said.

Neither soldier responded. As they finished binding the restraints, she noticed one of the soldiers had what appeared to be some high-tech prosthetic hand partially covered in a black glove.

That looks like something out of a Terminator movie, Alana thought, trying to avoid being detected staring at the behemoth-size soldier's artificial device.

Neither soldier spoke as they reached the end of the hall and turned to the last door on the right. It was a small conference room. The cinderblock walls were the same beige throughout everything she had seen in the facility.

A metal table was in the middle of the room, with one chair behind the table. A second door was on the opposite side of the table in the corner of the room, and a large mirror almost covered the entire wall facing Alana.

"I guess you have people behind the mirror watching," Alana said, looking up at the last soldier leaving the room.

Now alone in the room in the wheelchair, Alana looked into the mirror, and she could see herself for the first time in almost a week.

My hair is starting to grow out. Maybe there will be enough to brush in a month or so, Alana thought, allowing a smile that she noticed something so trivial given the conditions.

And suddenly, with no one else in the room, she heard a voice within her mind speak the Samoan words, "*Tatou te oti I up.*"

Before Alana could register a thought, she spoke the words aloud in English as she closed her eyes, "We die in words."

Alana kept her eyes closed and contemplated what had just happened. Still alone—the only sound being a slight hum from the lights in the room, she knew what she heard. It was something her grandmother had said many times on various occasions. But the voice she heard was almost childlike.

Then again, she heard in Samoan, "*E le o tuua na o oe. Ua ou sau e fesoasoani ia te oe.*"

This time, without uttering the words aloud, she understood what the voice was saying: "*You are not alone. I have come to help you.*"

There was instantly something reassuring about the voice—a feeling that whoever spoke to Alana could be trusted. She felt like she had heard the voice before.

She looked into the mirror and said aloud, "Fa'afetai," meaning "Thank you" in English.

Immediately, one of the soldiers stepped into the room carrying Alana's Bowie knife.

"I'm General Mason, Alana," he said, smiling.

"Why don't you take these restraints off of me?" she asked in a calm voice, turning her head to the side with a slight smile. "I promise I'll be good."

Mason laughed, responding, "No can do, little girl. I do have a few questions. Tell me what happened in the volcano on Maui?" Mason asked, smiling, keeping his eyes locked into Alana's as he lifted the knife, slowly sliding it between them near the middle of the table.

There is something wrong about him, Alana thought. She could not yet understand why he was making her feel this way. She refused to look at the knife, focusing on his eyes.

"Does a cat have your tongue?" he said, an almost sinister smile adorning his long face. "See the knife?" He picked it up and took it from its holster, exposing the blade—with what appeared to be remnants of blood still on it. "This is sharp. You could do a lot with this blade. Here's an example," he said as he stood and leaned over the table with the knife pointing within inches of her mouth. "I could cut your tongue out. If you won't use that little tongue to answer my questions, what good is it?"

Alana was stunned. Her first audible response was stopped in its tracks when she heard the voice speaking to her in English: *Know no fear. Do not speak your mind. We die in words.*

The angry retort on the verge of passing through her lips stopped. Instead, she looked at Mason and smiled without saying a word.

Stalwart, standing behind the mirror, looked at Roby. She wanted to ask him to step in and stop Mason, but she remained silent.

Roby had not moved the entire time. He remained standing in the same position since they entered the room, looking through the glass.

"You should be afraid, Alana," Mason said, placing the knife on the table.

"I'm not afraid of you," Alana said with no hint of fear in her voice or facial expression. "What do you really want from me?"

"I do have another agenda! Smart girl! I knew you were good for something other than those incredible tits and tight ass," he said, laughing as he spun the knife rapidly on the table, turning his eyes toward the blade.

"I'm going to take you with me when I leave. We're going on a field trip to Alaska together."

Alana did not respond. She continued to stare at Mason, refusing to answer.

"Here's a news flash for you, Alana. You have been to Alaska. You just don't remember it. "You were the guest of some really perverted kids," he said, standing and turning to look at the mirror, knowing Stalwart was watching.

"Hey, Margie, I'm guessing you're shaking in those magnificent high heels of yours right now," he said as he smiled and pecked his knuckles against the glass barrier in a succession of knocks.

"Some people think you're special. I'm not so sure. I just see a hot piece of Hawaiian ass in front of me. Maybe that's why Stalwart wants to keep you around?" Turning quickly to look back at the mirror, Mason asked, "Is that it? Do you want to have fun with Alana? I know you, Margie. I know what you like."

Immediately spinning back to face Alana, Mason leaned closely, within inches of Alana's face, saying: "Either way, we will find a use for you, or that will be it. Keep that in mind and act accordingly." Mason stood upright and began walking toward the door.

As Mason opened the door to exit, he turned and said, "I hope we have time to get to know each other better." His perverse laugh only ended after the door shut behind him.

Alana looked up at the mirror. She thought, *I know you're there. Tell me what to do. Where am I? Who are you? Please answer me, so I won't think I'm losing my mind.*

Sitting silently, she heard the same childlike voice say: *I'm here and will do all I can. But you must guard your thoughts and your words. We die in words. That may prove true. Aloha, I will see you soon.*

Alana nodded her head in affirmation and sat still, alone in the room.

CHAPTER EIGHTEEN
JONAS

Aaron had accomplished his mission.

That almost went too perfectly, Aaron thought as he stared at the young boy.

Aaron now had Jon Walker's son, Jonas, at the Order's designated safe house outside Twin Falls, Idaho.

The five-year-old boy had been sedated by Aaron. Following the instructions, Aaron conducted a brainwave scan on the child, using the equipment prepared for him to use, and forwarded the results over the dark web connection. He had no idea why the Order would be interested in a brainwave scan of a five-year-old boy living on an Indian reservation in Idaho. However, the one consistent thing in all his assignments was a lack of explanations.

The end result was flawless. An Amber Alert was in effect. Everyone in Idaho and Utah was on the lookout for Jon Walker—the abductor of his son.

Sitting in a chair across from Jonas, Aaron now fought the compulsion to look at the flip phone he had used to send Rebecca the last communication he had with her when he was leaving their apartment building. Pulling the flip phone from his shoulder bag at the foot of the chair, he opened it and read the message: *Rebecca, This is Aaron. Use this phone number to text me. Do not call or text my other phone. Just use this one. I love and miss you. Talk to you soon.*

Aaron knew he should not reach out to her again. Doing so could lead to her death—and then his.

Should I, or shouldn't I? he asked himself. He could not imagine how the Order could detect the communications on the old cell phone.

After a moment, the phone beeped with "New Messages" on the tiny screen. He scrolled to see that there were three messages.

Unlike newer smartphones, the messages were separate and distinct. Each one had to be opened by clicking on them before Aaron could read them. He clicked on the first message: *I miss you, babe. Hope you are doing well and thinking about me. I am constantly thinking about you. Love, Bec*

Aaron smiled and allowed himself a brief sigh of relief. The message had been sent the previous evening.

"I miss you, Bec," Aaron said, flashing a smile.

The second message had been sent early in the morning. It read: *I'm missing my bed partner. I couldn't sleep last night. I had a disturbing dream last night. I hope you are ok. No pressure, but when you get a chance, please text me and let me know you're ok. Love, Bec*

Aaron sat in the chair motionless, staring at the last text.

I can't respond, Aaron thought. *It will put her in danger.*

The hopelessness of the moment overwhelmed him—tears were in his eyes as the reality of having to give up the best partner he would ever hope to find was necessary for her safety.

The final text had been sent barely thirty minutes after the second message. This text was an image—and as the tiny screen unfolded, the graphic nature of Rebecca's nude body lying on the shower floor, blood all around, her wrist cut in a long, straight line from below her elbow to her wrist. A word message was part of the text image in all caps: *STAY FOCUSED. WE TOOK CARE OF THIS PROBLEM FOR YOU.*

Aaron jumped from the chair, releasing a primal scream that anyone could hear near the home. But no one heard…except Jonas.

241

Jonas suddenly awoke—groggily but still awake. The shock on his face was evident. Aaron was standing only a few feet away, holding the phone. Aaron looked at the boy and said, "Don't make a sound." Aaron sat back in the chair, looking at the phone as tears streamed down his face.

The flip phone suddenly began to vibrate—there was an incoming call.

Aaron stared at the boy and held his finger to his mouth to indicate the boy remained quiet. Clicking the tiny green button to accept the call, Aaron put the phone to his ear, his mind racing, his hands trembling.

"Aaron, as you can tell, we decided to give you some help. But after seeing that picture of her naked, I will say you have good taste. Everything is scrubbed. Nothing will link you to her. She is dead and gone as if she had never existed as it relates to you," General Mason said coldly. "You can thank me later in person."

Aaron could not speak.

After a brief pause, Mason asked, "Is the boy waking up?"

Aaron still could not speak. He was looking across at the boy but was in shock. For all of his training and experience, what he had just seen and heard had reduced him to silence.

"Aaron, is the boy waking up? I'm asking you, boy. Answer me, now, that's a goddamn order!" the General shouted into the phone.

"Yes, sir," Aaron said without emotion, "he is awake."

"He is not what we thought he was. He's Walker's son but not as exceptional as we hoped he might be. Proceed with a K and D on the boy. Make sure no one ever finds the body. If you need any new assets, you know how to reach out," Mason said.

Aaron looked across the room at the boy.

"After you finish there, we will need you to read the entire assignment on the encrypted access point. I'll give you a preview. We weren't as lucky with the detective in Maryland as with Amy Rodman. She is very close to identifying you and us. We are watching her, but your assignment is to return to Maryland and end her law enforcement career. We will have all of the arrangements and info on your chartered plane. Any questions?" Mason asked impatiently.

"Why did you kill her?" Aaron said, trying to hide his anger.

"Why did we kill her? That's on you, boy. You failed to follow my orders. Now get your fucking black ass in gear and do your job!" Mason shouted as he ended the call.

Aaron's anger erupted. He tore the flip phone apart. Then throwing it on the floor began stomping it until it was in tiny pieces as he shouted, "Fuck you!"

Aaron finally calmed enough to stop, looked at Jonas, and recalled his orders—K and D.

"Kill and dispose," he said aloud. And the longer he looked at the young boy, Aaron saw the causal point for all his pain and suffering—the death of his beloved Rebecca, his career in shambles, all because of an assignment. This assignment now demanded he kill the frightened little boy.

This boy is the reason Rebecca is dead, Aaron thought, his eyesight shrouded in angry tears. His face was red with anger and hate. Aaron stepped toward the boy to end the child's life. And then he heard the voice.

It was the boy…Jonas. Jonas was speaking wordlessly to Aaron.

You know this is wrong. Killing me won't bring Rebecca back. I am not the reason she was murdered. They are.

Aaron had never experienced a telepathic exchange with anyone except Roby. The words were repeating, gaining volume, then becoming deafening, momentarily causing Aaron to drop to the floor on his knees, covering his ears.

He screamed out loud, "Shut up! Shut up!"

The words suddenly shortened: *I am not your problem. They are.*

The words began to rise in volume until it was a deafening roar. Then, changing to sound like a chorus from an opera...over and over again.

Aaron could not stop hearing the chorus of voices. For a moment, he thought of taking the gun and blowing out his brains to end the maddening message. As Aaron remained on his knees, his head tucked downward toward the floor, there was finally silence.

In a voice from his past, he heard a soft female voice say: *Simon, do not kill Jonas. He is part of us. He is part of our family.*

It was his mother's voice. Falling face down on the floor, he began to weep.

"Forgive me, Mother!" Aaron shouted.

Aaron then heard Jonas. The boy was telling him what to do next.

For the first time in his life, Aaron was afraid. His thoughts turned to a question: *Can I do this?*

Aaron heard the voices of Jonas and his mother say together in perfect unison: *Yes.*

Stalwart

Margery Stalwart heard Mason's final threats hurled at Alana. She had now evolved from being shocked to completely terrified and now to being repulsed and angry.

Still standing in the room with Roby, her disgust with Mason nearly overflowed. Instead, she stood still and tried to think through her options.

How dare Mason speak like that to Alana and me, she thought. *He has never been interested in discovering what happened to the soldier. Mason wants Alana. But for what purpose?*

She knew she could no longer wait for a miracle to happen. It was time to take action. Looking toward Roby, the Observer, she sarcastically said, "Thanks, you've been a lot of help. When they called you an 'Observer,' they weren't kidding. All you do is watch."

As Stalwart reached for the doorknob to leave the dimly lit room, Mason abruptly opened the door and stepped in.

"I'm taking Alana with me," he sinisterly said through a dark smile.

Stalwart remained silent. Deep within, she knew that Alana had not killed the soldier. She was innocent.

Everything about Mason is sinister. I must stop him, she thought.

Mason then held Alana's knife in the air, gazing toward it.

"I'm going to keep this as a trophy. I'm sure you won't object, Margie. Speak now or forever hold your peace, Roby," Mason said, looking at the Observer.

The Observer did not speak or move.

Mason looked at Stalwart and said, "Margie, you look exceptionally yummy today. Tight black skirt, low-cut white blouse, high heels. You dressed perfectly for the occasion. I love black and white, my favorite colors," he said, laughing as he took far too long to look up and down her body.

Mason turned and left the room, humming an erratic tune loudly.

Stalwart looked at the Observer and turned, leaving the room. Suddenly, she heard his first audible words: "Take care."

Stunned, she turned and said, "You too."

After leaving the room, Stalwart went through the maze of corridors to the private office near the vehicle access point for the facility's level. Stopping along the way, she looked at her phone, contemplating sending a text to her supervising agent at headquarters in Washington. After standing for several moments, Stalwart decided against it, opting to leave the base first.

I'm getting out of here, she thought as she hurriedly walked down the hall. *There's nothing else I can do. I can do more once I get away on friendlier turf in DC*, Margery thought as she arrived at the door to her office. The room was secured with an eye scan, programmed only for her use. She put her chin in the small cup, and the door clicked. Before entering, she looked to ensure she saw no one else nearby. Stalwart stepped into the pitch-black room, reaching to turn on the light as the door was closing behind her. As she flicked the switch and the lights came on, she could now see she was not alone. Mason and the two monstrous soldiers were standing in the room.

Her first impulse was to scream—but she knew her screams would not be heard. The documentation she had returned to retrieve was in a locked cabinet behind Mason and the soldiers. She needed the file to make her case against Mason.

"How did you get in here?" she asked in as calm of a voice Margery could muster—her heart racing as the fear of the encounter now engulfed her senses.

"Margie, you've been a naughty girl," Mason said. "And naughty girls have to be punished."

Stalwart responded, "I'm not afraid of you and your goons." She then turned to leave, but one of the soldiers quickly stepped over and put his monstrous hand against the door. Stalwart was shocked, seeing a prosthetic device revealed outside the enormous soldier's glove. Turning back to face Mason, she said, "I sent the video to Washington, the one where you threatened to kill me. I'm not stupid, General. You and your command are over."

"I say you are stupid," Mason said, moving closer to her. "Your boss, the same one you assume tells me what to do, is not mine. Surprise! He works for me, Margie. You thought you were working for the FBI's SVU...the Special Visitor's Unit. What a catchy name. You people need to get a life and stop watching television," he said,

246

chuckling. "But in reality, I am in charge here. The visitors are running things just the way it should be. I've always been in charge. I give the orders. I can do what I want. And that includes you right now."

Stalwart swallowed hard, trying to find a way out without trying to frantically exit, knowing the two soldiers would stop her.

"You're in charge? You're a visitor? Tell me, what are you?" she asked.

"Don't you mean, who am I?" Mason responded cocking his head to the side, taking another step closer.

"No, I mean, what are you? You're not human. You're not like Roby and definitely not one of the kids. At least show me the respect to tell me what you are and what you're doing here?" Stalwart said, seemingly resigned to her fate.

"Visitors have rights, too, Margie," Mason said, amused with his comment. "You ask me what I am? If you had any real dignity or understanding of human's lowly place in the universe, you would never ask, 'What are you?' I am superior to you and the billions just like you in every fucking possible way. If we weren't here, you would have blown yourselves up like many others have. But we would never let that happen because you're here for a purpose, not necessarily one I agree with," Mason said as he glared at Margery. "You are the most racist beings I've ever encountered. The arrogance of thinking skin color dictates intelligence. Wait till you see my skin! You are slaves, and you don't even know it! And now, I will show you what real power looks like."

"Fuck you and fuck whatever you are!" Stalwart shouted.

"I disagree. We will fuck you first and show you just who we are," Mason said, licking his lips.

The General reached back and picked up Alana's knife on the desk behind him. He smiled and inched closer to Stalwart with the blade in his hand as the second soldier moved closer, now one on each side.

He looked at the soldiers and said, "Take that jacket off her and put her on the desk. Spread her legs." The soldiers grabbed her, each gripping her arms and legs, doing as instructed.

Stalwart screamed, despite knowing it would not be heard outside the soundproof safe room. Mason reached into his lapel pocket, pulled out a handkerchief, and said, "Open wide," as one of the soldiers forced her mouth open, pulling her jaw down. Stuffing the cloth in her mouth, Mason said, "Silence is golden, Margie."

Standing between her spread legs, the soldiers each holding one leg and arm, Mason placed the knife below her chin, the sharp side of the blade facing downward.

"Let's bare a little skin. I say, Margie, you first."

Terrified, Stalwart tried to scream, but only the guttural groans could be heard as Mason moved the knife downward. She shut her eyes—not wanting to see the horror she was experiencing.

Mason took the huge knife down the front of her neck—barely touching her skin. Taking the blade lower, he cut through her white blouse. Reaching with his other hand, he jerked the top, pulling the buttons from it and ripping the blouse open.

Using the knife, he guided it from the base of her neck down to her bra—and then, in a quick flick of the blade, cut the brassiere apart at the cross-section, freeing her breasts as they spilled outward from the confines of the undergarment.

"Very nice, Margie, very nice," Mason said, licking his lips and leaning down to slowly lick each breast. Stalwart opened her eyes and looked down, seeing what appeared to be an enormous, serpent-like tongue flick out and reach down to his chin in a fast, lapping motion on her breasts.

Unable to scream aloud, she moaned, but the only response was a tighter grip by the two soldiers.

I will survive, she thought to herself. *They're not going to kill me. They could never explain it.*

"Hold her still. I wouldn't want to hurt her," Mason said, and the soldiers obeyed, tightening their grip on Stalwart's limbs, temporarily confirming Stalwart's hopeful thoughts of how the horror would end—with her alive.

Mason slid the knife from her breasts down her toned abdomen to the top of her black skirt.

"It's a little tight. This might take two hands," Mason said, chuckling, as he placed a finger inside the skirt's waistband and inserted the knife. "Hold still, Margie!" the General said, and in a nearly savage motion using the knife, Mason ripped the skirt apart, from top to bottom. He pulled the torn garment out from under her, leaving her with only her tattered top and panties.

"You look delicious," Mason lustfully voiced as he licked the side of her face. "You'll make a fine meal! Tear the rest of her clothes off," Mason ordered the soldiers.

Stepping back, Mason said, "You wanted to know what I am? I'm going to show you. Since you've been so kind to show me your skin, I'll show you mine. Lift her up," he ordered the two soldiers. Still held by the limbs, her legs remaining spread, the soldiers lifted Stalwart, arcing her torso upward enough so she could see Mason standing in front of her.

The General removed his military jacket, pulled his uniform shirt sleeve upward, exposed his inner left arm, and turned his arm toward Stalwart.

"Watch this, Margie. I know you're going to be impressed," he said sarcastically.

Taking Alana's knife with his right hand, he made a deep slit from the pit of his inner elbow down his arm within inches of his wrist.

Minimal blood erupted from the wound, which appeared to dry almost as quickly as it found air.

"To quote a human, beauty is only skin deep," Mason said, pulling back one side of the pale epidermal layer to reveal a scaly, green, reptile-like skin beneath. "Isn't that beautiful? That's the real me," he said, smiling. "I would show you more, but I still have to leave this place, so that's all you get in show-and-tell."

Mason looked at the soldiers and said, "Lay her back on the table. Spread her legs as far as they will go. I want to make sure she feels all of me."

As they dropped her on her back on the metal surface, she squeezed her eyes shut as tightly as she could.

My God! They're going to rape me! But they can't kill me, Margery thought to herself, preparing for what she assumed would be the worst possible experience in her life. She kept telling herself, *Remember, this too shall pass.*

"Don't take this personally, Margie. My boys and I will enjoy you first...like this. Afterward, you are our main course. Bon appetite!"

CHAPTER NINETEEN
PARALYZED

Aaron had stood motionless in Allison Gage's closet for over an hour.

Arriving shortly before her return home, he had decided to wait, gun in one hand and the syringe in the other, for the right time.

The gun was needed only if the detective proved to be a challenge. The syringe was the first option—allowing him to sedate Allison to create what would ultimately be a scene suggesting her suicide.

There had been numerous opportunities to take her down, but Aaron failed to act. Aaron could not move.

He felt paralyzed.

The louvered design of the large closet doors allowed him to see within the room without detection. He had his first and best chance as she entered the bedroom, turning her back to him. But he felt frozen—unable to take advantage. As he stood watching, she had walked by a second time after undressing, going into the bathroom.

Yet, he had remained still.

What is wrong with me? Why am I hesitating?

While Allison ran the water for her bath, he recalled what had happened before leaving Idaho. It was the first mission he had ever failed to complete as instructed. And not only did he fail to carry out the mission, but he had chosen to lie.

Standing in the confines of the closet, Aaron remembered the words of William: "Cover-ups always fail."

What have I done? What happened to me?

Instead of killing Jon Walker's son, Jonas, and disposing of the body as instructed by General Mason, Aaron had chosen to return the boy to his mother.

As Aaron stood with his eyes shut, replaying his choice to not follow orders, he heard Allison run by the door. Opening his eyes, he briefly saw her wearing a towel.

Someone is at the door. How could I have fucked this up? Aaron thought, hearing the sound of a man's voice. Still standing in the closet, his target was joined in her bathtub by a much older man, a retired detective Richard Hopkins, Allison's long-time lover.

Aaron's conflicted choices seemed to chain him to the dark closet he occupied.

The file said he visited her often. How could I put myself in this position? I can't stay here. I have got to do what I came to do.

He heard the voices from the bathroom.

"I take it I won our bet?" the man said.

"I wouldn't call it a bet. I thought it was simply an agreement?" Allison answered, the sound of water suggesting the two were now both in the bathtub.

"You needed to leave all of that bullshit behind. I told you so," the man said, with a clear sense of superiority.

"I'm not giving up. Justice will be served," the woman said.

Aaron's thoughts returned to Idaho as the couple's intimacy continued in the bath.

I don't understand how the boy could speak to me like that. It was the same way Roby and I communicated. But I heard my mother's voice, too.

Jonas had told Aaron what to do, ensuring his safe return to his mother without detection.

I took orders from a kid. He orchestrated the whole thing. And the kid's great-grandfather knew me…and talked to me the same way. He told me I would meet my family soon. My brother and my father.

Aaron's thoughts turned to Rebecca's murder.

I will make them pay, he thought.

Aaron remembered the last thing Jonas told him as his anger grew: "You made a promise and took an oath to protect humans. Do as you promised. Do not let anger drown you."

Unsure of what to do, Aaron stood, waiting for something to release him from his self-imposed prison.

The sound of the couple leaving the bathroom drew Aaron's attention back to the present. He could now see the couple. Hopkins carried Allison into the room and then placed her on the bed. Both were still nude and wet, their bodies glistening from the bathroom light.

At first, Aaron felt ashamed to be watching them. But then he heard Allison Gage say to the older man, "I don't want this to ever cause a problem with your wife."

He's married, Aaron thought, gritting his teeth. *The bitch is cheating with a married man.* The memory of the file he had reviewed on the flight returned as his anger grew. *The man's wife has dementia, and he is cheating on her.*

Allison accepted the man with the unmistakable sense of the familiar as he began slowly grinding into her. Aaron was repulsed seeing the sight and shut his eyes.

Allison said, "I've missed you," between a steady stream of moans.

Aaron looked down at his hands—they were shaking. He continued to hold the syringe in one hand, the gun in the other.

After returning his gaze to the couple, Aaron sprung from the closet. He struck the man with the butt of his gun on the back of his neck. The man immediately dropped on top of Allison. In shock, Allison barely had time to scream before he jabbed the needle into the side of her neck as the now unconscious man's body restricted her movement.

As the syringe's contents worked, Aaron thought he could hear Allison faintly say, "Please don't kill him."

Standing back, looking at the two bodies on the bed, Aaron took a moment to think of what he should do now.

Aaron held the gun in his right hand, placing the syringe on the nearby dresser. Possibly in shock from the events he experienced, Aaron felt the need to bring a sense of order to the room, walking back to the closet and shutting the door. With his back turned, Aaron heard the sound of movement. As Aaron quickly turned, he saw Richard Hopkins rolling from the bed, reaching into his clothing for something. Aaron shouted, "Stop!" but saw the man pulling a gun from the pile of clothing. Again, Aaron shouted, "Don't do that!" as the man gripped the handle and began to turn to fire on Aaron. Before he could entirely turn, Aaron fired one shot into the man's temple.

"I told you to stop," Aaron said, shaking his head, then looking at Allison Gage, lying unconscious and nude on the bed.

Aaron again felt paralyzed.

"What have I done?" he said aloud as he sat in the chair in the corner of the room, surveying the blood-splattered wall.

To Be

Marc awakened to the sight of the man who had tossed him across the room like a ragdoll.

Still in pain from being thrown into a concrete wall, Marc mustered, "You know you're creepy, right?"

Roby stood staring at him without moving or blinking his eyes.

Marc's anger rose as he realized he was strapped in a hospital bed.

"Who the fuck do you think you are?" Marc asked through clenched teeth.

The man remained frozen—staring at Marc.

"Can you speak? Or is this silent treatment part of the General's bullshit?" Marc asked, dropping his head back in the bed and looking up at the ceiling.

"I was hoping to speak with you," the man suddenly said in an almost childlike voice, surprising Marc. "But you cannot hear me."

"You haven't said a word. There's nothing wrong with my hearing," Marc said in anger.

"The gift does not reside in you," the Observer said with a flat, monotone voice.

"The gift? How about giving me a gift and letting me out of here?" Marc said, staring into the eyes of the strange-looking man. Marc could now see why the man's eyes had appeared unusual—the pupil in one eye was larger than the other. And as Marc stared at him in silence, the man never blinked.

"Where is my family?" Marc suddenly asked in an authoritative demand. "I want to know."

Again, the man stood silently and said, "Your family is safe for now."

"Is that some kind of threat?" Marc asked as he tried to lift upwards against the restraints.

"No, it is just a fact," the man responded. "Do you care about your family?"

"Who are you?" Marc said, subconsciously deflecting the question about his family.

"I was hoping to speak with you. But you do not have the gift. Your family will die if you do what Mason says. And, if you try to do what you're thinking, they will still die, as will you. All your work for nothing but death."

"You listen to me," Marc began, his voice gaining volume as his hate began to spill over, but Roby interrupted.

"Please stop and listen to me," Roby said as he stood silently. "I am trying to help you."

"Get the fuck out of here!" Marc shouted.

"If you cannot find a way to stop the destruction of humans, you have one option: to stop the means of their destruction. Either way, your family will die. What you're thinking is insane revenge. And despite what you think will happen, you will give your enemies exactly what they want. Your thoughts betray you, as will your actions. Your death is your best option," Roby said coldly. "You should kill yourself at the first possible opportunity for the good of humanity."

"My family will die?" Marc asked as if he had heard nothing Roby had said. Scowling at Roby, Marc said, "You underestimate me. I can save them. I know I can."

"It is evident now your wife and children will die no matter what you do. You know this. I do not think your family matters to you," Roby said without any trace of emotion. "Do you really want to be responsible for the destruction of billions of humans?"

"How do you know that? How will they die if I find a way to safely remove the Axis Mundi?" Marc continued to shout. "I can produce a vaccine that will save humanity, not destroy it!"

"Not long after you first arrived here, you went outside, the only time you've been outside since you've been here. Do you remember?" Roby asked.

"What are you talking about?" Marc asked, bewildered at the query.

"When you were sitting outside alone, you said, 'To be, or not to be.' Did you not say this?"

"How did you know I said that? Are you listening and watching everything I do?" Marc said, stunned at knowing the answer to his own question.

"Dr. Walker, you take pride in being a logical person. When you said, 'To be, or not to be,' you applied logic to your situation. The philosopher Aristotle suggested the same thing, possibly not as direct and simple. Aristotle called this the excluded middle law. Are you familiar with it?"

"Yes," Marc answered.

"The law of the excluded middle says either A or not A; Being or not Being; but nothing in between. Do you understand this logic?" Roby asked.

Marc calmed his anger to listen and answer. After briefly pausing, he said, "Yes, I understand the logic."

"And that logic tells you that you have a choice. And no solution will save your wife and children. But there is a solution that will save your larger family."

"My family? You are referring to my family...of humanity?" Marc asked.

"Aren't you the human that suggested your family is extended far into the universe?" Roby asked.

Marc paused and thought.

Whoever or whatever this Roby person is or isn't, he doesn't understand being a slave. To live in slavery is not a life worth living. If we cannot live in freedom to reach our potential, humans will always be slaves. It is better to die in freedom. That is my choice for all of humanity. I will not be responsible for the slavery of billions of humans. If I cannot remove the Axis Mundi to save humanity, I will use the Axis Mundi against the creators and end humanity.

Without Marc uttering a word, Roby said, "I'm very disappointed. You are not a logical human. As long as there is life, there is hope for change. The death of billions of humans is not a means of revenge."

"If you know about Aristotle, you know about the history of my country, the United States of America?" Marc asked.

"Yes," Roby said.

"Use all of your logic and answer this. Would it not have been better if the slaves had a choice, a means to stop being slaves? And by stopping their slavery, they were consequentially ending the slavery that all of their children...and children's children...and their children...would endure? Would it not have been better if the slaves sacrificed themselves for their family's good instead of allowing the perpetuation of bondage to enslave their family for centuries? Answer that with your logic."

"As long as even one of those slaves remains alive, that single slave can change the world, even the universe. I know this is true. I've seen it happen. All it takes is one. That is what my logic tells me. And you are part of that family. And after all your family's suffering, do you choose to take away the only opportunity to change the outcome? You sound more like a child than a genius. And I can hear in your thoughts there is no hope for you to change your mind. Your anger and your rage have clouded and poisoned your reasoning. Dr. Walker, I urge you to kill yourself before you do more harm. That is the truth and logical."

Roby turned and left the room before Marc could respond.

Marc was alone with his thoughts. Looking around the room's walls, he said aloud: "I understand. But I can't stop."

Time was out of joint for Marc. After lying in bed for hours, the door to the room opened, and General Mason and Roby entered.

"Dr. Walker, I'm not a patient man. If you lie to me again, I will kill your wife and then each one of your children while I make you watch. And then I will end you. Do you already have a vaccine for the Axis Mundi? Yes or no."

"Yes. I have found a way to prohibit the removal of the Axis Mundi. I developed what you might say is a vaccine through a delivery virus I created in my lab," Marc responded.

"I thought so," the General said, nodding his head affirmatively as he turned to look at Roby, a sneer evident on the General's face.

Roby did not move or respond. He continued to stare at Marc.

"You possess the means to destroy humanity and save it. That's even something I applaud, Dr. Walker," the General said.

"Now, free my family. If you do, I'll give you what you want."

"Let's change that to make it work in everyone's self-interest. I will continue to hold your family. If you fail to do what I tell you, I will kill them and then kill you. You're in no position to bargain, Dr. Walker," the General said.

"I'll give you what you want," Marc said remarkably calmly.

"I'm going to have you taken to our lab. Remember, this is non-negotiable: your family will be the initial lab rats that you will test both the removal of the Axis Mundi and your vaccine. If it works, you and your family can count yourselves as survivors. Hell, you may even be considered a hero like your brother. But if you fuck-up either part of the delivery and cure, your family will die. Then you. Are we clear on that, Dr. Walker?"

"I understand," Marc said, quickly shifting his eyes to look at Roby.

The General laughed as he turned and left the room.

Roby continued to stand motionless, staring at Marc.

"What do you want?" Marc angrily asked.

"You equate freedom to death," Roby said. "That makes sense if only you choose to die, as you said, to self-sacrifice."

"I will do the right thing for my family," Marc said, looking into Roby's eyes. "But that doesn't change the fact you're creepy as hell."

Roby smiled and shook his head from side to side.

"Your thoughts betray you, Dr. Walker. One question. What does the apple not falling far from the tree mean to you?" Roby asked as he turned and left the room.

Departure

It was the first time in her life that Alana had ever wished she had remained asleep.

Death was never Alana's greatest fear. Her greatest fear was being trapped, held against her will, and imprisoned. Her worst fears were a reality. Looking up at the ceiling, it felt like the room was slowly collapsing on her—intense claustrophobia ripped through Alana as she struggled to breathe.

Alana heard a noise. It was General Mason entering the room.

"Hi, Alana. Now, let's get on with this," Mason said, lightly stroking Alana's arm.

"Get away from me, pervert," Alana said, her teeth clenched, repulsed by Mason's touch.

"Alana, I'm not a pervert. I'm taking you to Alaska," Mason said, continuing to stroke Alana's arm lightly, taking his other hand, putting it on her abdomen, and patting her stomach softly through the thin bedsheet.

"I'm not afraid of you," Alana firmly said.

"Yes, I believe you."

As he said the words, he reached under the bedsheet covering Alana and put his left hand between her legs—his fingers finding their way between her thighs, touching her.

Alana did not flinch.

"You brought me here to rape me?" Alana asked. In a sudden burst of crazed courage, she began to hysterically laugh. "You're not a man! You're something far lower. You remind me of a snake!"

Mason was shocked. He quickly jerked his hand away, leaving Alana exposed. Pointing at her face angrily in slowly paced words uttered in a deep growl, Mason said, "Do not mock me!"

"I'm just telling you what I think and see," Alana said through laughter.

"I am taking you to Adak Island off the Alaskan coast. If you aren't what they think you are, I will have my time alone with you. But not just by me. Do you remember the soldiers you insulted? They'll get to have their way with you, too. And afterward, you'll serve as our dinner. We just had your girlfriend Stalwart for supper," he said as he opened the door, shouting at the nurse: "Finish prepping her. We have to leave."

CHAPTER TWENTY
ALLISON

Allison awoke.

She was strapped to her office chair with tight-fitting plastic cable ties around her wrists and ankles. The chair was in the middle of her living room. Through the residual haze of the sedative, she could see the clock. It was 1:44. Looking through the glass at the top of the front door, she could see it was dark outside.

Her first impulse was to scream. But instead, she remained quiet. She looked down. Her only clothing was Ben's old T-shirt that she had worn earlier.

And then she remembered—Richard. She was in bed with Richard Hopkins when they were attacked. She recalled him dropping on top of her unconscious. And she remembered the needle being jabbed into her neck.

Where is he? Allison thought, momentarily shutting her eyes to try to focus on hearing any sounds. There was no noise—no sign of the person Amy Rodman called Andrew, known as Aaron by his mentor, William Hines—and to Allison by his real name, Simon Peter Carroll.

Then Allison remembered his mother's name. The information about his background began to come back to her.

Remain calm, she told herself.

As if he were a ghost immediately appearing out of thin air, Allison looked to her right and saw him.

"Hello, Simon," Allison said, trying to maintain her composure.

"Hello, Detective Gage," Aaron said. "You know the name on my birth certificate. I'm impressed."

"I know a lot about you and the Order," she flatly responded.

"Very good, Detective," Aaron said as he lifted a gun with a silencer and pointed it at her. "Please say whatever you want. I have fought my entire life to protect your right to free speech. Now is a good time to exercise it. You may never have another chance."

"Why don't you go ahead and get it over with? I don't want to spend the last few minutes of my life talking to you."

"I'm surprised! As hard as you worked to find me, I thought you would at least be interested in confirming if what Amy told you was true. But I guess I was wrong," he said as he pointed the gun at her and stepped closer.

"Did you kill Amy Rodman?" Allison asked, trying to reconcile her fear and the only way she knew she could remain alive: talking to him.

"No. I did not."

"You're a liar."

"Allison, I won't ever lie to you. One of the other members of the Order did. I was busy elsewhere."

"William Hines worked with you in the Order?" she asked.

"Yes. William was like a father to me. After my mother died, he stepped in and prepared me to be the person I am today," he said as he sat across from Allison, setting the gun on the nearby table.

"I'm sure he was proud. And you killed him?" Allison asked, now genuinely curious about everything Aaron would divulge.

"Yes, I killed him," he said. "We were playing chess. He was winning, but that wasn't why I killed him," Aaron said, unable to stop from chuckling. "I'm not that sore of a loser, Detective."

"And you killed the two boys?"

After a pause, Aaron answered, "Yes."

"Why did you kill them?"

"Because they interjected themselves into the middle of an assignment," he said, smiling at her. "They were collateral damage, considered acceptable by my employer, the government of the United States."

"Two innocent boys. You killed them in cold blood. That's not collateral damage. That is murder. You're a monster."

"How could I be a monster? I work for the government!" Aaron said as he laughed. "Please don't judge me so harshly, Detective. Excuse me for changing the subject, but who are you to judge me? What was it I witnessed earlier between you and the old guy? He's married, right?" Aaron asked. "And his wife has dementia. She will forget how you fucked around with her husband for years?"

Allison could not speak. She wanted to ask where Richard was but stopped herself.

"That's what I thought. Detective. There's no way to answer that, is there? The world is a complicated place, isn't it?" Aaron asked, standing as he reached over and patted her shoulder as he walked behind her. "It's hard to decide what is right and wrong."

Allison could not see him. While she had regained minimal composure, the sudden inability to see him made her tremble. Allison shut her eyes and tried to think of what to say. And then she heard him whispering in her ear.

"It's a fucked-up world, Allison, and you have a front-row seat."

Allison wanted to scream, but she knew she could not give in. She held still despite her impulse to try to move. Aaron now moved back in front of her…humming.

"Oh, the shark, babe, has such teeth, dear, and he shows them pearly white," Aaron began to sing, leaning within inches of Allison's face.

"Music…you love music, don't you?" Allison asked. "But your choice of songs sucks."

"Yes, I love music. I did a little research on you. Your husband killed himself right here. Why would he do such a thing, married to someone as observant of human behavior as you are? It is hard to imagine you did not see that coming. I'm not a detective, but I have to wonder, were you responsible for his suicide?" he asked, kneeling on one knee in front of her, brushing the hair from her face. "Were you the cause for his effect?"

"Yes. It was my fault."

"Tell me, how so?"

"It's none of your fucking business, Simon," she said, looking into his eyes, nearly spitting out his real name.

"Why not finish the story?" Aaron asked, returning to the chair beside his gun. "Please continue. I am truly interested."

"I told him I was having an affair. It broke his heart. We were finalizing our divorce when he killed himself." The truth seemed to be Allison's only defense—as she struggled to confess the deep pain continuing to reside within her.

"Was the man you were having an affair with the man in your bedroom?" Aaron asked, looking back toward the bedroom. "That man, Richard Hopkins?"

"Yes."

"And he was married?"

"He is married."

"Did his wife find out about you?"

"No, and we broke off the affair. You promised not to lie. Is Richard hurt?"

"He did not suffer," Aaron said, standing and walking toward the kitchen area.

"Did you kill him?" Allison said, using every bit of her inner strength to keep from breaking down.

"Yes, but it was in self-defense. Mr. Hopkins reached for his gun. I told him twice to stop, but he didn't listen. That is the truth."

Allison sat quietly, trying to remain in control of her emotions.

"He would be alive now if he wasn't having an affair with you. Maybe he'd be helping his wife, wiping the spittle from her lip?"

Aaron walked toward a picture of Allison and Ben hanging over the fireplace.

"Cute couple. Your husband, well, your ex, looks delighted. But I can tell in this picture. You can see it written all over your face. You did not want to be there."

Allison decided to speak truthfully—even to the sinister man critiquing the picture of her and her deceased husband.

"You are right...partially. I loved Ben. He loved me. But sometimes, love isn't enough. You said the world is a complicated place. It is. Love can only get you so far in life."

Aaron seemed surprised and walked back to sit down across from Allison.

"I was in love. I just found out less than forty-eight hours ago my employer unilaterally chose to end our relationship," he said, looking down. "They killed her and made it look like a suicide."

"The Order killed her? Like Amy Rodman?" Allison quickly asked.

"Yes, just like Amy Rodman," he said. "Except they made it look like she slit her wrist in the shower. Then they sent me a picture of it," Aaron said, shutting his eyes.

"I would be furious and want revenge," Allison earnestly said.

"Detective, I don't want to kill you. And I definitely didn't want to kill Mr. Hopkins. I was conflicted about coming here. The Order sent me to kill a five-year-old boy in Idaho. I wouldn't do it. I disregarded my orders. I took the boy to his mother and told them to hide. I wasn't sure what would happen here, but I felt the need to come to see you and to hear you. I truly appreciate you being honest with me."

Allison thought momentarily and then spoke: "Why don't you stop the killing? Stop now. I will help you bring the Order down."

Aaron laughed. "I have a few scores to settle with my employer. And if I do not kill you, that will lead to discovering my mission failures here and in Idaho. A five-year-old boy that I somehow feel connected with will die. As will his mother and his great-grandfather. Do you see my dilemma?"

"Is the Order truly part of the US government?"

"Yes, it's been in existence since the Revolutionary War. You can't imagine what they've done."

Allison summoned the strength to remain composed—it seemed like her only hope.

"Tell me what you know," she asked, sensing his need to talk.

"William served the Order for all of his adult life. They have levels within the Order, levels of assignments, and trust. William was the highest rung short of the top...what they call the Circle, the most powerful people in the country and the world. They are the people in control. He confided in me very few times, but I will never forget one thing. William described his role in the Kennedy assassination. He was on the Grassy Knoll. He also shared some of the history of the Order. The Order murdered Lincoln. It was a coup within the Order, an attempt to overthrow the US government. It was over race, as most things are. Even when it comes to money and self-interest, people are racists. Can you imagine being willing to risk everything they had over keeping slavery as an institution? The Circle had enough. Even now, they have some degree of loyalty to Booth as a martyr. They went as far as using their influence to preserve Booth's legacy not as an assassin but as an actor. Don't believe me? Google his name. You'll see Booth's name pop up as an actor. Imagine that. The little things, Detective, speak to the power of the Order. And I apologize...I didn't want to get your hopes up by suggesting you'd have the opportunity to do a Google search. You're going to have to take my word for it."

He honestly seems like he wants to find a reason to not kill me, Allison thought. *And the only way I can deal with this psycho is to get free and kill him like he killed Richard.* While her instincts as a detective had kept her composed outwardly, Allison's anger and hate for the man in front of her were nearly ready to boil over. And she knew that would be the end of her. *I want revenge*, she thought. The cold reality of the thought helped to gird the fortitude it would take to speak words she would have never thought of saying to another human being.

"They killed the person you love. You killed the person I love. You want revenge. So do I," she said coldly and truthfully.

"You want revenge? You were fucking another woman's husband. Your affair killed your husband. You're as guilty as I am. You killed your husband. You killed Richard. You're like a disease. There is a cure…a bullet."

Allison sat frozen—realizing her mistake.

"I will have revenge. On that…you can be certain. And there is a difference between us, Detective. The difference is you are a human being. But I've never felt fully human. It is like part of me is something else, something different. Humans are prone to making errors when they listen to their conscience. People say they have free will but admit to having something outside telling them what to do. That is strange, isn't it? I have a conscience. But it listens to me," he said, laughing hysterically.

Aaron composed himself and continued: "Regarding revenge, your goal is to kill me. I am directly responsible for the death of the man you love. That is all you care about…killing me. Fair enough. You have no interest in the Order. You have no interest in arresting me for three murders I admitted to committing. You just want me to free you so you can kill me. Be honest, Detective. Tell me if I am wrong,"

Aaron said, picking up the gun from the table as he walked behind her. "Killing me isn't doing your job. It just satisfies your hate. You swore an oath to protect and serve. And that would not include killing me if I was not threatening harm to you, would it? If you killed me in something other than self-defense, isn't that murder?"

As a tsunami of fear rushed over her, Allison remembered: tell the truth. *The truth is my only defense*, she thought before she spoke.

"I am a law enforcement officer for the state of Maryland. I swore to uphold the law, to bring the guilty to justice. I would not shoot you in cold blood as you have killed so many others. Even though you have admitted this to me, I am not a judge or a jury of one," Allison said, fearing it may be her last words.

Before Allison began to speak, Aaron heard in the same deep consciousness he had communicated with Jonas the words, "The truth is my only defense."

"I heard you," Aaron said, stumbling over the words, still trying to comprehend what had just happened. Aaron stood and walked across the room to the entryway to retrieve Allison's handgun. He asked: "Are you telling me the truth? Is the truth your only defense?"

Allison was stunned—it was as if he had some brief insight into her mind. *That's impossible*, she thought, calming herself as best as possible. After pausing to see him retrieve the gun and position himself directly in front of her, kneeling on one knee, she responded, "I'm telling you the truth."

Aaron could not hear any other wordless speech in his thoughts. Instead, the conflicts of his inner thoughts were smothering him: *Is this all an illusion or a delusion? Is this woman honest? Am I losing my mind?*

"I'm guessing you want revenge. You wouldn't be human if you didn't want to kill me."

"I didn't say I did not want to kill you. I do. But I would not kill you," Allison emphatically said.

"I've done this before. I am going to ask you a simple question. I've asked quite a few people the same question. Depending on how you answer will determine your fate," Aaron said, peering into Allison's eyes.

"I believe my fate is sealed," Allison said without thinking.

"It may be. But I want to hear your answer to this question. Here's the question. Why should I let you live?"

Allison sat quietly. The first thought running through her mind was, *This is the moment of truth.* After slowing her breathing, she responded.

"There is no good reason to let me live. I will never be a mother. I will never be a doctor or a nurse and help save people's lives. You're right. I caused the death of my husband. And I am to partially blame for Richard's death. I am guilty as you have charged. I have one value to the world and one true purpose. I bring the guilty to justice. I swore an oath to do so. I believe in equal justice for all. I truly would not treat someone differently because of their skin color. I can't judge the morality of what William Hines did in his life, but you killed him. And even more so, you killed two innocent young boys. You've admitted you are a murderer. And to answer your question, the only good reason to let me live is to bring you to justice. The voices of those boys are crying out for justice. You can't hear them, but I can."

Aaron stood straight up and looked around him. He heard voices—the voices of the boys. It was faint, but Aaron heard them say, "You killed us" repeatedly. Aaron growled as if he were a caged animal, unable to respond to the confinement of the prison of voices haunting his mind. His anger and frustration began to spill over into his words.

"Justice? What the fuck is justice? Justice is a perspective, nothing more or less. It's an opinion. People with my skin color were brought here as slaves. Is that justice? You can hear voices? Do you hear the boys? I can hear them, too. But that doesn't say anything more than we are probably both losing our respective fucking minds."

He paused, stepping closer to Allison.

"You want revenge, Detective. You want revenge! I want revenge!" Aaron shouted. "But neither of us will have it unless one thing and only one thing happens. You need to kill me. You need to be the judge and the jury. If you do not kill me, you will be solely responsible for those deaths to come, just like the death of your husband and your lover. They will fall squarely on you! If you don't kill me, you're as good as murdering many more…maybe even some innocent humans!" Aaron shouted, setting both guns down on the table by the chair, reaching into his pocket, producing a switchblade, and unleashing its blade.

Aaron stepped forward, putting his hand on Allison's cheek.

"You may want to act brave, but I know you're afraid. Like every human being walking the planet, you are afraid when they face even the idea of death. Death brings the entire human race to its knees. Death does not scare me, Detective. I fucking welcome death. Death is the only thing that will bring me peace," he said as he kneeled on the floor before Allison, holding the blade. Taking the knife and running it lightly from the top of her thigh down to her knee, Aaron lifted the edge under her shirt, hiking the T-shirt to her abdomen while keeping his eyes locked into Allison's. She could feel the point of the knife on her stomach.

Hearing his words, Allison resolved to confront her death with courage.

"I promise if I have the opportunity, I will bring you to justice," Allison said firmly, staring into his eyes.

Aaron leaned back—continuing to stare deeply into her eyes. He sat back, kneeling on both knees, moving the knife away, and then closed his eyes. Aaron then said, "Pestis eram vivus; moriens tua mors ero. Do you know what that means, Allison? *Living I have been your plague; dying I shall be your death.*"

"I will not serve as your judge, Simon," she said with cold, steady resolve. "I will do my job and nothing more…what I swore an oath to do."

"Let's see, Detective if you're telling the truth," Aaron said as he leaped to his feet and took the knife in numerous swirling motions before her face. "Your humanity will get the best of you. You want revenge. And revenge is all you will get, nothing more. You made a promise to me. I'll make you a promise. If you don't kill me, I will kill you and many others because of you. You have a choice to make. It's a life and death choice."

Aaron placed the knife below the cable tie on her right wrist, cut the plastic binding, and freed Allison's hand.

He reached back and picked up Allison's gun, placing it in her hand, and then forcefully guiding her hand, positioned the gun directly between his eyes as he knelt on the floor in front of her.

"For the sake of humanity, to avenge your lover's death and the two boys I killed at Deep Creek Lake, please…I beg you…pull the trigger, Detective, just pull the fucking trigger! You will have served justice on me," Aaron said without emotion.

"No! I will not give you what you want. This is not justice!" Allison screamed. "This is what you want. To give you peace! I won't do it! I told you the truth!"

"Did I tell you what I did after I killed the boys, Detective? I kicked the corpses of two innocent boys I killed. If you don't kill me, I will do something worse to your corpse. The choice is simple. You either kill me, or I promise I will kill you, just like I killed Richard Hopkins."

Tears streamed out of Allison's eyes. She trembled as she held the gun. She fought every impulse to pull the trigger.

I am not going to give him this, she thought.

Again, inexplicably, Aaron heard Allison's words without her uttering them.

Aaron quickly pulled back the gun from Allison's hand and repeated her thought aloud: "I am not going to give him this."

Allison sat stunned, looking at Aaron. "You can read my mind? What the fuck are you, Simon?"

Aaron stood and turned away from Allison.

"Detective, you're right," Aaron said. "I agree with you."

"What do you mean?" Allison said, in shock from the sequence of unfolding events.

Aaron knelt before Allison and placed the gun on the floor, picking up the switchblade he had dropped seconds earlier. Taking the blade, he cut each binding to free Allison. As she sat still, he picked up the gun and stood up.

"Do your job, Detective. I submit to justice," Aaron said as he handed Allison the gun.

For the first time in his life, Aaron accepted his guilt. And now, in surrender, peace of mind.

Allison stood, pointing the gun at Aaron, allowing the incredible turn of events to seep into her consciousness.

"Is this some kind of trick?" she asked, still confused.

"It's not a trick," Aaron said, feeling the immense weight of guilt falling away. "Do your job, Detective. I submit to justice. And I will help you prosecute the Order."

"You're doing the right thing, Simon," Allison said, gaining composure.

Allison was then directed to noise on the front porch directly behind Aaron. She saw a bright flash, blinding her. Immediately, the door burst apart with a blast that propelled Allison and Aaron to the floor, splintering the front door and shattering the windows in the room, glass and debris flying through the air.

Aaron had been knocked face-down to the floor with his back to the blast. Still stunned and trying to make sense of what was happening, he saw Allison, blood coming from the shattered glass embedded in her face and neck. She was still holding the gun, struggling to stand up.

"I can't see!" she shouted, pointing the gun toward the front of the house, emptying all of the rounds in rapid succession.

"Stay down, Detective!" was all Aaron could say before he saw Allison hit with a barrage of bullets.

Aaron crawled to Allison's fallen body and, as she took her last breath, said, "Detective, I promise I will avenge you."

The last thing Aaron felt was a long needle deeply penetrating his neck, losing consciousness as he lay by Allison's lifeless body.

CHAPTER TWENTY-ONE
THE ANCIENTS

Jon was nearing the *Canyons of the Ancients* near Cortez, Colorado.

Arriving in the late afternoon of a cloudless, beautiful spring day, he instinctively drove through a designated park area void of any visitors toward a site featuring one of the largest concentrations of Native American ruins in North America. Taking his backpack—his gun tucked away in it out of sight—Jon began to walk a trail along the ridge high above the flat desert stretched before him in the valley below. Just past the desert, Jon could see the snow-capped peaks of the Rocky Mountains.

I can see why they wanted to live here. It is beautiful. You can see the entire valley, Jon thought, making his way toward a pueblo ruin called "Painted Hand." A marker pointed down the ridge to an outcropping of sandstone where a tall tower's remnants remained. The dirt path led to a challenging climb down the rocky ledge to the enormous rock's flat surface, where the tower rose above the plain below.

Jon looked inside the crumbling structure, feeling the strong sense of having been in the tower before. Stepping out of the ruins, he walked to the edge of the ledge overlooking the desert basin below him. Backtracking to the far corner of the outcropping, he climbed down along the side to an area underneath the massive rock slab.

"I have been here," he said aloud as he made his way under the lip of the rock.

Tucked away in the far left-hand corner of the naturally formed rock shelter were faint petroglyphs—rock carvings depicting hands on the light-colored stone. Jon knelt and juxtaposed his hands over the hands carved on the stone in the prehistoric painting, careful not to touch the rock. His hand fit perfectly over the ancient petroglyph.

Despite dusk approaching, Jon wanted to go to an area in the ridge-line that formed a box canyon. Climbing to the higher ridge, Jon walked a quarter of a mile to the canyon that had grabbed his attention. He saw one of the large structures deeply inset in an enormous sandstone formation, the last sunset light falling on it. Even though the sunlight faded into dusk, Jon moved toward the ruins. On the climb up the rocky embankment below the ancient ruin, Jon heard something scampering on the ground. He turned and looked behind him, and sitting on a rock, seemingly commanding attention, sat a giant lizard.

Jon had seen others like it before in New Mexico—he remembered they were called "collared lizards" because the area around their neck gave the reptile the appearance of having a collar around their neck. While he had seen others, this was the largest he had ever encountered. Despite his love of nature, Jon was not a fan of reptiles.

"Sorry, dude, you're not my type," he said, laughing. Hearing Jon laugh, the lizard bolted from the rock and retreated to the cactus-strewn brush.

Jon turned and looked back down the narrow canyon.

This is a safe place, he thought. *Nothing comes in here unless you see it.*

Walking back amongst the rubble from various structures, Jon saw another grouping of rock paintings on the rear wall of the enormous overhanging rock. The most prominent featured wildlife seemed to jump out of the rock carving. It was a lizard. The reptile was standing taller than any of the animals on the wall. While the etching was a lizard with an intricately carved head and scaly skin, it stood erect with a human body.

"Lizardman," Jon said, laughing, walking up for a close-up look at the carving. "Even the ancients had wild imaginations…evidently a lot like mine."

Now inches away from the etching, Jon saw what appeared to be a series of faint wave-like carvings of lines directly below the sizeable lizard-like image. At first, Jon thought the waves were water. But looking around at the desert surroundings, Jon believed the waves represented wind instead of water. A gust of wind found its way through the ruins at that very moment. In the wind, Jon shut his eyes and heard a whistling…and words…kooni bai.

"The words…I understand them. The turn in time," Jon softly said as he opened his eyes.

Turning back to the large opening, Jon sat down on the edge. He looked past the jagged high rim of the canyon as the last rays of the fading sun arced upward above the mountains in the distance. Jon took out a water bottle and looked back at the fortress-like structure behind him again, feeling familiar with the place.

Suddenly, Jon felt the urgent need to take cover. He spun quickly and shuffled behind one of the structures, carrying his backpack and remaining as low to the ground as possible. Looking down the deep, narrow canyon below him through the many cracks in the surrounding structure he had taken cover within, Jon could see two men in the dim light moving toward his position. Pulling a pair of binoculars from his backpack, he zeroed in on the figures. Both wore fatigues and were armed. What was extraordinary to Jon was the sheer physical size of the two—they almost looked like giants trudging through the brush toward his position. The first soldier in the lead grabbed Jon's attention. While wearing standard fatigues, he had a black glove on his right hand.

They must know I'm here, Jon thought, taking out his gun.

Leaving his backpack tucked between fallen rocks, he stealthily circled behind the structures—always able to keep the approaching men in eyesight as they proceeded to near the steep climb upward toward the area where he had initially entered the rock formation. Jon looked down at the gun, shaking his head. He knew he could not take any aggressive, offensive action against them.

They are soldiers, just following orders, Jon thought. Hopefully, they will give up if they can't find me.

Jon's mind was a flurry of thoughts assessing their movement as they were now on the same plateau as him—less than fifty yards away. Looking nearby, Jon picked up a rock the size of a baseball and hurled it far into the canyon below to distract them—hoping to see how they would respond.

The sound seemed to echo off the steep canyon walls as it hit the hard ground below and rolled downward, immediately drawing their attention. Keeping his focus on the men, Jon saw one of the soldiers pull out what looked like a grenade or something similar in size from his belt. Both soldiers stepped to the ledge as the one holding the object heaved it toward where Jon had lobbed the rock.

Jon watched the object the soldier threw descend into the near darkness below. A burst of bright light lit the entire canyon. There was no sound or explosion, but the light had the same effect Jon experienced in Alaska. He was blinded—not nearly as bad as in the cabin, but still feeling pain in his eyes and suffering the inability to see clearly. The entire scene was now a blur to him. He froze, trying to avoid any movement that would give away his position.

He heard footsteps getting closer. Opening his eyes, he saw the two gigantic figures nearing where he was taking cover. Jon decided to outrun them down the outcropping face in the now nearly dark canyon. Seeing what looked like a smoother surface of loose rock and dirt, almost like nature's version of a slide, Jon bolted away from behind the standing stones. He jumped off the high plateau, hitting and sliding downward, performing a near-perfect controlled descent down the steep ridge. The move had surprised the soldiers, and they were slow to respond. Running through the brush, Jon turned the corner at the base of the box canyon and exited the sight of the pursuing soldiers.

I've left them behind, he thought as he vigorously increased his pace upward toward the ridgeline where his Jeep was parked nearly a half-mile away. Topping out on the ridge, Jon was now on a level plain of rock and dirt. As he rapidly went to where he had driven his Jeep, Jon's senses told him to stop and shut his eyes. Instinctively, Jon fell to the ground, tightly closing his eyes. The flash was still evident even though his head was tucked tight to his knees and his eyes shut.

Jon paused and looked up. His vision was intact. But as he began to lift himself off the ground, he saw one of the soldiers running full speed at him. Jon stood and waited, relaxing his body to prepare to respond to the attacker. As the soldier closed in, Jon used the enormous soldier's velocity to side-step and trip him, dropping him face-first with a severe impact on the hard surface. Jumping down behind the stunned, fallen man, Jon executed a powerful punch in the base of the soldier's neck, again driving his face down into the ground.

Jon heard the second soldier and turned, ducking at the last second as the soldier swung at Jon's head with a fully extended nightstick. Jon pivoted and unleashed a savage blow to the giant soldier's abdomen in the same defensive motion, his other hand still holding his gun. As the soldier leaned forward erect, Jon hit the soldier with an uppercut strike under the man's chin. The enormous soldier fell backward, hitting the ground as the dust rose from his loose dirt impact.

Turning to face the first soldier he had encountered, he could now see the monstrous-size opponent's glove he had noticed earlier. The soldier's glove was partially pulled off his hand, exposing a bluish-green scaly skin underneath. The soldier paused and picked up a huge rock using both hands, lifting the stone over his head and menacingly walking toward Jon.

"I don't want to hurt you," Jon said as he took several steps backward from the approaching man, appearing ready to crush him with the rock high over his head. "I'm warning you, soldier!" Jon shouted, taking two more steps backward in retreat. Finally losing his patience with the attacker, Jon lifted the pistol and pointed it at the soldier's head. "I don't want to shoot you...stop!"

The soldier was not deterred by the threat of the gun pointed at him and continued forward, now ten feet away, positioning the rock to crush it downward on Jon.

"Fuck this," Jon said, aiming the pistol down and firing one round into the soldier's kneecap, immediately dropping him to the ground, the stone falling on the soldier.

"I warned you, asshole!" Jon shouted. Before Jon could say another word, the second soldier reappeared and, with his massive, long arms, grabbed Jon from behind and lifted him off the ground.

Jon immediately threw his head back sharply into the face of the soldier holding him. The impact jarred Jon loose from the soldier's bear hug, and he crouched to the ground. Jon quickly spun on one knee and landed a punch deep into the soldier's crotch, causing him to double over. The soldier's head was now within inches of Jon, still on one knee, and using all of his strength, punched upward into the soldier's face, landing the blow squarely on the soldier's nose and mouth. The uppercut knocked the soldier backward, landing on his back in a cloud of dust on the ground. Jon quickly spun and saw the other soldier struggling to stand despite being shot. Jon ran toward him and landed a kick in his face, sending the soldier twisting to the side.

The fallen soldier then reached down toward his belt with his non-glove hand. Seeing the attempt, Jon jerked his arm behind in a rapid motion. Putting his knee on the soldier's neck, Jon saw what was likely the light weapon used against him. Out of the corner of his eye, he now saw the almost fully exposed hand of the soldier. The skin looked like snakeskin—reptilian—nothing resembling human flesh.

"What the fuck are you?" Jon shouted. "You're not soldiers."

Jon moved to stand over the head of the soldier with the glove. He pointed his gun at the soldier's head and said, "I've killed enemies for a lot less than this. You have until three to tell me why you're after me!"

Jon began in a slow cadence, "One…two…" and then he could see something dropping from the sky out of the corner of his eye. Quickly turning, Jon felt blasted into millions of pieces—as if he was coming apart. Jon saw rapid flashes of bright light and, within seconds, was lying face down on a dark metallic-like floor. He began to lift his arm in self-defense, but his gun was gone. Before he could focus, he saw a bright flash. Blinded, Jon shouted in agony, "No!"

A split second later, he felt a sharp pain in his neck and the darkness of unconsciousness.

Excluded Middle

Marc had completed his work.

General Mason had demanded Marc produce the viral agent that would effectively remove the Axis Mundi within seventy-two hours.

Knowing he was being watched each second in the lab, Marc accomplished the task less than twenty-two hours after initiating his work. Marc looked up at one of the security cameras in the lab and said, "General, it is done."

Looking down at the small canister in his hand, Marc thought, *I possess the means to destroy humanity.*

Marc was also ready to deliver the vaccine he had prepared to Mason. He had explained to the General that the viral cure would serve as a repellant against any attempt to remove the Axis Mundi. Similar to the toxin, the vaccine could be delivered airborne and would prohibit the lethal effects of exposure to the toxin.

Marc's wife and two children would serve as the test subjects. He created a liquid form of the vaccine for the test case—a shot given to his family before exposure to the toxin. Mason agreed to Marc's plan without hesitation or debate.

Marc understood he had no other options. It was all or nothing.

Releasing the virus in a small, confined space would bring about death to a human within a matter of seconds. Casting a large amount into the atmosphere, the toxin would eventually make its way around the globe, wiping out all human life in a matter of days.

The Axis Mundi was created with an airborne release in mind, Marc thought. *Humans never knew the fragility of life. The power to destroy humanity was always in the hands of our creators. We were always slaves, and as long as the Axis Mundi remains within, we forever will remain slaves.*

Marc had also shared with Mason how the toxin could be released—as part of a small-scale nuclear explosion to ensure its worldwide spread and the destruction of human life. The blast would propel the airborne virus into the atmosphere, and the wind would carry the virus to every corner of the planet in a manner that would ensure its worldwide presence and the extinction of humanity.

Destruction of an entire species accomplished without harming the planet, Marc thought. *Our creators knew what they were doing, except they never contemplated we would find the code and end our slavery.*

Marc's family had been held captive at APG, only two hallways from Marc. He was made aware of this only after he had agreed to create the toxin and the vaccine as Mason had ordered. Despite their close proximity, Marc had not requested to see them.

There is no middle option, only this or that, life or death, freedom or slavery.

General Mason entered the room, a smile on his face.

"So you have both the toxin and the vaccine?" Mason asked, knowing the answer.

"Yes. I have done as you asked," Marc responded.

"Not everyone gets to use their wife and children as lab rats in an experiment. You must be certain you have perfected the vaccine?" Mason asked, pausing for Marc to answer.

"I am confident. I wouldn't do this if I did not know exactly what I was doing. Right, General?" Marc answered with a question.

"It would appear that is so. You know there are no second chances. The life of your family hangs in the balance. If you're ready, let's begin."

Marc was escorted to a small room with a large, black screen dominating one wall. He was alone in the room with his thoughts.

I just surrendered the means to wipe out humanity to General Mason. But I know what he is and what his intentions are. There is no other way to free humanity. The universe will know I did not allow the human race to submit to slavery.

The die is cast, Marc thought as he silently stood in the room. *By the power of truth, I, while living, have conquered the universe. That is how I will be remembered.*

Mason, Roby, Dr. Allen, and an enormous soldier walked into the room. No words were exchanged. Mason motioned Marc to sit in the only chair in the room.

Pulling a control device from his pocket, he pressed a button pointing at the giant screen. Immediately, the screen image broadcast the live feed of the nearby room where Marc's wife and two children were being held. They were all strapped down in three wheelchairs. Each of them had tape over their mouth. His teenage sons were looking at their mother—her back to the camera. Each of them was attached to monitors.

"Can I speak to my wife and kids before we do this?" Marc asked without a trace of emotion.

"You haven't acted interested before. Why now? If this works, you can join your wife and children. You can all be together, one big, happy family," the General said. "But that's only if this works. Otherwise, you won't have a family to be with," Mason chuckled.

Dr. Allen then spoke uncharacteristically in defiance of Mason.

"This is not right. This is not the way to treat humans. We aren't lab rats. They are his family," he said, looking at Mason. "Even if he thinks he has created a vaccine, this is not how to test it. Using his children and his wife. What is wrong with you, General? Where is your humanity?"

"You can't imagine how funny that question is. I take it you disagree with the test?" Mason asked as if he was considering another option for the experiment.

"I disagree with this completely, and you know I have, General. Dr. Walker should have never created the toxin and then had the arrogance to believe he could create a vaccine after handing over the means to extinguish life to you...to the military. The fool gave you what you wanted. We can find a way to test it without putting his family at risk like this. This is inhuman."

"On that, we agree," Mason said, now loudly laughing. Mason put his hand on Dr. Allen's shoulder and said, "I have an idea. It's true, it is inhumane. But you're wrong about one thing: removing the Axis Mundi will not end all life on the planet...just human life. But I'll give you credit where credit is due. You pointed out a fallacy in the test: we need a control subject, an unvaccinated human."

The General looked at the soldier and coldly demanded, "Take Dr. Allen to the room to join the Walker family. Except, in his case, do not administer the vaccine. He can serve as the control in this experiment."

Allen shouted, "No! No!" as the soldier grabbed him by the arm and the back of the neck, nearly carrying the world-renowned evolutionary biologist out of the room.

"I'm guessing that did not turn out like Dr. Allen expected," Mason said, shaking his head in mock astonishment. "Humans, you never stop surprising me."

Marc and Roby did not speak or move.

Within minutes, the video screen erupted in chaos as the soldier wheeled Dr. Allen into the room strapped into a wheelchair. He was not connected to a monitor. A second gigantic soldier stepped into the room, holding three syringes.

Allen started to shout, "You only have three syringes! Where is mine? Where is my vaccine? This is murder!"

Using the same remote device, Mason pushed a button and said, "Dr. Allen, you've seemed to change your mind about the efficacy of what Dr. Walker has created. Soldier, shut him up. He's upsetting the Walker family."

The soldier kneeled over Dr. Allen, placing a significant strand of tape over his mouth as Allen continued to protest, his words now muffled and reduced to groans.

"Good work, soldier," Mason said. Turning to look at Marc, the General continued, "Allen will serve quite nicely as a control subject for the toxin. That is Allen's first good idea since he's been here! I guess it took him time to evolve into the role of a lab rat."

Marc remained silent, refusing to look at Mason as he stared into the livestream at his family.

"Before we start this, do you have any last requests? Other than talking with your family," Mason said, looking at Marc.

"May I join them? Can I be with my family? I do not want the vaccine. My work is complete."

"No! You have more work to do," Mason said, pausing. "I may be wrong, but I do not believe you need a vaccine. You're different, aren't you?"

Marc was puzzled by the General's last comment, unsure of what the General was saying.

"You aren't going to let my family live, are you?" Marc asked, never turning his head from the screen.

"Your family is leverage. I know you would never do anything to hurt them. That is one of the few universally shared traits: humans are loyal to their families."

"I knew we would never get out of here alive," Marc said without emotion, briefly turning to look at Roby. "And General Mason, you are more interested in the Axis Mundi as a weapon, correct?"

"Fuck yes! It's always been a weapon!" the General said, laughing loudly. "Just like your family, the vaccine is leverage."

The soldier abruptly returned to the room and stood directly behind Marc. Roby remained in the corner. Mason pushed the button and said, "Seal the room. On my order, deliver the vaccine to Ms. Walker and the two children."

"I don't care, but it looks as if you're sacrificing one of your soldiers. Is he another control subject?" Marc asked, allowing a chuckle to follow his query.

"If this is what you say it is, it will not have any adverse effects on him," Mason said, laughing. "In a way, he is a control subject in the test, but not in the way you think. I'm assuming we are like you. You're immune to the toxin, as are we."

"Just what I thought. I wanted to hear you say it," Marc said coolly. "But I'm not like you. My ancestors do not include reptiles."

"You've known for some time. You also know your legacy. You're directly responsible for the destruction of humanity."

"We were already as good as dead," Marc softly said, dropping his head forward. "That is how and why we were made. As you said, we are lab rats."

Mason looked at Roby and then turned to the monitor, pushing the button, saying: "Release the toxin."

"*Vi Veri Veniversum Vivus Vici*," Marc said flatly.

Mason briefly turned and looked at Marc. "What was that you said?"

Marc had his eyes shut, refusing to answer.

After less than ten seconds, the heads of Marc's wife and children drooped. They were unconscious. Allen's head dropped seconds later. Marc remained seated motionless with his eyes shut, refusing to see the events on the screen.

After waiting several minutes, Mason broke the silence: "Check the monitors. Are the Walkers still alive?"

Marc continued to stoically sit with his eyes closed.

The soldier leaned over and looked at each monitor. Looking up into the camera, he took his hand and turned his thumb downward.

"What about our control subject, Dr. Allen?" Mason asked.

The soldier leaned over, felt his neck, and gave the same response with this thumb. Mason turned to look at Marc.

"Dr. Walker, you are only half as smart as you think. Your vaccine didn't work, but the toxin achieved the expected results. Congratulations, you got that right, and that was what I was most interested in. The bad news is that your wife and sons are dead, as is Dr. Allen. I have what I want. But I'm going to keep you alive so you can see the final outcome of your work," Mason said, chuckling. "Just for being a pain in my ass, you'll see how you're remembered."

Mason looked at the soldier behind Marc, saying, "Take him back to his room and strap him down. I want him kept alive."

CHAPTER TWENTY-TWO
THE CONFEDERACY

Mason was alone with Roby.

The silence in the large room magnified the tension between the two. Serving as an Agent and Observer, their respective roles placed them in direct conflict.

Finally speaking, Mason, the Agent for the alliance known as the Confederacy, said, "It proves what I've been saying. If you give these humans enough rope, they will ultimately hang themselves. Humans are dangerous," After a brief pause, both still looking at a vacant section of the room where a holographic image of the members of the Council would soon appear, Mason said, "The timing could not have been better to keep peace within the Confederacy."

The Confederacy was one of the countless galactic alliances between various life forms across the vast universe. Alliances were primarily for protection both from within and without.

"Imagine what I have facing me. My home planet is nearing destruction. Four hundred million of my family could die at any moment. And I'm here, trying to keep a lid on a bunch of renegade slaves...slaves your family created," Mason said, filling the silence.

As in most interactions, Roby, serving as the Observer for the alliance, did not speak. He listened.

The two had traveled to a location near Adak Island, off the coast of Alaska. They now had what the Council of the Confederacy had requested and awaited orders on the next steps. The five members forming the Council were the acknowledged power-sharing leadership group of the Confederacy—an alliance of over one hundred planets harboring life reflecting nearly as many separate and distinct species. The two would address the Council with their findings in a few moments.

"What gives me hope is an obvious solution to both problems," Mason said, failing again to draw a response from Roby.

The familiar and safe confines of the Anguis mothership fueled Mason's confidence. Again, breaking the silence, Mason smugly said, "This feels like home."

Roby understood the dual inferences Mason was sharing, calling both the enormous spaceship and its present location on Earth "home." Unlike Mason, Roby enjoyed being anywhere except where he was now, submerged deep below the ocean off the coast of Alaska in a room with the Anguis General. The awkward silence continued as they waited for the Council to join them.

Unexpectedly, Roby broke the silence.

"General, I must say I am surprised. I thought you hated Earth?" Roby asked in his soft, childlike voice.

"Hell...I'm the one surprised! I thought you were just going to sit there and not say anything. You need to speak honestly and openly about what you see here," Mason said, avoiding Roby's question. "We do not have to be friends...or enemies. I am counting on you. So is the Council."

Both Mason and Roby understood there would never be a friendship forged between the two. At best, respect and adherence to their respective duties and roles had been their focus over the many Earth years spent together.

"General, do you not hate Earth?"

Mason was a general—a former military leader for the Anguis chosen by the Council to serve on Earth as an Agent to ensure compliance with the Confederacy's *Rules of Engagement*. The rules outlined the boundaries for what they could do, leaving minimal room to take any independent action. Almost all the galactic alliances adopted the same standard for engaging with colonies throughout the universe.

"No, I do not hate this island. It's the inhabitants I despise," Mason said.

"Thank you, General, for the answer."

As an Agent, Mason served in an operational capacity. Though limited, the "General" helped to bridge the Confederacy's oversight of the Earth colony in his role as a liaison to the human's most powerful military, the United States of America.

"You're welcome," Mason said, chuckling as he briefly turned his head to look at Roby. "We both have jobs to do."

"You have changed," Roby said.

Mason's military background kept him in line, following orders, Roby thought. *But his thoughts fully betray his role and intentions. He will do anything to protect his family and his species. We share that in common.*

"I've changed because the situation has changed."

"General, I appreciate this sharing of ideas. Please continue," Roby responded.

"The Circle, the leaders of humans, are the worst possible representatives for humans. They don't give a fuck about all those billions of humans on the island. I actually care more about humanity than they do," Mason said.

Outside of a select group of military leaders, only a small group of humans known as the Circle was aware of the roles of Mason and Roby and the Earth's status as a colony of a galactic alliance known as the Confederacy. The primary function of the Circle was to maintain a strict veil of secrecy by keeping order and ensuring Earth's compliance with the rules and mandates governing a colony within the Confederacy. Their wealth and safety were dependent on hiding any presence of a technologically advanced overseer.

Loyalty had been purchased at a relatively small price by the Confederacy. But distrust of humans remained a constant. This was true for all members of the Council, including the species responsible for the creation of humans…the Newe.

"We agree. Humans are far more formidable," Roby said.

"I agree."

"The truth is the truth," Roby.

"I thought your fondness of humans would prejudice your perspective. You surprised me by sharing the reasons you believed Aaron is gifted. I would have never suspected him. Maybe you have changed, too?" Mason added.

Being Newebean, Roby carried with him the conflict of assisting in policing and enforcing oversight on the creation of the Newe that had originated millions of years earlier.

"The past is the past. I am not a prisoner to it," Roby said softly and sincerely.

"I'm not a prisoner to it, but the Anguis were," Mason sneered. "Prisoners as in slaves. It's one of the few things we share with humans."

Roby chose not to respond.

"The danger with humans is their nature. They are aggressive and arrogant. The Circle knows they are a colony. They know they are technologically inferior. But they talk down to me as if they are superior to me! Just because of how they look! What is just way too fucking funny for me is their belief that skin color is important! All but one of the Circle are white males. Imagine if they saw their creators, the Newe, and realized the race that had created them had predominantly black skin color! And if they knew what I looked like under this covering, they would shit themselves! Humans are the most racist species in the universe. Their racist, aggressive, arrogant nature makes them a threat. Especially if they somehow find a way to make more exponential jumps in their technology."

Despite the millions of years to grow and mature as civilizations, racism remained a universal reality. To bridge the consequences of universal racism, alliances adopted a set of agreements to address the challenge. The one uniting theme that brought consensus from the multitude of alliances was an aversion to full-scale galactic war, and the credo echoed throughout the vastness of space and time: "No One Wins."

"We are here to ensure that never happens," Roby responded.

"Let's admit that our distrust of each other is because we are different," Mason said.

"I do not distrust you because we are different."

Appearing to overlook Roby's comment, Mason continued. "Different families trying to find a way to coexist. That is what keeps the peace."

"The means to destroy another family must be closely guarded. Otherwise, no one wins," Roby said, allowing a hint of a smile.

"Yes! Power must not be in the hands of the few. We know what happens when that occurs," Mason said, nodding his head in positive affirmation of Roby's comment. "Power must be shared."

"General, do you find it somewhat paradoxical that the Collective is an immense concentration of power?" Roby asked, referring to the small group of alliances ruling over the rest.

"To use an Earth saying, the Collective is a necessary evil."

"Did you just say evil?" Roby asked, moving his head slightly in mock surprise.

"You know what I mean," Mason snarled.

"Being different is risky," Roby said after a brief pause.

Mason immediately responded, quoting part of the Charter of the Collective, "Each species has the right to exist."

"And that includes humans?" Roby quickly queried.

"I have no problem with the existence of humans as long as they are not a threat to the universe. Each alliance decides what to do with a self-destructive, dangerous species. Humans are a direct threat to the Newe and the Anguis," Mason said through a tightened jaw.

The Newe and Anguis were two of the Confederacy's original five founding families of species—the alliance that controlled Earth. In the distant past, the two species had been at war and finally found peace in the common ground of survival. The Newe and the Anguis finally accepted each other's existence when the threats from outside were much more significant than their own conflicts. Earth had been a source of disagreement since the Newe had first sought to colonize it.

After a pause, Mason turned in his chair to face the empty space of the room. Roby did the same as silence filled the room.

"You cannot deny the history. Creating a Newebean colony on Earth was unfair to my family. The Newe did this! Your species enslaved many other species, including my own family! That is what happens when too much power falls into too few hands," Mason angrily stated.

"Correction, General. I have never enslaved anyone," Roby said, speaking louder and more forcefully than Mason had ever experienced.

"You're right. I apologize," Mason sincerely said. "But your family, the Newe, did. And they did it because they had the power. What has happened before can happen again. And that will not happen on my watch!"

After a lengthy and awkward pause, Roby spoke: "General, neither of us can deny our pasts. As you spoke of human nature, we both have our own."

"Time is running out, Roby," Mason said in a much quieter and softer tone than Roby had ever witnessed in his time with the General.

"My home island will die soon. And so will millions of my family. Something must be done to save them."

"I understand. Time is of the essence," Roby said, breaking the silence.

Time was a problem for the Anguis home planet. The planet was being pulled closer and closer to the star it orbited. No engineering miracle could alter the magnitude of moving millions of Anguis over the vastness of space in a relatively brief time. The sheer travel distance limited the time a mass exodus could safely remain in deep space and reach their destination intact. Only one planet within the Confederacy uniquely matched the needs of the Anguis—both in the predominance of water and large enough and close enough to relocate four hundred million of their race: Earth.

"Survival for my family hangs in the balance. The solution is simple. What stands in the way is a slave race threatening the Confederacy, a species the Newe created. The Axis Mundi confirms that!" Mason said, his emotions bubbling over as he spoke. "If the Newe were facing near-term extinction and there was an option, a way to save your family, would you not pursue it?"

"I would pursue every path to save my family," Roby said.

"The Anguis paid an enormous price serving the Confederacy at a great loss of life in conflicts, especially in the Great War. The Anguis helped preserve your family. We deserve to be treated similarly," Mason said, nearly pleading his case.

"I understand, General," Roby said with sincerity.

"I know the prejudice. I know the fear the Newe and others have for my kind. But that is why we agreed to form an alliance for our mutual protection and benefit. Alliances are not one-way paths, Roby," Mason said, furthering his perspective.

Of all the species, the Anguis were viewed by most in the Confederacy as uncontrollable and even disgusting. In their most primitive form—something that seemed to lurk close to the surface—the Anguis enjoyed feeding on other species. The scornful joke floating through the universe was, "If an Anguis invites you to dine with them, beware: you are probably the meal."

Roby saw truth within the humor. Mason and his soldiers seemed unhinged and capable of doing anything, including making a meal of other species.

Ultimately, their nature betrays the Anguis, Roby thought.

"I'm not falsifying the threat of humans. I can prove it. They have nuclear weaponry and are destroying their own island. They are finding ways to change their own cellular structure. They are expanding their capabilities in artificial intelligence. They have checked all of the boxes as threats. The existence of humans is the greatest danger to the Confederacy since the Great War," Mason said, returning his gaze to the vacant area of the room.

Witnessing a species knowingly and greedily destroying their own island significantly threatened alliance members. Self-destructive behavior of any kind was frowned upon by the Confederacy. The consequences of being found guilty of this type of self-destructive behavior were severe by the overseeing Council.

"And what makes humans the most dangerous threat is this infection of the gift. That magnifies the danger," Mason added, crossing his arms.

The most looming danger the Confederacy perceived was humans' capacity to alter their cellular structure. Roby understood the fear and the conflict. He was more than a Newebean—he was gifted. While this had never been fully evidenced, several members of the Council considered it a strong possibility.

"I understand your concern," Roby flatly responded.

"It's not just my fucking concern, it is yours too! The gift puts the power in the hands of very few! It almost destroyed the Newe!" Mason nearly shouted as he turned to look at Roby.

Roby maintained his fixed stare at the wall in front of him.

"I want to know how humans were given the gift?" Mason plaintively demanded, sounding as if he were seeking an answer from Roby.

"Do you think it is some kind of conspiracy, General?" Roby responded with his own query.

"Yes, I do," Mason emphatically answered. "And that is what I will tell the Council."

The history of the gift helps to support Mason's conspiracy theory, Roby thought. *The gift has one source—the Newe.*

"The gift remains specific to the Newe since the time of your Newebean queen, Isa. There has never been a gifted Anguis. Why? Is that because science does not allow it? Or is it simply a choice by the Newe to not share the gift with other species?" Mason broke the silence with another flurry of questions. "Yet this rogue Newebean creation, humans, has now benefited from the gift. How the fuck does that happen, Roby?"

"General, if your hypothesis is true about a conspiracy, then there must be an intention. For what purpose would humans be, to use your term, infected with the gift?"

"What species is responsible for placing the gift in humans?" Mason asked again, briefly turning to look at Roby as he finished his query. "We both know the answer, as will the Council. It had to originate with the Newe."

For the Anguis, the threat from humans was a blessing. Humans were now a threat, and Earth was a potential new home for the Anguis.

The long silence between the two was broken by Mason: "Here is my hypothesis. The humans are being prepared to be used as gifted soldiers controlled by the Newe. It is the remnant of your Queen Isa and the Dogoa Rebellion. It is the nature of Newebeans to be dominant. And allowing the Anguis species to be destroyed removes one of the last hindrances to their plans."

"My advice is to stick with what you know, General. I will," Roby said, looking at Mason, meeting his gaze.

"I thought you would say that," Mason said.

The flickering of light patterns began to form in the room's empty space opposite the two.

Mason smiled and quickly turned away from Roby, cheerfully saying, "Here we go."

Roby was now in the middle of the conflict, where he had planned to be from the beginning.

CHAPTER TWENTY-THREE
THE COUNCIL

Roby sat and listened as Mason began speaking to the five members of the *Council of the Confederacy.*

"Esteemed Council leaders, I have an update on the issues related to the Earth Colony. The report will be troubling to some, but all I will share with you is the truth."

Mason turned slightly to look at Roby before continuing his presentation: "My Observer will confirm what I am reporting to you is factual, without prejudice or exaggeration."

The holographic image of the Council in front of Mason and Roby was from a distance—not allowing them to see the expressions of Council members as they heard the report.

"We have found the Earth Colony to be violating three areas in the *Rules of Engagement.* These include developing and using nuclear weapons against their own species, destroying the island's environment, and cellular manipulation."

The Newe's Council representative, Lintoo, interrupted Mason, "The law does not read 'manipulation' as you suggested,' Lintoo said, correcting Mason.

"You are correct. But to avoid reading the entire law, I tried to keep this concise and simple," Mason said. "I know your time is valuable. Any rebellious and illegal acts, on their own, would be enough to warrant taking immediate action against the Earth colony."

"I urge you, General, the Council is not short on time. And please, do not tell us how to respond. Now, please continue," the massive

Newebean Council representative said with a significant degree of authority.

"I apologize for my error, Council Member Lintoo," Mason said, holding back a sneering contempt for the correction offered by the Newebean representative.

Mason's thoughts were transparent to Roby, as they had always been.

I wonder why he does not say what he is thinking. Mason would enjoy eating Lintoo. Lintoo's size would keep Mason fed for days. Roby's sense of the absurd almost caused him to smile, but he remained statuesque as he sat by Mason.

"This next fact may prove incredibly troubling," Mason continued.

This may be enough to give him approval for the decree of annihilation of humans, Roby thought, awaiting Mason's disclosure of the presence of the gift in humans.

"How did mere Earthlings, what is truly nothing more than a slave, unlock the mind's abilities through cellular alteration? We all laughed at *The Prophecy of Isa* and the ridiculous prediction this could come true on Earth. The prophecy was true. The gift has infected humans," Mason continued but was again interrupted by the Newebean representative.

"Excuse me, General, we thought your presentation was a sharing of facts? Bringing up an ancient prophecy and simultaneously calling it ridiculous and true suggests what you are offering us is a prophecy of your own choosing," Lintoo interjected, laughing as he continued. "Is this creation 'The Prophecy of the Agent'?"

The Anguis representative immediately interrupted.

"The General is one, if not the greatest, of the military leaders in the history of the Confederacy. I would appreciate hearing what the General is saying without further interruption. Please show the General the proper respect he deserves."

300

Mason paused and waited to see if anything else would be said.

"I am speaking truth in facts. In *The Prophecy of Isa*, the writing directly referred to a quadrant in Middle Time of 78M102. We are in that quadrant of time. The prophecy directly referred to 'The Five,' five humans given the gift by a Newebean royalty member. As you all know, the prophecy said that The Five would lead a rebellion within the Confederacy and ultimately end our alliance during this time quadrant. The prophecy says the Atobean Revolution would spread throughout the universe, freeing civilizations from slavery, restoring power to the many, and removing power from the few. Based on the facts, what we know to be true, I undertook an exhaustive search for The Five. I have now captured four of the five. I now hold them in the Anguis Base here on Earth. I will continue my search for the fifth so-called gifted human. I commit to the Council I will have the fifth in custody very soon." The General paused, hoping the Anguis Council representative would now speak what was necessary.

"The General has done outstanding work. While I am dismayed to hear that an ancient prophecy may have some validity, it is better to take the next and most necessary step. Given the heinous violations by the rebellious Earthlings and the capture of what appears to be gifted leaders of a would-be revolutionary movement against the Confederacy, I now move to annihilate the humans on Earth," the Anguis representative said. "My esteemed Council members know this can be done quickly without harming the Earth island."

Mason was relieved and waited before he would speak.

"I second the motion of the esteemed Anguis representative," the Seda representative immediately followed.

Before calling for a vote of the Council members, the Newebean representative interjected.

"Respected Council representatives, hear my plea. The annihilation of any species has never occurred in the long history of the Confederacy."

The Newe representative's comments were spoken over by the Anguis Council member: "That is because no other colony has ever achieved this level of terror! We cannot allow slaves to hold the whip, or we may find ourselves slaves. And while none of my Council colleagues have experienced this, I can attest my family endured slavery."

"I agree with the proposed action," the words of Lintoo shocked every attendee, especially Mason. "We cannot ignore the threat. But first, before my approval, which is required to annihilate a species, we need confirmation of the threat. I request the so-called 'Five' be brought before us and tried here. If they are what the General says, we can proceed with the actions to remove the human threat. By bringing them here, we can make an example to benefit all of the Confederacy and the Collective. This will remind all of the consequences of revolt by any species anywhere, anytime," Lintoo, the Newebean representative, stated.

"I agree with my honored and respected Council member," the Anguis representative said, smiling. "But the time to allow their presence here will not remedy us of the threat. I would amend the motion to evaluate the captured members of 'The Five' on Earth to ensure they are truly gifted. After testing, I suggest the Council examines 'The Five' remotely before transporting them from Earth. This will also afford the General time to find the fifth gifted human. After this examination, the Council can declare the final order to annihilate the human species on Earth while the gifted humans are transported here for full effect and universal benefit. Is this acceptable to all?"

Even though he was light-years away from the Council, Roby could read the minds of all the members. *Lintoo approves of this plan. It is done,* he thought, briefly closing his eyes in frustration. *The General is correct: this is the Turn in Time as prophesized.*

After completing the unanimous vote, Lintoo said: "General, you will only execute the annihilation after final approval by Council following the examinations. You will rely on the means developed by the Newe to exterminate human life. We will begin plans to make this available to you. Is that clear?"

"I will do as ordered," Mason responded with a hint of frustration. "Hail the Confederacy!" Mason said, the Council echoing the words as the holographic image disappeared.

The General is trying his best to be the savior of the Anguis. With that would come great power. And with that power, he could finally tip the control of the Council against the Newe, Roby thought.

Roby sat quietly beside the General. He clearly heard Mason's thoughts and was unsurprised: *"I must find the last member of The Five. I hoped to have Alana for a fine meal, but that can wait. Instead, maybe I'll eat Roby.*

Hearing this, Roby did not flinch. Seeing out of his peripheral vision, Mason slightly turned to look at him as if the General was serious about his appetite.

Before Mason could speak, Roby said, "Congratulations, General. That went very well. Are you hungry? Maybe we could dine together?"

Mason responded, "Not yet, but maybe soon," offering the comment with a sinister grin lighting up the General's face.

The General thought Jonas was one of The Five, but the tests proved negative, and Mason ordered the boy to be exterminated, Roby thought. *The General does not understand the power of the gift and even what a young boy can do. The power of the one and the few will destroy the control of the many. He believes Marc Walker is one of The Five. Once tested, the General will be proven wrong. He does not understand why I identified Aaron as gifted and the consequences. Mason does not know the identities of the other gifted humans. Only two possess complete knowledge of this: Isa and me.*

Adak

Mason believed he had successfully abducted and now held all but one of the gifted members of "The Five." He had moved four of them to the Anguis underwater base on Earth south of Adak Island in the Aleutian Island chain.

Adak Island appeared nearly lifeless. Once a thriving military base for over six thousand World War II US soldiers, the base was now deserted. The harsh weather conditions ensured only a tiny population on the island.

The submerged Anguis mothership near Adak was the only Anguis base on Earth. The Council dictated the Anguis outpost in a compromise agreement to allow the Newe the right to colonize Earth.

The Confederacy's other two alliance bases on Earth were similarly located in remote, underwater locations to avoid detection. The Seda's base—again in an enormous mothership—was north of Easter Island. The Newe's permanent underwater base was in a deep ridge between Madagascar and Reunion Island.

The most extensive permanent base in the original colonization of Earth remained deep within the artificial satellite, the Moon. The Newebean leader at the time, Isa, had brought the sizeable orbiting object across the vast distance between the alliance and Earth to ensure a military presence was available to protect the island from attack. The artificial satellite appeared to be Earth's natural Moon, but its precise location and other unique, unusual anomalies suggested something much different. The exact orbital placement allowed the artificial Moon to appear the same size as the sun around which Earth orbited. Isa wanted this for numerous reasons, including a reliable tidal pattern, but there was more to the exact placement. Isa's desire for equality of all beings throughout the solar system was portrayed in what could be seen from Earth.

Built deep into the satellite, with access on the unseen side of the orbiting object, the military base was comprised entirely of New-ebeans. This fact continued to cause friction within the Council.

Only two obstacles stood between the General and the Council's approval to clear the path for the Anguis to begin their desperate relocation to Earth: testing the captive humans to ensure they were indeed gifted and finding the final, remaining member of The Five.

Should the Council change its decision on annihilating humans, Mason was prepared to do so alone. Mason and his small Anguis crew were secretly in the final stages of completing the delivery system to spread the virus to remove the Axis Mundi, ending all human life on Earth. A nuclear warhead was placed on the western slope of Mount Adagdak, a volcano on the northern tip of Adak Island.

The island's location and the consistent high winds—Adak was known as the "Birthplace of the Winds"—offered the perfect location to release the humanity-ending viral toxin that would effectively clear the Earth of human life.

As he walked toward the Observer's room on the gigantic Anguis mothership, Mason thought: *My family's life and every Anguis on our home planet, Draco, is at stake. I need Roby's help,* the General thought as he grew closer to Roby's cabin. *Maybe I won't eat him after all if he doesn't prove to be a hindrance.*

The thought made Mason chuckle as he walked down the spiraling halls of the massive mothership to Roby's quarters.

Before Mason could press the call button, the door opened as if Roby had been waiting for him.

"May I come in and speak with you?" Mason asked.

"Yes, General, please enter," Roby answered.

Mason looked around the cabin. While any hint of personal belongings was unexpected, the lack of almost anything in the large room paused Mason.

"Where do you sleep?" Mason asked, perplexed. "You do sleep, don't you?"

Roby offered a grin as he responded: "Of course, General. I'm not what humans call a vampire?"

"They actually enjoy being scared. That was a design flaw you Newebeans fucked up," Mason said, nearly chortling. "No offense intended."

"None taken," Roby responded, now smiling. "How can I help you, General?"

"We need to proceed with the brainwave scans as the first step in documenting each of The Five we now hold are gifted," Mason said, disgusted with the final word.

Roby heard Mason's thoughts and considered his response—the brief pause frustrated Mason.

"Are you gifted?" Mason blurted out. But before Roby could answer, he heard Mason's thoughts, something the General could not conceal. "I'm just kidding with you. If you were gifted, you'd be tried and executed," Mason said.

"You are right," Roby said, offering a flicker of a smile.

"And Observer's took a vow to never lie, so two strikes!" Mason said, laughing. "I'm positive you're not gifted. And please, don't take that as an insult."

"Thank you, General," Roby answered.

"We need to move forward with the examinations. The Council is in a hurry."

"I heard they wanted to be sure the captive humans were, in fact, gifted," Roby said, accentuating the word "gifted" to infuriate the General.

"I hate that word. It probably makes Newebeans feel special. It reminds me that we had been slaves once and had to fight to avoid extinction. At least your race did not have the opportunity to put a timebomb in our DNA," Mason said, a nervous laugh betraying his diminished confidence. "I understand that humans want to survive. But so do fucking ants," Mason said.

"I will meet with each of the captives and conduct the brainwave scans," Roby began but was interrupted.

"We will meet with them together. First, I want some time alone with each one. You may observe, but I want you outside the room. You have your tests. I have mine," Mason said. "And we need to move quickly."

"I agree," Roby responded, shocking Mason. And then he surprised Mason with a much more unsettling statement: "Dr. Walker is not gifted."

Roby was telling the truth, and that reality touched Mason's sense of what he was hearing.

Mason thought: *Why would he lie? But how could a human find something like the Axis Mundi? He may be using it to slow the process, making it two unknown humans I need to find.*

Roby knew Mason's thoughts would mirror the confusion it created over Dr. Walker.

Mason angrily said, "Impossible. Why the fuck haven't you said it before now?"

"I have not done any tests. What I have witnessed can be confirmed in the testing. There is one trait all gifted Newebeans possess, and that is their value of family. In the case of Dr. Walker, he gave you the power to destroy his family. You believe Dr. Walker failed in perfecting a vaccine. I believe he knew exactly what he was doing. Dr. Walker knowingly sacrificed his wife and sons. That's not normal for any Newebean or Anguis. I am certain he is not gifted."

Roby knew Marc Walker was not gifted—and the brain scan would prove this. Once the scan was available, it would force Mason to tell the Council that he had not found all of The Five—slowing the annihilation of humanity. This would force Mason to either reject the Council's order and attempt to take unilateral action to wipe out humans to save his own species or try to spend the time to find the final two members of The Five on a planet of eight billion humans.

Roby stood silently, listening to Mason's thoughts.

They're on the list. The gifted fucking creatures must be listers, Mason thought.

The listers (the genetically edited beings on Earth) were part of a record of all genetic edits made by the Newe. The list had allowed Mason to identify Alana and Jon Walker.

As Mason continued to think, he turned his back on Roby. Roby continued listening.

Mason thought, *If I am missing one, maybe two, then there is a conspiracy, a Newebean plot to conceal their identity.*

Mason slowly turned back to face Roby.

"Let us proceed as planned," Mason said calmly. "I would appreciate you working with my team to review the entire list, from top to bottom, for the missing edited humans."

Mason turned to leave, and his thoughts were now much different and alarming.

"I want to examine Alana first. I believe she knows more than the others," Mason said as the General's thoughts offered perverse images of him having violent sex with her and chewing on her while she remained alive.

Roby struggled to respond stoically, knowing the General's thoughts: "I agree."

Gifted

The room was even smaller than Alana's previous confinement.

At least I'm not strapped down in a bed, she thought, surveying the surroundings.

Alana had awakened from the drug-induced sleep to find herself in another prison cell.

She was nude, lying on a small cot-like inset when she first gained consciousness. The walls were smooth and black. The only light came from each corner of the high ceiling. The effect of the black walls and ceiling and dim light was unsettling. The bed was barely padded. A blue one-piece jumpsuit was on the floor beside the bed. The tight-fitting clothing was made of a material she had never seen before. There was no zipper. When she pulled the jumpsuit on where the material met across her chest, it bonded without any Velcro.

The room had a metal sink, commode, and shower area without any privacy enclosures. The door was barely visible—the crevices around it so tight a razor could barely fit. There was no means of opening it from inside. Despite the surreal setting, Alana felt much more in control and confident.

I'm no longer afraid, she thought. *I am here for a reason. I must be prepared to see this through*, Alana thought as she pushed a button on the sink's faucet, leaning over and drinking the cool water.

She immediately recalled the words of her grandmother: Know no fear.

Am I really in Alaska? The entire room feels like it is moving.

Alana sat back on the small bed and shut her eyes, her back against the incredibly smooth dark surface covering the walls, ceiling, and floors.

This place is floating. It's a ship. It's like when I'm surfing, on top of the board in calmer waters. The motion feels like gentle waves.

Even though Alana could not remember the last time she had eaten, she felt invigorated and stronger than ever.

As a test, Alana dropped to the floor and began doing pushups. She realized she was not fatigued as she counted the repetitions, passing one hundred. Alana stood, jumped, and touched the high ceiling.

The ceiling is probably fifteen feet high. How can I jump that high?

At that moment, the barely visible door abruptly opened. The General and the same two gigantic soldiers Alana had seen in the last location stepped into the small room.

"Hello, Alana. I hope this room meets your approval," Mason said.

"I am hungry," Alana said without emotion.

"I am hungry, too," Mason said, looking up and down her body. He turned and looked upward at the soldier to his right, "Bring our lovely guest some food."

The General and the second soldier remained standing, looking at Alana.

"I would like to have a private conversation with you. I'll tell you why you're here and answer any questions. But you must promise you won't attack me, or I'll have my friend return and ensure you're held down. Will you be a good little girl?"

"If you touch me, I will hurt you," Alana said firmly.

"I guess we are going to have to agree to disagree," Mason said, laughing. "If I want to touch you, I can and will. But I promise, for this conversation, I promise I will not touch you. You have my word."

"Your word?" Alana chuckled. "I don't trust you, and I'm not afraid of you."

Looking at the second soldier, Mason said, "You may leave, but stay close, just in case our gifted guest changes her mind."

When Alana heard Mason say "gifted," she understood how he meant the term with some level of respect and possibly fear. Sensing this from the General gave Alana more confidence, even though she did not know why. She knew he remained in control.

As the soldier left the room, the other enormous guard returned carrying a metal tray with two silver metallic containers and a cup.

"This may not be exactly what you like, but it is nutritious for your kind," Mason said, taking the tray from the soldier. "You can leave, but stay close."

Mason presented the tray to Alana, and she took it, sitting on the side of the bed. Her hunger pains had awakened. As Mason watched, she opened the round metallic container. It looked like it contained soup. It smelled like a chicken soup her grandmother had made for her. Opening the rectangular container, she saw two pieces of pita bread. There were no utensils. After smelling the soup again and taking a sip, Alana gulped down the contents of the container. She then took the bread and devoured both pieces, keeping her focus away from Mason, who continued to stand by the door, his arms crossed, a grin on his face.

Looking up at Mason, Alana calmly asked, "Why am I here?"

"You are here because you are an exceptional, unique human. You have a gift that makes you this way. I'm sure of it. You will have some tests not long from now that will confirm what I said is true. You are gifted."

"What does that mean…gifted?"

"You are different from other humans," Mason said.

"Where are we?"

"You are submerged near Adak Island, approximately one thousand feet below the surface. The island is off the coast of Alaska," he said.

"This doesn't have anything to do with being a suspect in a murder, does it?"

"No! It's not because of what you've done but your potential to create chaos," Mason responded as his eyes narrowed in a more intense stare. "That is why you're being held here."

"You aren't a General in the US Army, are you?"

"Yes and no. I am like you. We are this, and we are that, two different things simultaneously."

"How am I two different things at the same time?"

"You are part human and part Newebean."

"What is Newebean?" Alana asked, somehow already knowing part of the answer to her query.

"The Newe is the species that first colonized Earth. The Newe are your ancestors. And before you start feeling good about the Newe, they created humans to be slaves, never to be as evolved as you are. You are a hybrid, a human with a rare gift the Newebeans bestow on a fortunate or unfortunate few. I need to understand why you are the way you are and who did this to you," Mason said with the most sincere tone she had heard.

Then Alana heard something...a voice.

No, it's not a voice. It is Mason's thoughts!

In astonishment, Alana almost sprang up from the bed, nearly dropping the tray from her lap to the floor. She immediately placed the tray on the floor.

"Are you alright? You look like you were frightened?" Mason asked, unsure of Alana's strange reaction to what he had said. "I'm not threatening you. I'm here to find answers. And if you help me, it will make it easier on both of us."

"You believe I am all of the things you say I am," Alana said as a statement, not a question.

After briefly pausing, Mason crossed his arms and answered: "Yes, I do. I am sure of it. We have some tests to prove you are gifted. The tests will not hurt you. They will simply confirm the type and volume of your brainwaves and brain utilization. They are scans. We will not touch you. I will give you instructions to follow. If you follow the instructions, you will not be touched, and the test will not take long. After that, we will talk again," Mason said, turning to leave the room and stopping to ask. "Will you follow orders?"

Alana stood and said, "You fear me."

Mason smiled as he closed the door and said, "Yes, I do."

Before the door closed, Alana responded, "You should."

CHAPTER TWENTY-FOUR
ENEMY OF MY ENEMY

Mason and the two soldiers walked down the hallway to the cell where Marc was being held.

As they opened the door, Marc met the first soldier with a vicious punch to the enormous soldier's jaw, momentarily knocking the giant soldier backward into Mason.

Mason stepped back and said, "Dr. Walker, you need to calm down. Or I will do it for you."

The two soldiers stepped into the room as Marc backed against the wall. The soldiers stood less than three feet from him, forming a barrier between him and Mason as the General entered the room.

"I came here to chat with you, but you decided to act human," Mason said as he started to laugh. "The next time you move to attack one of us, I will order these fine soldiers to break your left arm and then the right. You get the picture, Doc?"

Marc stood still—fearing to move a muscle.

"Don't make me hurt you because I will," Mason glared. "You've been relatively accommodating so far. Please don't fuck that up," Mason said.

"What do you want?" Marc asked. "I've done everything you asked. I know how this all ends. I'll be dead."

"Why so dramatic? I am going to run some tests on you. Don't worry, there's no probing," the General said, chuckling. "Only the Sedas do that shit. We are actually trying to find out just what you are."

"What kind of tests?"

"To test your brain utilization...brainwave scans...to see if you are what we think you are."

"What do you think I am?" Marc asked, unsure of where the conversation was leading.

"I want to see if you are gifted," Mason said.

"And if I refuse?"

"Refuse? That is not going to happen."

"You have what you wanted from me. I helped give you your doomsday weapon. Why aren't you using it?"

"I will in time. I promise. First, I need to test you. My colleague and I have differing opinions on your mental skills whether or not you are gifted. I think you'd appreciate my perspective more than his.

"What do you mean by your perspective?"

"I think you are gifted. There's no way I can fathom you aren't gifted. What you've done is remarkable, Dr. Walker. I'll be the first to say that. A human discovering the Axis Mundi is extraordinary. My colleague, Roby, do you remember him?"

"Yes, I remember Roby. Tall, weird, and creepy as fuck."

"Yes! See, we can agree on some things, Dr. Walker. He thinks you're not gifted."

"If I'm not to use your word, gifted, what does that mean?"

"I'm not sure. But the consequences for you—they're probably the same. I'm not going to lie to you. You will die, but we all do...eventually," Mason answered.

"You're going to kill me. Why should I do anything to help you?"

"I am shocked by your considerable concern over your mortality. Aren't you interested in knowing your ancestry?"

"I'm ready to die."

"Again, you're confusing me with someone that gives a fuck. I have to say, your reaction to your family dying also nags at me. Did you love your family?"

"Yes, I loved my family," he said. "Enough to free them from slavery," Marc said, growing angry. "There are worse things than death."

"The Newe are the ancestors you raved about. They are your family. You are right. Humans were created as slaves by the Newe. The Newe put a time bomb in each human. If they wanted to rid the Earth of the species, it could be done easily without harming the island. Implanting each human with what you call the Axis Mund is sick, warped, criminal behavior."

Mason paused before continuing: "I am not Newebean. I did not create you and put you in slavery. My family...my species, the Anguis...were enslaved by the same species that created you. That is the truth."

Marc was stunned. He leaned back into the wall behind him. He could not speak.

"Don't you want to know who you are?" Mason asked.

Sitting motionless, Marc shut his eyes without responding to the General's question.

"Your brother is here. I have no doubt he is gifted. You will see him soon if you comply with the brainwave scans."

"What do you mean my brother is here?"

"Because he is gifted," Mason said.

"My brother has no part in this. Let him go," Marc said, trying to comprehend why Mason had brought Jon to this place.

"He may now have an even larger role than you will," Mason said, turning his back on Marc to leave the room.

"Wait!" Marc said, still not moving from his position against the wall.

"Yes, Dr. Walker," Mason said as he turned.

"Are you going to use the toxin and wipe out humanity? There's an ancient proverb on Earth: the enemy of my enemy is my friend. If what you say is true, humans could be an ally against the Newe."

"Before we try to find common ground, I need you to be tested. Do you agree to be tested?" Mason asked.

Marc shut his eyes and dropped his head, responding in a low voice, "Yes, I agree to be tested."

"Good," Mason said as he left the room, leaving Marc alone.

Brothers

After his experience with Marc Walker, Mason allowed the two soldiers to step into the room ahead of him.

Jon Walker was sitting calmly on the bed. He appeared to be relaxed with his legs crossed and his muscular frame leaning against the wall.

"Good morning, Jon," Mason cheerfully said.

"I wouldn't know," Jon said, smiling.

Despite the conditions, Jon had found solace in having time to piece together all the seemingly random events he had experienced over the past two weeks. While he did not fully understand everything, he knew his experiences had a purpose. And Jon had found peace in the knowledge Jonas was much more than Catori and even he expected.

I'm not losing my mind. I think I've finally found it, Jon thought.

"It looks like you're in a good mood. I'm General Mason. Perhaps you've heard of me?"

"I know who you are," Jon said. "I heard you were an asshole years ago."

"Well, Jon, we have something in common. I heard you were an asshole, too," Mason responded.

Jon quickly spoke, "You should get better troops around you, General. These two need work. They are pathetic."

One of the soldiers released an audible growl.

Jon looked up at him and smiled. "Next time, I'll finish you."

"Boys, let's all get along. Let me share some good news from one asshole to another: we've brought you here to be with some of your family. It's going to be quite a reunion," Mason said, smiling.

"Where the fuck am I?" Jon asked mockingly.

"You're closer to home than you can imagine. You're near Adak Island. But you're submerged a thousand feet or so."

"Adak Island? That's a bit remote. Why did you bring me here?"

"Because you are gifted, Jon!" Mason boisterously said, moving closer, standing slightly behind the two giant soldiers blocking Jon's path to the General.

"I'm gifted?" Jon chuckled. "Maybe you have the wrong person, General," Jon responded, looking down as he clinched and unclenched his fists.

"No, I disagree! We're going to run some tests on you to make sure. Will you be so kind as to try your best not to resist?" the General asked.

"What kind of tests?"

"We actually need you awake and engaged in the test," Mason said. "I promise it won't hurt a bit or take long."

"Maybe I don't want to be tested? Have you thought about that?"

"Of course I have! That is your nature! Jon…listen to me. Please don't make us hurt you, even though my friends here would enjoy it," Mason said as a smile formed.

"They couldn't stop me before. How could they now? I don't see any rocks around here, right, dumbass?" Jon said, looking at the soldier still favoring his knee, wearing a glove to cover the hand Jon had severed in Alaska. "By my count, you're a hand and a leg down in the body count."

318

"Jon, let's be civil. What if I tell you that if you do not consent to be tested, it will not be you we hurt? What if I tell you we have some-one else here close to you? Your brother is here. If you choose to not be tested, I'll have you watch me kill him. And if you attack any of us, I'll have him killed," Mason said. "Would that change your mind?"

"Why the fuck would you have my brother here?"

"You'll see him as soon as we get you two tested. And the test will work like this. We will leave. I'll speak to you over a communication network here, open the doors, and guide you to a small room down the hall. You'll go in the room, lay down on a table, and be still for less than a minute. That's it. You'll then return to this room, and we will get you something to eat. I promise it won't hurt. It's not a trick. It's just a test for brainwave utilization. I promise."

Even though Jon distrusted the General, he could sense he was tell-ing him the truth.

Brainwave scan, that is really funny, he thought.

"You've been chasing me all over the country to see if I know my ABCs?"

"Not even that much. Depending on the outcome of the test, you will be out of here in less than a day or two at the most."

"Can I see my brother after the test?"

"Yes! I was planning a bit of a reunion!" Mason buoyantly an-swered.

"Is my brother here because of his genetic work? I'm guessing you saw it as a weapon? I thought of that the first time he mentioned it to me. He thought I was crazy. I told him I was thinking like the military thinks," Jon said as he looked at Mason.

"You can't imagine how close to being exactly correct you are! I think you'll be disappointed when you hear about some of his choices," Mason said, laughing. "He let his family die and didn't blink."

"Let his family die?" Jon said as his smile disappeared and his eyes narrowed, focusing on Mason. "That is the last thing my brother would do and help you make a bioweapon. I'm disappointed, General. Now you're lying."

"I am telling you the truth. Your brother let his family die. You can ask him yourself! It was his failure and his choice. He either fucked up, or he sacrificed them. I think you care more about your family."

"I don't believe my brother would knowingly let his wife and sons die," Jon said, hoping to move past the General's comment about family and possibly Jonas. And even though Jon said he did not believe Mason, he again sensed the truthfulness of the General.

There's no way Marc would do something like that. There's got to be more to this. I need to see Marc to find out what is happening.

"If you get tested, I will make another promise. If you submit quietly to our scan without a fight, I will leave you in a room like this with the man who killed your son, Jonas."

"What the fuck did you say?" Jon said, bolting up from the bed.

The two soldiers closed ranks in front of Mason.

"There's no reason to get mad at us. We didn't do it! We are holding him here, just down the hallway from you. I promise, Jon, I will give him to you on a golden platter. You can do what you want to with him."

Unexpectedly, Jon heard Mason's thoughts.

It's more than a sense. It is what Denali shared with me. Mason thinks he is telling the truth, but Jonas is not dead. I can also sense that.

"My son is not dead," Jon said before he could control his utterance.

Do not speak my thoughts. I should have learned that by now. Shut up, Jon, keep your big mouth shut.

"I beg to differ. Jonas is dead. He was on an Indian reservation in Idaho. The killer murdered your son and buried him somewhere outside of Pocatello. I wouldn't tell you this if it wasn't true. Just do what I ask, and I'll give him to you soon. Revenge will be sweet. Do we have an agreement?"

Jonas is not dead, but I need to see my brother, Jon thought, pausing before responding to Mason.

"Ok. Test me."

"That's a deal, Jon. And I promise I will help you get your revenge."

Unhinged

Mason and the soldiers left Jon's cell and walked to the next cell where Aaron was being held.

Unlike Jon, Aaron's captivity had unhinged him. Aaron wanted to die. He did not care about anything.

The sight of the door opening made him fly into a frenzied attack on the soldiers as soon as they began to step through the door. Aaron's fighting skills had not diminished in his pain.

Leaping forward before the first soldier could move, Aaron landed a direct punch to the near-giant combatant's throat. The soldier fell back, stunned and gasping for air. The second soldier was already on Aaron by the time he had pulled back his fist, but he was ready for the soldier's aggression.

Twisting and using the soldier's momentum, Aaron slung him hard against the wall. Landing an array of quick fist blows to the soldier's face, Aaron kicked the soldier's knee. Unbeknownst to Aaron, this was the same knee that Jon had shot less than forty-eight hours earlier. The soldier fell in a heap, the excruciating pain and face punch incapacitating him.

Aaron then turned to Mason—the person he knew had issued the kill order on Rebecca.

"Your turn, General," Aaron said as he moved toward Mason. The first soldier stepped in front, struggling to recover from Aaron's attack seconds earlier. Using all of his strength and momentum, Aaron landed a vicious punch into the face of the enormous soldier. Aaron saw Mason turn and run away down the dark exterior hall as the soldier fell back. Instead of immediately following, Aaron spun the nearly unconscious soldier around and viciously twisted his neck, the sound of the break audible. Looking at the other soldier still writhing in pain on the floor, Aaron viciously kicked the soldier in the chest and ran out of the room down the hall in the direction Mason had left.

The corridor was narrow and curving. Running at full speed, the lights in the hallway went dark. Aaron could not see anything. Walking down the hall, touching the sides of the wall for guidance, he shouted, "Mason, I'm going to fucking kill you! Trying to hide won't help. I will find you!"

As his anger propelled him into the pitch-black darkness, Aaron suddenly met with an impact that touched every part of his body. The unseen force knocked him backward. Nearly unconscious, Aaron saw Mason standing over him, holding a truncheon in his right hand.

"I guess we will do this the hard way," Mason sneered. A bright light flashed, causing immense pain and immediate blindness. Aaron felt something pierce his stomach as he lost consciousness.

Aaron awoke, barely able to see—his vision still blurred. He was locked down to a flat metal table. The bindings on his wrists and ankles were metal, allowing almost no movement in his limbs. Looking around the room, he saw Mason walking toward him.

"Wake up, you fucking insect."

Amid the turmoil, Aaron heard someone speaking to him. It was Roby.

Do as you are told. You have something essential you will need to do.

Aaron immediately stilled and remained silent.

"You killed one of my soldiers," Mason said, leaning over him, a drop of fluid from Mason's mouth falling on Aaron's cheek.

"I apologize. I meant to kill all of you," Aaron said calmly.

"We will have time to play later. First, we are going to run a little test. I would tell you to stay still, but I don't think you have many options on that," Mason laughed as he stepped away.

The room went dark, and then a dim light glowed above Aaron. While he could feel no physical sensation other than the cold slab of smooth black metal he was lying on, his mind reacted with memories resurrecting from his past.

For Aaron, it was like some had said of the experience before you die.

My life is flashing in front of me, he thought.

Aaron saw his past speeding by from his earliest memories in a swirling tide of thoughts that made him close his eyes. There was his mother and then Rebecca. And then the Detective. And then he heard the audible crack of him viciously breaking the soldier's neck.

Breaking into the stream of memories was a vision of Roby standing next to him in the hospital. His mother was lying in the bed near death.

You were there from the beginning. You've always been in my life. How could I forget?

The vision ended with a sound and vibration.

Aaron opened his eyes, and Mason was gone. The metal clasps had been released. Mason's voice boomed through unseen speakers in the room.

"Go back to your room. The door is open. It is the only open door you will see. You cannot go anywhere else. If you try to do so, you will be brought down like the ant you are."

Again, Aaron heard Roby.

Do exactly as you are told.

Aaron responded in thought to Roby, *I will.*

Walking out of the room, he proceeded down the narrow corridor past numerous other sealed doors to his room. Aaron entered, and the door closed behind him immediately.

"Out of all your family here, I will enjoy seeing you die the most," Mason's voice sounded in the room. Even though Mason was not in the room, Aaron could hear his thoughts momentarily.

The General isn't lying, Aaron thought. Then he heard Roby's words.

I am here. I will see you soon, Roby said.

I need you, Aaron thought, realizing it was one of the only times he had admitted he needed help. Sitting on the bed, Aaron lowered his head, covered his face with his hands, and cried like a child.

Reunion

Mason had completed the tests on each of his captives.

While Roby was not privy to the testing outcome, he read Mason's thoughts and knew the results.

"You were right. Marc Walker is not gifted. Thank you for your honesty," Mason said with painful sincerity. "All three of the others are gifted. And surprisingly, the most powerful of them all," Mason said when Roby interrupted.

"Alana is the most powerful."

"Only a Newebean could compound the stupidity of putting the gift into a human by placing it in a woman," Mason said, looking for a response from Roby.

Roby knew the Anguis culture's unsettling perspective of the female gender.

"I would assume they are all very powerful," Roby responded, deflecting from Mason's comment.

"Yes, but they are part human. I've traveled large quadrants of the universe and know of no other species as disgusting as humans. Why would anyone implant the gift into a human? Since you're Newebean, I thought if anyone knew, a Newe would know?" Mason mockingly laughed.

"Does that unsettle you, General?" Roby asked.

Mason was surprised by Roby's sarcasm, sparking Mason's simmering rage.

"Would it unsettle you if an Anguis or Seda was similarly gifted," Mason responded quickly, barely able to contain his anger.

"Neither of those species has ever been a recipient of the gift," Roby said with no hint of emotion, deflecting Mason's query.

"You fucking arrogant Newebean. Your people created humans to be slaves. And then your people engineered a way to kill off an entire species they created with one breath of air. That's cruel and immoral," Mason said in a slow cadence, the volume of his voice rising as he spoke. "You believe you're intellectually and morally superior to us? All evidence to the contrary."

Roby concurred with Mason's perspective. Roby was not loyal to either the Newe or the Confederacy.

He will see where my loyalties are soon, but not yet, Roby thought.

"I understand your perspective, General," Roby said in response.

"I beg to differ," Mason said, growling, almost spitting the words out as his long tongue briefly appeared in his anger. "My family were slaves, much like the humans. We had to fight to gain our right to survive. If we had trusted your species to do the right thing, there would be no Anguis today. You enslaved your creation, part of your family. How the fuck can you or any Newebean judge me because of my appetite?" Mason asked. "That's my nature. And I control it. But slavery is your choice! Be careful. Someday, your species may decline and ours in ascendancy. And on that day, you may be the main course for a hungry Anguis!"

Mason cultivated the threatening insult by swiping his long tongue over his lips. Roby did not speak. The General continued as if the other comments had never been made.

"Roby, I have two problems, as do you," Mason said in a conciliatory tone.

"We do not have all of the gifted," Roby interrupted the General without any emotion in his voice.

"You said we! That is refreshing!" Mason nearly shouted. "We are in this together! And you're right! We only have three of the gifted: Alana, Jon, and Aaron. Jon's son is dead, but he was not gifted. There are still two gifted humans that have not been detected. The Council turned all of their Newebean intellects on this, looking at every recorded lister. Based on what they are saying, they do not know the identity of the undetected gifted humans."

Roby knew Mason's thoughts and waited.

"There remains a simple solution to both find the two gifted humans. My idea is this: we request the Council approve the toxin release. Whoever, wherever he or she is, the gifted humans will remain alive, and the rest will die. It's simple and effective. No humans…no problem. Afterward, the gifted will be detected easily."

"We do not know if the toxin would kill a gifted human. That's an assumption. We know this: removing the Axis Mundi will kill humans. But the gifted are, to use your word, half-breeds," Roby said, using Mason's words to give him more confidence in speaking his mind with him. "The toxin may or may not work as you assume. And I heard the Council, as you did. They want the genetically enhanced humans brought back alive to make an example of them. That is as important to them as killing off nine billion humans."

326

"I knew you would say that!" Mason laughed and looked upward for a moment as if in contemplation. Then, quickly dropping his head back down, looking at Roby, continued: "I've got a solution. We will test the airborne toxin on the captives we have."

"This would most certainly kill Dr. Walker," Roby stated but was interrupted by Mason.

"And your point? The human that sold out his family will be our control subject!"

As Mason laughed, Roby responded: "The Council wants all of the gifted to be returned for public trial and execution. If the toxin kills them, what then?"

"I've thought of that, too," Mason interrupted. "I will talk to the Council and present our dilemma. I am sure they will agree with my plan," Mason confidently said.

He is right. The Council will probably accept this as an option. He does not know that Jonas is still alive and gifted. And the General does not know the identity of the final undetected gifted human.

But Roby was genuinely concerned that the toxin may prove deadly for even gifted humans.

It's a risk, an unknown, Roby thought.

"May I make a suggestion, General?" Roby asked after pausing.

"Be my guest," the General said, bowing as if in honor of Roby's request.

"Let us first meet with them as planned, in a group setting, before we take the next step you suggested," Roby said. "This will take minimal time and will not cause any issues in the next steps. By doing so, we may learn more. One of the answers we seek is to find who enhanced humans with the gift. This may prove pivotal in finding out. It is one of the steps we told the Council we would do, and they approved it."

"It's like you could read my mind," Mason said, looking at Roby skeptically. "The second concern I had that I haven't voiced is exactly how dangerous these gifted humans are? Intellect is more than brain capacity and mental abilities. Alana is the most powerful but shows limited intellect. The only thing that impresses me about Alana is her ass," Mason chuckled. "Unless her brain is there, you can rule out her intellectual gift. She does not even know how much power she has. If she had control of one percent of her power, I'd be dead right now," he said morbidly, snickering. "She cannot harness what she does not know she has within her. The same goes for Aaron. My greatest concern is Jon. He is already showing signs that he is something greater than any human."

"You are more concerned about him because he is a warrior?" Roby asked.

"Precisely. Jon knew what his brother found could and would be weaponized by the military. The funny thing is I think he hates humans as much as I do. Unlike his brother, he holds his tongue and is light years more intelligent and perceptive. He is the most dangerous of the group, in my opinion."

Roby paused. He could hear Mason's thoughts coming to terms with going through with the suggested examination. Allowing the General more time to think through the consequences, Roby remained silent.

"We can do this examination quickly. And it will serve our purpose. I want to give Jon the gift of revenge. I want to watch Jon tear Aaron apart, and he will once he hears Aaron say he killed his son."

"Isn't it more about your own revenge, General?"

"Revenge is a two-edged sword in this case. Aaron killed Jonas, and Aaron killed Nosmon, one of the most loyal Anguis to ever live. Nosmon did not deserve to die like that, at the hands of an insect...a lowly human. The way that creature killed Nosmon reminded me what humans can do when left up to their human nature," Mason thought-fully said. "Let's bring them all together and see what happens."

CHAPTER TWENTY-FIVE
ALL TOGETHER

Mason called each one of his captives by intercom to the central arena, one by one.

He ordered each to leave their cell separately and directed them to individual small rooms containing a metal chair. Surprisingly, all complied without resistance, including Aaron. None of them had an opportunity to cross paths—each assuming it was another step in the testing process.

Mason directed them to sit in the single oversized black metallic chair, dominating the space in the small, closet-sized rooms. Immediately after each one was seated and putting their hands and legs in position, as Mason requested, metal bindings appeared, securing their ankles and wrists and holding them in place.

After each captive had been confined to the chair, Mason turned out the lights in their respective confinement areas. The General would let them sit alone in the darkened space for several minutes before bringing them down to the center of the cavernous room.

The Anguis referred to similar spaces in their native language as the *Tua Nukkanna*, translated as *arena*, in English. The arena offered the Anguis a setting for fights to the death, the only sport enjoyed by the species. The large circular room below the mothership's flight deck was immense. The ceiling was over twenty meters above the floor at the center of the arena—a pronounced slope leading down from the top of the area to the bottom created the atmosphere the Anguis sought, despite its location inside a spaceship.

At the top of the arena were a dozen rooms spread equally around the circle, typically used as spaces for individual Anguis gladiators, four now holding Mason's captives. Each of the four holding rooms would remain closed, hidden from the rest of the arena. This would allow Mason to open the doors and bring them together to the center.

Mason was now excited with Roby's insistence on examining the gifted humans in a communal setting.

"The one thing humans had right was gladiators! Their ancient arenas looked very similar to our own. I'm unsure if you've ever seen Anguis gladiators in a fighting pit, but this is the smaller-scale version. It works perfectly for our purposes. We will wheel them all out and down to the floor simultaneously. We may even see a battle to the death," Mason almost giddily shared as he stood with Roby in the center of the arena.

The Anguis love individual combat, Roby thought, wanting to smile but suppressing the desire to show his emotions at the General's enthusiasm. Roby turned from the General and surveyed the massive room as Mason stood patiently enjoying the thrill of being in total control.

The Anguis mothership had initially held a crew of forty-four on the current tour of duty. That number had now diminished to Mason, the gigantic soldier Damron (the brother of Nosmon, the soldier Aaron had killed), and three other Anguis soldiers.

Roby now understood why so many of the original Anguis crew had vanished.

The confinement to the mothership had likely led to infighting, Roby thought. *The popularity of blood sport battles probably accounted for many deaths to entertain themselves and find closure in any conflicts between each other. And, while they had tried to keep it hidden from other species, the Anguis history was peppered with multiple stories of insurrection and mutiny against their own leaders. The bloodlust of the Anguis has helped to thin out the soldiers, which will help serve our purposes.*

Given his objective, Roby was relieved that fewer Anguis soldiers were onboard the craft.

Despite its enormity, the spaceship only required a single pilot. The craft contained a fleet of smaller vessels, including six V-shaped craft and two larger elliptical-shaped vessels. Mason, Damron, and Roby all had the prerequisite abilities to pilot the massive spacecraft and smaller vessels, as did the three remaining Anguis soldiers on board the mothership.

Distracting Roby's thoughts, Mason declared, "Let the games begin!" he said in a loud, ringing voice as he pushed a button on a hand-held controller, opening the door to each of the holding cells high above the pit. He waited a moment for dramatic effect and then pressed a button that began the movement of each of the chairs, gliding the captives slowly down to the arena floor.

Simultaneously, each one of the captives started the slow descent toward Mason and Roby. Each struggled with the much brighter light Mason had chosen to temporarily unsettle their vision as they left the pitch-black room for the enormous arena space.

Jon looked to his right and saw his brother in the next closest chair. Marc was not looking around. Instead, he was staring straight ahead. Jon then looked to his left and saw a woman. She seemed to look familiar to him.

I recognize her, Jon thought. *She is an Olympic athlete. She's calm, like this is no big deal. Either that or she is a hell of a good actress.*

Looking directly opposite him was a man Jon had never seen. His senses about the unknown man reminded him of what Denali had told him, that he would meet his brother.

Mason said one of these would be the person responsible for killing Jonas. I know Jonas is alive. I sense his presence. Mason said the killer was a man. Is this the man? Jon questioned in his thoughts.

Despite the lengthy confinement, Alana continued growing in her confidence to survive the captivity. As the chair she was secured in glided down, she briefly surveyed the entire room, looking for exits first. She then briefly glanced at each of the three men confined to chairs.

That is Dr. Marc Walker, she thought, having seen him many times in news reports over the past few years.

She then remembered he had a twin brother, a war hero.

That must be his brother, she thought, taking a quick glance at the man. *They look alike but are definitely not identical twins.*

Turning to look at Aaron, Alana had an immediate revulsion.

Something is wrong with him, she thought, turning back to look at Mason and then Roby.

Alana had to suppress her desire to smile at the tall, strange-looking man near the General.

I know you. Hello, she thought. Immediately, Alana heard a silent response from Roby.

Hello, Alana.

"Welcome to my home away from home," Mason said as all four reached the arena's pit.

"I'm sure you all have lots of questions. And we will try to answer some of them. You can look at this as a group interview and a way to be introduced to each other. I am going to ask some questions. If you want this to go quickly and painlessly, just be honest," Mason said as he slowly spun in a circle to see each of the captives as he spoke.

"First, some introductions. I am General Mason. I am a US Army General and a General in the Anguis military, the greatest military force in the universe. As some of you have guessed, I'm not human.

But neither are some of you, one of the reasons you've been brought here."

Mason paused and walked in a circle close to each chair of his captives.

"I thought that might get your attention. One of your human sayings is, 'You can't tell a book by its cover.' That fits nicely. I'll use myself as an example. I appear human, but I am not a human. I am Anguis. As much as I detest it, I will continue to wear this skin covering so you will find it easier to communicate with me. In my natural form, I would surely intimidate you, maybe even frighten some of you."

Mason walked to the front of the chair Jon was bound in.

"This is Jon Walker, a war hero. But Jon is afraid of the dark. Look at Jon. All of the muscles and strength. But he's a drug addict and an alcoholic. Like I said, you can't tell a book by its cover," Mason chuckled and paused. "Jon has done extraordinary things, primarily killing other humans. He killed humans because he was ordered to protect his country," Mason said as he leaned over Jon, inches from his face, as he continued.

"God bless America, right Jon? Have you thought about who you were fighting for? All those deaths just to help satisfy the pitiful greed of a few select humans," Mason turned, shaking his head. "I can't say he woke up to this paradox because Jon never sleeps. Finally, something clicked, and Jon figured out he had been used. Jon's hatred and distrust of humans drove him to move as far away from people as possible. But you can run only so far, Jon," Mason said, interrupted by Jon.

"Who the fuck invited you to our planet?" Jon asked, his anger overflowing as he stared at Mason.

"Who said it was your planet, Jon?" Mason calmly answered. "I think the creators of humans would strongly disagree."

Mason stepped away from Jon's chair and walked toward Alana.

"This is the lovely Alana, an Olympic athlete. She is undoubtedly the top female athlete on Earth. She is beautiful, and she can be deadly. Alana is trained in just about every human discipline to harm others. Why would she train in everything from knives to guns? Three men sexually assaulted her a few years ago. They would have had their way with her if she wasn't as strong and gifted as she is. Three men attacking a woman, imagine that. It was in their nature, as it is in so many humans. The three men that tried to rape her are now free, enjoying life. The human justice system chose to deliver justice where it could be afforded. Humans talk about justice, but how was justice served? Alana isn't a fan of humanity, in general. Can you blame her?" Mason asked, turning his back to Alana. "We share that in common. I hate humans. They disgust me."

Pausing to turn and lean over Alana, within inches of her face, Mason said, "We share something else in common. Alana hates being confined, a slave to someone else. I, too, despise the idea of being a slave. Long ago, my family was slaves to a species called the Newe," Mason stood erect and paused. "I share that in common with humans. Humans are slaves to their creator, the Newe," Mason said, pointing to Roby. "Who are the Newe? Our Observer, Roby, is a Newebean. Say hello to the species that created humans and simultaneously enslaved them."

Turning back to look at Alana, Mason continued: "While you may hate me, you cannot deny we both hate humans. Don't we, Alana?"

Alana refused to answer.

Mason walked toward Jon and said, "Jon, you hate humans, don't you?"

"Not necessarily humans. I just hate windbag assholes," Jon responded.

"A windbag asshole? There's no better way to introduce Jon's brother, Dr. Marc Walker," Mason said, smiling as he walked toward Marc.

"You can't tell a book by its cover. Dr. Marc Walker helped save millions of lives, finding a cure for a pandemic and then for cancer. Married with two children, Dr. Walker won the Nobel Prize and was acclaimed by millions as the world's smartest man. But Dr. Walker isn't what you think he is. Dr. Walker cheated on his wife more times than even a genius can remember. And he voluntarily gave me the means to end the human race, the ultimate weapon. Making things even stranger, his failure to produce a vaccine to protect humans killed his wife and sons when he was testing it. He agreed to use them as the lab rats," Mason stopped as Jon interrupted.

"You're a liar! My brother would never do that!"

Turning slowly to look at Marc, Mason crossed his arms and asked barely audibly, "Dr. Walker, am I lying?"

Marc sat with his head down in silence.

"Silence is an answer, Jon," Mason said as he dismissively shook his head. "I'm telling you the truth. Why lie?"

"Marc, just tell this alien piece of shit he is a liar," Jon pleaded.

Marc remained motionless, refusing to answer.

"Dr. Walker will go down in the universe's history for his part in ending human life on Earth. No need for applause," Mason said, patting the metal tightly securing Marc's hand. "Interestingly, despite his accomplishments, Dr. Walker appears to be different from each of you. He is the only human in this room. That strongly supports my thesis that there is nothing a human wouldn't do to further their self-interests, including sacrificing their family."

Marc said nothing. Jon looked at him. Despite faintly hearing Mason's thoughts, he could hear nothing from his brother.

"Marc, please say something," Jon nearly pleaded.

"That was awkward," Mason chuckled. "Moving along, three of you are well known. Some might even say celebrities because of your accomplishments. I'd like to introduce a person who makes it his life's work to be unknown. In his life of anonymity, he has several identities, but let's go with calling him Aaron to make it easy. Aaron is a shadow, the darkest side of humanity. In this case, he may not initially appear to be a bloodthirsty assassin who has killed countless people, even innocent children. But Aaron is. He killed two teenage boys in Maryland. After killing the boys, Aaron shot another round into them. If that wasn't horrific enough, he kicked them. Imagine the type of sick being that kicks dead children," Mason said with disgust.

Jon vividly remembered the appearance of the two boys in Canada by Monte Lake.

But they told me they were killed by my brother, Jon thought, trying to make sense of the flood of information being shared by Mason.

"Aaron takes his orders from a secret organization within the US government called the Order, but similarities to Jon and other soldiers end there," Mason firmly stated as he moved to stand directly behind Aaron.

"In his defense, Aaron suffered just like each of you from racism. There are different responses to the pains inflicted by ignorant, prejudiced humans. Some, like Jon, rise up and fight. Some, like Alana, become accomplished athletes. Some, like Dr. Walker, pursue academic achievement to prove the prejudiced assholes are wrong. But some join in. Instead of lifting up, they go low and try to fit in. Doing so, they perpetuate the worst traits of humans. Imagine a slave working for the slaveholders, killing other slaves. This is the case with this creature," Mason said, angrily smacking Aaron on the back of the head. "Aaron hates humans even more than I do. Given what I've said, that may sound impossible, but it is true. And what I am going to share will prove my point. Aaron has intimately touched the lives of two of you in this room. He killed a soldier and created a crime scene in a volcano in Maui to pin a murder on Alana," Mason said, looking at Alana. "Alana, everything you went through can be placed squarely on the shoulders of this shadowy scum."

Alana maintained her silence and kept a fixed stare downward.

"The second person this murdering thug has touched is you, Jon," Mason offered in an attempt to sound empathetic. "Aaron kidnapped your five-year-old son, Jonas, from a reservation in Idaho and killed him, burying the body somewhere outside Pocatello."

Jon glared at Mason but refused to speak.

Suddenly, Jon heard Alana speaking to him in his thoughts. *Jonas is not dead. Aaron kidnapped your son but returned him safely to his mother.*

"Aaron, am I lying?" Mason asked.

"You are telling the truth. I was ordered to kill and dispose of Jonas. I follow orders. I killed him and disposed of the body," Aaron said without hesitating. "It is true, I cannot recall how many humans I have killed, and I hate humans. And yes, I killed two boys in Maryland."

Jon again heard Alana. *Aaron is lying to protect Jonas. Mason thinks your son is dead. Your son is alive because of Aaron.*

"See how he takes pride in killing?" Mason asked.

"I killed Jonas on orders. You gave the orders, General. And I also killed one of your goon soldiers trying to protect you from me," Aaron said.

Before Aaron could continue, Mason stepped closer and unleashed a vicious smack across Aaron's face with his open hand.

"You will pay for killing Nosmon. His brother will make sure of that," Mason snarled.

"General, are these the same two soldiers that I kicked their asses? If they are, I'm not impressed with ending one of them. They definitely aren't soldiers," Jon joined in laughing.

"This assassin killed your son, and you're laughing? Jon, I am shocked. Maybe you are more human and less gifted than I thought," Mason said in frustration.

"General, may I ask a question?" Alana interrupted, hoping to deter Jon from speaking his thoughts aloud.

"Yes, please."

"What is gifted?"

"Being gifted separates you from humans. You were all brought here because we believe you may be a genetically enhanced, altered human. If so, you are half human and half Newebean," Mason said.

"Why is that important to you?" Alana quickly followed up.

"Gifted half-breed humans represent a danger," Mason answered. "Humans are enough of a threat without having enhanced abilities."

"What is your problem with humans?" Alana asked.

"What has humanity done in its history? Kill and destroy. Killing other humans is as much of human nature as breathing and eating. Humans even build monuments to killers. Humans slaughter other humans over lines drawn on a map and a flag they wave. Humans, much like their creators, practice colonizing and enslaving. Humans believe they are superior to other humans because they are different in skin color or appearance," Mason's voice rose as he continued. "Humans kill other humans out of greed, prejudice, and arrogance. And what they can't kill, humans destroy. Humans destroy everything they touch. This very planet is suffering from the human infestation. Is there anything I am saying that is not true?"

Pausing, Mason slowly turned to look at each of his captives. "I laugh when I hear humans proudly and reverentially refer to their species as the 'human race.' Here's something you don't know, but it is true. Racism is universal. Racism is present throughout the entire vast universe. And the Newe is one of, if not the most, racist species in the universe," Mason said, turning toward Jon. "And those are the ancestors you can thank for putting the Axis Mundi in humans to keep them in line as slaves forever!"

"Every human has a ticking bomb inside, courtesy of their creator," Mason said. "That is how humans were engineered to be easily annihilated. Dr. Walker's work in genetics got their attention, finding the bomb, what he calls the Axis Mundi. The lab rats were learning how to fight back. And now, with the help of Dr. Walker, I have the same power as the Newe, the power to destroy every human on Earth. Thank you, Dr. Walker."

"Did you create a bioweapon to destroy human life?" Jon asked, looking at Marc.

"No," Marc responded, shutting his eyes. "The bomb was already inside of us. I gave General Mason the fuse to light the bomb."

"What is wrong with you?" Jon asked.

"Nothing is wrong with me. I've made choices you may disagree with, but everything I have done is for the good of humanity," Marc responded.

After a brief silence, Mason spoke: "Please, Dr. Walker, explain what you have done. I would like to hear your answer, too."

"I did not create a weapon. In my research, I discovered the DNA signature code, the Axis Mundi. If the Axis Mundi is removed from a human, the human will die," Marc said. "This was the intent when it was engineered into human DNA by the creator of humans, the Newe, to annihilate human life without harming Earth. The Newe have held this power since they first created humans. Using an airborne virus to remove the Axis Mundi, the Newe could kill every human in hours. I developed this capacity and gave it to the General. He is telling the truth. Humans were created to be slaves and easily exterminated. The end was always inside every human, waiting for their creator to end human presence on Earth. The General will destroy humankind, not me," Marc said soberly. "By ending human life before becoming slaves, humans defeated their creator. The final victory for humans is in extinction. My conscience is clear. There are worse things than death, Jon. One of them is slavery. I choose freedom in death, not life in bondage," he said as he tried to move his arms and legs as evidence. "There was no other option."

"Why give up? We can fight!" Jon shouted.

"That's a nice thought, Jon, but it is impractical given that the Newe have the weaponry right now to destroy every human on the planet. Your brother's choice to not submit to your creators as slaves is brave and logical. The only way you can win is choosing to die in freedom," Mason nearly shouted as he stepped toward Aaron, "not giving those slave-creating assholes what they want!"

Mason turned and looked briefly at Roby before continuing.

"I believe, ultimately, humans were created to serve as soldiers, to fight and die for their creator," Mason stated. "If this was allowed, humans would inflict death across the universe, all for the benefit of the Newe. I commend Dr. Walker for fighting back the only way possible. It is the most humane thing I've known a human to do!"

"Why don't you join humans and fight with us? Lead us if you're serious about fighting to free slaves?" Jon asked.

"My species are no longer slaves," Mason answered. "We were forced to agree to allow the Newe to colonize this island, or, as you call it, a planet. We are in an alliance with the Newe in the Confederacy."

Jon interrupted Mason, laughing, "The Confederacy? That seems to be a perfect name for it."

"I guess it is, given your human history. But we've been around much longer than humans. And we may have been around longer than the Newe. They just found a way to gain more power," Mason said.

"If you are part of the Confederacy, and support the Newe, then I have two words for you, General: fuck you," Jon said coldly.

"I understand how you feel. But now, I want you to listen to me closely. What I am about to say does not apply to Aaron and Marc. They are as good as dead. But Jon and Alana," Mason said, walking first toward Alana's chair, "I want to offer the two of you an opportunity to live. By living, you will have the opportunity to fight the Newe. I promise."

"You said Marc is human, but the three of us are gifted," Jon said, pausing. "Is the assassin my brother?"

"Bravo, Jon, you are truly gifted. Aaron is your brother! Or should I say, Aaron is your half-brother. You two shared the same mother, a mother neither of you knew, probably off-world. I'm not sure about who your respective father is. But that doesn't matter at this point," Mason said, gleaming. "Jon Walker, say hello to your long-lost brother and the murderer of your son. Damn, that is keeping it in the family!"

"Is Marc my brother?" Jon asked.

"You'd have to ask the cook, the one that mixed you all up in their own perverse genetic concoction," Mason answered. "When it comes to the Newe, family lines get blurry. But just like I know Aaron is your half-brother, I can tell you, truthfully, that even though you were twins and shared the same mother, you were intentionally given the gift, and Marc was not. How fucked up is that?" Mason laughed. "That is what the sick, warped science of the Newe will do. They find a way to fuck up family reunions!"

Alana had been able to read Mason's thoughts the entire time. Roby had been quiet until now, but after Mason's words, she heard him silently say, *Do not believe what Mason says.*

I do not believe him. But are humans slaves? she asked in silent thought.

Yes, as long as the Axis Mundi is viable as a means to initiate extinction, humans are slaves. But you are different. You were created to help humans gain freedom. You are more. So are Jon and Aaron. In that Mason is speaking the truth, Roby thoughtfully responded. *But Mason does not understand everything you are and what you can do. If he did, he would kill you and me.*

What do I need to do? Alana asked.

Be patient, Roby responded. *Aaron is an assassin but lies to protect Jon's son from Mason. The boy is similar to you, Jon, and Aaron. He is gifted.*

I will be patient, Alana responded. *I knew Jonas was gifted. I could hear Aaron's thoughts.*

I thought you could, but I wasn't sure, Roby silently responded.

Mason stood before Alana, asking, "Will you help me, Alana?"

She stared at him and said nothing.

Mason shrugged his shoulders, turned away, and walked back to Jon.

"Jon Walker, will you help me? I promise to help you. And to prove it, I'll let you have your revenge on the person who killed your child," Mason said cocking his head in confidence as he finished speaking. "You can put an end to your half-brother, Aaron."

Jonas is still alive. Mason truly believes Jonas is dead. And that is good for Jonas. There is safety in Mason believing he had died, Jon thought.

At that moment, with Mason a foot away, Jon heard Alana's thoughts speaking to him: *Aaron is protecting your son, saying he is dead. Do not do what the General says. Do not kill Aaron. He is here to help us protect humans.*

Jon was stunned but controlled his emotions.

"Why aren't you answering me, Jon?" Mason was asking.

Jon spoke in his thoughts to Alana: *I do not believe the General. But I am going to play along for now.*

"What do you want me to do?" Jon asked, responding to Mason.

"Just follow orders and do what I tell you to do," Mason said.

"And I can have my revenge?" Jon asked, smiling.

"Absolutely, I want to see that. That will come soon, but not yet," Mason said.

"I have trouble following orders. Let me think about it," Jon said as he spoke his thoughts to Alana. *This will hopefully give us a chance to get free from Mason.*

I hope you're right, Alana responded.

Mason suddenly clapped his hands together in a single loud sound, drawing attention.

"First, we're going to give you all a test. You're going to all be exposed to Dr. Walker's toxin. Then we will see who is left alive," he said as he walked up the slope toward an opening at the top of the arena. Turning before he left the room, Mason laughed and said, "What did your evolutionary scientist call it? Oh yes, survival of the fittest. We will see who is fit."

CHAPTER TWENTY-SIX
ON TRIAL

Roby remained in the room.

Hearing Mason's words, Roby immediately spoke to Aaron in his thoughts.

Exposure to the viral toxin should not harm you, but I am not sure. Stay calm. I need your help.

Aaron listened. But hate was drowning out everything happening around him.

Aaron hated humans, and he fervently hated Mason. He hated Marc Walker. Most of all, Aaron hated himself. The people he had loved were dead. And Aaron knew the reason. He had himself to blame, but he felt those in power had used him as a pawn. He felt his entire life had been a lie or, worse, a horrible joke played on him.

Aaron looked up at Roby, and his rage spilled over into words. "Fuck you!" he shouted and dropped his head down. The others were not sure who he was yelling at. But Roby knew.

Roby was concerned. He knew Mason would be expecting him to leave the arena and was probably watching and listening to what was happening in the room.

He wordlessly spoke to Alana next. *The toxin should not harm you. Know no fear.*

It won't harm me. I know there is more to do, Alana responded as she sat calmly.

Roby turned from the four and left the arena.

Jon Walker looked at Marc, realizing what delivery of the toxin would do to humans.

"Marc, does the toxin really work?"

"Yes. I created it. It will work, and it has already worked. My family is dead."

"If Mason is telling the truth, the toxin will only kill humans," Jon said but was interrupted by Marc.

"It will only kill humans. I am the only human in the room," Marc said, still appearing relaxed and distant. "It's not your time, my brother. But we all die, Jon. For me, this feels like we are on trial."

"On trial? What do you mean?" Jon asked.

"It feels like much more than gifted beings and now the toxin. It feels like humanity is on trial. The verdict hangs in the balance," Marc said, refusing to make eye contact with Jon.

"Why did you agree to help Mason?" Jon asked.

"You've never trusted me, Jon. I'm not surprised you do not trust me now. But I've always respected you, even though you have wasted your life. You've spent most of your life trying to avoid reality. Your world has been built around believing in good and bad, right and wrong, and thinking you know the difference. You haven't learned it yet, but it is easy to swallow a lie if you want to believe it," Marc said, looking at Jon briefly and saying, "That's the truth."

"That isn't fair," Jon responded but was talked over by Marc.

"You've drunk yourself into hideous intoxicated stupors, thinking that would take away the pain of living a lie. How dare you even hint at judging me! I'm immersed in reality. I know what is real and what isn't real. That's why all of this is a shock to you. Now you're presented with reality and can't run away to a remote cabin or find a bottle to hide in. It's your fate, my brother, the one you constructed," Marc said, looking into Jon's eyes. "You've cheated death, and you've cheated life. And now here you are, submerged near an Alaskan island, forced to come to terms with what I've discovered. We are slaves. We are in bondage. We always have been. It's a hereditary trait implanted by our creator and enforced by our kind and family. As long as we live, we will always be slaves. We cannot escape what we are. Fuck the creators. I'm going to send them a message they'll always remember."

"I forgive you," Jon said softly, looking at Marc, trying to find closure.

"I don't want your forgiveness! I am doing what is necessary. Doing what is necessary isn't as easy as pointing a gun and squeezing the trigger at someone you are ordered to kill. There are no orders here, just choices. I've made mine, my brother. Fuck your forgiveness! I don't want it!"

Mason stepped back into the room and paused at the top of the arena.

"When I leave the room, we will deliver the toxin into this space in a few minutes. It is odorless. You won't sense anything, at least that is according to Dr. Walker," Mason said, chuckling. "If it works, it will happen within a few minutes. Dr. Walker will probably be the first to know. This may be the last time we are together. To quote one of the few humans worth quoting, 'The past is prologue.' And thank you, Dr. Walker, you helped prove what most of the universe already knew: humans deserved their fate…extinction. I bid you all farewell until the next time."

Mason smiled and left the room, the door sliding shut behind him.

All four sat silently until Alana spoke.

"We aren't going to die from this."

"How are you so sure?" Marc asked. "Are you a fortune teller now?"

"I know. None of us will die from the toxin."

After several minutes, nothing had changed. They were all sitting without any effects from the airborne release of the toxin in the room.

Mason and Roby were standing, looking at a monitor outside the arena.

"You were wrong, Roby. Dr. Walker is gifted. That means we have all but one of the gifted here. That will speed things up," Mason said, turning away from the screen to look at Roby. "I want to be sure of this before we talk to the Council. But if the testing is flawed, then you are flawed. And how can I really know if any of these Newebean slaves were actually gifted in the first place? Or was it all a hoax?"

"The testing is not flawed. The results were correct," Roby said, still staring at the screen.

"That's impossible. I see Dr. Walker alive and well in that room. I know his wife and children, and Dr. Allen died from something. He's either gifted or the toxin is not what it is supposed to be," Mason said. "I want some fucking answers!"

"Dr. Walker administered a vaccine to himself some time ago."

"That's impossible! We administered the vaccine he prepared to his family, and they died!" Mason snarled, shouting at Roby. "How can you say that?"

Roby turned from the monitor and looked into Mason's eyes.

"The tests were accurate. Dr. Walker is not gifted. He is fully human. The only way Marc Walker remains alive is by taking a vaccine that works. What he created in captivity, given to his wife and children, was not a vaccine. And he knew it."

Mason paused and turned back to look at the screen.

"There are not many things I would ever say I could trust about humans," Mason said, shaking his head, "but the one thing I would say you can trust is that a father would never knowingly kill his sons and wife. That's colder than I could ever imagine."

"How is it humans killing other humans a surprise to you, General?" Roby asked. "You were saying this a few moments ago in the arena. Anguis kill other Anguis. They do it for sport. And despite the technological advancements of my own species, we chose to create a subservient species of slaves."

Mason stood looking at the monitor and quickly turned, grabbing Roby by the throat.

"You fucking Newebean. I swear if you are lying to me, I will kill you and have you for a meal," Mason said, his eyelids flashing evidence of his species. After a second, he released his grip and turned toward the monitor. Mason could hear voices from within the room and listened.

"How are you alive?" Aaron asked, matter-of-factly looking at Marc. "I thought you were human?" he asked, laughing.

Marc did not say anything. He shut his eyes as if he were no longer present in the room.

"You are gifted," Jon said with a hopeful tone. "They were wrong. That explains how you've been able to do all of this. You are gifted."

Marc opened his eyes and glared at him before Jon could finish speaking.

"Jon, shut the fuck up!" Marc shouted.

Aaron looked at Alana and asked, "How did you know none of us would die?"

Alana looked at Marc and said, "He is unlike the three of us. Dr. Walker is fully human."

Jon erupted, "That's impossible! He is still alive! Explain that!"

Aaron turned his gaze toward Jon and said, "You should listen and shut the fuck up. You're embarrassing yourself."

"Don't you tell me to shut up," Jon said, glaring at Aaron, his face growing red and the veins in his neck and arms popping out as his anger flowed.

"Calm down, soldier. Get a grip and listen. Just think for a moment about what you know. Your brother is alive. His family is dead. How does that happen?" Aaron sarcastically asked, smugly chuckling.

"I would guess, no, I know what Dr. Walker did. Do you want to hear it?" Aaron asked. "Or have you figured it out? No, that's not possible. You'll only understand if someone gives you orders about what is happening."

Jon's anger held his response in check long enough for Alana to speak, directing her words to Marc.

"You created a vaccine and used it. It protected you. But it didn't protect your family? That only makes sense if the vaccine you used on yourself was different than the one you gave to your family," Alana said, looking at Marc. "You made a choice, didn't you? You chose to kill your family. You gave them a placebo. You let them die. And you chose to live."

The room fell silent for a moment before Marc responded.

"The power to create is the power to destroy. Would humans share a vaccine with other humans? Or would they use it as leverage? We know the answer. Imagine if a nation or even a small group of people had the power to detoxify people it chooses and then threaten to use the viral toxin as a weapon. Forget blackmail. Imagine using the vaccine as a weapon, withholding it from so-called enemies. A vaccine makes a quick, clean genocide a reality. In the last pandemic in 2025, the richest countries hoarded and controlled access to the cure, leaving poorer countries and even poorer people in their own countries waiting and dying. Imagine that with something that could kill any human that did not have the vaccine. What would happen if I took the vaccine to a drug company? The vaccine would be worth more than diamonds; only those with enough to pay for it would live. There was never a way to deliver a vaccine to all of humanity without turning the vaccine into a weapon. Can you think of a way? Tell me and leave your self-righteous judgments of me out of it," Marc said coldly. "The vaccine is as deadly in the wrong hands as the toxin. Humans are to blame for that reality."

"You killed your own family," Jon said. "You hypocrite. You're no brother of mine."

"I did not kill them. I gave my family freedom. It was a choice," Marc said. "They died a painless death, something that is far from cruel. They were already dead, as you are, Jon, and the rest of you. The difference is you're still breathing, but it won't be long before you meet your end. And I'm not a hypocrite. I'm just honest," Marc said, turning his attention to Alana and Aaron, saying, "You know I did the best thing for my family."

After pausing, Marc continued as the three remained silent: "Here is the reality I spoke of earlier. Almost every significant discovery, from nukes to vaccines, is tightly held as the property of those who can control it. They use it for their benefit at the expense of others. They gain power from it. Now, think of survival of the fittest. That's what humans do to survive. The 'fittest' is not defined by physical traits. Being fit to survive is having the power to survive. Possessing power makes the survivor fit."

"You're taking that choice from humans, the power to survive," Alana said.

"You want humans to choose? Hasn't anything I said sunk in? Even a being from another planet understands human nature better than you do!" Marc laughed. "There is an economy of survival. 'What's in it for me?' is true north for humans. Humans always do what is in their personal self-interest. Humans are selfish by nature."

"If anyone is selfish, I think it's you," Aaron said, almost spitting out the words. "Economy of survival? You shortchanged billions of humans just so you can say, 'I know best because I'm smarter than any of you.' I'm a sociopath. I understand what I am. But you do not know what you are, Dr. Walker."

"Reality check. Sharing the vaccine was not humanly possible. Humans would have destroyed billions of other humans out of greed and

351

fear in their own self-interest," Marc said, pausing, slowing his speech, and evening his tone. "Knowing this, I destroyed the vaccine after I tested it on myself months ago," Marc admitted. "Now you dare to judge me, assassin? Do you want to know what is toxic? It is humans. We are toxic. We do not deserve to live. And living as a species of murderous, greedy slaves more inclined to destroy each other than join together to fight against our oppressors was never an option for me. I know humanity all too well. I know myself and what I am. I've been called a genius. But knowing what I know about myself, I know what humans can do," Marc said, stopping to look upward.

"I cured cancer, up to that time, the deadliest killer of humans. And what happened? I received death threats for putting so many people out of work making a living from caring for people with cancer! I was ridiculed for not making a fortune from selling it to the highest-bidding pharmaceutical company. I learned from experience. That is all I need to know. Humans are no better than their secrets. And if you are honest, you know every human is guilty...as charged. The crime is being human."

"You're a murderer. You're no better than me," Aaron responded.

Marc said, pausing: "Yes. I chose to allow my family to die a painless death. And I will do all I can to help Mason do what he intends: destroy the rest of humanity, the rest of my family, before they are used as soldiers and slaves. They will all die a painless death."

"You fucking asshole," Aaron said, sneering. "I agree with Alana. You took away the chance to fight for freedom," Aaron said. Turning to Alana, Aaron said, "And I disagree with you, too. I have my doubts about whether Dr. Walker is actually human. He doesn't sound human."

"What is a human being? Do you even know? Do you want to lecture me on the value of human life? Human beings are what to you...targets? Mission objectives?" Marc said, glaring at Aaron. "You said it. You are a sociopath. You admitted you killed Jon's son and two teenagers, and how many others? How many dozens or hundreds have you killed? Did you really lose count? Or do you have a notepad somewhere with a list of your kills? Admit it, assassin. You're like Jon. You take orders. And then you kill whoever you are ordered to kill. But that is not an excuse. You want to kill because you hate humans. You hate humanity. You have no right to judge me as a human being. The one thing we know for sure is that I am the only human being in this group. I alone speak for my species! I know what is best for my species."

Aaron sat silent as Jon lowered his head. Alana spoke.

"You asked a question. You asked, 'What is a human being?' Why don't you answer that for us? I would like to hear that since you claim to be a human," Alana said calmly.

"I don't want to hear anymore. Dr. Walker is convincing me humans should die," Aaron said. "Maybe the fucker is right? If Walker is a human, I want him dead!"

"Shut up! I want to hear his answer. Dr. Walker, what is a human being?" Alana nearly shouted.

"Every living creature shares one common trait: they are a resource. No matter how big, powerful, and intelligent, we all serve as a resource. Even in death, we help fertilize the ground. Human beings thought they had climbed to what they believed was the pinnacle of the evolutionary pyramid. We were the ultimate consumers, and everything else was a resource. For us, the law of nature is to eat or be eaten, and humans choose to devour everything. They grew blind to the reality: eat all you want, but you're always a resource."

Marc chuckled at the absurdity of his last point.

"I can say this because I am a human. When we looked around the planet, we didn't see life. We saw opportunity. We ate creatures that were smarter than us and even more moral. We devoured everything not because we had to or needed to but simply because we could do it. I'm guessing eight out of ten people in the US are obese. Yet, some areas of our planet have people dying of starvation. How can you defend that? I do not doubt that the universe sees the hubris of humans and says, 'They need to go.' Would you tolerate something like us? And now that at least a few humans know we are not at the top and someone else is in control, we need to look at humanity from a much more honest and realistic perspective. The truth is that humans are a resource. Not only were we greedy, selfish killers, we were ignorant! We are slaves, a resource made for this purpose. We cannot deny our history of enslaving each other destroying other species and our planet. The fact we are all bound to the chairs we are now seated in attests to not being in control. Someone else is."

The large room fell silent. Marc dropped his head and was barely audible.

"I found a way to remove the creator's means of destroying us, but I could never find a way to remove the same inherited traits that remind us we are very much like our oppressors, something we just didn't know till now. Do you want humans to kill others, serving as slaves for a species light years away? Is this what you want? If you do, then you are inhumane, not me."

"Just because they view us as a resource does not mean we submit to them," Alana said. "You said it yourself: every species fights to live. Why not us? Why take that away from billions of humans?"

"Humanity is already dead. I choose to make it a choice that is painless for humans and painful for the slaveholders. In death is our only victory."

"Bullshit! I was a victim, but I learned to defend myself so that wouldn't happen again," Alana said.

"It did happen! After that, you were abducted. Look at you now, strapped down in a chair! For all of your 'gifts,' you couldn't stop being a victim, again, could you?"

"We can submit, or we can fight! What you're missing is the power to survive. A human being fighting out of greed is not as powerful as a human fighting to live on. You're taking that power away from billions!" Alana passionately responded.

"Power corrupts. Power even corrupts the will to survive. Humans are never satisfied with what they have. That thirst, craving, lust for more. Does all of that originate from the need to survive? It's a perversion of what you call the will to survive. And we can't tell the difference! Which human traits are more prevalent? Love... generosity... empathy? Or do they sound something like this? Pride... greed... lust...envy...gluttony...wrath...sloth? Jon knows what those are. Do you? Those are the Seven Deadly Sins. Seven words that fit humanity like a tight noose. We do not need a compromise with our creators. We need a conclusion."

Marc paused before continuing, turning to look at Alana.

"They control us. They can wipe us out in one blast of a nuclear warhead on Adak Island that will spread the viral toxin around the earth in twenty-four hours. You choose to fight? You say the greatest power humans have is the desire to survive? I say an even greater power is choosing to not survive. That power goes against evolution, genetics, and what has been drummed into us by the forces of nature and nurture throughout our lives. Forces that began with a corrupt creator. We do have a choice. And I'm making it for my species. The only weapon we possess is the power to destroy what they want. And they want us. We have the power to destroy their resources. That's all we have! I rest my case. Humanity has a choice, and I'm making it count."

"I heard you quote the creator of the nuclear bomb. What did he say when he realized the destructive power of what he created?" Alana thoughtfully asked.

"Oppenheimer quoted Hindu scriptures, the *Bhagavad Gita*: '*Now I am become Death, the destroyer of worlds*,'" Marc responded.

"And now you are death, and you are destroying a world. And your choice to end billions of lives makes you the same as our creators: a tyrant," Alana said. "And if being a tyrant is hereditary, then we can choose to rebel against it. It's a choice, not a genetic certainty. And I promise I will do everything possible to stop you and them."

"You sound so brave and courageous. But you're bound to a chair. You have no power. Whatever your gifts are, they are not serving you very well. You're like us. You're a resource. I know Mason. I can only imagine what he has planned for you. You're going to have horrific things happen to you before you die. Death is something you will wish for," Marc coldly said. "That's reality, and there is no escape."

"If I could escape, I know what I would do," Aaron said, interrupting Marc. "I'd ensure you got what you want so badly for humanity. I'd end you with prejudice."

"I'm sure you would," Marc said smugly. "You need to understand what I'm doing to help Mason. Three hundred years ago, if you were captured and onboard a slave ship sailing from Africa, and you knew what would happen in the future, all of your family, your future generations, would be enslaved and face horrific pain and suffering, I am sure you would do the same as I am now. You'd revolt and ensure the ship sank with all on board dead and end the horror before it was allowed to continue. You would understand it is better to stop the chain of events before your family endures it. Nothing ends slavery better than removing the slaves from the equation. Am I right, assassin?"

"Being right about slavery does not give you the power to choose for others," Aaron said. "I'm glad you weren't my ancestor."

"The highest state of being is to be free," Marc responded. "That is what I am creating through self-destruction. You aren't human. You're a much lower life form. A creature that kills women and children. You're slightly more evolved than pond scum but far less moral than a virus."

"Moral? Did you just say moral?" Aaron said, laughing. "And who killed their wife and children? That wasn't me, Doc. What you can't stand about me is I am a mirror. Looking at me, you see what you are, but in more detail. Shine a light in the dark places of every human, and you'll find me. You have decided you are the judge for humans. How am I different? Even on my best day, I will fall short of killing eight billion. And if I get a chance, I'll show you what pond scum can do," Aaron threateningly said as he glared at Marc.

As soon as Aaron had finished speaking, Mason and Roby entered the arena. The two walked down to where the four were bound in the metallic seats. The enormous soldier, Damron, entered on the opposite side.

"Dr. Walker was right. Humanity is on trial," Mason said as he used a controller to move Alana and Jon upward from the center area of the arena. Once they were moved halfway between the floor and the top rung, he said, "Let the games truly begin."

Mason released the binding around the wrists and ankles of Aaron and Marc. Both were shocked and stayed seated momentarily, trying to comprehend what was happening.

Aaron understood. Roby spoke to him in thought, *No!*

But it was too late.

Aaron bolted from the chair and sprinted toward Marc.

Marc responded, barely able to get out of the chair before Aaron began his attack.

Jon shouted, "No! Stop!"

Aaron threw Marc backward against the chair and began viciously punching him in the face. Marc appeared to submit, offering no defense against the attack.

Putting his hands around Marc's neck, Aaron shouted, "You want freedom? Breathe in eternity!"

Using all of his strength, Aaron choked Marc to death. Marc put up no defense as he gagged for his last breath.

Marc had given up.

"You fucking killer! I will end you!" Jon said, in shock from witnessing Aaron strangle his brother to death.

Mason turned to Roby and said, "One less problem to deal with."

Aaron remained over Marc and did not see Damron quickly moving on him, plunging a device into his neck.

Falling over on top of Marc, Aaron lost consciousness, his hands still around Marc's throat.

Damron walked next to Jon, stabbing the needle into his neck, and then followed, doing the same to Alana.

"The verdict is in for humans," Mason said, smiling, looking into Roby's eyes. "Guilty...and the sentence is death."

CHAPTER TWENTY-SEVEN
PASSION

Alana awoke lying on the cool metallic floor.

Through the murkiness of regaining consciousness, she heard a noise and saw Jon Walker lying beside her. They were both nude.

Jon began to awake and turned to look at Alana. Neither of them spoke, choosing to remain quiet.

Mason's voice began to sound within the room.

"We will have you both back in the arena for examination by our Council very soon. But I thought I would do this first...call it a win-win for all. You now have the opportunity to enjoy each other's company. It may be the last pleasure you have while you are alive. And while you may not be happy with it, I'll be watching. That's a win-win. You're both together, gifted, and as partial human beings, you are both appealing, so act accordingly."

Both of them sat up and instinctively moved away from each other. Alana sat with her back against the wall, crossing her legs and covering her breasts with crossed arms.

Jon moved against the wall across from Alana, seemingly out of respect. They faced each other in silence.

Alana hoped Jon could hear her wordless voice. She thought, looking at him, *Can you hear me?*

Jon heard her. Without changing his expression, he responded, *Yes, I can hear you.*

We only have one advantage. Mason does not know we can communicate like this, Alana shared in silence.

I understand, Jon responded. *What can we do?*

Let's think for a moment, Alana responded. The two remained motionless, looking into each other's eyes.

Mason's voice boomed into the room.

"This doesn't look like what usually happens when two humans are nude together," Mason said, chuckling. "Time is wasting! You two should take advantage of this treat. If you don't, I may have to intervene. And I doubt you would like that. I'm doing this to give you both some pleasure. Call it my gift to the two of you."

Without speaking, Alana looked at Jon and crawled across the room on her hands and knees, stopping at his feet.

We need to do this to have any chance of getting out of here. I know Mason's threat is genuine, Alana spoke in her thoughts.

Jon looked at Alana. While he knew she was speaking out of necessity, he was overwhelmed with a desire to be with her. *This was meant to be. I want her. We need to consummate this passion.*

Jon's thoughts were immediately known to Alana.

I feel the same. I'm unsure of everything happening to us, but this is part of what was destined to happen. I want this.

Putting his right hand to Alana's cheek, Jon leaned forward and silently responded, *Yes, this is part of our destiny. I want this, too.*

Alana climbed on Jon's lap as he remained sitting up, his back against the wall. Sharing deep, passionate kisses, both caressed each other's sculpted muscular bodies. Their passion was unbridled.

Despite knowing Mason was watching, they both became lost in their need to share all they felt. Both moved in perfect synchronicity, a dance meant for them to perform and be joined in together.

They stood together, still kissing and gently touching each other. Alana moved back against the wall. Jon placed his hands on her hips, lifted Alana upward, and entered her as she wrapped her legs around his thick, muscular back. As they rhythmically moved in a symphony of passion, both shared the same thought: *The future is now.*

Their intensity profoundly affected Mason as he sat alone, watching Alana and Jon on his monitor, his long tongue flicking across his lips.

I hoped for this, but more is happening here, something I can't explain, Mason thought. *Did I make a mistake letting them be together?*

The doubt quickly faded. As Mason watched, the General's natural instincts began to elicit different emotions and desires. He wanted to interact but feared it would interrupt what he was thoroughly enjoying.

"I'm going to have some of that, too," he said aloud as he continued transfixed by the imagery, his long tongue gliding out and nearly down to his chin as he lustfully licked his lips.

After nearly an hour of endless unrestrained passion, ending with them locked together on the floor, Jon and Alana held each other tightly.

I know you want to kill Aaron, but he has a purpose. I do not understand it yet, but I know he is meant to be here and help us. Please, do not kill him. I believe you can speak to him as we are now. You will need to listen to him and talk to him silently.

Jon was stunned. He held Alana tighter, but his thoughts betrayed him.

If I have a chance, I will kill him. He killed my brother in front of me.

Alana's words intruded on Jon's thoughts: *I know how you feel. But there is more here to seeking revenge. You must promise me, do not kill Aaron. You may need to help him. Can I count on you?*

Jon responded: *I will do my best. But how can a serial killer, a sociopath who killed two boys, help us save billions of lives?*

His presence here is not an accident. This was destined. This was meant to be, just like us being together. Please, listen to your heart and trust me. Now, hold me tighter.

Jon obliged as Mason abruptly broke the silence in the room.

"Thank you both. I hope you enjoyed your time together. That wasn't so bad, was it?"

Neither responded to Mason as they held each other with their eyes shut, waiting to see what he would say next.

"As we have done before, you have a choice. You can either comply with what I'm asking or you enjoy another forced sleepy time. Damron is waiting outside if you choose non-compliance. Will you do as I ask?"

Both responded in unison, "Yes."

"Good! Now, Jon, I will open the door, and you will exit to your right and walk down the corridor to the next open room. There you will find clothing and food," Mason said as the door opened.

Jon looked at Alana and wordlessly said, *Stay safe. We will do this together.*

Alana responded, *Yes, stay safe. And do not let revenge overwhelm you. You can do this. I know you will.*

She smiled as Jon nodded slightly as he stood and walked out of the room. After Jon left, the door closed, and Mason spoke.

"You will do the same, Alana, except exit to your left and proceed to the next open room. There is food and a shower to clean up from your romp in your room. Please do so, act accordingly," Mason said sinisterly, laughing.

The door opened, and Alana walked out of the room and down the narrow, spiraling walkway to the next open door.

She entered and found food and water on a small table. Needing nourishment, she devoured the soup and bread and drank all the water in the container.

Alana walked to the shower and stepped into it, turning on the water. The water cascaded over her, helping her regain some normalcy and reinvigorating her for whatever was next.

Stepping out of the shower, she picked up a towel off the table. What appeared to be the same clothing was lying on top of the small cot in the room's corner. She dressed and sat down in thought.

What are my gifts? I need to know. Alana sat silently and closed her eyes as if awaiting an answer. And then she heard a single, faint word.

Isa.

She heard the name and understood, buried deep within her mind, was the answer.

How do I find out what to do? Please tell me how.

Silence, as Alana focused and attempted to quiet her mind.

Isa.

Again, Alana heard the name. And after a moment of silence, she heard a faint voice speaking. But Alana could not make out the words. The language was different—something she could not understand. Finally, she heard a voice she immediately recognized. It was her grandmother speaking to her.

Do not think. Know the outcome. Trust your senses. Know no fear.

Tears of joy began to stream down her face. The voice brought peace.

After moments of silence, Alana heard her grandmother's voice saying one word.

Isa.

Is this Isa? Alana asked, deep in thought.

Yes.

How do I not think? Alana responded. *I do not understand.*

Trust your senses and know the outcome.

What is it I must do? What is the outcome? Alana asked, frustrated in her failure to understand.

You will know. Remember: know no fear.

And then the voice disappeared into the darkness of her thoughts.

Mason's voice suddenly rang into the quiet space of her confines, startling Alana.

"Alana, it's time to talk to some of the Council. Will you be a good girl and follow instructions? We're almost finished here, and then you'll be on your way to your new home."

Alana nodded her head affirmatively.

The door opened.

I'm stepping into my fate and destiny, she thought as she left the room. *Isa, help me.*

Arena

Jon was sitting on the bed, his legs crossed over his knees, his eyes shut.

Can you hear me?

He was trying to reach out to Alana. But there was silence.

Jon began to think through everything that had happened. Two thoughts were battling for his focus: Alana's plea to not kill Aaron and his rage and desire to seek revenge on the assassin for killing his brother.

The memory of his time with Alana ultimately triumphed in Jon's mindful conflict, allowing his heart rate to slow and his anger to subside.

Did that really happen? I've never felt so connected to another. It was like we knew each other forever. I felt at peace with her. I trust her.

Mason's voice interrupted Jon's thoughts.

"Jon, will you be so kind as to follow instructions and avoid another forced sleepy time?" Mason asked, laughing. "I know you rarely sleep, if ever, but this is getting a little frustrating."

"What do you want me to do?"

"Just follow my directions. We're going to chat with our Council soon. Now, I'm going to open the door, and you be a good soldier and follow orders and walk down the hall to your left. You'll find the small room you were in earlier. Sit down in the chair. You'll be strapped in. But not for long, I promise," Mason responded.

Jon walked out of the room and down the hall. As Jon followed the hallway, he thought of Alana—hoping she could hear him and know he was moving. But he heard nothing.

After following the curving corridor, Jon saw a door open on the left. Inside was one of the oversized, metallic chairs. He stepped into the room and sat down, careful to have his hands as he had positioned them earlier. Immediately, the bindings wrapped around him, securing Jon. As it had before, the room went dark. Jon hated the dark and tried to calm himself as he waited to be rolled into the arena.

After several minutes, the door slid open, and the bright lights of the enormous space momentarily blinded him. The chair began its slow descent toward the pit in the center of the room. Jon was surprised to see Damron and Aaron waiting at the bottom.

Damron was the enormous Anguis Jon had twice encountered—severely injuring the soldier both times.

Also sitting bound in a chair was Aaron. He was still unconscious, his head drooping over. According to Mason, Aaron had killed the soldier's brother, Nosmon.

Once Jon's chair arrived in the pit, Damron walked to Aaron and, taking the same syringe-like instrument the Anguis had used before, stabbed it into Aaron's neck.

Immediately, Aaron woke up, groggily looking around.

Jon began to do what Alana had asked. He began focusing his thoughts, attempting to speak to Aaron.

This is Jon. Do you hear me?

Jon felt foolish, and then, looking at his brother's killer, he grew angry and stopped. Damron pulled a truncheon-like weapon from his utility belt. The weapon appeared to have a rounded, clear tip protruding at the end.

The giant soldier walked toward Jon, standing directly in front of his chair.

"I see you looking at this," Damron said, holding up the truncheon. "This is what I call a 'motivator.' It motivates humans," he said, a sneer appearing on his enormous face. Damron was holding the instrument in the same hand Jon had severed in his cabin in Alaska. A glove still partially covered the soldier's hand.

"Do you need a hand with that?" Jon smugly asked. "I think I know where you left one."

Damron took his left hand and backhanded Jon with a vicious slap across his face, sending saliva flying from the impact.

"You will lose a lot more than your hand. I'll make you feel pain like you've never felt before. That insect killed my brother and your brother," Damron said in his growling voice. "I will give you a chance to kill him for both of us. If you win and kill him, then you and I will fight to the death. And I will kill you and feast on you. If he kills you, know this: I will kill him and avenge your brother and mine. That is the Anguis way. We avenge the death of our family members. But first, a chance for you to do so."

Jon looked at Aaron and again tried to speak in his thoughts to the assassin, remembering Alana's plea and his promise to her.

Can you hear me? We need to work together to stop him. Can you hear me?

Seeing Jon's attention focused on Aaron, Damron pressed the truncheon instrument into Jon's abdomen. The pain was intense as if the weapon was a torch burning Jon's skin. He shouted in pain, trying to gather himself and avoid passing out. Jon looked down, expecting an injury or at least some damage to his clothing, but there was nothing. The pain slowly subsided as he tried to regain a semblance of normal breathing.

"That's why I call it a motivator. It hurts, doesn't it? The longer it touches you, the worse it gets," Damron said, growling. He then turned and walked toward Aaron as Jon continued trying to communicate with his brother's killer.

Can you hear me? We need to work together.

But Jon heard nothing.

Aaron remained seated, bound in the chair. Damron took the truncheon and pushed it into a similar area on Aaron's side. Jon winced, expecting a similar reaction, but instead, Aaron sat calmly as if the weapon had no impact on him.

"You feel pain. You're just hiding it," Damron said, taking the stick upward and placing it on the right side of Aaron's neck, between his ear and shoulder.

Again, Jon thought this would bring about an immediate reaction, but Aaron sat looking into the soldier's eyes as if he were unfazed. Angrily, Damron turned and walked back to Jon and stabbed the weapon into the middle of his stomach.

Jon shouted out in pain, "Fuck you!"

Damron laughed and said, "Now I know it is working."

Damron reached down into his pocket and pulled out a small remote. He touched a button, and Aaron's bindings disappeared. Damron then smiled and released Jon.

"The General will watch this later. He is busy fucking the girl. Then we will eat her," Damron said, snarling, looking at Jon. "Our crew has already enjoyed your brother, but nothing will compare to the girl." The soldier licked his lips, a smile forming across his face.

Jon leaped from the chair and charged Damron, but he was met with the truncheon in his face. The impact and force in the club

367

knocked him backward to the metallic floor. The pain was excruciating. Looking up, Jon saw Aaron moving toward him.

At first, Jon thought he heard something and then possibly a grin from Aaron. But the assassin jumped on top of him and unleashed a flurry of punches to Jon's stomach. Still feeling the pain from the truncheon, all Jon could do was try to block the blows from Aaron's onslaught.

With Jon nearly incapacitated on the floor, Aaron stood and looked at Damron and said, "Watch what I do with him. And remember how easy it was for me to kill your brother. I'll do the same to you."

Damron audibly growled. Jon heard a loud hiss from the giant Anguis.

"Continue, insect. I will enjoy eating you, too," Damron said as he held up the truncheon in Aaron's face.

Jon tried to stand but continued suffering from Aaron's beating. Rolling over to his knees to gain stability to lift off the ground, Jon suddenly felt a crushing kick to his abdomen. Falling back down, the breath knocked out of him, he could see his attacker. It was Aaron. After a series of repetitive kicks as Jon lay curled on the floor, trying to protect himself from the vicious attack, he heard Aaron's voice.

"This is what happens when someone receives military training. What a wimp. I expected more from the great Jon Walker!" Aaron gleefully shouted. The pause allowed Jon to rise from the floor momentarily, but he was met by a punishing blow to his temple before he could fully stand.

Aaron's punch dropped Jon back to the floor. Again, the assassin stood looking down at Jon, taunting him.

"Jon Walker, the hero. Hey, Jon, heroes die. Get ready to meet your maker," Aaron said as he began a barrage of sharp kicks into Jon's side. Aaron looked down at Jon, shouting, "Can you hear me? Can you hear me?"

With all his strength, Jon rolled away across the smooth pit flooring, retreating from the kicks.

Aaron repeated in a mocking tone, "Can you hear me?"

Is he trying to speak to me? Mustering all of the self-control Jon could summon, he shut his eyes, opening himself to another defenseless attack.

Can you hear me? Jon thought as Aaron deliberately walked toward him.

And he heard Aaron speaking to him.

We both take him out when the giant lizard gets close to us. Understand? Just say 'Yes' out loud if you hear me, Aaron silently communicated to Jon.

Aaron was nearing him, and Jon shouted, "Yes! I fucking hear you!"

Aaron's face lit up in a smile. He turned his back to Jon and wordlessly spoke, *Grab me, start to choke me. This is our chance.*

"I'm going to beat you like this, Anguis scum!" Aaron shouted, mocking Damron with his back to Jon.

Despite being in intense pain, Jon jumped up and grabbed Aaron from behind, wrapping one of his massive arms around his neck as he held Aaron aloft, facing Damron.

Seeing Jon choking Aaron, Damron laughed and said, "Finish him! Then I will finish you!"

"Watch closely, you fucking reptile freak! I'm going to get my revenge! Something you couldn't do!" Jon shouted, taunting Damron.

The enormous soldier could not control his rage. Damron quickly responded, charging the two with the truncheon in front. As he closed, Jon released the grip on Aaron's neck, freeing him. Seeing this, the soldier responded by pushing the weapon into Aaron's face. But nothing happened.

Instead, Aaron landed a solid punch to the side of Damron's cheek, causing the enormous soldier to stagger. Jon then lowered his shoulder and charged the Anguis. Picking the giant soldier off the ground, Jon slammed Damron on the floor, spearing him with his body weight.

Stunned, Damron struggled to breathe. Before he could gather his senses to offer a defense, Aaron was stomping on the soldier's face with repeated vicious stomps and kicks. Jon flailed away at the soldier's stomach, landing punch after punch into Damron's abdominal area.

Out of the corner of his eye, Jon saw the truncheon fall to the floor. While Aaron continued his brutal assault on the soldier's face, Jon lifted the weapon and, feeling a button at the top of the grip, pressed it and shoved it into Damron's mid-chest.

A loud squeal erupted, and then a long hiss. Aaron backed up as Jon pressed the weapon deeply into Damron's body. Quickly moving it upward, he stuck it under the soldier's chin, the soldier responding with another screech of pain, but not as loud, and then a low hiss as the soldier's body stopped its frantic shuddering.

"He's dead. You can stop now," Aaron flatly said, but Jon pressed it deep into Damron's neck. "Hey, I said he's dead!"

Jon released the truncheon and stood back from Damron's massive body.

"You've had your fun. We have work to do. Come with me," Aaron ordered Jon.

"I'm not taking orders from you," Jon said, still enraged from the battle with Damron.

Alana may be dead. The toxin has already been taken to Adak. We have to move now! Aaron said in silence. *Are you deaf?*

"How do you know?" Jon asked aloud.

Dumbfuck! Those Anguis assholes could be listening to us! Don't say another word. Roby told me. We need to move now! Aaron silently conveyed the urgency of the situation to Jon.

Roby is talking to you? Jon asked as he followed Aaron up the ramp toward the top of the arena.

He has been all along, Aaron responded as a door to the corridor slid open. *We must find Alana before the General kills her.*

Confused, Jon continued to follow his brother's killer into the depths of the massive Anguis mothership in search of Alana.

CHAPTER TWENTY-EIGHT
TROPHY

Mason's voice over the intercom completed the instructions for Alana to be seated.

"Sit back. Make sure your arms and legs are just right, and the locks will snap into place," Mason said remotely. "This won't take long."

Alana was not in one of the small rooms accessing the arena. Instead, she was in a room similar to her cell. But there was only a table on the far wall and a black metallic chair. The lights were dimmed. She gripped the armrest, pushed her ankles against the chair, and shut her eyes as she felt the metal bindings grab her wrists and ankles.

Know no fear, she repeated to herself. Remembering the words of Isa, she thought, *Do not think. Know the outcome.*

She thought this repeatedly as she sat strapped in the chair alone, awaiting whatever would happen next.

A door slid open, and Mason entered the room carrying her Bowie knife.

"Alana, I thought I would return this for old time's sake. It is my favorite trophy from my time on Earth. I will always cherish it," he said as he held the blade close to his face in the dim light, admiring the steel and the reflection of his image in the metal.

"Take it as a gift," Alana said. "It's the least I can do."

"That's funny. But the Anguis do not steal. We only take what we win in battle. What's the human saying, 'To the victor go the spoils.' I earned this, Alana. I've spent far too long on your island and worn this skin far too long. But all of that is changing very soon."

"How so, General?" Alana calmly asked.

"We have now delivered the nuclear warhead containing the toxin to the side of a volcano on Adak Island. You will miss out on the explosion, but it will happen soon. We could not have picked a better place to end the human pestilence! Adak is called the 'Birthplace of the Winds.' It's a perfect island with a continual tempest! We've been forced to be here. It was our prison while we police the human species. After all this time, this place, and the wind, they finally serve the Anguis. This was fateful, Alana. I believe in fate," Mason said, nodding his head. "As perfect as it is to end human life, I must admit, we hate this weather: it's far too cold. But the wind, Alana, the wind is amazing! The explosion and the wind will blow the toxin into the atmosphere, poisoning all human life on Earth. In a matter of hours from now, there will be no human life on Earth. Only an island needing recovery from the human insects' infestation."

"You're not destroying Earth?" Alana asked.

"Far from it! My species, the Anguis, desperately needs a new home. With its marvelous temperatures and water, your planet will make us a perfect place to live and prosper. And we will leave the Confederacy behind and start something new, far from the Newe," he laughed. "It is a brave new world! And soon, it will be our world!"

"It's hard for me to believe you have such a warm fuzzy feeling about Earth," Alana flatly said, trying to understand the purpose behind Mason's commentary.

"In many ways, we will be better stewards of the Earth Island and avenge the billions of dead earthlings. The Newebeans did this, not us. We will put an end to Newebean rule and dominance. The Anguis will be welcomed and respected by other species throughout the universe. We owe much of this to Dr. Walker, you, and the rest of your gifted family. The gifted were the key to unlocking the potential on Earth. Thank you for your service to the Anguis family!"

"I'm not going to say, 'You're welcome.' I hope you understand," Alana sarcastically responded.

"It's about control, Alana. Humans have this insane sense of control. They think they are in control of everything. They evidently inherited that from their ancestors, the Newe. But control is an illusion. The one-half of you that is human gives you a sense of control. And even though you're bound to that chair, and I'm holding a knife, you try to anger me with your words? You're not in control, little girl. I am," Mason said, a sinister smile lighting up his face.

"I'm guessing the Newe already know what you're doing. The nuclear bomb will not be set off. They do not want the outcome you speak of, General. And you admitted it yourself. They are much more intelligent than any other species, including the Anguis," Alana said, smiling.

Before she could blink, her chair flipped backward, allowing a slight tilt. The metal forming the arms and legs re-imagined themselves in a split second to create an X shape. Alana's arms were lifted upward above her head. Her legs were spread far apart. She could barely see Mason because of the nearly flat position she was being held.

"They can't stop me! They are too far away and do not know what is happening. The Sedas are also here, but they are intelligent enough not to get involved. They, too, will prosper, and hopefully, we will remain aligned with them. You don't remember the Sedas. I call them the kids. But they had a lot of fun with you," Mason chuckled. "The only thing that stops the toxin spread is what the Anguis need the most: water. But the bomb is above ground, and the winds will blow the toxin freely without resistance from the Newe or humans. The Axis Mundi is a natural killer. There's nothing but time till it happens. But before all that, I will have fun with you and then devour you. You will supply the ultimate feast!"

Mason, holding the knife, walked toward Alana. She began to recite Isa's words spoken to her earlier, but fear was drowning out her thoughts.

Then she remembered: *Do not think.*

Stepping between Alana's legs, Mason leaned over and burrowed his head deep between her legs, making a hissing sound.

"You smell so good!" Mason said as he lifted the knife. He pulled back the center opening to her jumpsuit, baring her breasts, and placed the blade inside the tight-fitting fabric below her navel. Slowly pulling the knife toward him, Mason shredded the material. He cut and tore off the remaining shreds of Alana's jumpsuit using the knife.

Mason returned to the opposite wall and placed the knife on the table.

"I'll use that again when I prepare you for dinner after I finish having my way with you," he said, snarling the last words.

Alana felt the grip of terror momentarily paralyze her. But then, the voice.

"Know no fear. Know the outcome," Alana repeated the words, barely audible.

"What did you say?" Mason asked, still laughing. "You remember Stalwart? I thought she was the finest fuck I would ever have on this island and the tastiest meal. But you will be even better. I watched you and Jon. I want you to do that with me. You can't escape. You might as well enjoy it, right, Alana?"

Mason dropped out of Alana's sight and buried his head in the exposed flesh between Alana's legs. She felt his long tongue swirling and probing. For a moment, fear reigned. Then, her courage was restored.

"Know the outcome," she said calmly as she shut her eyes and relaxed her body.

Mason heard something but did not hear what Alana said. Stepping back, he began taking off all of his clothes. In seconds, he was nude, standing between her legs.

"Earthlings have a saying I enjoy as it applies to beauty: 'Beauty is only skin deep.' Alana, I've worn this skin for four decades. I've been forced to be two things at once. It's time you saw me for the Anguis I am."

Mason returned to the table, took the knife, sliced it into the skin below his elbow, and began cutting through the covering. Only a trace of blood appeared—and then it vanished after exposure to the air. After making cuts down his other arm, chest, and legs, Mason slowly took the blade from the top of his forehead to his chin in a thin cut.

He sat the knife back down on the table behind him and began to pull off the human skin covering his bluish-green reptilian skin. After shedding the entire skin covering, he stood as an Anguis before Alana.

"I'm aroused by you, Alana, even though you're not my type," Mason said.

But Alana was not afraid. Her body remained relaxed, her breathing slow and steady.

"General, you said you wanted to experience what you watched. Why don't you release me? I will show you real pleasure. Don't you want that? You're not afraid of me, are you? General, you do not frighten me. You arouse me, too. Release me, and I promise I will please you like you've never been pleased before," Alana provocatively said. "Then you can do whatever you want to do to me. Grant me that for the benefit of both of us."

"You're good, Alana, I'll grant you that. But you only want me to release you so you can defend yourself with all of the kung fu bullshit you've learned!" Mason said, his voice now noticeably different, a hiss finding its way into his speech. "I didn't become a General in the Anguis military being foolish, falling for something like that. I will have my pleasure. I'm not concerned with what you can do for me. Just being there, like this, is just fine. But thank you for the offer," Mason said, moving closer to Alana. "I'm recording this to look back at our special time together. It will be a cherished memory."

Mason stepped between her legs, poised to enter.

Lifting her head up, Alana sternly said, "I'm not afraid of you," as she looked into the Anguis General's eyes.

"That is why I'm going to enjoy this even more," Mason said. "I think you want this."

"I do, General," Alana said as she shut her eyes and loudly said, "Know the outcome."

Focusing on the outcome, the knife on the table behind Mason began to loudly rattle against the metal surface. Mason heard the sound and turned just in time to see the blade, its sharp point flying toward him across the room, penetrating his throat.

Alana again said aloud, "Know the outcome. Know no fear," as the bindings around her ankles and wrists released.

Sliding off the table, she stepped in front of Mason. The Anguis General was leaning back against the X-shaped chair, holding the blade frantically, attempting to dislodge it from his throat.

"I'm in control, General," Alana said as she glided the blade with one hand and took it down the entire length of Mason's torso, splitting the Anguis open, his organs spilling onto the floor in a slimy, blue-green pile at Alana's feet.

"Goodbye, General," she said as she smiled, stabbing the blade deeper and upward, jutting out of his back. As the last signs of life evaporated from the General, Alana reached within his chest, pulled Mason's still-beating heart, crushed it in her hand, and threw it on the floor.

Live On

In the halls of the mothership, Jon and Aaron continued to search for Alana frantically.

"Where is she?" Aaron said aloud as they ran down the corridor.

"I thought you knew?" Jon shouted in response.

"I'm not talking to you!" Aaron answered without breaking stride. "Roby isn't responding."

"We can't keep running in circles," Jon said, stopping. Aaron stopped and turned.

"Let me see if Alana can hear me," he said as the two stood still. Incredibly, Jon heard Alana's voice silently speak to him.

I am nearby. The door is open.

"She's nearby!" Jon shouted.

"The door is open," Aaron said as he resumed running, interrupting Jon. "I hear her too."

A door was open in the corridor. Aaron and Jon were both stunned to see what was before them.

Alana was nude and picking up what looked like Mason's shirt, putting it on as they entered the room. A pile of remains of some type of animal was on the floor—and some of the same remnants were visible on Alana's body.

"What happened?" Jon asked, still in shock.

"I'll tell you later," she said, walking past both of them carrying the Bowie knife.

Aaron laughed and said, "That's Mason. Or what is left of him!" as he followed Alana out of the room into the corridor.

Jon paused, looking at the remains, and said, "Fuck you, General," quickly sprinting to catch up with Alana and Aaron.

"Roby is in here," Alana said, stopping where it appeared there was no door.

"Here?" Jon asked.

They all stopped as Alana pressed her hand against the black wall. Suddenly, a door slid open. Inside the large room, Roby was unconscious, bound in one of the oversized metallic chairs.

Alana stepped inside and stood still as Aaron ran past her toward Roby.

Aaron immediately stopped as he heard Alana speak in thought, *Stop, we are not alone.*

Jon heard the silent words and stepped forward, standing beside Alana. The crushing blow knocked Jon face down on the floor as Alana dropped to her knees to avoid the truncheon swung at her.

Aaron pivoted to see what appeared to be a nearly seven-foot-tall lizard-like figure behind Alana. Before he could react, Alana spun and stabbed the creature in the abdomen, ripping open a giant wound. The beast fell, pulling Alana to the floor. Despite the gaping cut, the Anguis began choking her with its enormous reptilian hands. Alana's knife had been knocked from her grasp and was out of her reach.

As Aaron leaped over Jon's motionless, outstretched frame to help Alana, he could sense the impending impact. Another Anguis crew member of the mothership tackled him, sprawling them across the floor. Rolling away from the creature, Aaron stayed on his back as the beast positioned itself on its hands and knees, making a hissing sound. The Anguis bolted toward Aaron through the air.

Aaron met the Anguis's leap with his knees tucked against his chest with a powerful upward kick against its chest, using his legs to propel the creature several meters away. Looking toward Alana, he could see the first Anguis twisting its head and thrusting downward savagely, biting her neck.

The second Anguis recovered from the fall and grabbed Aaron from behind. The beast picked him into the air and tossed Aaron across the room near the chair where Roby was held captive.

Aaron saw one of the truncheons on a table built into the wall less than a meter away out of the corner of his eye. At the same time, the Anguis saw it as both dashed for the weapon. Aaron reached it first and met the Anguis assault with a sharp blow to its head, momentarily stunning it. Pushing a button on the gun, Aaron thrust the truncheon into the chest of the Anguis, the creature squealing and hissing in pain as it fell backward. Immediately, Aaron thrust the weapon again into its chest.

The Anguis died in a matter of seconds.

Turning his attention to the other side of the area, Aaron could see the first Anguis had subdued Alana, retrieved the knife, and held it over her, preparing to strike.

At the exact moment, Jon regained consciousness and rolled to his side. Still stunned, lifting to his knees, he saw an Anguis on top of Alana, ready to plunge the blade into her. Springing forward with all of his strength, he tackled the Anguis.

As they rolled over and over in struggle, Jon felt the sharp blade penetrate his stomach. The Anguis twisted the knife deep inside of Jon.

A vicious blow from behind knocked the Anguis from Jon. Aaron continued the repetitive impacts on the Anguis's face as it was on its back, ending its life and reducing its face to a greenish mass.

"No! This can't happen," Alana said as she crawled toward Jon, bleeding from the bite to the neck. She put her hand on his massive wound to stop the blood spilling from his abdomen.

Aaron could see the severe injury Alana had sustained from the bite of the Anguis. Dropping the truncheon, he knelt on the opposite side of Jon's body.

No words were spoken, but all three heard each other's thoughts.

I'm so sorry, Alana. I let you down, Jon spoke, his thoughts conveying his pain.

You saved me. You did not fail, Alana responded. *I failed. I allowed fear to distract me.*

Looking up at Aaron, Jon's silent words were directed toward him.

Thank you for saving my son. Now help Alana, protect her, and Jonas, Jon pleaded.

I will, Aaron responded.

You did all you could do. You will live on. I promise, Alana silently voiced to Jon.

At that moment, Jon Walker died.

With tears in her eyes and blood pouring from the wound inflicted by the bite of the Anguis, Alana looked up at Aaron.

For all of the gifts, I could not save him. I failed. I was distracted by my own pain and fear. Don't let the same thing happen to you. We need you to do what is necessary to protect human life. Do not fail as I have. Please save them.

Alana fell unconscious onto Jon's chest.

Aaron ran back to Roby. He could not find a release for the chair. Quickly surveying the room, he saw a device he recognized on the table where he had found the truncheon.

The syringe works both ways, Aaron remembered as he grabbed it and stuck it into Roby's neck.

Immediately, Roby awoke. The bindings released, and the tall Newebean stood and looked toward Alana.

We must take care of her, or she will die. If she dies, all hope dies with her, Roby thoughtfully spoke to Aaron.

A door opened behind Roby, and he ran into the now-opened area. He retrieved a small packet and rushed toward Alana.

I've never seen him move like this, Aaron thought as he followed Roby to Alana's side.

Roby pulled what appeared to be a gauze-like material from the container and placed it on the bite wound on Alana's shoulder. He reached inside and pulled out a similar-looking device to the syringe-like weapon the Anguis used. He pushed it against her neck.

Looking at Aaron, he said aloud, "There is very little time. We must stop the nuclear weapon from exploding the toxin into the atmosphere."

"Tell me what you want me to do," Aaron said.

"We need to move her and take her to Adak."

CHAPTER TWENTY-NINE
PEACE

Aaron hurriedly followed Roby out of the room down a spiraling corridor to what appeared to be a dead end. Aaron carried Alana in his arms. A door appeared in the wall as they closed in.

"You're opening the doors with your mind," Aaron said aloud. Despite the uniqueness of their telepathic conversations, Aaron wanted to hear Roby's voice.

"Yes, you have the same abilities. The mindful force you have within you will be called upon soon. Listen to me and remember this: Do not think; Know no fear; Know the outcome."

Aaron had heard this before, many years ago.

"You were always there from the beginning. Why couldn't I remember?" Aaron asked as they ran down a narrow hallway.

"It was better you did not remember everything," Roby said without slowing.

"William used to say that to me. Know no fear," Aaron responded. "I ignored it."

"William was one of us," Roby said.

The pain of what he had failed to see for most of his life struck Aaron.

"I killed William. I was following orders," Aaron said, closely following Roby, maneuvering through another opening in the spacecraft.

"Remember, do not be distracted by your pain," Roby said. "William always understood how everything would end. Everything is for a purpose, leading to now. You are where you are supposed to be."

Aaron remembered Alana's words as he looked down at her face as he carried her into the next area within the massive mothership. Entering a large chamber, in front of them was an array of spacecraft. Most were V-shaped. The closest and largest was elliptical.

"Is this what people saw and called a Tic Tac," Aaron said as a door on the side of the craft opened, and they entered.

"Yes, this is the craft we will use to retrieve the cube housing the nuclear weapon and toxin. It must not explode into the atmosphere," Roby reiterated as he sat down behind what appeared to be the craft's control panel.

"Can you remind me why we are interested in protecting the human species?" Aaron asked in frustration.

Appearing to ignore Aaron's question, Roby said, "We will retrieve the cube from Adak. If the cube is not fully submerged in the ocean when the nuclear warhead detonates, the toxin will spread, as Dr. Walker said."

"How long do we have?" Aaron asked.

"We have thirteen Earth minutes. We must ensure Alana is safe. We are first taking her to a bunker on the island. Lay her down and be seated," Roby said with a directness that had rarely been apparent in his voice. "We do not have any time to spare."

After laying Alana on the craft floor as instructed, Aaron sat down in a large seat to the right of where Roby had already been seated. In front of Roby, a dimly backlit blue circle resembling a clock face appeared. The circle was divided into four equal areas, with a cross formed by the dividing lines. The circle's lines were in a North, South, East, and West positioning.

"Is this how you fly this craft? It looks simple," Aaron said, amazed at the spacecraft's controls.

Wordlessly, Roby responded as a bay door of the mothership opened below them—the dark water visible through a window shield that simultaneously appeared. *Watch closely. This is critical for you to learn.*

"You're teaching me how to fly this? Now? Roby, I'm not sure this is a good move," Aaron said.

"It is necessary. The craft moves directionally by bending gravity and space. All you need to know is the directional abilities. Watch and learn. It is simple," Roby confidently responded.

Aaron watched as Roby placed one hand on the circle and slid it down. The craft immediately responded to the movement of his hand.

"Speed is determined by the exertion of force you place on the wheel by your touch," Roby continued.

"A wheel makes sense," Aaron thought, amazed at the simplicity of control over a technology that far outdistanced anything humans possessed.

The craft dropped into the ocean, but there was no vibration or impact as the vessel moved below the mothership and sped through the water. Roby moved the elliptical ship, remaining below the surface without any trace of the water's friction.

"I can't feel any motion. It feels like we are sitting still," Aaron said, amazed at the experience.

"There is no resistance. The craft bends the space around it. It is essentially frictionless," Roby said as the vessel neared the water's surface.

Watching Roby, Aaron could see him sliding his hand slowly upward as the craft responded accordingly, gliding upwards, breaking the surface of the ocean and lifting into the air.

The craft flew in a matter of seconds to the coast of Adak Island in the sun's breaking light.

Aaron looked back at Alana.

"Will she be alright when we leave her in the bunker?" Aaron asked, his concern for Alana's welfare evident in his spoken words.

"Yes. I have cared for Alana's injury. I have a blanket to wrap her in and a packet of food, water, and clothing. She must survive. The hopes of countless species across the universe depend on her surviving this and carrying on toward her destiny."

"Did Mason go rogue on the Confederacy? I'm guessing he decided to take things into his own hands and get rid of humans so the Anguis could make Earth their home planet?" Aaron said, trying to understand the events leading up to the present.

"Yes. Mason's intention was to always wipe out human life on Earth," Roby quickly answered. "The timing was not working out, waiting for the Council to approve the extermination. Mason felt the need to act. The Anguis home planet is on the verge of destruction. He subdued me and began executing his plan. The General wanted to save his family. That I understand. We are doing the same and more."

As he spoke, the craft seemed to immediately drop without any maneuvers other than Roby sliding his hand. Without wind friction, Alana remained unmoved, lying on the floor. A large barren field positioned in a narrow valley between the mountains was visible in the light from the rising sun as they descended. The remnants of an airstrip were nearby, and some abandoned structures. Roby guided the craft to a small hill protruding from the field's flat terrain and landed.

"This was a bunker from what humans called their World War II. This is where we will leave Alana. We must move quickly," Roby said, lifting out of the seat.

Aaron picked up Alana and carried her, following Roby down a flat plank to the soggy ground below. Roby was carrying a packet, leading him toward the now visible opening. Stepping onto the island's surface, the footing was tricky—the bog-like grass gripping and challenging every step. After trudging across the grass, they finally reached the concrete outside the structure. Roby began to run toward the abandoned concrete bunker. Aaron ran on solid ground, keeping up with

Roby despite carrying Alana. The structure had no light or power, but Roby threw light sticks as he descended two flights of nearly dilapidated steps so Aaron could navigate the stairs.

A large vault-like door was at the bottom, which swung open before they reached the landing.

That's amazing, Aaron thought, trying to comprehend Roby's mental powers.

You're no different. I'm just more practiced, Roby responded in thought.

Behind the door was a row of bunks. A small kitchen appeared at the end of the long, narrow room.

Aaron laid Alana down on the first cot as Roby pulled a blanket from the pack and placed it over Alana, still only wearing Mason's shirt.

Tossing several light sticks around Alana, Roby ran out of the room back up the stairs with Aaron following close, the large vault door closing behind them.

"We only have a few minutes left," Roby said aloud, anxiety apparent in his voice.

Aaron heard Roby say as they exited the building, "We are running out of time. Get on my back."

Roby stopped before stepping on the thick, wet grass and leaned forward. Aaron complied by jumping onto Roby's back in one rapid motion.

Immediately, they were off of the ground, flying over the thick bog surface toward the craft.

You can do this with your mind? Aaron silently asked in awe.

This and much more, Roby responded.

The sun was now nearly over the horizon. As soon as they entered the craft, Roby lifted the vessel, flying over the small island to a volcano on Adak Island's north side in seconds. After dropping over the top, Aaron could see the cube's reflection shining in the dawn light.

"I see it!" Aaron said, standing by Roby, looking through the window.

Standing by the cube was a soldier.

"Is that an Anguis?" Aaron asked.

"Yes, be prepared," Roby said. "It is the last Anguis. And he may be a passenger on board this craft in seconds."

Unsure of what Roby meant, Aaron shook his head in affirmation.

Roby quickly positioned the craft above the cube. Aaron could see a dot within another smaller circle beside the primary guidance wheel. Roby touched the small dot, and Aaron felt the wind blowing into the craft. Behind them, a hatch door below the vessel was now open, the barren cargo hold behind them filling with the force of Adak's swirling winds. Despite the continuous pressure of the wind, the craft remained perfectly stable in the air.

On the surface, an amber-colored beam shone around the cube. The Anguis soldier, still disguised as a human, leaped atop the cube as it lifted into the air.

Roby stood and turned, moving in front of Aaron toward the opening. Aaron turned and wanted to stand side-by-side with Roby, but there was not enough space in the front compartment. As the craft hovered over the side of the volcano, the cube, with its Anguis passenger, rose in the air and into the vessel.

Aaron saw the Anguis soldier on top of the cube as it lifted entirely into the vessel. Before the bay door was closed, the soldier jumped from his position on top of the cube, drew a standard-issue US Army military pistol, and fired the weapon, striking Roby three times in the chest.

Seeing Roby stagger and fall to the side, Aaron charged the soldier, drawing his attention and fire. A bullet struck Aaron in the shoulder, spinning him but failing to stop his momentum as he closed on the soldier.

Aaron speared the soldier with the full force of his body weight, knocking the soldier against the cube, the pistol dropping from his grasp. Momentarily distracted by the pain from the wound, Aaron remembered: *Do not be distracted by your own pain.*

Despite the gaping wound, Aaron lifted the soldier over the cube by his neck and slammed the Anguis soldier repeatedly against the cube's top. Still seeing life in the giant soldier's eyes, Aaron gripped the head of the Anguis and twisted the soldier's head in a complete three-hundred and sixty-degree turn, instantly bringing death.

The blood loss from the wound made Aaron dizzy, and he feared losing consciousness. He heard Roby's silent voice in his thoughts: *Know no fear. Know the outcome.*

Pausing for seconds, he stopped and stood still. Focusing his mind on the wound, Aaron willed it to cease bleeding out. The blood flow to the open wound immediately stopped. Aaron ran to Roby lying on the floor between the two seats in the front of the craft. Tears were in Aaron's eyes as he looked at the Newebean.

"Do not be distracted by your pain. Submerge the craft near the mothership. *Know the outcome.*"

Aaron stepped over Roby and sat down in the seat Roby had used to pilot the vessel.

Putting his hand lightly on the wheel, the craft responded, racing toward the volcano's steep slope. Aaron moved his hand upward, and the ship flew directly upward at an incredible speed, gaining altitude to over ten thousand feet in a split second.

"Oh shit!" Aaron shouted, temporarily losing control of the craft.

Aaron lightly moved his hand to the side. Seeing the ocean on the south side, he directed the craft first over the coast and then in a deep plunge below the water's surface. Despite striking the water with a force that would have shattered any human-constructed vessel, there was no impact.

Bending gravity, no friction, Aaron thought as he took the vehicle deep below the surface. He could barely see the enormous mothership in the dark waters. Pushing forward, he brought the craft close alongside the mothership.

Standing and stepping back from the control panel to kneel beside Roby, Aaron said: "Save yourself! I know you can do it!"

"My time is over," Roby said.

"I am sorry. I let you down," Aaron said through tears.

"You've done well, my son," Roby said in a calm, barely audible voice.

Aaron knew. Roby was his father.

"Father, forgive me for not knowing. I've done horrible things. I've killed so many humans and inflicted so much pain. Please forgive me."

"You are forgiven and redeemed. This is your purpose, your destiny. You are saving billions of humans."

"I fucking hate humans!" Aaron cried out, ashamed at his admission. "I can't lie! Let's leave. I don't want you to die!"

"One of our kind once said, 'Love your enemies.' It is the greatest sacrifice to die in service to others, especially those you believe to be your enemies. You swore an oath to protect and serve. You are fulfilling that oath. Through Alana, countless species across the universe will be freed from slavery. There is so much more to what you are doing. Know no fear. We will both die soon, but death is a part of life for all beings. It is my time to pass," Roby said as he shut his eyes. "My son, be at peace."

"I love you, father!" Aaron shouted.

And then, in silence, Aaron heard his father's final words: *Do not be distracted by your pain. Know no fear. I love you, son.*

Aaron stood and looked at the cube. He knew it would explode in a few moments deep below the ocean's surface, ending the threat to humans and destroying the Anguis mothership. Suddenly, Aaron heard a voice behind him. A screen appeared in mid-air in a holographic image. On the screen was a human-like face, but longer with a much more pronounced cranial region—the forehead dominating its face. The face spoke to Aaron.

"You are not a human. You are Newebean. You must serve your family. Take the wheel upward into Earth's winds. I order you."

Aaron laughed.

"I'm through with taking orders. I like it here. It's a good place to die."

"You hate humans. Why would you do this against your family, your own kind?"

Suddenly, the voices of the past began to echo in Aaron's thoughts. William, Allison, Roby, and Rebecca were all crying out to him, saying in unison: "This is your purpose."

"Who the fuck are you?" Aaron asked, looking at the image on the screen. "Not that I care, but I am curious."

"I am Lintoo, the Newebean representative to the Council of the Confederacy. I am part of your family. Your father is a close friend of mine. He will be very disappointed if you do not do as I am telling you to do."

"My father is dead. And he is not disappointed. He died making this happen, you lying fuck!" Aaron shouted.

"Roby was not your father," Lintoo said. "He is a liar and a revolutionary. You've been told many lies. Now, hear me. Humans need to die. We now see the revolt for what it is. This is not what we wanted. Humans must be annihilated."

"You want me to believe you and die based on what you say? And in the process, kill billions of humans?" Aaron asked, laughing. "I guess the Anguis General was right about some things!"

"I am telling you the truth as a member of the Council of the Confederacy. If you die there as you are, the universe will be thrown into chaos. You can keep order. Fly above the surface. You will be known throughout the universe for exterminating humans. But if you help to preserve human life, no one will know your name. You will have died in vain and doing harm to your family, the Newe."

"You swear on the Confederacy?" Aaron sarcastically laughed. "Whatever you are, remember this: I don't give a fuck about the Confederacy."

"If you think this will save humans, you are wrong. Your death only prolongs their existence until we can exterminate our slaves," the Newebean forcefully stated. "We have this power."

"Humans are your slaves. That may be the first truth you've spoken. Let me share some human wisdom. Many humans ask themselves a question: 'Why am I here?' They do not understand their purpose and why they live. I'm not human, but I know why I am here. I was meant to be here. This is my purpose. I'm here to bring peace."

"Your mind is dark," the Newebean responded.

"This thing of darkness, I acknowledge mine," Aaron said, quoting from his mother's favorite Shakespearean work, *The Tempest*. "How beauteous mankind is! O brave new world, that has such people in it!"

Lifting his hand toward the monitor, slowly turning his closed fist—the knuckles toward the face of the Newebean Council member—Aaron slowly raised his middle finger. "As you from crimes would pardoned be, let your indulgence set me free."

As Aaron's last words were heard by the Newebean Council member, the explosion ripped apart the cube behind him, creating a nuclear explosion below the ocean's surface, prohibiting the toxic virus from

reaching the Earth's atmosphere. The nearby mothership was immediately ripped apart by the blast, resulting in a second nuclear-like
blast.

"We have failed," the Council leader said, turning to look at the
other four members. "But this is not the end, far from it. Peace is just
a prelude to war."

Freedom

The force of the nearly simultaneous blasts knocked Alana from the
small cot in the underground bunker on Adak Island.

Awakening to the explosion in an unknown environment, Alana
looked up at the vault door, now vibrating with the after-effects of the
nearby explosions.

Alana could sense Roby and Aaron were dead.

The pain in her neck and shoulder was intense. Alana remembered
what had happened and how Jon had given his life to save her.

Tears flowed down Alana's cheeks, then she remembered: *Do not
let your pain distract you.*

"I failed," she said alone in the concrete-walled room. Through the
dim yellow glow of light sticks on the floor, Alana could see flakes and
chips of the ceiling fall to the floor as the ground continued to rumble
and shake around her. After shutting her eyes and sitting still for several minutes, Alana opened her eyes and looked down at the backpack,
barely visible in the light from the glow sticks. She felt a presence—a
voice locked within.

Opening the backpack, Alana found packages of the nutrients she
had onboard the spacecraft and several water containers. And in the
bottom corner, she felt something small: two cubes.

Alana pulled the objects out and held them in her hand. They looked like dice without the indentations. Alana laid them on the cot and knew they contained instructions from Roby.

But how? she asked herself in thought.

Alana picked up one of the cubes and held it tightly in her hand. Closing her eyes, she heard the message and saw the messenger. It was Roby.

"You are now alone in an abandoned bunker on Adak Island. Knowing that you are experiencing this message confirms my death. These are what we call mental blocks. I hope you are smiling, knowing what this means in human language."

Alana smiled and felt Roby's comforting presence.

"The blocks can be reused to leave messages to others in your journey. There is much to tell you. Please drink water and replace the bandage I placed on your neck. The nutrition is not very appetizing, but it will suffice for now. After you complete these actions, we will resume in the same way. But first, do as I have requested. I promise I will be here."

"It sounds like you are here," Alana said aloud.

Alana could both see and hear Roby. She was more interested in what he would say next than drinking water and re-dressing the injury she suffered from the Anguis. She waited and was surprised by what she heard.

"I'm waiting. I know you haven't put the block down. Please do these steps first. They are for the good of your being," Roby said.

Uncharacteristically, Roby smiled.

Alana laughed, put the block down, and did as instructed.

After eating and drinking, she replaced the dressing on her shoulder. The injury was already healing, but the pain remained intense.

Alana picked up the block and continued.

"Good. Your grandmother always told you to be patient. Patience is important. Never run to your own demise. Now, let me help you with the pain. Your eyes are closed, and you see me. Now, I want you to focus on the pain and the points where it is originating. Know the outcome. Do not think. Focus on healing. The outcome is no pain. The outcome is healing. Focus, Alana. Now, set down the block and continue to focus. When you have fully healed, we will resume."

"Healed?" Alana said aloud. The injury inflicted by the bite of the Anguis was severe, and the pain was intense. But she trusted Roby and the outcome.

Placing the block beside her on the cot, Alana kept her eyes closed and cleared her mind of distracting thoughts. Focusing on healing as the outcome, the pain began to rapidly diminish. Her shoulder and neck began to have a slight tingling sensation.

She continued. And the pain went away.

Opening her eyes, Alana pulled back the bandage and looked at the area suffering the significant injury. It, too, had vanished. Alana's shoulder and neck evidenced no sign of the Anguis attack.

Picking up the block, Alana closed her eyes and saw Roby smiling again.

"Never doubt what you can do when you know the outcome," Roby said, still smiling. He then paused and continued.

"The toxin was released deep underwater in the ocean. Humanity is safe for now. But the threat remains and will only become greater in time. You are part of a universal revolt against the slavery enforced on many species by the majority of alliances. The power of the few, the alliances, and their respective leaders enslave the many. The Confederacy is just one alliance. I am Newebean, but my species, my family, has inflicted incredible pain and death throughout the galaxy. From what you would know, a hundred thousand Earth years ago, a leader sought to change the Newe and other alliances. The leader's name is

Isa. You are a direct descendant of Isa. You are gifted with the same powers she developed. You will develop your own gifts in time."

"I've heard her speak to me. She saved me from the General with her words," Alana responded.

"Alana, you have been distracted for much of your life about your family. You ask, 'Who are my father and my mother?' You will learn soon. But this I can tell you, to give you peace of mind. Soon, you will understand your place in the universe and know your family. This is your purpose and your destiny. There are no coincidences. Nothing is random in the universe. All are part of all, as all remain connected."

"What do you want me to do next? I'm sure I will be pursued. And I never want to be imprisoned ever again," Alana said, the memory of what had occurred fueling her anger and frustration.

"You have two points in your near-term journeys that are critical. The first is to travel to Idaho, to Fort Hall Indian Reservation. There, you will meet Jonas, the son of Jon Walker. The mother's name is Catori. And you will meet Denali, the boy's grandfather. Denali will help you convince the mother to let you take Jonas with you for his protection. Jonas is one of the other gifted beings on Earth. You are one. He is one. And there is a third."

Alana's thoughts drifted toward seeking the identity of the third gifted being.

"I can hear your thoughts even now. You will discover the third gifted being's identity only after you and Jonas travel to the second point in your journey. That place is in the Atacama Desert in Chile. You will not need directions for this travel. You will know where to go. You will be taken to Chile from Idaho. Once in Chile, you will know where and when you must be. Be patient. Time will pass. At the given time, you will also know the identity of the third. There, you will briefly find refuge and freedom together. You are now in what is called 'The Turning of Time.' This is the time for freeing countless species across the universe if you and your family succeed."

"My family? My family will help me?" Alana asked.

"There are many other things you will learn in your journey. The first step will begin in a few moments. A helicopter will land outside your bunker. A Newebean outcast on Earth, part of our revolution against the Confederacy, will help transport you to Idaho and Chile. While you can trust him for your travel, always beware. Trust, but ultimately, know the intentions of others around you as you know the outcome they seek. Trust is not blind. Never rely on your thoughts to confirm realities about those you will meet. Even those closest to you may seek to destroy you and the revolution. Remember this: even those closest to you may conflict with your purpose. Know the outcome, and do not be distracted by your own pain. Freedom demands a sacrifice, and that sacrifice will be painful in many forms. Know this is true: death is not the end."

After saying those words, Roby smiled again. And Alana could sense his presence—a reassuring connection beyond words.

Alana thought, *Mauna Kea, hope is alive, and death is not the end.*

"I was there with you then and am with you now and always. Remember the words you have heard. Remember the words of your grandmother, Nohealani. Listen to the words of Denali, the grandfather of Jonas. Your family is all you have, and not all of your family will help you. I have a family. My son, Aaron, died with me, helping to preserve human life on Earth. Remember him as redeemed in his final act."

Momentarily, Alana's thoughts again turned to Jon Walker.

"I know you want to blame yourself for what happened to Jon Walker, but that is unnecessary. He lives on in another form, as do I. Jon Walker served his purpose, and I served mine. It is now left up to you to serve your purpose. You will learn the truth. Know freedom for all. Make it known to the universe."

"Will I see you again?" Alana asked, tears now forming in her eyes.

Deflecting from her question, Roby said: "There is one last message. After you reach Idaho and travel to Chile with Jonas, pick up and hold the second mental block. If you try to access it before then, the message will not be available. You must be in Chile at a place and time you will know to listen. For now, goodbye, Alana. The freedom for countless other families across the universe depends on you and your family. Know the outcome. Peace…love…and hope."

As the message ended, Roby's image faded away. Alana sat in silence and focused on what Roby had shared with her.

Standing up, Alana looked around the confining space of the dimly lit bunker. Reaching into the pack, she found one of the jumpsuits she had worn on the mothership. Taking off Mason's blood-splattered shirt, Alana put on the form-fitting clothing and packed everything into the backpack. As the light sticks faded, Alana walked to the vault door. Without touching the door, she willed it to open, and the massive door immediately responded.

The cold chill of the air and wind from the surface blew down into the bunker. Alana shut her eyes and focused on her body temperature and immediately felt comfortable despite the near-freezing temperature on the surface.

Walking up the steps, she looked out on the haze of a barely visible, early morning sun through a thick bank of clouds smothering the small island—the remnants of the massive offshore explosions. Alana walked onto the bog-like grass and felt the sensation of sinking into the spongy soil. Standing motionless, Alana focused on rising above the grass. While her feet barely touched the ground, she could move across the bog without hindrance.

Standing in Adak's near hurricane-force winds, Alana felt freedom—the first time she had experienced the sensation in many weeks. Her life had changed forever on that distant day when she ran up the volcano and was abducted.

"Never again will that happen to me," Alana said, looking at the swirling clouds above as the constant winds helped to clear breaks in the thick covering overhead.

Alana remembered the original abductors were not Mason and the Army. Her abductors were the Sedas, what Mason referred to as the "kids," the grey alien species.

Her memory of the past quickly faded as she heard the sound of a helicopter. Looking up into the foreboding sky, Alana saw it begin its drop to the abandoned airfield where she was standing. The aircraft touched the surface, and the door opened as steps dropped to the airfield's broken cement.

A tall man stepped from the helicopter, bending over as the propellers continued to turn. He walked to within a foot of Alana, held out his hand, and said: "Alana, I'm Isaiah Williams. Roby sent me here to help you."

Alana shook his hand and said, "Let's go. We have a long trip ahead."

EPILOGUE
TERRORISTS

Alana sat quietly on board the helicopter as it lifted off the ground from Adak.

Her thoughts returned to Roby and what he had said about family.

Family is all we have. Earth is an imperfect world populated with imperfect human beings.

Aaron was Roby's son. Every human being lives today because Aaron fought and died to preserve life. Yet Aaron was a killer, an assassin. It is fitting that humanity was saved not by the noblest but by one so flawed. Perfect imperfection. I see that now. No one will know what truly happened at Adak. No one will know Aaron's name. Aaron died as he lived, in the shadows.

Looking out the window, Alana's thoughts returned to Jon.

Death is not the end. I believe it. I hope to know this as a reality. I still feel your presence. Thank you, Jon, for saving my life. You will always be with me.

Now over the Bering Sea and looking back to Adak, Alana remembered her grandmother's words about islands: "We live on sacred ground. Honor the island where you live. Maui is an island, part of the bigger island, Earth."

Earth is an island, and we, the indigenous inhabitants. We, all of humanity, are terrorists fighting for our land. This is a fight we cannot lose.

Isaiah asked Alana over the din of the helicopter, "Is there anything I can get you?"

"No, thank you. I have all I need for now."

400

The news release informed the world that terrorists had detonated a nuclear warhead off the coast of Adak Island near Alaska.

According to the information released by the US Department of Homeland Security, "All of the terrorists perished in the explosion near Adak Island. The entire population of Adak Island perished in the explosion, a total of forty-eight civilian casualties."

The press release stated the only known US military fatalities were two Army personnel: General Mason and retired Sergeant Jon Walker. The two military personnel had "personally thwarted the terrorist's plans, sacrificing their lives to protect humanity."

The terrorists were depicted as a group of former Soviet military and KGB officers. In all communications, it was clear that all the terrorists behind the explosion were dead.

The official release from the US stated in closing, "The terrorist threat is over."

A separate press release three days later announced Dr. Marc Walker and his family had died in a fiery single-car accident near Anchorage.

The news of the twin brothers dying so closely together brought shock and sadness to many in the US and around the planet. A large memorial service was held in Dallas, with the President of the United States and other leaders from around the world attending.

The news cycle continued to evolve. After several weeks, no major news agency mentioned the deaths of the twin brothers from Dallas and the nuclear explosion near Adak Island.

Behind their veil of secrecy, the United Nations Security Council planned to meet with the members of a small group of wealthy, influential people called "The Circle."

The Anguis replacement crew was closing in on leaving interstellar space and reaching the solar system's outer bounds where the Earth Island resided. They would arrive approximately three Earth years following the explosion near Adak Island. The Anguis home island (planet) remained on the verge of destruction, threatening an end to the Anguis family.

ACKNOWLEDGEMENTS

From the blank page to publication can be a lifetime.

In many ways, every person I have met has served as an influence in placing words on blank pages. But some people have proved more influential than others in this, the first book of *The Family* trilogy.

I wish to thank Lisa Kiernan and Vulpine Press for their valuable assistance, trust, and confidence in making this trilogy a reality.

As always, my deep gratitude to my immediate family and Alan Kalisky, a dear friend and part of our extended family.

And to you, the reader, I offer my heartfelt thanks for giving the time to read these words and this story. Welcome to *The Family.*

"The bond that links your true family is not one of blood, but of respect and joy in each other's life."

– Richard Bach, *Illusions: The Adventures of a Reluctant Messiah*

Luke Lively worked as a bank executive for over thirty years, leading three banks as CEO. Following his career in financial services, Luke pursued his passion for writing. In 2009 his first novel, *A Questionable Life*, was published, earning excellent reviews.

The Family: Tempest is the first book in a planned trilogy.

Luke enjoys time with his family, living on the US East Coast.

Find Luke online at: www.lukelively.com